## Praise for *WHATEVER LIFE THROWS AT YOU* by Julie Cross

"Loved this book! Great characters, great story, and so much swooning!"
—Cindi Madsen, *USA Today* bestselling author

"[A]llows readers an all-access pass into the lives of professional athletes and their families." —SLJ

"An addicting and gritty story about family, friendships, falling in love, and choosing to follow your own path. *Whatever Life Throws At You* is a story that combined my love of sports and YA romance in a way only one other YA author, Katie McGarry, has done." —*Mundie Moms*

"Julie Cross once again delivers with this swoon-worthy, laugh-out-loud romance between a sexy rookie baseball player and the new coach's daughter." —Yara Santos, *Once Upon a Twilight*

"An irresistible story about family, first love, and following your heart."
—Jen, Jenuine Cupcakes

## Praise for *CHASING TRUTH* by Julie Cross

"An enjoyably twisty, romantic, and thoughtful prep-school mystery."
—*Kirkus Reviews*

"A fun whodunit for teens. It has more depth than most teen mysteries and could be recommended easily to fans of Harlan Coben, Ally Carter, and Jennifer Lynn Barnes." —Charla Hollingsworth, HNGC Library

"Fans of *Veronica Mars* are going to love this!"
—Jaime Arkin, *Fiction Fare*

"A whodunit-style read that had me clicking the pages all through the night." —Erica Chilson, *Wicked Reads*

"I love the witty banter Julie always incorporates in her novels, and the swoon-worthy chemistry that always occurs between the two main characters has her books making my favorites list again and again."
—Kirby Boehm, *The Preppy Book Princess*

# BREAKING THE ICE

a Juniper Falls novel

JULIE CROSS

Also by Julie Cross

***OFF THE ICE***
***WHATEVER LIFE THROWS AT YOU***
***CHASING TRUTH***
***HIDING LIES***

# JULIE CROSS

# BREAKING THE ICE

Entangled Publishing, LLC
2614 South Timberline Road
Suite 105
Fort Collins, CO 80525

Entangled Teen is an imprint of Entangled Publishing, LLC.

Visit our website at www.entangledpublishing.com.

Edited by Stacy Abrams
Cover design by Clarissa Yeo
Interior design by Toni Kerr

ISBN: 978-1-63375-898-8
Ebook ISBN: 978-1-63375-899-5

Manufactured in the United States of America

First Edition December 2017

10 9 8 7 6 5 4 3 2 1

entangled teen
an imprint of Entangled Publishing LLC

*To the dancers and cheerleaders of the world.
Know that you are a special breed—both artist and
athlete combined. Keep doing what you love.*

# Chapter One

*T*ap...*tap*...*tap, tap*...*tap*...*taptaptap.*

   I zoom in on the purple ballpoint pen, willing it to stop, sending it silent threats. But it won't listen. It's currently under the mercy of the blonde occupying the seat in front of mine.

   *Tap, tap, tap...tap, tap...*

   Maybe it would be easier to deal with if a sense of rhythm were involved. Maybe it would be easier to deal with if I didn't have the hangover from hell. And if I hadn't gotten up at five in the morning to hit the weight room before hockey practice.

   *Taaap, tap, tap, tap...tap...*

   My head is seriously about to explode. I shift my focus to the garbage can clear across the classroom. At least the nausea (and puking) subsided by the middle of hockey practice. I need to hydrate right now. Unfortunately, I'm trapped in this classroom for another seventy-two minutes before I get a water break.

I'm barely paying attention to what Mrs. Markson is lecturing about, and she's been at it—emphatic arm-waving and all—for thirty-seven minutes.

*Tap…tap, tap…tap, tap.*

I try to focus on the flowchart explaining the U.S. government chain of command, but the damn pen won't shut up. I blow air out of my cheeks and wipe sweat from my forehead. I probably smell like a brewery. Or possibly the rancid beer spilled on the floor of said brewery. I shouldn't have gone out last night. I shouldn't have even been in Longmeadow last night. Longmeadow is for Saturday nights. Not Tuesday. Not when I'm enrolled in a stupid-ass summer-school course (which I only signed up for so I could have room in my schedule for a dual-credit college Calculus class this fall). Not when I'm working my ass off to earn a starting position on varsity this fall.

For three years, I've been fine with JV, fine with whatever amount of game time I got. But thirty seconds on the ice in the state tournament last March changed everything. I'm hooked. It's all I can think about. This fall is my last year playing hockey, and if the Otters make it to state again, I need more than thirty seconds of ice time.

*Tap, tap, tap…*

The sun emerges from behind a cloud and floods the room, making it hard to read the flowchart projected on the wall. Mrs. Markson heads over to adjust the window blinds. The tiny break is a sign. An opening for me to take action.

Half standing, I lean forward and wrap my fingers around the hand gripping the misbehaving purple pen. The pen stills, and I sigh with relief.

Haley Stevenson jumps, like she'd been in a daze and I've just burst her bubble. "What the—"

"Your pen. It's distracting."

"Distracting?" She looks about ready to shove me out of her personal space—the smell is probably getting to her. "How can a pen be distracting?"

I move my hand over hers, forcing the pen to tap several times against the desk—and I make sure to create the most gratingly inconsistent rhythm possible. "That's how."

"I have *not* been doing that," Haley insists.

We're in the very back of the room, so only a few students take notice of my impulsive handling of the tapping situation. Most are still scrambling to copy down notes. Mrs. Markson could have a career as an auctioneer if she wanted, the way she spits out information like we've all got five brains we can simultaneously use. Normally, the first day of school is a dud. Nothing gets done. But with summer school, the first day equals the first week. No time for small talk or wasting time.

I'm leaning over Haley's shoulder, her big brown eyes staring up at me accusingly. I have a clear view of her notebook. The flowchart, or any of the other projected notes we've been reviewing for more than thirty minutes, is nowhere to be seen. But she has written her name in several different styles of cursive, sometimes including her middle name—*Allison*—and sometimes adding an initial. She's also doodled some hearts, a few badly drawn geometric cubes, and, crammed into the side column of the page, written with slanted print a "Hump Day To-do List."

I refrain from snickering at the "Hump Day" reference. I'm too old for that. But, while holding her pen still, I do read this very important life-changing to-do list consisting of seven tasks essential to one's mid-June Wednesday survival in Juniper Falls, Minnesota:

*1. Write cheers for July 4th demo*

*2. Teach Kayla B. (and maybe Kayla S.) newest 3-8 counts of competition routine*

*3. Check UCF site for tryout/clinic dates*

*4. Day 5 of teeth whitening*

*5. Underwear drawer*

*6. Download calorie counter app Jamie mentioned*

*7. Tumbling at 6 then make dinner for Dad*

It isn't really my style to engage in conversation during class. Especially to comment on this list. Where would I even start? I mean, what happens if you miss Day 5 of a teeth-whitening adventure? Or I could comment on the ambiguous *underwear drawer*. That one definitely has my pounding head working on overdrive. But I don't comment on anything.

Now that my concerns have been addressed, I let go of Haley's hand, freeing the purple pen, and she immediately gives two quick taps against her desk.

All right. That's the last straw.

I pluck the pen from her fingers, tuck it behind my ear, and sink back into my seat. "I'm gonna have to hang on to this until the end of class."

Haley spins halfway around to face me, the surprise in her expression telling me that the most recent taps hadn't been *F*-you taps. "That's my only pen—"

"Miss Stevenson," our highly caffeinated teacher says, looking right at Haley. "If the president and vice president can no longer serve, who becomes president?"

Haley's face flushes before she's even fully facing forward again. "Um…the first lady?"

The entire class laughs. Our middle-aged teacher—who takes Civics very seriously—doesn't laugh. Her face pinches like Haley's answer causes her physical pain. "Look at your flowchart, Haley. The answer is right in front of you."

Mrs. Markson's already swiped the flowchart from the projector and replaced it with the Bill of Rights. In front of me, Haley's entire body stiffens. I guess that's what happens when you're consumed with thoughts about your underwear drawer instead of copying notes.

*Jesus Christ.* Now I'm consumed with thoughts of Haley Stevenson's imaginary underwear drawer (imaginary not because it doesn't exist—I'm confident that it does—but because I've never seen it before). My gaze roams from her ankles, traveling the length of her smooth, very toned, bare legs until I reach the hem of the frayed jean shorts resting high on her thighs. Shorts she'd never be allowed to wear during the regular school year. And yeah, I get this dress-code thing now. I'm completely distracted. I've never had a class with the Princess of Juniper Falls before. It's a small town—one middle school, one high school—so we've always been in proximity to each other, but never this close, I guess.

Two rows over from us, Jamie Isaacs shoots his hand in the air. "It should totally be the first lady. Or a vote. Women voting. A whole bunch of women all voting at once."

"Thank you, Jamie, for granting women the right to vote," Mrs. Markson says drily.

I'm about to laugh with the rest of the class, but my sluggish hungover brain is too busy catching the fuck up. What the hell is Jamie Isaacs doing in summer school? Didn't he graduate last week?

That's one of the downfalls of all those dual-credit classes at the community college, and spending all but one week of junior year practicing with JV. I'm not up on all the latest gossip. Not that I'm close enough to the inner circle to get that info anyway.

"What is *currently* the governing rule, not what should, may, or will be in the future?" Mrs. Markson continues, gliding down the aisles with the largest stride her knee-length pencil skirt will allow. "Civics is not about creativity. It's about understanding the law and our rights as citizens of this country. So, who can tell me the position that is third in line to become president of the United States of America assuming the first two were deemed unavailable?" She scans the room, and her gaze finally rests on me, a hopeful expression already forming on her face. "Mr. Scott?"

I can feel Haley's and Jamie's eyes on me. I lay an arm over my notebook and lean on it. After several seconds, I finally shake my head. Mrs. Markson rolls her eyes and turns around, heading back toward the front of the room. With a great amount of force, she snatches the Bill of Rights and slams the flowchart back into place. She grabs a red dry-erase marker and makes a big effort out of circling "Speaker of the House."

We go through eight more projector slides before we finally get a break. By that point, I'm close to passing out from dehydration. I stumble out of the room and lean over the water fountain, chugging for a good minute.

When I fall back into my seat, already regretting the water binge, Haley Stevenson is turned around facing me.

"I need my pen back," she says.

"Sorry. Can't do that." I flip over another page in my notebook (at this rate, I'm gonna need a new notebook for tomorrow) and rub my temples. "I've confiscated it for the greater good. Executive decision."

In a motion quicker than I ever would have expected from her, Haley reaches out and rips my glasses right off my nose. Her face blurs in front of me. She carefully folds my glasses and then drops them into the front of her backpack. The backpack is scooted over until it rests between her legs.

Haley folds her arms across her chest. "My pen for your glasses."

I stowed her annoying pen in my back pocket when I got up to get a drink. I reach for it, but hesitate. "No tapping," I warn.

My vision isn't clear enough to be sure, but I think she rolls her eyes. "I did not—"

"Yes, you did." I hold the pen out, but grip the end tight.

Haley does the same with my glasses, not giving them up quite yet. "You owe me some notes. I couldn't write anything down for the last like hour or something."

I lift an eyebrow. "I didn't realize you needed the pen to take notes."

"What else would I need it for…" Her voice trails off, her neck and face turning pink. She drops the glasses onto my desk, snatches the pen, and turns around.

After my glasses are back in place, my forehead relaxes and I watch Haley turn several pages over in her notebook, hiding the "Hump Day To-do List" she made earlier.

If I were Jamie Isaacs—or any other guy on my team for that matter—this would be the point where I'd bug her relentlessly about the underwear-drawer mention. I might be vying for more time under the hockey spotlight, but I'm not Jamie Isaacs. I'm not the guy who cracks jokes all the time and always talks a big game. It used to bother me, I used to wish I were more like him or Leo or Hammond, but I'm over it now.

Mrs. Markson gives us a five-minute warning. Since I'm already in my seat, I'm debating getting in a short nap when Haley turns back around to face me.

"What now, Haley?"

She flinches in surprise. "Do I...I mean...have we had a class together before?"

Haley Stevenson doesn't know my name. And I used hers so easily it probably seems like I'm the type to silently worship the popular kids. Whatever. She can think that if she wants.

"No," I say, and she turns pink again. She's embarrassed by my assumed embarrassment. "Not in high school," I add, then wait a beat before finishing. "But in day care, you used to shove Cheerios up my nose."

Her mouth falls open, forehead wrinkling. "You're kidding, right?"

The reaction is satisfying despite my headache. I shake my head, but offer nothing more.

She eyes me skeptically. "I would remember that."

I shrug. "You don't remember my name, so maybe you forgot other things?"

Haley sweeps her hair up into a ponytail, tying it with a band from around her wrist. "Forgetting and never being informed are two different things."

The textbook lying on my desk provides an opportunity for me to look busy and end this chat. Even though I've enjoyed messing with her, the fact that she doesn't know my name is a bit of a conversation killer.

Ten seconds later, Haley shouts out triumphantly, "Fletcher Scott!"

I glance quickly around the room, taking in all the faces now turned toward us. I slide down in my seat. Clearly the conversation reins have been swiped from me. "Well done. Now turn around and take those notes you're so worried about."

But Haley doesn't move. "Coach put you on varsity right

before the state finals. When Joey Petrie pulled his groin. I had to scramble to find you a locker buddy. Luckily Becca had some free time."

Too many people are looking at us right now. My gaze shifts to the clock above the door. Isn't it time for another flowchart? "Tell Becca thanks for the oatmeal cookies."

"Aren't they the best?" Haley sighs. "You're lucky, you know? All the guys fight over Becca—" Instead of pink, she turns bright red this time and then shakes her head. "God, I didn't mean fight over her like that…"

"Like what?" I offer, playing dumb.

"Everyone wants Becca as a locker buddy," she clarifies unnecessarily. "Anyway…so the cookies? I helped her with that batch. They were good?"

No idea. Considering eating them probably would have killed me. "Best oatmeal cookies I've ever seen."

She looks pleased with herself, and I'm hoping that will result in her turning around. "I still don't believe you about the Cheerios at daycare thing. So what else do you know about me?"

Apparently, I've stepped unwillingly into an I-know-more-about-you pissing contest. What *do* I know about Haley Stevenson? Probably not nearly as much as she assumes. First off, she really did shove Cheerios up my nose when we were three. I know she dated Tate Tanley for a long time, but they broke up.

The other thing that I know about Haley Stevenson: my fifteen-year-old cousin, Cole, is hopelessly in love with her. Though I doubt he's ever said more than two words at a time to her. I also doubt that Haley realizes rising-star freshman varsity player Cole Clooney is related to me.

Haley huffs like my silence proves her win.

"I know that you…" I say, and Haley lifts an eyebrow,

waiting. "Have tumbling practice at six."

Her mouth falls open. "You read my—"

"I also know that you should probably focus on note-taking instead of socializing." I wave my hand, suggesting she turn and face forward again. "Sounds like you have some catching-up to do."

She blows the loose hair from her forehead and waits, like she's considering this carefully. "Whatever."

I sigh with relief when she finally turns, giving me a view of the back of her white tank top again. Our break ends, and Mrs. Markson goes back to her lecture.

For a while, I'm taking notes and enjoying the quiet. My body relaxes, and even my headache begins to fade.

The peace lasts about ten minutes. Then I hear the *tap, tap, tap* again. Not from the pen this time, but from Haley's leg bouncing up and down.

Hopefully, Mrs. Markson is willing to edit her seating chart. Otherwise, I'm never gonna make it through the summer.

# Chapter Two

## -HALEY-

can't believe he read my list. Could I get any more cliché?
God, what a disaster.

I'm too distracted the rest of class to actually learn
anything. I've written random words in my notebook, but
most likely I'm missing too much information for any of it to
make sense. And to make matters worse, when I'm walking
out of the classroom, Jamie beside me and Fletcher Scott
two paces in front of us, Mrs. Markson stops me.

"You two…" Her eyes narrow at Jamie and me. "Given
the fact that you both are taking a second stab at this class,
I highly recommend that you seek out different partners for
our group work, understood?"

Jamie laughs, his head still held high. I turn bright red,
of course. I hate this part of my life. The part that defies
the typical Juniper Falls Princess résumé. Over a hundred
years of princesses in this town, and I bet not one of them
dropped out of Civics because they were getting a D. And

that's without even mentioning how much I had to pester Mr. Smuttley, our guidance counselor, to get him to remove evidence of that *D* from my transcripts.

Now that I think about it, changing a transcript might be illegal. Does this mean I can't run for a political office?

Maybe if I had aced Civics, I'd be able to answer that question.

But I have too much to do today and can't stand around contemplating a future career in politics. I shove Jamie toward the door, promising Mrs. Markson that we won't sabotage our grades by working together.

Jamie, who can't receive his diploma yet because he failed this class the first time around, is completely calm and unconcerned with Mrs. Markson being onto us. As soon as we're in the hallway, he shouts to someone standing less than ten feet away, "Clooney! What's happenin', little dude?"

Cole Clooney opens his mouth to respond to Jamie, but stops when he sees me. His face goes completely red, and he's suddenly lost the ability to speak. It takes great effort on my part to not roll my eyes. I keep telling myself that any day now he's going to grow out of this afraid-to-talk-to-girls stage. The better he gets at hockey, the more he ends up hanging out with my friends. I'm now running low on one-sided conversation topics.

Still, I flash him a smile and try yet again. "Hey, Cole."

He turns a deeper shade of red and looks anywhere but at my face.

Before I can even contemplate making a bigger effort to engage the kid, Fletcher Scott eyes him and silent words seem to flow between the two of them. I think he's lying about the Cheerios. He has to be.

I stare at Fletcher, studying him. He's not an easy guy to read, not so far, anyway. Or maybe I've gotten too used to the arrogant, say-everything-on-my-mind hockey players. Jamie and most of the other guys on the varsity team love to hear themselves talk. I can pick all their voices out of a crowded hallway. Fletcher is much quieter. But unlike Cole, when he plants his feet somewhere, there's no awkward shift from one foot to the other, and his head isn't angled downward, toward the floor, or up above everyone's heads.

Jamie snaps his fingers in front of me, and I immediately shift my gaze from Fletcher to him. I rub away goose bumps from my arms and will my face not to turn red like Cole's.

Okay, that stare drifted way past acceptable length. So Fletcher Scott is nice to look at. Big deal. *Pull yourself together, Haley.*

Jamie lifts an eyebrow, and I quickly turn my attention to my cell. Being both cheer captain and Princess of Juniper Falls means receiving more than twenty text messages during one four-hour summer-school class. I scroll through the first few.

> **LESLIE: what color ribbon for the hair bows??**

> **BAILEY: pls tell Leslie no freakin polka dots this year!**

> **AMANDA: silver wired ribbon would be amazing for the cheer bows! Just sayin...**

> **KAYLA: Kyle totally apologized for the other night. He was so sweet, srsly Haley, you have to believe me!**

The last text knots my stomach. When you know your best friend's boyfriend is an asshole and you tell said best friend this more than once and she chooses not to take your advice, well, that's where I'm at with Kayla right now. I have no idea what else to do except be civil and distance myself. I can't enable. That was my mom's advice, and I think it's the best plan.

And because Leslie goes nowhere without Kayla lately, Jamie Isaacs has been forced to become my new BFF. Which probably means I'll be stuck in these ridiculous hockey conversations on a daily basis.

I tuck my phone away, holding off on reading any more texts. Otherwise, I'll break my own rules and reply to Kayla regarding what I think about her supposedly apologetic boyfriend. I tune back in to the hallway chat and take a good, but much shorter, look at Fletcher Scott. The program for the state finals listed his height as five eleven. I'd bet my crown on that being a two-inch lie. Not that those two inches make much of a difference to me. I'm only five one, so standing beside either of these guys makes me feel like a garden gnome. With his hoodie on, I can't really tell if Fletcher is built underneath it. He's broader than Cole but smaller than Jamie. Without realizing it, I let my gaze linger on Fletcher a bit too long again, trying harder to read him, to see him—everything about him seems to be buried just out of my reach.

My phone vibrates in my pocket, probably reminding me of a task I'm late to complete. I tug on Jamie's sleeve—he's my ride today. "Isn't it your feeding time?"

Jamie perks up. "You're feeding me? Let's go."

I wasn't planning on feeding him. I meant that we should hurry so he could get home and feed himself. But whatever, I can make him a sandwich. Or five.

Before we walk away, I point a finger at Fletcher. "I want those notes tomorrow."

His eyes widen. He lifts a hand to shove his glasses back into place. They're quite a distraction from his blue eyes. He has nice eyes. I got a good look at them when I stole his glasses earlier.

And nice teeth, too.

I run my tongue over my own teeth. It's time for day five of whitening. *God, he read that in my notebook.* I can't even imagine how that list looked from Fletcher Scott's perspective.

The situation is too hopeless to improve, so I leave the conversation hanging in the air—my demand of notes tomorrow already submitted—and drag Jamie outside toward the parking lot.

"Haley," Jamie says. "Did the captain of the cheer squad just force the smart, quiet kid to hand over his notes? I didn't think you were that type, and I'm a little turned on by this."

I smack him on the shoulder. He's such a flirt. It's like he can't even help it. I know he's not really into me; Jamie's heart belongs completely to older women—he's a bit obsessed if I'm being honest. I'm about to tell him he's full of it, but then I stop and rewind. I did kind of do what he's suggesting. But only because Fletcher stole my pen. Not that I'd been taking notes anyway, but I couldn't leave with him thinking I'm a stereotypical dumb blonde cheerleader.

But seriously, why does that even matter?

I scrub my hands over my face and groan. *Just forget about it and move on, Haley.* That's the mantra I've been trying to adopt over the past several months. It's working so far. Sort of. Mostly.

Okay, sometimes.

At least I'm no longer creating heartbreak-filled set lists to try to get the attention of my ex-boyfriend who did not, in fact, want to give me his attention.

"What year is Fletcher?" I ask Jamie once we're in his truck. Across the parking lot, Fletcher and Cole climb into a newish-looking SUV.

"Same as you." Jamie gives me a sideways glance. "He wasn't the only junior on JV last season."

"I know that." I shrug, hating that he read my thoughts. "He played in the state finals."

"For less than a minute," Jamie says.

"Was it a good less-than-a-minute?" I don't know why I'm drilling him for information. Maybe I'm planning ahead to make sure I win the next I-know-you-better contest. I totally won today. And humiliated myself in the process.

"Don't know. I was too busy playing. The whole fucking game." Jamie looks at me again. "He doesn't go in much 'cause he's got that thing."

"What thing?" We're on the road now, so I crank up the radio and roll down the window.

"You know…" Jamie clutches his chest with one hand and makes weird gasping noises.

I stare at him, completely confused. "What? A heart attack?"

"Not a heart attack. Like when you can't breathe…what's that called?"

"Asthma?" I guess.

He snaps his fingers. "Asthma. That's it. Remember him in grade school? He was always sick. He missed two years of school."

"Nobody misses two years of school." But now I'm trying to remember him. Believe it or not, our tiny town actually has two elementary schools. Jamie went to West school. I went to South. I'm guessing Fletcher Scott went to West.

"Fine. Don't believe me. Just ask him yourself."

I wave a hand, indicating that it's not important and probably none of my business.

"But before you do that," Jamie continues. "You should probably break his cousin's heart. That kid is two seconds from stalking and shrine building in your honor."

I'd been scrolling through texts on my phone, but my

head snaps up. "Who?"

"Clooney. He's got it bad for you."

"Cole and Fletcher are cousins?" I refuse to address Cole Clooney's apparent little-boy crush on me. He'll find his way eventually and meet a girl his own age to practice on. Then break up with. Because that's what happens with your first love. That's what happens with all high-school loves. Either that or you don't break up and end up accepting too many of the other person's faults. Imagine if Tate had gotten back together with me? I probably never would have seen the light and wormed myself out of the pain-in-the-ass I'd become. Exactly why I've decided to hold off dating until college. I was definitely not my best self while dating Tate, and especially not right after we broke up.

"I know, right?" Jamie says, but doesn't elaborate on why he finds their familial connection shocking.

I lean against the window, feeling way too overwhelmed for such a beautiful summer day. I need to figure this class out. I need to be so much better than I am. How do I make that happen?

I flip my notebook open and start a new list.

*Ideas for Getting Ahead in Civics Class*
*1. Sit by someone who knows the answers.*
*2. Ask more questions.*

A few more items on the list and my confidence will make its way back.

"Jamie, we gotta pass this class. No fucking around."

"What's that you say?" Jamie grins wide. "You want to fuck around with me?"

I give him a look that indicates the exact opposite. The grin fades, and his expression darkens, his gaze refocusing on the road. "Yeah, okay."

Guilt washes over me after seeing Jamie, who never worries, nearly as tense as I am. I touch his arm. "You're not failing again. I won't let you. You're gonna pass, get your diploma, and in September you'll be flirting with college girls instead of student teachers, got it?"

"Student teachers *are* college girls," Jamie points out, but he nods and blows air out of his cheeks.

I add Jamie's name to my list. He's my friend, and the one thing I have a perfect record at is being there for my friends. He's not failing this class again.

I add another item to my getting-ahead list of ideas: *bring more than one pen to class tomorrow.*

# Chapter Three

"Just say it," I snap at Cole. "Just fucking say it."

Apparently hungover me forgot to inspect my backseat this morning before taking off. It was dark out. I couldn't see. But Cole can see clearly now. And since I'm his ride home from summer school—at least for today—I get to enjoy his awkward silence all the way out to the country where my grandpa's farmhouse sits.

Cole chances another lightning-quick glance into the backseat and then turns forward again, his face redder than when he'd laid eyes on Haley a few minutes ago.

"I didn't say a-anything," Cole stutters.

I rub a temple with one hand. "But you want to, so go ahead."

"Did someone…I mean did somebody actually…" He snorts out a laugh, reminding me how much maturing he'll do over the next couple of years. "Did someone wear those?"

After turning the car out of the parking lot, I look over my shoulder at the backseat, counting quickly. "Probably four someones."

"Probably?" Cole says, his voice rising an octave. "You don't remember?"

I shake the fog from my head. I remember bits of last night. Basically, everything before my fourth shot. But I think that was around six o'clock, and it was after midnight when I finally fell into bed. A lot can happen in six hours. A lot of panties can happen. Obviously. Considering my backseat is littered with four different pairs.

I'm hit with a flash of me jumping in the lake buck naked. My guess is that I didn't swim alone.

"I was drunk," I tell Cole after remembering that he's waiting for my answer. "Now, I'm hungover. In case you haven't noticed."

He goes silent, and I feel like an asshole for being such a shit example. I glance at him before turning onto the bumpy country road that will take us home. "Hey, just so you know, this is a very bad way to wake up in the morning."

"You mean hungover?" He relaxes into the seat. "I know that. But usually you don't do that on a school night."

This is true. Very true.

"A bunch of people from work took me out for my birthday, and we got carried away. Next time I wake up with several pairs of thongs in my backseat, I'm gonna be damn sure that I remember how they got there, okay?"

He turns red again at the mention of the thongs. "People from work?"

The word *work* comes out as a squeak. Before he starts getting the wrong idea, I elaborate. "People who are also employed at my place of employment. Friends. Obviously, some female friends."

"So, you didn't…"

When he can't finish the sentence, I do it for him. "Screw four girls in my backseat?" Cole nods, and I shake my head. Then with a smirk, I add, "Not last night, anyway."

That gets him to laugh and loosen up a bit. But he still works way too hard to keep his eyes forward. "Dude, if you can't even look at a pair of panties without freaking out, how are you supposed to have a conversation with a girl?"

Cole drops his gaze and picks at my leather seat. I smack his hand to stop him. This car is my most-prized possession. "I have plenty of conversations with girls."

"Really?" I stare at him. "What girls?"

"Just a few from school." He shrugs, not even coming close to pulling off this lie. Seconds later, he sighs, giving in. "I only like one girl and she's…she's—"

"Haley fucking Stevenson." I roll my eyes. "With her pen-tapping and you picking at my seats constantly, you two are a perfect match."

He straightens up, looking a little too hopeful. "Really? You think so?"

"You know what I think? I think you can't know if you're a perfect match until you actually talk to her."

Cole picks at the seat again and then stops himself. "Do you do that? Actually talk to girls? I mean, I know you do other things with them…"

"I talk to Ricky and Angel all the time." I can't escape even one shift at work without those two forcing me to verbally express some kind of feeling. "And you heard me on the phone the other day, listening to Rosie's roommate drama for more than an hour."

"That's different," Cole says, and then he's silent for such a long time I'm sure that he's dropped it, but then he adds, "I mean talk and you know…"

"Hook up?" I suggest, already hating where this is going. "Date?"

"Yeah."

Once. Only once. Two years ago. A girl from work who was much older than I was. I had a massive crush. She didn't. That's pretty much how our story played out. "Crushed" is the best word to describe what that did to me. Now I prefer to keep the physical and emotional separate. Much easier this way.

"Yeah, not really my style. The whole relationship thing. Why do it when you can skip over it and go right to the good stuff?" When his face reveals clear disappointment, I add, "That's just my way. Doesn't have to be yours. In other words, talk to Haley before this crush gets any bigger inside your head."

"Why did I have to take Health instead of Civics?" He scrubs his hands over his face. "We could have been in class together."

Knowing Cole, he still would have turned red at the mere thought of eye contact with Haley. The entire summer. And I know why he didn't take the class with me. My aunt Lisa—his mom—is so fucking competitive, she'd have ripped him apart every day he came home with any grade lower than mine. Doesn't matter that he's almost three years younger. And school is nothing compared to how she is about hockey. If that kid burns out by junior year, it will be completely his mom's fault.

This is why I didn't ask him if he wanted to go to his house or mine. The kid needs a break from that shit.

I'm driving uncharacteristically slow down the rocky dirt road. Cole smirks at me when I start to get that pre-nauseated look from all the bumping around. I pull the car into our long driveway and park near the barn. The doors are open, and my older brother Braden's boots are visible.

All three dogs leave Braden's side and charge at Cole and me the second we step out of the car. Prancer and Dancer are chocolate labs and Vixen—she's mine—is a yellow lab. Cole is taller than me by an inch, but he's light as a feather, and those dogs plow him over every time.

Braden pokes his head out of the barn and laughs at Cole. "Dude, if I didn't know better, I'd say you don't stand a chance against varsity defenders."

While Cole is rolling around on the gravel with the dogs, I head for the backseat, hoping to remove the remaining evidence of last night's birthday celebration. I've got three pairs of panties scrunched in one hand and I'm reaching for the fourth when I notice Braden leaned over my shoulder.

He lets out a low whistle. "Hey, Gramps! Come check this out."

I elbow my brother in the ribs, but he's bigger and stronger and gets his arms around me, forcing me to release the panties in my hands. Before I know it, Grandpa Scott, with his gray hair, worn jeans, and muddy boots, is opening the other door to the backseat and looking things over.

"Yep." He shakes his head, mock shame on his face. "I told your dad, this is what happens when you don't go to church."

Of course, my dad chooses right then to bring the tractor up to the barn. He hops off, and Grandpa Scott shouts the same warning about church at him. My dad takes off his hat and sunglasses to get a good look in the car. He gives away a small smirk but says nothing more.

Dad reaches down and grabs Cole's shirt and pulls him to his feet. "You boys hungry? Let's go make some lunch."

"But we still have—" Braden protests, but Dad waves away his concern.

After I've tossed the panties and we're all filing into the big kitchen, I'm as surprised as Braden that they're gonna stop for lunch. We only get about ninety-six frost-free days each year in northern Minnesota, so it's pretty rare during one of those days to see Grandpa, Dad, or Braden inside when it's light out. I'd be out there with them, but Dad and Braden have both made it clear that my job is school.

Well, that and Saturday nights in an old warehouse right outside Longmeadow. A job they love to tease me about, but I don't mind. I'm doing something I enjoy. Dad is all about enjoying the moment. It's kind of his thing. And the job pays a shit-ton of money. Especially lately. I've really been bringing in the cash over the past six months. That's how I was able to buy the used SUV.

Lunch in a house with four men means everyone opening cabinets, drawers, and pantries all at once, throwing meat and bread together. Cole isn't a Scott like me, but he joins in with no apprehension, piling turkey breast onto a piece of bread as fast as I'm slicing it.

"Hey, enough." I shove his hand away from my blue cutting board. "I'm gonna be here all day slicing meat."

"Cut me some, will ya?" Braden says.

I groan, the hangover hitting me hard. I need food. And food has always been the most complicated part of my life. Thanks to Grandpa Scott's system, our kitchen is the easiest place for me to eat. Blue cutting boards are mine. Blue baskets in the fridge and pantry are mine.

And this turkey breast is mine. I roasted it myself all day on Sunday. I'm about to tell Braden to cook his own, but Grandpa Scott has already pulled a ham from the fridge and is slicing it on a white cutting board. Braden snatches four thick pieces of ham.

Fifteen minutes later, we're all spread out around the

dining-room table, our plates piled—mine with at least a pound of meat, three baked potatoes, and one of each fruit in the basket on the counter.

Dad glances at my plate, does a double take, and then lifts an eyebrow. "So you really are going for this bulking-up, starting-defense-position thing?"

I shrug. I don't want to jinx it.

"It's summer," Grandpa says. "Why the hell are you boys skatin' around on ice in the middle of the goddamn summer?"

"He was up before five this morning," Braden says. "I thought those practices were optional?"

Cole and I look at each other. We both laugh. "Optional as in everyone knows the starting positions are determined from summer training and scrimmages," I answer.

"You don't see the football team out there before August," Dad says, his mouth full of sandwich. Grandpa, Dad, and Braden all played football. And apparently, a generation or two of Scott men before them. They love to rip on the hockey team, rightfully so. I can't imagine what it must be like to play a sport other than hockey at Juniper Falls High.

Cole tears the crust from his sandwich. "And you don't see anyone talking about the football team. Like, ever."

We all crack up because Cole rarely dishes out the dirt when my elders all gang up on us.

"Guarantee that came straight from your mother's mouth," Grandpa says, and Cole's face flushes.

That does sound like something Aunt Lisa would say.

The subject moves back to teasing me about the panties in my backseat—which always includes mention of the misuse of the skills my late grandmother passed on to me— and eventually we end up on Cole's infatuation with Haley Stevenson.

"Haley Stevenson," Braden mutters. "Why does that name sound familiar?"

"Probably because she's the current princess of our town and her name is everywhere." Juniper Falls Princess is described as a political position for a chosen high-school girl to represent the local youth each year, but it's really just a popularity contest that's been around for more than a hundred years. I turn to Cole. "Why don't you just grow a pair and talk to her? If she shoots you down, then you get to move on." She will definitely shoot him down. But he needs to learn this for himself.

"You're in class with her." Braden points his fork at me. "Why don't you chat Cole up to Haley?"

My eyes widen. This is not something I would ever do. And Braden knows that. I don't really socialize with people at school. All small towns have their gossip, but Juniper Falls takes getting in other people's business to the extreme. My family has a history of being the center of town rumors for some very private matters, and though we've fallen off the radar for several years now, I'd like to keep it that way. I haven't heard gossip about my parents in years, my grandmother only through stories Grandpa Scott tells about events before I was even born. My brother's brushes with the law in the past seem to be old news now. And I've managed to go from being the-one-to-harass to the-one-I-can't-remember, proving that how people perceive me is very much within my control.

"Haley doesn't want to talk to me." That's my best excuse. "Cole's the star varsity hockey player. He's got a better shot at conversation with her than I do."

"You're the one in class with her. Besides, Cole isn't even ready to ride the bench when it comes to chatting up girls," Braden says, then he tosses Cole a sympathetic look. "Sorry, man, but it's true. I've seen you in action. It's pathetic."

Cole stabs a piece of meat, poking it several times before forking a bite. "Yeah, I know."

"And if Fletch can get all those panties in his backseat, obviously he knows his way around the opposite sex." Dad flashes me a sly grin, like it's completely his genes that contributed to my apparently wild night last night.

"The panties were a joke," I point out.

Dad shakes his head. "Scott men are known for having a way with women. It's one of our best qualities. And really, it's not rocket science. It all comes down to understanding the differences in male and female pleasure."

I expect Cole to turn red again, but instead, he's wide-eyed, looking ready to take notes.

I roll my eyes. "We're corrupting a fifteen-year-old. Maybe we *should* go to church."

"We are not corrupting him," Grandpa Scott says, even though he made the church joke earlier. "We're providing him the same education you and your brother both received."

"That's right," Dad agrees. "Just because he's not a blood relative of mine, Gramps, or your brother's, doesn't mean we don't care about his future."

I still remember clearly the first time I admitted to fooling around with a girl to Dad, Gramps, and Braden. I was probably close to Cole's age, maybe a tad older, and the first words out of Dad's mouth were, "Did she enjoy the experience?"

If I were someone who had friends at school or on the team—good thing I'm not—then this approach to fathering and grandfathering might seem really weird, but I guess I'm used to it. *To them.* Grandma Scott, before she passed away two years ago, had a big hand in my "education" as well.

After a lot more prodding, I finally agree to say

something nice about Cole in front of Haley. I only say yes to get them off my back. Today's conversing with her already took too much of my patience. But after lunch, when Cole and I are sprawled out on the couches watching a baseball game, I have this strong desire to grab a notebook and create my own "Hump Day To-do List." I wonder what Haley is doing right now. It isn't time for tumbling practice yet—that's scheduled for six o'clock. Maybe she's whitening her teeth or teaching Kayla Squared some eight-counts.

Maybe I won't change my seat tomorrow.

# Chapter Four

## −HALEY−

tried to read the three assigned chapters last night. I really tried. There was all this drama over the cheer bows, plus Kayla S—not my BFF Kayla but a different one—has been all insecure about not being able to learn our new choreography, so I spent three hours going over it with just her and me. She's doing awesome, as I knew she would if she could just stop worrying about what everyone else thought. But still, three hours is three hours. Then Leslie got on my back about blowing off Kayla B. If Leslie would just join Team Don't Enable the Girl with the Asshole Boyfriend, I think Kayla would crack. But she won't. Anyway, I ended up reading half of the assignment, retaining nothing, and falling asleep at my desk, drooling on the textbook.

So when Mrs. Markson announces that she'll be drilling us with questions on the reading and scoring our participation, I'm a hot mess. My palms are sticky with sweat, and I have to keep wiping them on my jean shorts. Several students stumble to answer questions, but many of them still get the answer right. I hold my breath when Mrs. Markson says, "Jamie?"

He jolts up, a red mark on his cheek from leaning against one hand. "Yeah?"

"Who is the father of our country?"

Before I can even think the name George Washington, Jamie is shouting, "God!"

Mrs. Markson purses her lips. "George Washington." Then she makes a note in her gradebook.

Shit. That was Jamie's first grade in this class, and he just flunked. A minute later, she's glancing my way. "Haley, a U.S. senator is elected for how many years?"

Oh God, I know this. I *know* this. The president is four years. So, a senator is either two or six years and a house rep is whichever the senator isn't.

"Uh…I think it's…" I toss the two numbers back and forth in my head, and then I feel a soft kick against my seat and the word *six* is coughed out skillfully. "Six," I blurt out.

Mrs. Markson nods and spins, turning her back to me. I blow out a huge breath and then glance over my shoulder. Fletcher Scott is busy scribbling in his notebook, not making eye contact with me. But he just gave me the answer. Unless I imagined a six in that cough. I didn't imagine it. And I didn't miss the fact that Mrs. Markson obviously gave Jamie and me two of the easiest questions. I've got to step up my game. I grab my pen and begin a new list.

*Ways to Step Up My Civics Game:*
*1. Study twice a day.*
*2. Get to bed earlier.*
*3. Ignore Leslie's guilt trips.*

*4. Make flash cards (color code them).*

*5. Memorize any answers that contain a number by making up a cheer or song ("six is for senators, four is for presidents, two is for house of rep...").*

"Fletcher, the house of representatives has how many voting members?"

Fletch shifts in his seat behind me, but he doesn't hesitate before quietly answering. "Four hundred thirty-five."

I wait to see if Mrs. Markson says he's wrong, but like with me, she nods then turns to someone else. Never in a million years would I have answered that question correctly after simply reading the assigned chapters (*note to self: add house of rep head count to the Civics number song*). And this gets me thinking about the guy in the seat behind me and his apparent secret—or not so secret, I guess—genius.

When we get our midmorning fifteen-minute break, after Fletcher rises from his seat and heads out the door, I turn around and snatch his notebook from his desk. I flip back through at least twenty pages of meticulous notes. By the looks of it, he hasn't missed a thing Mrs. Markson has given us, and that's practically an impossible feat considering her race-car pace of delivering information.

I spot Fletcher's black Nike slides crossing the doorway and return his notes to the original page and place the notebook carefully back onto his desk. I have to be really smart about this development, because in Fletcher Scott's eyes, I'm the girl who can't answer the most simple Civics questions, who skips note-taking to write to-do lists that scream ditzy blonde cheerleader, and only brings one pen to class (I have five today). I'm not exactly study-partner-of-the-year material. This could be a problem. But it's nothing a little charm and genuine kindness won't solve. That and finding out what it is Fletcher Scott wants as much as I want to pass this class.

No, I *need* to pass this class. I will pass this class. And so will Jamie. If I can pull off an *A* in Civics, then my GPA will be a 3.2. It's not the 3.6 average for UCF incoming freshmen, but it's better than 3.1.

Fletcher slides back into his seat, and I spin around and straddle mine. "Hey, Fletch."

The nod he gives me screams dismissal, and let's be honest, I'm not someone who gets that kind of nod too often, so it's a little disheartening. "I take it you're doing all the 'optional' summer varsity workouts?"

I glance at his chest. Varsity hockey players practically live in their JFH spirit wear (most of which they get for free from the boosters). But Fletcher is wearing a T-shirt that says No, I will not fix your computer.

"Yep." He keeps his eyes down and flips a page in his notebook, leaving a clean sheet on top.

"How was practice this morning?"

"Fine." Fletcher lifts his head, eyeing me cautiously—this reaction isn't unjustified. I've seen plenty of popular kids pull some pretty shitty stuff with the, uh, *less*-popular kids. "How was tumbling last night?"

My cheeks warm at the reminder of my stupid to-do list. He's trying to force me to turn around. *What's his deal?* I plaster on a grin and sit up straighter. "It was killer, actually. I'm working on a back full. Do you know what a back full is?"

He shakes his head.

"It's a layout back flip, and while you're upside down, you add a full twist. I only got my layout about six months ago, and one of my coaches—Andrea—is like hard core, and she says you gotta have a layout for a whole year before twisting. And then there's Jonas who's like, go for it. Just don't break your neck."

"Was it Andrea or Jonas last night?"

I'm caught off guard by the intense way he's listening now. It makes me immediately self-conscious of all the words I'm choosing. I dig my fingernail into the wooden chair I'm sitting in, tracing a pattern. My knee bounces up and down. "It was Andrea, and she had me doing all this awesome strength training, and by awesome, I mean terrible. Terrible today, anyway. My abs are screaming at me."

*Okay, Haley, enough about you. Focus on him.*

"So, hockey," I say, shifting subjects. "It's going well? Are you excited for a full season on varsity? It really is a different world."

He stares blankly at me. I take notice of his stylishly messy dark hair. He's got nice skin, too. "I didn't realize you played varsity hockey."

"I don't, but I've spent plenty of time on the bus with the team. Talk about needing a reality check. It's like, how many people can we crown king of the world at the same time?"

Fletcher cracks a smile and then smooths it out before I can react. "What do you want, Haley? Is this your attempt at an apology for the Cheerios? If so, I accept. Let's both move on."

I still don't believe him about the Cheerios, but now's not the time for that debate. "I don't want anything." Not yet anyway. "Just making conversation. I was really impressed with your knowledge of last night's reading. She nailed you with a tough question."

Being part of the Juniper Falls Women's League has taught me to suck up better than anyone else.

"Right." Fletcher scratches the back of his head, his

eyes darting around like he's debating something. "I, uh…I studied."

"I can tell."

"I mean…" He folds his arms, gripping his biceps. "I studied with my cousin. Cole. You know Cole, right?"

My forehead wrinkles. "He's not in this class, is he?"

If so, shouldn't he be learning from inside the room?

"No, but he's a planner. Likes to think ahead and prepare…" He focuses on something over my shoulder, and it almost looks painful when he adds, "You'd like him. You guys should hang out sometime."

"You want me to hang out with your cousin?" This conversation has taken an odd turn. To keep my hands busy, I reach in my bag and retrieve a granola bar.

"I don't want you to do anything," Fletcher says, his gaze now hyper focused on the granola bar I'm about to take a bite of. "It was just a suggestion."

Okay, someone is grouchy today. Maybe he's hungry. I hold the bar out to him. "Want some?"

He actually leans back, away from it. I roll my eyes. "I've got another one in my bag if you're afraid of girl cooties." I bend over and grab another Kashi bar, tossing it onto Fletcher's desk.

His eyes widen. "No thanks. And can you please not eat over my desk?"

Jesus. This guy really does *not* like me. I look down at the desk, and to Fletcher's credit, there are a few crumbs. *Oops.* I use my hand to brush them away. "Sorry. I'm such a—"

My voice cuts off when Mrs. Markson comes up behind me and snatches the granola bar right from my hands. "No food in class, Haley!"

My mouth falls open. I look at her over my shoulder, and I'm about to protest her food stealing, but she's staring at Fletcher. "Do you need to leave?"

I look back at him, and his face is flushed. He drops his eyes, and then in the lowest voice possible, he says, "Yeah, I have that appointment. Thanks for reminding me."

Okay, maybe she was behind me because she had been in the back of the room to remind Fletcher that he needed to leave. I didn't think absences were excused in summer school. Maybe he's in therapy. That would explain a lot; he needs an attitude adjustment. I mean, it's summer, we're gonna be seniors in the fall, so why the moodiness? Although, this could be his normal disposition. Guess I really wouldn't know otherwise.

Fletcher is up out of his seat in less than two seconds, his books tucked under his arm. He heads out the door before I can say a charming good-bye or anything at all. Obviously, becoming study buddies isn't something we're going to achieve in one day.

Mrs. Markson watches him leave, and then she hands me back my Kashi bar. "I mean it, Haley. No food." Her voice rises, and she addresses the entire class. "That goes for everyone. Five points off to anyone who breaks that rule."

There's a grumble going through the class, but most didn't seem to notice Fletcher's departure. Only the fact that I reminded our teacher to remind us of this super-important no-food rule.

After that fiasco is over, Mrs. Markson returns to teaching and passes around handouts for our Constitution projects—an assignment we'll need a partner for.

The twenty pages of meticulous notes flash in my mind. Bad attitude or not, Fletcher Scott is going to be my partner. I just need to create a plan of action. I need to do something special to make sure he knows that I'm the one.

Okay, not that *one*. Finding that *one* is on my summer to-don't list.

# Chapter Five

## —FLETCHER—

"Take a seat, Fletch," Coach Ty yells at me, pointing to the bench.

I skate over to the boards and remove my helmet. "I'm fine."

Ty assesses me and shakes his head. Okay, I am wheezing a little, but it doesn't feel like the type of wheezing that will get worse. Several of the guys out on the ice have looked over this way, taking notice of the exchange.

"Sit," Ty repeats firmly.

From across the ice, Coach Bakowski turns to face us. "He said he's okay, Ty. Let the boy practice." He releases a quick, sharp blow of his whistle. "Scott, face off with Red."

I don't look at Ty. I shove my helmet back on and skate over to the blue line as fast as I can. Bakowski smacks the top of my helmet with his clipboard. "Stay on your feet, son, understand?"

Yeah, I get it. He'll let me play, but I have to promise

not to get myself killed. Little does Bakowski know, I start each day off with the goal of not getting myself killed, so I don't need a reminder.

I grip my stick, lean forward, and wait for the whistle to blow. When it does, I put every bit of force I own into charging Red. I know it's his spot we'd both be fighting for. Assuming I'm even a contender. But even if I don't get Red's spot, I could make second line. I'd play half the game, most likely. That's way better than thirty seconds. I want all the seconds I can get.

Unfortunately, this morning I only get three seconds before Red has me flat on my back. I'm sliding across the ice, waiting to bang into the boards, when Jake Hammond grips my practice jersey and pulls me up. I shake off his hand and skate far away from him, going after Red again. *I can fucking get up myself.*

Coach blows the whistle, and we start the drill all over again. This time, it takes Red a couple of seconds longer to plow me over. A truck is now sitting on my chest. If I didn't have gloves on, I'm sure my blue fingernails would tip everyone off to what's going on inside, but still I'm grinning. Progress is progress.

"Clooney!" Coach yells, charging after Cole. "You take that goddamned shot when you've got the chance. What the hell are you waiting for? Think Tanley might doze off if you give him a couple of seconds?"

Cole drops his head and skates back to his starting position. Bakowski rarely yells at me. I've only practiced with varsity for a total of eight days now, but I've already figured out that Coach is hardest on the most talented players. I'm not on his hate list. And I need to be. Somehow.

・・・

When I walk into Civics class, I'm holding a bag of ice to my hip, my body weak from waiting way too long to use my inhaler today. The abrupt halt I make after reading the chalkboard is painful. In huge letters across the board, Mrs. Markson has written

## "NO FOOD IN CLASS."

I duck my head and chance a few glances around. I don't know what she said to the class after I left. I couldn't stick around with Haley rubbing her granola bars all over me. I retreated to my car, downed a bunch of Benadryl, and clutched an EpiPen in my hand, waiting for the familiar pre-anaphylactic shock signs. Luckily, they never came, but I was too drugged up to drive home, and Braden had to come get me.

I'm hyperaware of my classmates this morning as I make my way to my seat in the back of the room. I wait to feel eyes on me, but I seem to be as invisible as always. I release a breath and slip into my seat. From the back, it's easy to keep track of glances my way and whispered conversations at my expense. Little pockets of chatter pop up from different areas of the room, but it's nothing out of the ordinary and no one is paying any attention to me. Relieved, I re-tuck the bag of ice into my shorts and get out my notebook and pen.

Five minutes before class starts, Haley and Jamie Isaacs walk into the room. They're being themselves and talking loudly, laughing at jokes only a select few are in on. So, I'm more than surprised when Haley glances around, obviously searching, and when her gaze lands on me, she grins and speeds up her pace, heading in this direction.

Jesus, what now? I already made an idiot of myself trying

to drop Cole into our conversation yesterday. That kind of bullshitting isn't something I'm good at. Obviously. But I tried, just like I said I would. I can't help it if being direct is more my thing. Direct or keeping my mouth shut. I don't do much in between.

Haley drops her bag onto the floor and hands me a sheet of paper from her folder. "Snagged an extra copy of the handout for you. We went over this after you left. What kind of appointment did you have, anyway?"

"College counselor." I'd already rehearsed this lie in my head before walking into the room, so it comes out smooth and easy.

"Oh." Haley looks surprised, or maybe disappointed. But the grin returns shortly after, and she takes her seat before dropping a card on my desk.

"Fletcher" is written in glittery gold cursive across the front of the envelope. Is this a birthday-party invitation? I haven't gotten one of these since third grade. "What's this?"

"It's an invitation."

"To…?" I flip it over, slide my finger through the sticker, unsealing the envelope. Inside is a black card with beautiful handwritten calligraphy covered in gold glitter. Sparkles fall from the paper onto my desk.

*You are Cordially Invited to be my Partner for the Civics 125 Constitution Project*

*\*Refreshments happily provided by me*

*When: Out-of-class meetings scheduled at your convenience, I'm flexible*

*Where: Your place might be best due to piano*

*lessons every half hour at my house, but a neutral location is also fine*

*RSVP: Haley Stevenson, 832-9745, blonde&cheering@gmail.com*

*P.S: I truly believe we will make a fabulous team! Go Fletchly! (that's our team name, btw)*

My mouth falls open, but no words exit. Have I landed in an alternate reality? What the fuck is this? I flip the card over a couple of times, searching for clarity. Finally, I look up at Haley. "You want me to be your partner for the Civics project?"

"Yes," she says, all serious. "But no pressure. I understand if you want to weigh your options."

I glance down at the card again and then back at Haley, shaking my head the whole time. I don't know whether to laugh or be creeped out. I mean, who does this? "You could have just asked me. No need to pull out the calligraphy pen."

Haley shrugs. "It's an important project, and I wanted to make sure you knew how much I appreciate your consideration."

I'm half tempted to tell her to drop the Junior League bullshit, but it's kind of amusing. What she's doing, it's the type of thing kids like me would get ripped apart for. Caring too much about something like a school project or being too enthusiastic. Somehow, Haley gets away with it and still remains the Queen Bee around here. It's interesting at the very least. I'm not too jaded to appreciate irony.

And honestly, I'd rather not have any partner for this project. Given Haley's less-than-stellar Civics knowledge displayed thus far, partnering with her might be as close to no partner as I'll get. Besides, if we study at my house, I can invite Cole over and maybe give him a better opportunity to talk to Haley. Not that it will help his cause—not that anything will—but it beats me sucking at talking *about* him to Haley.

I toss the sparkly invite to the side. "Yeah, sure. Whatever."

Haley pulls herself up straighter, her eyebrows lifting. "Are you saying yes? You don't want to think on it and call me later? I'm totally okay with that."

Did I read that card wrong? Is she proposing marriage or asking for a kidney? *Jesus.* "It's fine," I mumble. "We can work together."

Haley releases a squeal, clapping her hands. "This is so great!"

I glance sideways and slide down in my seat after seeing that several other students are looking over here now. If she stands up and announces to everyone that she's taken, I'm done with this school. I won't be back on Monday.

"Now I can give you these. For ethical reasons, I had to wait until you said yes." A large tin emerges from Haley's bag, and she thrusts it in front of me. *Oh God, not again.* "Just don't open this in class. I think Mrs. Markson might be on a crash diet or something. Or she has a bug or mice phobia."

I hold my hands out in front of me. "I really don't need any gifts."

"I used Becca's cookie recipe. I know how much you like those oatmeal cookies." Haley grins and shoves the container right under my nose.

I lean back, my eyes wide and pleading. "Can you just put that away? Please."

Hurt flickers across her face, but she forces a smile. I wait for her to drop the tin back into her bag, but she goes for mine instead.

"No, don't." I grab her wrist, stopping her, then lower my voice to a whisper. "Please Haley, just put it in your bag."

"Why? What's the problem?"

"I don't want them," I snap. "I'll be your partner, just don't give me anything. It's a stupid Civics project, that's all."

Her face turns bright red, but she says nothing more. The cookie tin—full of walnuts, I'm sure—gets zipped into her bag, and I'm careful not to put myself anywhere near it during the entire class.

And yeah, maybe it would be easier to tell Haley the truth. I'm sure I will at some point, but not right here, right now. Not when she's going to jump in Jamie Isaacs's truck after class and tell him everything. And then he'll talk about it with the guys on the team, and I just want to go to practice and class this summer without any drama. Without people noticing me when they didn't before. Plus, we've got some assholes on our team, and I wouldn't put it past them to "test out" my weakness as some varsity initiation. Something along those lines happened to me in third grade. It's the reason I dropped out of school for two years.

It only takes one near-death experience to get paranoid at the sight of a granola bar or tin of cookies. And those cookies are a triple threat for me—wheat, eggs, and nuts.

I'd be dead before I could even choke out the word "EpiPen."

After class, when we're filing out of the room, I look through texts that I missed during class and groan at the first three from my mom.

**MOM: Lisa said you needed your inhaler during practice. Have you talked to Dr. Webber about all this extra cardio?**

**MOM: Braden had to pick you up from class**

*yesterday?! What happened? Should I talk to the school counselor?*

*MOM: I'm calling your father.*

I figured Aunt Lisa was way too busy yelling at Cole and taking notes on his performance to provide any kind of report about me to my mom. And she's calling Dad? Is that supposed to be a threat? Dad's just going to tell her to back off like he always does. Neither of them will admit this, but I'm positive I'm the reason they're not together—they were never married, but we all lived together, for a short while, at least. Every fight they've ever had has been about me—*should he be homeschooled or go back to school, is it okay to play sports?* When I lived with my mom, I spent too much time worrying about her worrying, reassuring her. My dad needs less from me. It's easier to live with him.

I continue scrolling through texts—I've got twelve from this morning alone.

*ROSIE: hey sexy, what are you wearing Sat. night? Less is more, Baby!*

*HENRIETTA: I've been without panties for 3 days, just thought you shld know*

*LEXI: u r mine tomorrow.*

*ANGEL: my leg will now touch my face. I'm sending u a pic. Try to imagine it draped over your shoulder...*

*BRITTNEY: been waiting a year for you to turn 18, Scott. Now it's legal to touch you in private*

Cole comes up beside me, so I tuck the phone away. Before we reach my car, though, I hear someone call my name from across the parking lot.

"Fletch! Wait up." Haley is jogging toward us. I glance quickly at her hands to make sure she's not offering me any more cookies. She stops in front of us, her face flushed. "Can I call you Fletch? And...when do you want to get together? I'm free all weekend."

Haley Stevenson is free all weekend? How is this possible? Even without a boyfriend—at least I don't think she has one at the moment—she's still like the social center of all things...well, social.

"I work on Saturday night," I say.

"Cool, where do you work?" Haley asks.

Beside me, Cole snorts back a laugh. I turn to him, shooting a glare in his direction. If he wants to hang out in the big kids' club, he needs to learn to keep his damn mouth shut. I turn back to Haley. "I work outside of town."

"Really?" Unfortunately, she looks genuinely curious. "Doing what?"

"It's just, you know, odd jobs. Freelance..." I scratch the back of my head. "That kind of stuff."

"All right, then." She rolls her eyes. "Don't tell me."

*Okay, new subject.* "Tomorrow morning, does that work? Maybe around ten or eleven?"

She agrees, and I give her my address and phone number. Before I have a chance to absorb the fact that I've just signed up to spend extra time with the world's most infuriating girl, I focus on a plan of action—two birds with one stone and all that shit. Once we're safely in my car, I turn to Cole. "You busy tomorrow morning?"

"Wait...so you guys are like studying together?" Cole asks.

"Partners. For a project." I toss the glittery invitation onto his lap and then back the car out of the parking space.

He's very carefully touching the card, like it's actually

Haley instead of just made *by* Haley. I keep glancing his way, waiting for him to say something, but he's still staring at the card, his face reflecting either hurt or jealousy, maybe both.

"Relax, man." I take the card away. "This is a classic case of popular girl using nerdy guy. She wants me to do the project, and she wants an *A*."

"She said that?"

I shake my head and laugh. "No. She'd never come right out and ask, but it's implied. Trust me. And I couldn't care less. I'd rather do it myself, anyway."

"Won't it be weird for me to hang around during your study session?" Cole asks, but I can tell by his tone that he wants to.

"It's fine. You're family, you're supposed to hang around." I give his shoulder a light punch. "It's time for you to grow a pair, okay?"

# Chapter Six

## −HALEY−

**ME:** *should I bring anything? Chips? Soda? Pimento loaf?*

**FLETCH:** *pimento loaf? Wtf is that?*

**ME:** *don't know but my mom keeps telling me "there's pimento loaf in the fridge if ur hungry." That was days ago. I'm afraid to look.*

**FLETCH:** *yeah, u should be. Don't bring anything*

**ME:** *nothing?*

**FLETCH:** *nothing. Srsly. I got it covered*

. . .

'm breaking one of the first Junior League rules that I learned—don't show up at someone's house without bringing something. But then again, I brought Jamie. Maybe that counts. Maybe I should have warned Fletch about the additional guest, but I was too afraid he'd be scared away, and Jamie could really use some of Fletch's Civics knowledge to help him pass this class. But it's probably better if I don't mention that part to Fletch.

I set one white sandal onto Fletch's driveway, the car door only halfway open, when a herd of dogs comes running at us. Before I can even process this development, the back door flies open and Fletch is jumping in front of the dogs, commanding them to stay. The big yellow lab sits immediately, but the other two brown ones fuel their energy into pacing in a circle, knowing they aren't supposed to jump on us.

"Holy shit," Jamie says, stepping out of the car and assessing the property. "You ever thought about having a party out here? It would be kick-ass."

Fletcher does a double take after hearing Jamie. But he doesn't say anything about this extra guest.

I throw Jamie a warning look. *We're serious academics, remember?* Then I smile at Fletch. "He's kidding."

Jamie eyes the lake out past the barn. "I'm totally not."

"Jamie's looking for ideas for his project," I say. "He's here for inspiration."

Even I think that's crossing the corny line, but Fletch doesn't say a word. I look him over for the first time since arriving. He has on jeans and boots, like he's been outside working. I know they run some sort of farm here, but I don't know much about it. His hair is messy as usual, and he attempts to smooth it like he'd forgotten we were coming over. He's also wearing a T-shirt that says I'm MENTALLY CORRECTING YOUR GRAMMAR.

Yep, I'd say I picked a good partner.

"Not much of a party guy," Fletch says. He pats the yellow lab on the head, whispering "good girl," then he leads us inside. The house is pretty old, but the kitchen is immaculate—brand-new steel counters and cabinets, spotless tile floors, all the appliances sparkling. The living room is more lived in and a little closer to what my house looks like inside. Except minus anything remotely feminine. This place is a man cave, no doubt. Fletch waves a hand at the coffee table, where someone has laid out some odd-looking crackers, sliced meat, and lots of fruit. By fruit, I mean pieces of fruit randomly strewn across the table. "Help yourself."

The big man-cave flat-screen is playing a baseball game, muted. Someone moves in the recliner facing the TV, and I spot a pair of skinny legs resting on the wood floors and some blond hair poking from the top of the chair—Cole Clooney.

I turn quickly to Fletcher, my eyes narrowed. He shoves his black-rimmed glasses back to the bridge of his nose. He's done that move three times in questionable situations. I'd say that's a habit to take notice of.

Jamie is busy examining the strange crackers and shoving meat in his mouth while trying to say hi to Cole. I almost elbow him to remind him to use his manners, but then I remember that we're in a man cave and those rules might not apply. Instead, I tug the sleeve of Fletch's T-shirt. "I forgot my bag in the car. Can you help me get it?"

"I'll do it," Jamie says, more out of obligation than actual willingness.

"Nope, I need Fletch to keep the muddy dogs from pawing my white dress."

Fletch looks annoyed by my comment about his dogs, but follows me anyway. When we get to my car, I reach in the back and grab my bag, slinging it over my shoulder. I spin to face Fletch. "What are you up to?"

His eyes widen, all innocent-looking. "I'm not—"

"Yes, you are. I thought your 'you should hang out with my cousin' comment the other day was odd, but now it makes sense." I tap my foot and wait for him to confess. He doesn't, of course. "Are you so naive that you think I'm not aware of Cole's little crush on me?"

The dogs choose that moment to exit the barn and come barreling at us. Fletch lifts a hand to stop them, but I shove it away. "It's fine."

The two chocolate labs are the first to get a dirt-covered paw on me, leaving several marks up my dress. But the yellow lab hangs back.

I laugh at the paw prints and then reach a hand out to pet the yellow lab. "Look at you, you're the good one, aren't you?" I bend down and sit on the gravel driveway with the dogs, then look up at Fletch. "He or she?"

"They're all girls," he says, then pats the yellow lab on the head. "She's mine. Vixen."

"Vixen?"

He nods and then points to the other two. "Prancer and Dancer. They were born on Christmas Eve."

I turn my attention back to Vixen, my hands now rubbing under her ears. She licks my cheek and wags her tail. "She's so happy. Are you sure she's *your* dog?"

Fletcher kicks a rock in my direction, but there's a tiny hint of amusement on his face. "She's not happy. She's fierce. Vixen! Attack!" he commands, snapping his fingers.

The other two dogs sprint toward the mailbox and start barking at nothing—there's nothing around here—but Vixen stays put and continues licking my cheek and sniffing my neck.

I've forgotten why we even came out here. My dog addiction took over. "I've always wanted a dog, but my dad's allergic. Cats, too." I look into Vixen's brown eyes. "You would come with me if I invited you, right? You can sleep in my bed and lay on a pile of clean laundry if you want." The other day, Jamie's mom screamed at their dog, Alpha, for sitting on clean laundry. I wanted to strangle her after that. The way his little head hung down when he trotted away, it was heartbreaking.

"Maybe if you make her a glittery invitation..."

Fletch has his thumbs jammed into his pockets, and he's leaning against my car. For a quiet, nerdy type, he has an ease about him. He's comfortable in his own skin. This is probably my biggest issue with Cole. It was the same thing with the sophomore I dated briefly last fall. Call me horrible, but when a guy talks to me—especially when he kisses me—I want him to be in control, I want him to be sure of himself. I'm over the boys.

But speaking of Cole...

"So, Cole..." I pull myself back on my feet and dust off as well as I can. "It's not gonna happen. If that's the only reason you agreed to be my partner, then I think you should change your RSVP to no."

Fletcher stares at my dress and then shoves his glasses again. *Hmmm...*

"Is that the only reason you agreed?" I press. Of course I figured he had some ulterior motive, but I assumed he either wanted me to shut up and saying yes might make that happen, or he thought maybe all the partnerships were figured out since he'd left class early that day.

The way he diverts his gaze and scratches his head, I already know the answer. "Does it really matter? I'll do the project. It's no big deal. Just go in there and talk to him for a few minutes."

"I'll talk to him, and you'll do the project?" I'm trying not to ball my hands into fists, but seriously? What the hell?

"I'm not saying you have to lie to him or anything," Fletch explains. "You're into helping people and all that shit, right? The kid needs practice talking to girls. Just help him out. And don't worry about the project. I got it covered."

I blow the loose hair off my face and then draw in a slow, deep breath. *Don't yell, Haley. Or swear at him. Be a lady.* "You know what I think? Cole's not the only one who needs lessons in how to talk to girls."

Vixen must be one of those dogs who sense when humans are upset, because she moves to my side immediately, rubbing her sweet, happy face against my thigh. See? I don't need a boyfriend, I need a dog. I reach down to pet Vixen again. "You are so sweet. Just don't let that grouchy guy rub off on you."

Fletcher folds his arms across his chest. He looks pissed. Good. "So I'm mean now? Why? Because I didn't accept your fucking cookies? Are you really that self-involved, Haley? I'm a horrible person because the Princess of Juniper Falls gave me a gift and I didn't want it?"

I swallow back the overflowing anger. His words are too close to the ones Tate shouted at me so many months ago. Back then, he'd been kind of right. I was scared and thought I needed him, but my words and behavior had been shallow and selfish. But I've come a long way since then, and I'm not about to let Fletcher Scott label me as that girl again.

"I'm gonna go in there…" I point a finger at the door. "And I'm going to talk to your cousin because you're right, I do like helping people. But as far as the project goes, you don't get to do it by yourself. You're stuck with me. Consider it your punishment for being an asshole."

Fletch's mouth falls open in surprise, but I don't wait for him to come up with some asshole reply. With my bag on my shoulder again, I fling the back door open and stomp inside.

# Chapter Seven

## —FLETCHER—

Haley's sitting on my couch, her back perfectly straight, her face calm and relaxed—not like someone covered in dirt who called me an asshole fifteen minutes ago. Jamie's sprawled out beside her, piling the last of my smoked turkey breast into his mouth. Cole is pretending to watch the baseball game, but really, he's sneaking glances at Haley's legs.

When she sat on the driveway with my dogs, her short dress drifted up high enough for me to see a flash of pink panties. And I hadn't looked away. So yeah, maybe I am an asshole.

"Cole?" Haley says.

My pen slips from my hand. She really is going to talk to him.

Cole spins the recliner so he's facing us, his cheeks already bright red. I refrain from rolling my eyes, but Jamie doesn't. He even shakes his head. And I honestly have no idea what Jamie is even doing here. Is he Haley's bodyguard? Are they dating? It doesn't seem like they are.

"While we're both here," Haley says to Cole, "can I ask you a few questions for the Otter blog? I'm doing a guest post in July."

"Me?" Cole's voice cracks.

Haley keeps her head ducked, writing something in her notebook, and then she looks up again, plastering on a smile. "Yep, you. We have almost no interviews with underclassmen."

When Cole doesn't initiate further conversation, Haley continues as if he had. "What position do you play, again?"

Jamie and I are both watching this exchange the way you'd stare at a car accident—horrified yet curious.

"Uh...forward," Cole manages to say with his eyes down, picking at the skin around his thumbnail.

Haley, on the other hand, is looking right at him. "Eye contact, Cole. It's essential in an interview." She smiles broader when he actually looks at her. "Think about when you're in the NHL and SportsCenter wants to talk to you... this is all training for that."

Jamie stifles a laugh.

"So...a forward does what, exactly?" The way Haley locks eyes with him, I'm right there, mesmerized. She's got some weird power of persuasion. "Can you give a game scenario or recap a play from state, maybe?"

Cole drops his head again, exhaling. State is a huge sore spot for him. In the final game, he plowed into Tanley and knocked him unconscious, forcing him out of the game. Which forced us to put in a cold goalie, not nearly as good as Tanley, and then we lost.

"Or sections," Haley adds, probably realizing her mistake. "Eye contact, Cole."

And to my surprise, my little cousin dives into an in-depth explanation of the third period of the game that took us to state. I tune him out and turn to Jamie. "So...who's your partner for the Constitution project?"

"Don't know yet." He snatches up a banana and then tosses his feet on the coffee table. "Markson said me and Haley weren't allowed to work together, so she's hooking me up with someone."

"Markson's hooking you up with a partner?"

Jamie points at the blonde beside him. "No, Stevenson is playing matchmaker. She's working on a few leads. She got you, so I know she'll come through for me. You know this shit, right? Aren't you doing college stuff already?"

Haley glances at us when Jamie says that. I clear my throat. "Um yeah...I've been taking some gen eds."

"Really?" Haley asks. "Since when?"

"Freshman year," Cole answers for me and then recoils when I glare at him.

"I haven't even looked over the assignment yet. Have you guys?" I lay the handout in front of me and pretend to read it.

"I have," Haley announces; she's proud of this fact. "I really love option number five. I have a bunch of ideas. I was thinking we could dress like Thomas Jefferson and his wife—I'm pretty good with a sewing machine—and then we can stage a conversation about signing the Constitution, and since we're supposed to use theatrics to put our own twist on it, Thomas can offer the pen to his wife. He'll let her sign instead of him, and that will be symbolic of women's voting rights to come in the future."

I stare at her in disbelief. "You're kidding, right?"

Haley's neck flushes. She yanks out the messy bun on top of her head and lets her hair fall down to cover it. Her gaze falls back to the worksheet, her thumbnail in her mouth. "Yeah, that's probably stupid. I have some other ideas—"

"I think it sounds cool," Cole says, even though I look over at him like he's nuts. Nuts for Haley is more accurate.

Jamie tosses a few grapes into his mouth. "Hey, can you sew me a costume, too?"

Haley tucks her hair behind her ears and shakes her head. Her pen is tapping against the coffee table. "No, it's stupid. What were you thinking we should do, Fletch?"

If my dad or Grandpa Scott were in the room right now, they would both smack me on the head for "making a woman feel unheard," as Dad has told me so many times never to do. And my parents may not be together, but my dad still has it going on with the ladies. And he's pushing fifty.

"It's not that I don't like your idea," I say, putting on my best face. "But I'm not really into live-action performance."

A laugh bursts out from Cole, but he quickly turns it into a cough. I swear that kid is going down if he doesn't cut that shit out.

Some of the life and energy returns to Haley's face, and I'm surprised by how relieved that makes me feel. She sits up straight again. "That's okay, I get it. Let's do something else." She hands the sheet to Cole. "What do you think?"

"Well...I'm not like...you know, in the class," Cole stutters.

Haley sends her direct eye contact his way again. "I asked you a question, Cole. Answer it. Or politely decline. I'm aware that you're not in the class."

If those words weren't dripping with patience and sweetness, with Haley's pretty birdlike voice, they'd be mean as hell. Maybe that's a tip for future me. I can say whatever I want to her, I just need to use the right tone.

"Okay, right." Cole nods and takes his time reading the paper.

Jamie tosses an apple at me to get my attention. I catch it before it smashes against my glasses. When I look up, he mouths: *this is fucked up.*

I snort back a laugh and then internally freak out because I just shared a joke with Jamie Isaacs. I'm not ever in the general vicinity of Jamie's jokes. Before I get all twisted up about this, I make small talk with him—another first. "So, have you gotten any info about Minnesota State? When do they start workouts?"

Jamie sighs. "Last week. But I gotta pass this damn class or lose my spot. But me and Leo are keeping in shape."

"Really?" I take a bite of the apple. "What kind of workouts are you doing?"

"We scored some ice time," he says, "and we're doing cardio every night, weights at the gym…that kind of shit."

"I'm doing weights in the morning. Trying to catch up with Red."

Jamie laughs and then quickly smooths out his expression. "No offense, dude. But Red's a monster. Besides, he's predictable. The guy can't turn worth shit. All you gotta do is check him while he's turnin'—" Jamie stops abruptly and stares at me. "You're serious, aren't you?"

I shrug and try my best poker face. But inside I'm dying for Monday-morning practice so I can test this theory.

"Don't fucking downplay it," Jamie accuses. "You want a better spot next season, you sure as hell need to be able to say it." He drops his feet to the floor and leans forward. "Is that what you want?"

I debate shrugging again. I like my quiet existence where my goals are locked inside my head and not there for anyone to see. But for some reason, I tell him. "Yeah, I guess that's what I want."

"You guess?" His eyebrows rise, then he leans back

against the couch again. "If you decide you're sure, then come to the rink Sunday night. Around nine. Me and Leo have the place to ourselves."

Wait, is he gonna let me train with them? I start to ask, but Jamie cuts me off, nodding toward Cole and shaking his head. Okay, so this is a secret. I can handle that.

"...Cheerleading is going great, Cole. Thanks for asking," I hear Haley say. "We're working with a really great choreographer for our new competition routine."

An hour later, we've decided on a PowerPoint presentation but haven't really gotten anywhere toward completing the assignment, but it's nearly time for me to head to work and Haley has plans. I leave Cole in the living room and walk both of them out. Jamie, who's not as fond of the dogs, gets right into Haley's Honda Civic, but she stops to pet all three.

Feeling like we left things unfinished earlier, I bite the bullet and apologize. "I'm sorry for tricking you into coming here."

Haley stands up and faces me, her dress covered in dusty dirt. She's braided her hair into a long, intricate braid over the last hour — the girl does not stop moving — and she grips the end of the braid, twisting it around her finger. "I just thought you *wanted* to work with me. I guess that was my fault for making an assumption. I mean, why would you?"

"Especially after the Cheerios," I joke.

Haley gives a half smile at that, but her eyes show defeat. I scrub a hand over my face and do something I know I'll regret. "Look, let's start over. Tomorrow, you and me. Making the most awesome Constitution project ever, okay?"

Her whole face lights. "Together? Fifty-fifty?"

"Fifty-fifty," I confirm. *Please don't let this suck.*

Haley throws her arms around my neck, and I'm so shocked I don't move to remove them. In fact, I return the hug, wrapping an arm around her tiny waist. The urge to pull her against me, grind our hips together, and swing her around hits hard and fast. I'm startled by this new development and release her, stepping back before anything else happens.

Haley blushes, realizing my reaction. "Sorry. I'm a hugging person." She nods toward her car. "Jamie, too. So watch out. He'll crush you before you can ask him to let go."

I shove my glasses back to the bridge of my nose. "I'll be sure to keep my distance. From Jamie," I add. *And you. Jesus. What the hell?*

Haley turns quickly and opens the car door. "See you tomorrow, Fletch. I'll come about the same time?"

"Yeah, sure."

When I walk back into the living room, Cole has the recliner lying all the way back, and he's staring up at the ceiling, his hands behind his head.

"I think that went well," he says, a big grin on his face.

My stomach twists. I should just tell him that Haley's not interested. But I can't remember the last time I've seen Cole this happy, and I can't bring myself to tell him. Besides, he thinks his chat with Haley—which was like a bizarre academic lesson in basic conversation—went well. He might not even believe me. Then I'd be the bad guy who told him he doesn't stand a chance. Truth is, give it a couple of years and Cole might stand a chance with someone like Haley. Hell, that's what happened with Tanley and Claire O'Connor. But right now, Haley and Cole are in very different places.

The other reason that I don't want to tell Cole what Haley said: I can't get her out of my head—the feel of my arms around her…she's the perfect size for me. I could lift her with a couple of fingers.

So yeah, I need to get my head somewhere else ASAP.

Lucky for me, the girls from work have been texting me all morning to come in early. I kick Cole's foot. "I gotta get ready for work. Are you hanging out, or do you want a ride home? Braden's bartending tonight, so he won't be around."

Cole pops the recliner upright. "Think I can go with you guys?"

I look him up and down and then laugh. "Uh-uh. You aren't ready."

"I am. I totally am," he says so earnestly, like I might actually say yes.

"Where's your fake ID?" I lift an eyebrow, waiting.

He deflates. "You've been going for two years, and you just turned eighteen…"

"As an employee," I remind him. "Ricky's had very strict rules in place for me."

This is sort of true. I wasn't allowed to take customers back in the private rooms. And they were all warned to keep their hands out of my pants, but that only made women—and sometimes men—more determined and creative. Thank God for bouncers.

Cole doesn't press me further about joining me at work, and we spend an hour playing Xbox together before I drop him off and head out on the two-lane highway that leads to Longmeadow. I'd planned to get to work early with the intent of putting in some extra rehearsal time, but the second I walk through the door, Rosie and Henrietta clobber me with "birthday kisses," and before long, we're knocking back way too many shots of tequila and rum.

# Chapter Eight

## -HALEY-

Fletch never answered my text about bringing something over today, so I took that as a yes. When I pull into his gravel driveway for the second day in a row, I'm not empty-handed. I knock on the door a few times, and after no one answers, I ring the bell. I'm standing there nearly five minutes when I hear the dogs barking. An older man with jeans and boots and silver hair comes walking up from the lake behind the house, then a middle-aged man hops down from the roof of the barn—he's got Fletch's dark hair.

Both men walk toward me at the same time, assessing me. The oldest one eyes the bread in my hand. I plaster on a smile. "I'm Haley Stevenson. Fletch and I are supposed to work on a project today…"

The man with dark hair pulls off his work glove and reaches out to shake my hand. "Jeffery Scott. I'm Fletch's dad." He points to the older man. "And this is my dad."

"Haley Stevenson, huh?" Fletch's grandpa looks me over

again. "Guess he took our advice." He plucks the bag from my hand and opens it immediately, burying his nose in it. "Whatcha got here?"

"It's not cookies," I say right away.

Okay, where is Fletch? And where is his mom? I'm really great with moms.

"Cinnamon? Apples? Oats?" Grandpa guesses.

Far in the distance, a motor or engine of some kind starts and then putters to a stop several times. Both men are frozen, listening, and then Fletch's dad swears under his breath.

"I better go check on that tractor," Mr. Scott says, then he flashes me a grin that's the polar opposite of his son's usual sullen expression. "Nice meeting you, Haley."

"Come on." Grandpa nods at me and opens the door, leading me through the kitchen. He ties the bread up tight again, and when he disappears into what looks like a closet, I swear to God I hear the thud of my homemade bread landing in a garbage can. But when Grandpa emerges, he grins big and says, "That'll be great with dinner. Now let's see what our boy is up to…"

I stand awkwardly beside him while he knocks on Fletch's door, getting no response. Before I can offer to come back later, he's swinging the door open. The first sight I take in is the completely immaculate room. Nothing on the floor, no clutter anywhere. Shelves with large plastic-lidded bins line the walls.

Fletch is sprawled on his stomach, one leg hanging off the twin-size bed. He's wearing black dress shoes and black dress pants, a red button-down shirt untucked, probably partially unbuttoned, and barely on him. His hair is sticking up in every direction, like dozens of fingers have made their way through it. Smudges of red are scattered all over his face, his bare forearms, and the strip of flesh exposed on his side.

Even more alarming are the various colors of lace—suspiciously resembling lingerie—poking out of the pockets of his pants. I take a step into his room, wanting a closer look. The faded green bills attached to Fletch's waistband catch my eye. "Is that money?"

"Oh boy." Fletch's grandpa eyes me warily, then he touches a hand to my shoulder. "If he asks, you let yourself in, okay?"

I don't even get to respond because he abandons me, walking quickly across the house, and the sound of the back door opening and closing follows him. And yeah, I could do the same. Obviously, I've caught Fletch at a bad time, so leaving is the wise thing to do. But now that I've seen all this, there's no way I'm gonna take off before figuring this shit out.

This is like a frat prank gone wrong. Maybe the community college has fraternities and Fletch is pledging?

I walk all the way across the military-clean bedroom and stand over him. I was right. Actual money is stuffed in his pants. But I go for the lace-filled pockets first. Fletch is sleeping like the dead and doesn't even stir when I pluck the first pair of panties from his pocket. I release it onto the immaculate floor right away and go for another one. Between both pockets, he's got two black pairs, a green, and two red. All thongs. I go after the cash next, my fingers brushing his skin in the process.

Before long, a pile of bills is stacked up on the bed, and I'm more confused than ever about my supposedly nerdy Civics partner.

# Chapter Nine

## -FLETCHER-

I wake up with a pounding headache, my eyes refusing to open. Okay, this is not happening again. I'm two steps from an afterschool special. Maybe three steps from a twelve-step program.

"Look at you sitting there like such a good girl," a soft yet familiar feminine voice says. "What is Fletch going to buy you with all this money? You deserve a new toy, maybe some treats…"

Oh no…no way. My eyes finally open, and the first thing I see is the digital clock beside me: 11:30. Then I lift my head and look around for the body that goes with that voice.

Haley is sprawled out on my floor, Vixen curled up beside her. And a bunch of cash sorted into piles is stacked in front of her.

Shit. Oh shit.

I pull myself up to a sitting position, my mouth too dry to speak. A cold breeze from the vent above my head hits my stomach, and I glance down at my bare chest, taking in the lipstick smudged all over it. I yank my shirt together, buttoning it quickly.

"Good morning, sunshine." Haley flashes me a devious grin. "What a night, huh? Four hundred and eighty-two dollars. Is that what you usually pull for those...*odd jobs*?"

Oh God, this is bad. Really bad. Like moving to Duluth to live with Mom bad. My stomach twists, and I stumble out of bed, heading straight for the bathroom. I don't even get the door all the way shut before I'm leaning over the toilet, puking up way too many shots of rum. Never again. Never again.

I wait for the heaving to stop before flushing the toilet and leaning over the sink to rinse my mouth. Still a bit unsettled, I sit down on the bathroom floor and lean against the tub. I almost forget Haley's presence in my house until the door creaks all the way open and she's standing in front of me, holding a glass of water.

She hands it to me, surprisingly lacking the judgmental look I'd been expecting.

"Thanks," I croak out after taking a long drink. "Sorry. About sleeping through our study session or project session or whatever..."

Haley squats down and assesses me. "Your eyes are really red. You're not a drug addict, are you?"

"Shit. My contacts." That would explain the glued-together feeling my eyes had this morning. And the fact that they're burning right now. I pull myself to my feet and fumble around in the medicine cabinet for my solution. Relief hits the instant my eyes are free of those things. But the world blurs in front of me. Haley walks out of the bathroom then pops back in, holding my glasses.

"I didn't know you wore contacts," she says.

"Just to play hockey."

"And for work, right?"

The grin I saw right when I woke up returns to her face. This little screwup on my part is going to cost me. Big time. I put my glasses on and spin to face Haley. "I went out with my older brother last night after work. He likes to mess with me."

She smooths out the grin and offers a nod. "Okay, so your older brother likes to mess with you by covering your body in lipstick, stuffing thongs into your pockets, and dropping…oh, like, four hundred dollars into your pants. That makes perfect sense. I don't have a brother, but if I did, I'm sure that's what he'd do to me."

Well, it is partly true. I hung out with Braden after work, but we were still at work and there were lots of others around, too—mostly female others. And Paco. And Danny…I think Rowdy, too.

"I'll tell you what, Fletch," Haley says, reaching around me and turning the knobs on the shower. "I'll give you two choices…one, you can tell me the truth about that little job of yours and I'll leave you alone with your hangover. Or two, you can clean yourself up and get your head together and do some work with me, and I'll forget about the panties and the money and the lipstick…"

I doubt she'll forget anything, but I have to hold out hope at least. I glance warily at her. "Option two. Definitely two."

The smirk on Haley's face is gonna be forever etched into my memory. She knew I'd pick option two. She points to the shower and gives me a little wave. "I'll be in the living room hanging out with Vixen."

I lock my bedroom door behind her and then the bathroom door. I down the entire glass of water and then brush my teeth for nearly five minutes before hopping into the shower. By the time I'm out and dressed, I feel 20 percent less hungover.

Haley is stretched out on the couch with Vixen. Today, she came prepared for dog interaction, wearing long jean shorts and a dark tank top, along with running shoes. Her wavy blond hair is up in a ponytail. She turns around when she hears my door open.

Her gaze sweeps over me, her eyes landing on my gray baseball T-shirt with Meh written across the front. "I think I like it better when you're mentally correcting my grammar."

Yesterday's T-shirt. I lean against the door frame, not sure how to proceed with this studying thing after the start we've had today. "Why is that?"

Haley stands and then shrugs. "I like thinking about people thinking about me inside their heads. Guess I'm self-centered like that." She doesn't give me room to comment or protest. "You should probably eat something. Otherwise you might get sick again."

My eyebrows shoot up. "You sound like someone who knows her way around a hangover." Subconsciously, I'm digging for dirt on Haley. I need some collateral, just in case.

"Yep, I've had a few," she says, no hint of regret in her voice. "Not my finest moments, but it happens."

I haven't moved much, so Haley takes it upon herself to shove me from behind, toward the kitchen. "I'm going, I'm going."

"Good, because I can't be here all day. I've got this arts and crafts with Girl Scouts thing to do later." She opens my fridge and glances around. "Damn, this is like the cleanest kitchen ever."

I laugh, but there's nothing funny about the truth behind that fact. "My grandpa runs the kitchen. He keeps a tight ship." After nearly killing me once, he calls it his penance.

"I make great omelets," Haley says, still glancing around the fridge. "That's a surefire hangover cure. With lots of cheese. And bacon if you have it."

I've already got a pot on the stove, and my water and oatmeal measured out. "No thanks."

Haley actually looks disappointed, and after careful observation of her while I'm cooking and then eating, I think it's because she can't stand not having something to do. She kept folding and unfolding napkins, braiding her hair three different ways, scribbling cheers in her notebook, practicing turns on my kitchen floor.

Finally, after fifteen excruciating minutes, I dump my bowl into the sink and glance at my room before deciding that I can't possibly be trapped in there with Haley. I grab her backpack from the floor and toss it over my shoulder. "Let's work on our project outside."

"Outside?" Her nose scrunches, but she follows me anyway. She snaps her fingers once, and Vixen comes trotting in and heads straight for Haley's side.

I stare at her, my mouth half open. "What are you doing to my dog?"

"Just giving her plenty of love and attention. Maybe you should try it sometime."

My only response to that is to glare. I give my dog plenty of love. *Jesus.* I blow out a breath. "Come on, I wanna get this over with."

. . .

"Haley," I say for the third time. Finally, I lean over her and remove her sunglasses.

She jolts to life, rolling over quickly onto her stomach. "Do you ever sit on the roof of the barn? I bet the view is amazing from up there."

I scrub my hands over my face. For a full forty-five minutes we managed to outline the basics of our Constitution presentation and begin writing the material, then I lost her, though she seems in denial of this fact. The weather outside is perfect—seventy-two and sunny—so I'm not too burned up about being out here in this project hell.

Haley leaps up from the grass and heads to the barn, glancing over the sidewall and the roof. "I could climb this…" She turns to me. "Can I climb this?"

"Whatever."

I watch her place her foot in the exact place I've used to hoist myself up a thousand or more times. She glances over her shoulder. "Spot me, okay?"

Instead, I climb behind her, barely keeping up. When we get to the top, I sit down on the slanted roof, taking in the view. I never get tired of it. My entire life I've been looking out here, and it's still amazing. The giant lake behind Grandpa's house is visible, plus his ten acres of cornfields— even Braden and Dad on the tractor are easy to spot. Haley takes five seconds to look out, and then she's walking up and down the side of the roof like it's a balance beam.

"Hey Fletch?" She pauses to make sure I'm listening. "Is it true what you told Jamie yesterday? About wanting to take Red's spot?"

"I didn't—"

She lifts her sunglasses and gives me a look. "You did. You want a better spot. Right?"

"Who doesn't?" This conversation is making me very

uncomfortable. "Statistically speaking, if I'm on the varsity roster for an entire season, I'll get at least three hours of playing time. At least. So I'm already in a better position."

"That's your wall, huh?"

I look up at her, completely confused. "My wall?"

"Yeah, your wall. The thing you put between you and people." She increases her pace, spinning on the ball of her tennis shoe when she reaches each end. "It's obvious that I'm ruining all your plans. You throw your smart-person mumbo-jumbo stats at people, if you even bother talking to them—"

"Haley!" I bolt upright, watching her foot slip in slow motion. One foot comes out from under her and then the other. My heart jumps up to my throat, my arm shooting out, hooking around her waist. I grab her, preventing her from falling, then pull her down as quickly as possible, forcing her to lie on her back on the slanted side of the roof.

# Chapter Ten

## -HALEY-

The breath is sucked out of my lungs, my heart on a high-speed chase. My head slams against the roof a little harder than I would have liked, but luckily, I'm not on the ground dead or paralyzed. Vixen barks from below, showing her concern.

Fletch's arm is around my midsection, his weight half on top of me. I can feel the rapid rise and fall of his chest, his heart slamming against his rib cage. He smells like cinnamon. He swears under his breath and then his lips are right next to my ear. "Do not. Stand up. Again. Understood?"

Goose bumps spread all over my body. I can't breathe or speak. I nod my head up and down several times.

I think I just experienced a true adrenaline high. Or maybe I'm in the high right now.

Fletch exhales and then raises his head, his eyes meeting mine. My heart drums faster. "Haley? You okay?"

He's scanning me top to bottom like maybe a limb fell

off or something, but the look on his face, the way it's open
and inviting—that's the Fletcher Scott I want to get to know.
A laugh escapes my mouth. "I think I'm having one of those
epiphany things. Like when what's-his-name got hit in the
head with an apple and figured out gravity."

"Isaac Newton," Fletch says. "Except it's not confirmed
that the apple actually hit him in the head. And we still don't
understand everything about gravity—"

I wave a hand in front of his face. "There's the wall again.
Now you don't get to hear my epiphany."

His mouth forms a thin line, jaw tensing. He quickly
withdraws his arm from around me and slides back, putting a
good two feet between us. "I hope this epiphany is something
along the lines of 'wandering around on my barn roof will
get you killed.'"

I turn my face toward him but stay lying on my back.
"I just realized that this wall you have up…it's probably
not there all the time. I've caught a few glimpses of Other
Fletcher when you aren't on your game."

A sly grin spreads across his face, and all I can think is,
*there it is, Other Fletcher*. "You have no idea what you're
talking about, Haley."

"Not completely," I agree. "But I'm onto something.
The you that hangs out with Cole Clooney and has panties
stuffed in his pockets is a very different guy than the one
sitting behind me in Civics. Am I wrong?"

The grin fades from his face, and he stares at me for a
beat too long before he pulls himself up to his feet. "We
need to get back to work."

I roll my eyes. Should've seen that coming.

• • •

Jamie glances at the Girl Scouts climbing the playground like little ants on a log, then he turns back to me, fighting laughter. "Let me get this straight…you think Fletcher Scott is a stripper?"

It sounds ridiculous when Jamie says it out loud, but seriously, the guy had several hundred dollars stuffed in his pants. What else am I supposed to think? I catch Cole looking our way from across the playground and give Jamie a warning. "Shut up," I hiss. "Why would you bring Cole? Are you trying to feed into this crush of his? That's not very nice, you know."

Jamie shrugs. "He's my little wingman."

"Wingman? For who? The Girl Scouts?" I groan and step around him, heading for the picnic tables where Leo is unloading my box of supplies.

"You know what I hate more than anything?" I say to Leo. "When my cheerleaders screw me over and don't show for something they willingly volunteered for."

Leo drops containers of beads onto the table and then looks up at me, grinning. "Is that your way of thanking me for being here?"

"Sure." Just as I'm about to cast a cheer-curse on Amanda and Bailey, Amanda's car rolls into the parking lot, windows down, rap music blasting. I throw a glare in their direction and then walk toward the playground. "All right, Girl Scouts, let me see you line up!"

The twenty-or-so girls in brown shorts with sashes across their chests abandon the playground and run toward me. Jake Hammond—who had been helping little girls across the monkey bars—heads over to stand beside me. The girls must be eager to hang out with the current Prince and Princess of Juniper Falls, because they form that line faster than I thought possible.

"I need all of you to raise your right hands," I tell them. Amanda and Bailey shuffle toward me, hanging out beside Jake and me. Before they can utter some lame-ass excuse, I start talking again. "Repeat after me." All the girls stand straight, chests puffed out. It's adorable how serious they are. "I promise…"

They repeat the words in unison.

"To never show up late to any of my commitments." I wait for them to recite the words while my cheer-mates stare at the ground, shuffling their feet. "To always be responsible for my actions, especially when very nice, adorable Girl Scouts are counting on me."

Thankfully, Amanda and Bailey have enough sense to keep their mouths shut while I explain the craft we're doing and the girls take their seats to make beaded pins to attach to their sashes. Finally, I step away from the table and turn to face my teammates.

"Both of you are on probation—"

"We volunteered for this—" Bailey starts.

I lift a hand to shut her up. "Exactly. Next time, don't bother. Especially if you're going to roll in here blasting music with f-bombs in every line. Do you guys possess any amount of common sense?"

Neither of these girls have younger siblings, probably don't work with kids at all, so cutting them some slack wouldn't be the worst thing ever. But I'm an only child, and even I can figure out that rolling into a park in the middle of a summer weekend day with inappropriate music might reflect badly on me. When it comes to my girls on the cheer squad, I don't cut any slack. We live in this constant hole created by the cheerleader stigma, even worse in Juniper Falls because it's always all about hockey. Even with cheerleading. While I'm captain, these girls are gonna act like decent people, keep in shape, respect themselves, not get caught passed-out drunk by the pond. The basics.

Both of them mumble sorry, and I wave them toward the table, indicating that they should help out. Bailey plasters on her cheer smile and attempts sucking up to me by saying loudly to all the Girl Scouts, "How many of you are going to be Princess of Juniper Falls like Haley?"

Sixteen of the twenty hands shoot up in the air. I roll my eyes. Now we have to teach them basic math, considering they're all between eight and ten years old. Mathematically, that leaves room for two, maybe three princesses in the group.

"How many of you are going to be hockey players like Jake?" I say.

A few hands shoot up in the air—including Jake's little sister, Maddie—and I look at those stats and sigh. I love my town, I really do. I want to live here forever and for my kids to live here. But it sucks that all these girls get pushed into skates like the boys, but then when they reach high school, it's like, cheerleading or volleyball or maybe basketball or track. And of course, impressing the town elders for that princess nomination.

"I'm gonna play football!" a tiny messy-haired girl says.

I walk past her and give her a high five. "Who's going to be in honors classes like Jake?"

Conversation breaks out among the group, all the girls talking at once about what they'll be into when they go to JFH. I must look incredibly frustrated, because Jake comes up to me while the girls are still elbow-deep into their craft.

"You okay?" he asks.

For a majorly hyped-up hockey star, Jake is incredibly genuine, but I still feel this barrier between him and me. Like he's all about the game. Nothing will change that.

And last fall, we had this drunken hookup incident that left things a bit weird between us. We talk, but there's no casual touching like there used to be.

"I'm fine." I flash Jake a smile just to prove it. "Just trying to keep my cheerleaders out of the town gossip mill."

"You're going all dictator on them, aren't you?" Jake gives me his charming Jake-Hammond grin to show he's kidding. "I saw you guys out for a run at like six in the morning. What's up with that?"

"Cardio. It's crucial to getting through an entire competition routine." I walk behind Jake's sister, Maddie, and examine her pin. Like her brother, she's a hockey phenom, even at the age of nine, but her artistic skills aren't in the same universe. I grip the end of her pin to keep the beads from falling off.

"Dang it." Maddie looks up at me, her cheeks flushed. "Can we play on the playground again?"

"Finish your pin first," I tell her, even though I really don't care. I may have come up with this craft activity, but at Maddie's age, I would have steered clear of the craft table and instead been digging in the mud and climbing all over the playground. But God forbid I send a Girl Scout home without a pin.

She sighs. "I suck at this."

"Maddie," Jake warns, imitating his mom's disciplinary tone.

They are pretty prim and proper in the Hammond household. I know this because our mothers are good friends, and my mom does her best to imitate Mrs. Hammond when possible.

Cole Clooney slides into the empty space beside Maddie and takes the pin from her hands. "I'll help you. I'm good with beads."

Jake stares at Cole, his forehead wrinkling like he's completely confused by this. Cole must have felt Jake staring, because his face flushes and he mumbles something about his older sister making jewelry.

I give Cole's shoulder a pat. "I'm gonna fire Amanda and Bailey and hire you for all the volunteer events."

The second the words are out of my mouth—while Cole flashes a beaming smile my way—I regret them. The last thing I want to do is lead him on. But I can't undo what I've just said without stumbling over my words and probably making things worse. Instead, I walk away and put some distance between him and me.

Jamie walks up beside me and whispers, "Look at little man over there, laying his charm on the Girl Scout."

I give Jamie a look. "That's Jake's sister. She's nine."

He shrugs. "Hey, practice is practice."

I shove Jamie. "Go get the cookies, will you?"

Jamie jogs over to my car and emerges with containers of homemade cookies and lemonade. Everyone jumps in to help distribute the snacks except Cole—he stays in his seat, putting the finishing touches on Maddie's pin. I offer him the container, and he grabs a handful of cookies.

"At least you haven't taken up Fletcher's cookie-rejecting habits." It's another string of words that slips out without thought. Why am I bringing up Fletch right now? Why am I comparing him to Cole?

"That's because it'd kill him," Cole says with his mouth full of cookie, his gaze focused on the pin and beads in front of him.

I nearly drop the tin in my hands. "What?"

"My mom says cookies make people fat," a girl across the table says. "And fat people die."

"Everybody dies," Maddie says, handing Cole a big green

bead. Her pin is Otter green and silver. "Even if they don't eat any cookies."

Jake claps his hands together. "Okay, don't you girls have a theme song or something? Let's sing that instead of talking about…"

The girls all look up at him, waiting for the sentence to be completed. Luckily Amanda and Bailey decide to be useful and both lead the JFH fight song—something the Girl Scouts are much more familiar with than any Girl-Scout songs that might exist.

While they're singing, I nudge Cole. "What do you mean, cookies would kill Fletch?"

"He's…allergic," Cole admits reluctantly.

I fold my arms across my chest. "To what?"

It's obvious by Cole's expression that Fletch would not be happy about this conversation. Which is probably why Cole puts an end to it by shrugging and saying, "Cookies."

Maybe Fletch is allergic to nuts? I think those people can die if they eat nuts. Why couldn't he just say that instead of making me feel like an idiot?

On impulse, I pull out my phone and send him a text. I'm not gonna rat out Cole, just poke Fletch a bit and see if he admits to anything.

*ME: apparently ur cousin doesn't mind eating my cookies*

*FLETCH: I'm not even…*

*ME: Jesus. Get your mind out of the gutter. I meant literal cookies. I guess good manners don't run in the family*

*FLETCH: He'll eat whatever u give him b/c HE IS IN*

*LOVE WITH YOU.*

*ME: whatever. He's nice. Ur...something else. And love? Doubtful. Infatuation? Maybe.*

*FLETCH: OK, I'll give u that. Love is obsolete.*

*ME: obsolete with Cole? Or in general?*

*FLETCH: don't know. Not an expert on the subject.*

*ME: Thought maybe u were, considering all those panties stuffed in ur pockets...*

*FLETCH: more proof that love is obsolete. Panties and love have zero connection. I can get one without the other.*

*ME: gross. And TMI*

*FLETCH: I meant that hypothetically*

*ME: sure u did*

*FLETCH: Haley?*

*ME: yes...?*

*FLETCH: butt out*

I fight the urge to throw my phone across the playground. He's got the brooding-asshole act down a little too well. And yet, part of me wants to prod him some more, if only to get another glimpse of Other Fletcher—the one without so many walls.

How can someone be so infuriating and so interesting at the same time?

# Chapter Eleven

## -FLETCHER-

"No, no, no!" Jamie shakes his head at me. "You're reacting instead of predicting. It's too late at that point."

I bend over, panting. "How can I react if there isn't anyone to react to?"

"Dude…" Jamie skates toward me and twists to a stop before crashing into me. "You gotta trust us."

Leo is behind Jamie, sliding the puck around the ice. "You get these drills down, and you'll be ready for the real thing."

I pull in a breath, the air barely able to enter my lungs. As much as I hate to bring out the asthma meds in front of these guys, I'm too far into this workout to quit now or risk passing out. I snatch my inhaler off the wall and take a few puffs.

"Need a break?" Jamie asks.

I shake my head, holding the medicine in my lungs for

several seconds. Relief comes instantly, my fingers tingling with feeling returned. "I'm fine. Just ready to learn how to plow Red over."

Both guys laugh, and then Leo says, "You aren't Jamie or Red. First rule of hockey is to know yourself well enough to hone your strengths and work around the weaknesses."

"You can skate, man," Jamie says. "Your balance is better than big guys like me and Red. You're more agile. That's the shit that will catch Bakowski off guard. Especially if you pull it out during the scrimmage game against Longmeadow in August."

Did Jamie Isaacs just use the word "agile" correctly?

Leo rolls his eyes. "The practice game that isn't supposed to decide anything. Right."

Right. Despite my lack of varsity experience, I know this unspoken rule about the end-of-summer scrimmage game: October tryouts are just a formality. The real tryouts are in August. With the exception of the occasional new freshman—like Cole last fall—who may surprise Coach.

I inhale a deep, less-obstructed breath and nod. "Okay, what now?"

Jamie and Leo exchange glances, and then Jamie drops a puck in front of me. "Same drills—back crossovers around the cones—except this time, you do it with the puck and with Leo in your way."

"Got it." I twist around, taking my position, and put every ounce of energy and mind power into repeating these drills over and over again.

"Speed up!" Jamie shouts at me from his seat on the wall after another thirty minutes. "You should be doing this in your scary-fast zone right now."

"Don't be afraid to get a little uncomfortable," Leo adds.

I push myself through the cones, increasing my speed

with each trip. After three more times through, Jamie points a finger at me, grinning big. "Yes! That's where it's at."

Of course, I completely wipe out after that. Sliding across the ice on my ass. I recover quickly, still managing to keep control of the puck. That wins me a nod of approval from Leo.

It's nearly midnight when we finish up—six hours until I have to be up again for practice—and I'm beyond exhausted. But it feels good. Like I'm one inch closer to my goals. After helping Jamie and Leo lock up the rink, we all walk out together, skates slung over our shoulders. Leo gets a call, answers it, and then hops into his truck to continue talking.

"Give me your number, and I'll text you when we score some more ice time," Jamie says, holding up his phone.

I pull my cell from my pocket and try not to think about how weird it is that we never hung out while we were both in school together. Okay, I guess we're in summer school together, but I doubt Jamie had planned to be around this long. I'm long past having any desire to be in the cool kids' circle, but here I am, spending my weekend with them.

"So…Haley thinks you're a stripper," Jamie says, so casually I have to replay his words in my head to make sure that I heard them right.

My mouth falls open, my body tensing. "She told you that? When?"

I was right this morning—everything is ruined. Duluth with Mom, here I come…

"Saw her this afternoon. She was pretty sure about it." Jamie glances over at my car and then back at me. "I thought she was nuts, but you do have a pretty sweet ride, and you won't tell people where you work. I figured you were writing essays for Longmeadow's varsity team. Those guys are bigger idiots than me."

My entire body goes into defensive mode. It's something I'm familiar and comfortable with. I avoid direct eye contact, keep my distance, keep my answers short and precise. "My mom bought me that car. And I promise, I'm not a stripper." One truth. One lie. Not necessarily in that order. I've done this act ever since I started back at school in seventh grade. But for the first time, I feel a little guilty about lying to Jamie. He and Leo spent a lot of time helping me tonight. They didn't have to do that. I'm both appreciative and uncomfortable about this fact. I don't ever want to be in debt to someone, especially someones with as much social influence as Jamie, Leo, and Haley have. I look over at Leo. He's behind the wheel, the phone to his ear. I can see him laughing, but I can't hear him with the door shut and the windows up.

Jamie shrugs. "Whatever, man. Haley's the one freaking out over it, not me. But if you were a stripper…" He glances over at Leo and then back at me. "Hypothetically speaking, would your audience be of the male kind or the female kind?"

"Okay, so not only am I a stripper, but I'm a stripper in a gay strip club?" I pinch the bridge of my nose and force my shoulders down. "Haley really loves her juicy gossip, doesn't she?"

Jamie folds his arms over his chest, looking much less amused. "Hey, don't blame Haley for this. She'd fucking kill me if she knew I told you what she said."

I blow air out of my cheeks, my exhaustion rising a notch. "Then why are we having this conversation?"

Jamie nods in Leo's direction and lowers his voice. "I'm just looking for a place for my man to meet some people… *you know*, like him."

Okay, so senior MVP Leo Rose is not a ladies' man. I

guess I can see that. Now that it's being pointed out to me. I wonder how many people know.

"Kennedy Locust is a fucking prick. And you should see these dudes online he's been talking to. They're fucking nutcases. I just thought maybe if he had more options—"

"I'm not a stripper," I repeat. This conversation needs to end ASAP. "But I'll keep my eyes open for gathering locations of dudes who like dudes, okay?"

Jamie narrows his eyes. This is the intimidating enforcer I labeled him as a long time ago. "Not a word to anyone about this, got it? Not about what Haley told me, either."

I wave a hand, like I'm fully informed, but my stomach jolts, a small ounce of fear returning from my bully-infused elementary-school days. I shove those feelings back down where they belong. "I swear not to tell anyone that Haley is certifiably insane and has a big imagination."

Jamie heads toward Leo's truck but stops before opening the door. "Someday, when you manage to ditch that fucking chip on your shoulder, you're gonna hate yourself for being an ass to Haley. That girl is more loyal than anyone you'll ever meet. She'll lay down in traffic for you if you're friends."

He's giving me an out, a free pass to leave without explanation. I should take it, but I can't for some reason. "Who says I've been an ass to Haley?"

"Not her," Jamie admits. "But she about threw her phone into the park fountain today after texting with you, so I figured you must have been an asshole."

He hops into the truck and shuts the door before I have to answer. I head for my own car and wait for guilt to punch me in the stomach. It does. But it's quickly followed by anger. I didn't ask for this. I didn't fucking ask for Haley Fucking Stevenson to invade my personal space. Everything was just fine before she started tapping her pen against the desk in front of mine. Everything was exactly how I wanted it to be—how I need it to be. And now, just because she's decided to use her calligraphy skills and too-much glitter on me, I'm supposed to fall over and thank my lucky stars?

Fuck that shit. I don't work that way. Not anymore. Not ever.

# Chapter Twelve

## -HALEY-

"A C isn't that bad," Kayla says when we're cleaning up the mats after cheer practice.

I groan to myself and put a little more force into folding the mat at my feet. "I want an *A*." I *need* an *A*.

Leslie, another senior cheerleader, adds, "It's just the first test, right? How many more do you have? We can do the math and figure out what you need in the rest of the class to get an *A*."

"I'm starving," Kayla whines. "I can't do calculations without food. Let's go next door."

I hesitate, chancing a glance at Leslie. She knows I'm not doing the socializing with Kayla thing much, but really, it's the one-on-one BFF sessions that I've openly boycotted. So maybe lunch with the three of us will be fine. But if she brings up Kyle Stewart, I'm not going to patronize her justifications.

"Does this *A* in Civics have anything to do with your recent obsession with a certain college in the middle of

Florida?" Leslie flips her dark hair over one shoulder. She's probably the most responsible cheerleader on the squad, otherwise I'd get on her about the lack of ponytail today and safety issues that go along with this violation. "Seriously, Haley...*A* or not, how the hell are you going to convince your parents to let you go to school all the way in Florida?"

"Out of state tuition is insanely expensive," Kayla adds. "What's wrong with Minnesota State?"

I glare at her. She sounds like my parents. "Besides the fact that their cheer squad is about the same skill level as a third-grade Pop Warner?"

"Cheer snob," Leslie sings, wagging a finger at me.

And yes, I'm obsessed with the University of Central Florida, more specifically their cheer squad. My cousin Serenity graduated from UCF, and when I was in eighth grade, we visited her in Orlando and went to a football game—she was in the marching band—and I quickly set aside my tomboy ways and decided cheerleading was exciting and athletic enough for me. But it was only very recently, after helping my ex-boyfriend's new girlfriend get brave enough to pursue her own far-away-from-Juniper-Cove dreams, that I looked into actually attending UCF. And it's just for four years, just to cheer. Then I'll be back. I'm not headed for Broadway fame like Claire.

"I've emailed the cheer coach a few times," I admit to my girls while we're walking across the street toward O'Connor's tavern. "And he told me they have a few out-of-state tuition waivers for cheerleaders." It's a long shot, but if I can get myself there for a visit, then who knows? Maybe it'll happen. Someone has to make it on that team, and someone has to get awarded those tuition waivers. "Jonas is helping me learn partner stunts."

"I thought Jonas was a tumbling coach? You didn't

mention that he did stunting," Kayla says.

I shrug. I don't want to get too excited. I've just begun learning the basics of stunting with a guy. We have an all-girl cheer squad, and UCF actually has more guys than girls. All the girls are flyers on that team. The crazy shit they do... it's amazing.

When we enter O'Connor's, Claire and her dad are both behind the bar. Claire's dad had a horrible brain tumor last year and has only recently been able to return to work. He's improved dramatically after several surgeries, but he still has issues with motor function and needs someone to, for example, hold a glass while he fills it at the tap.

Claire flashes me a huge grin and waves. I haven't seen her in forever, and I'm dying to catch up, but later. Without Leslie and Kayla. Neither of them can let go of the idea of Claire as the older girl who stole my boyfriend. Technically she *is* with my ex-boyfriend now, but how it happened is far different and more complicated than Leslie and Kayla will ever understand. On some level, Tate has belonged to Claire for a very long time. Neither of them figured that out until recently, but it's true. Depressing for me, but true.

On our way to a table in the back, I spot a guy sitting in our usual booth—Fletcher Scott. He's wearing a black T-shirt with the words "Reindeer Crossing" printed in bright red across his chest. He's pressed all the way to the window, headphones on, a stack of college-looking textbooks in front of him, along with a notebook and several pens. We didn't talk much in class this morning—I was still pissed at him for his little "butt out" comment yesterday, and I was really nervous about the first test. He's focused on his notebook, his body leaning forward, pen moving swiftly across the page. He doesn't look up when we approach.

As much as I'd love to stay pissed off at him, I can't help

but stare at this less-defensive, more-vulnerable Fletch. The image of him lying in his bed with panties and cash stuffed in his pants is replaced by this Fletcher, alone in the booth looking completely…lonely.

Fletcher Scott is lonely.

My heart lurches, and my hand lifts on its own, the corners of my mouth rising in time with my hand. "Hey, Fletch," I say, giving him a wave.

He jerks up, his eyes wide, muscles tensing. He glances around quickly and then his blue eyes fall on me. And instead of returning the smile, he shoves those glasses up to the bridge of his nose and stares at me, his mouth hanging half open like he's waiting for the punch line.

Beside me, Kayla mumbles, "Nerd alert."

And Leslie elbows me in the side and whispers, "Smart move, babe. I bet he can help you out with that grade of yours."

I cringe internally because that's kind of what I had thought, as well, but not like that. I was only following Mrs. Markson's advice about choosing a partner who had a good chance of passing the class. And I never intended to have Fletch do the work. I want to earn my *A*. That part is just as important as the grade itself. I think *I'm* more of a nerd than Fletcher Scott will ever be.

Leslie mimics my wave to Fletch and plasters on the most fake of fake-cheer smiles. "Nice shirt. Are you one of Santa's elves?"

*Seriously? Since when is five nine elf height?* I don't say that out loud because I know these girls are only teasing and there's no vindictiveness behind it, but it seems different today for some reason.

He offers a two-second glare and then looks back down at his book as if silently pointing out that he chose to stay quiet, to not care about me or Leslie or Kayla. I stare at him for a beat too long, and then Leslie pushes me from behind, the three of us falling into a booth not far from Fletch.

The second we're tucked into our seats, I glare at Leslie, keeping my voice low. "Are you trying to shove us into the mean-cheerleader box? What is wrong with you?"

She blushes, guilt all over her face. "Sorry. It's just…"

Habit. That's the word she had to swallow. And it's a terrible excuse. One I would never use for myself, therefore I refuse to let her get away with it.

"It's just you being an asshole for no reason," I snap.

"Look at him," Leslie says, pointing a finger at Fletcher's booth. "He couldn't care less. That's just how he is." Leslie turns to Kayla before I can get in a word of argument. "You don't think I'm being awful, do you?"

"Don't bring her into this." I shake my head. Sometimes I hate my friends, but if they weren't my friends, then who would be responsible for straightening them out?

"She's the one who made the nerd-alert comment," Leslie says.

"Lower your voice," I hiss. And yeah, I forgot that Kayla did make that comment. "Both of you suck at being nice. Work on it."

Kayla mumbles sorry, but Leslie waves a hand like she doesn't think I'm serious. I totally am. If Fletcher and I somehow manage to pull off an amazing grade on this Constitution project, I will flip out if I hear any mention of me bribing a nerd or whatever. Goofy T-shirts and glasses aside, Fletcher Scott is not even in the same universe as the word *geek*. It's not my fault if these closed-minded girls can't see what I can.

I sink back in my chair, this realization hitting me hard. Oh shit…

Am I into Fletch?

# Chapter Thirteen

## -FLETCHER-

"Seriously, Kayla... Stewart is only gonna wait so long before he finds someone else. What are you so afraid of?"

"Shut up," Haley says. "She's ready when she's ready. Leave her alone."

I've been forced to eavesdrop on their conversation for thirty minutes. Okay, forced is not entirely truthful. My vehicle is still mid–tire rotation across the street, and my headphones are in, but the battery died on my cell and I don't have an outlet at my table. If it wasn't pouring down rain outside, I would have left the second Leslie called me an elf. What the fuck?

I've sat in this same booth so many times—my great uncle Manny works in the kitchen—during the two-hour gap I had last year when I went from community college classes to JFH classes in the afternoon. Manny always makes sure it's wiped down for me, no trace of anything anywhere. No one seems to care if all I order is bottled water.

"Haley's right," Leslie says. "Stewart is a punk-ass if he keeps pressuring you. You guys do other stuff, right?"

Jesus. Ear plugs. Now.

I shove a few books into my bag and glance out at the rain. Maybe it's not coming down that hard.

"Hey, Scott, how's it going?"

Startled, I jump and look up. Tate Tanley is hovering in front of my booth, preparing to slide in across from me. He's wearing a bright-blue T-shirt with CRITTER CRUSADER written across it. Several mice and a raccoon hang from a ladder at the bottom of the shirt.

Tate points to the seat across from me. "Mind if I sit?"

"Go ahead."

We're both quiet for a long minute, and then Tate picks up my British Literature textbook and flips through it. "College course, right?"

I nod.

"I think Claire has this book for a class at Northwestern." He glances at the redhead behind the bar and then back at me before setting the book on the table again. "I heard Jamie and Leo ran you through the ringer last night. Are you really trying to get Red's spot?"

Apparently, it isn't such a secret practice, after all.

"I'm not gonna say anything," he offers, then after waiting a few seconds for me to respond, he adds, "besides, I might join you guys next time. I wouldn't mind some practice without Bakowski breathing down my neck."

I twirl a pen around my fingers, imitating Haley's restless behavior. I don't have a concrete reason not to trust Tanley, but all I've done for years is avoid being noticed in Juniper Falls. Still, it was my choice to play varsity hockey; I'm the one who set that ball in motion. I guess it comes with the territory. In fact, it's a big problem if I go unnoticed on the ice, especially with Coach Bakowski. I kind of need him to notice me or else I'm stuck riding the bench all season. Or worse—I'm cut before the season even begins.

"You've got the old house out in the country with the lake view, right?"

I narrow my eyes at him. "You know where I live?"

"I was over there last week," Tate explains. "Mice under the stove, I think?"

Oh, right. The exterminator Grandpa called. "Didn't realize you were part of the Critter Crusaders."

Tate grins. "If I wasn't, you wouldn't catch me anywhere near this T-shirt. The job's not so bad, though. I've been using the money to fix up cars. My stepdad and I are working on a 1965 Mustang."

"Seriously?" My guard drops a bit. I lean forward in my seat. "You guys know what you're doing?"

Tate shrugs. "We're learning. After the Mustang, I want to work on a Dodge Dart I saw at the junkyard last week, but it'll be like starting over. Every engine is a different animal."

"Yeah, I bet." I debate adding that I love old cars, but it feels weird, sharing anything personal with one of my team-mates.

"You gotta check out the Mustang," he says as if sensing the words stuck inside my head. "If you're into that sort of thing."

Both of us stop talking when Kayla and Leslie pass by. Seconds later, Haley appears in front of us, her gaze following her friends until they're out the door and then falling back on me. Her hair is up in a ponytail, her tight pink tank top hugging her in all the right places. I glance lower and get a nice view of her legs in those short cheer shorts, but I quickly force my gaze up. Tate lifts an eyebrow. Caught in the act by the girl's ex. Real smooth. What the hell is wrong with me?

I'm no stranger to hot girls and usually have plenty of self-control, so I don't know why I keep finding myself in these situations when Haley is around.

"Hey, Fletch," Haley says, oblivious to this silent exchange I'm having with her ex. "Got a minute for our Civics project?"

Tate's eyebrow shoots up even higher, but he stands, preparing to leave us alone. "Come check out the Mustang sometime if you want. Roger likes to show it off."

"Yeah, okay," I say, though I'm not sure if I will ever take him up on that offer. I know we're practicing together and all, but that's just about hockey, not about changes to my Juniper Falls social life. I like it just the way it is.

Tate surprises me by resting a hand on Haley's shoulder. With his girlfriend behind them watching. "You all right? Leslie and Kayla giving you a hard time?"

Haley flashes him a smile that I've come to recognize as her more forced effort. The Princess Smile. That's what I'm calling it from now on.

"They're here to remind me what a shallow bitch I used to be. It's karma, right?" She shakes her head. "I'm kidding. They aren't that bad. They'd commit murder for me." Her forehead wrinkles. "Well, maybe not Kayla, since that's against the Ten Commandments, but she'd wish she could murder for me. The sentiment is there."

Tate gives her a squeeze and then releases her. "Jamie and I would murder twice for you. Each. So, you're completely covered."

She gives him a sad-but-real smile this time. "Thanks, Tate." Haley waves both hands. "Now go see your girlfriend and quit feeling sorry for me. Fletch and I have work to do."

He stares at her for a beat longer and then turns around. The smile immediately fades from Haley's face. She slides into the booth beside me, but keeps her eyes on Tate and Claire. My muscles are screaming at me to flee or at least appear busy with my notebook, but instead, I'm studying Haley, studying her ex and his new girlfriend. I can't tell what she's thinking, but when Tate touches Claire, an almost wistful look fills her face. My stomach twists in knots. This bugs me. I don't know why.

I pick up my pen and twirl it again. "Karma, huh?"

Haley jolts out of her haze and looks at me. "I went to the dark side for a little while last fall. The whole Juniper Princess race was an ugly obsession."

"And now?"

"Well, I won, so maybe I didn't learn my lesson." She sighs. "I don't know…I like it for different reasons now. Less for the title and more for the influence I can have on people, on the town. And hopefully something bigger. Someday."

"Very diplomatic answer. Maybe we should include this in our Constitution project." Over at the bar, Tate has his hands in Claire's hair. He's twisting it in a knot on her head, securing it with an elastic band. I turn my attention back to Haley, watching her eyes gloss over a little. The sunshine fades from her face. I nod toward the lovebirds behind the bar. "What's that like? Fighting the urge to commit one of those murders?"

"I don't hate either of them, if that's what you're wondering." Haley grabs a strand of hair that fell from her ponytail and twists it around her index finger. "I hate that I thought I understood everything and then…well, it turns out I didn't know anything about relationships or love."

This reminds me of our text exchange yesterday. I shift

in my seat, uncomfortable with a return to that conversation.

"I'm not even sure I knew much about Tate," Haley admits. "But Claire did. Claire *does*. And that's the most difficult part. I thought he was mine, but he's not, and he never was." She plasters on a smile. "Which leaves me with no one to bitch to and to control, right?"

"You do have a way of forcing people into things," I say, thinking about our academic partnership. "Do you always get your way?"

She rolls her eyes. "Not without great effort and persuasive skills."

I lean on one elbow, studying her. "See? That's scary."

Haley's face fills with mock surprise. She leans into my personal space, her eyelids fluttering, all innocent looking. "Are you scared of me, Fletch?"

Afraid of sharing space with the Princess of Juniper Falls? Definitely. Afraid of a beautiful girl leaning closer? Not even a little. "No. I'm immune."

"Immune, huh?" She touches my wrist and slides her fingers higher.

My heart gives a loud thud, like it's jolting to life for the first time. I attempt to pull my hand away, but Haley applies more pressure, preventing this.

Her face breaks into a grin and then she laughs. "I'm kidding. It's not like that with me."

"Just so you know, I don't believe a word you say," I tell her. "Not after I've seen your manipulation tactics—fancy calligraphy and glitter can influence the masses and establish world peace. I bet that was your princess campaign platform." I nod toward the bar again. "I bet you even use homemade invitations to get guys to ask you out. 'To my future boyfriend, here is a list of when, where, and how we will meet and fall in love'—since you're so into the love thing."

"I am not into the love thing!" She looks both annoyed and surprised by my lengthy speech. Hell, I'm surprised by it. Guess I've stowed up a lot of Haley Stevenson details over the past week.

"Right," I say. "So, if I were to ask your ex if you're into the love thing, he would tell me—"

Haley presses her palm to my open mouth, cutting me off. The tip of my tongue touches her skin, and I taste both salt and something else.

"Leave Tate alone," she orders. "And for your information, I have zero interest in inviting or being invited to date anyone at the moment—" Her voice cuts off, concern filling her face. Her fingers touch the collar of my T-shirt, pulling it aside. "Fletch, you've got red—"

My heart takes off in a whole different kind of race. After shoving Haley's hand away, I flip my arm over and nearly panic when I see the red welts forming. As if on cue, my throat tightens, my tongue now thick and fuzzy.

Shit. Oh shit.

I stuff the loose items into my bag and push Haley hard enough to send her out of the booth. She stays on her feet and unfortunately follows me out the door.

# Chapter Fourteen

## —HALEY—

Oh my God, I think Fletch is dying. Maybe he ate nuts? Why would he do that?

"Shit," Fletch says, his eyes trained across the street. "My car."

He's reaching down into his pocket, trying to pull out a phone. Already, his breaths are shallow, red welts spreading farther and farther across his neck and arms.

"I'm calling 911." My phone is already out, my fingers poised to dial.

"No!" Fletch says with such conviction I stop. He appears to be struggling to breathe.

"I'll drive you to the hospital, okay?" I say, and with some reluctance, he nods. I attempt to tug him by the arm toward my car, but he jerks away, holding his hands up in surrender.

"Don't. Touch. Me."

A dozen different emotions swirl inside my head, but the urgency of the situation wins, and I jog toward my parents'

Honda Accord, flinging the door open for Fletch.

He's barely in the seat, his seat belt not quite on yet, and I've already made it around the car and into my seat. It's a manual transmission (my dad forced me to learn), which freaks me out for a second because I don't have a free hand to do CPR or abdominal thrusts or whatever if I need to.

I peel out of the parking lot, causing Fletch to lurch forward and then for his head to slam against the seat when I've got the car in drive. I shift quickly through the gears the second we're on the main drag. We've only got about a mile to go before I can pull up at the emergency-room doors. We hit a red light, and I glance at Fletch. He's got something in his hand now. It looks like a marker, and before the light switches to green, he stabs himself in the thigh with it, holding it there for several seconds.

I hit the gas again and zoom around cars. Ninety seconds later we're staring down the bright-red emergency-room lights, and Fletch seems to be breathing better. Probably due to the shot he gave himself. I try to help him out of the car, but he pulls away again. Instead, I run inside to get help. Juniper Falls has minimal emergency-room services, and we also have lots of down time between the drama—I mean trauma—so Fletch gets a team of three nurses, two doctors, and an orderly.

And yeah, I'm panicking about Fletch maybe dying, but at the same time, I'm soaking up the adrenaline rush. I totally got him here faster than an ambulance. Maybe I should become an ambulance driver. Is there a college degree for that?

"Did you already use an EpiPen, Fletcher?" a nurse asks him. She knows his name. Is he a regular here?

"Food allergy?" a young doctor asks.

The orderly shoves Fletcher into a wheelchair. His red

welts have spread to his face, and his upper lip is swelling to a very abnormal size. I stop moving and stare. I can't help it.

"Nuts, dairy, wheat," the nurse recites. "Right, Fletch?"

Another nurse walks briskly toward us. A nurse I know. Mrs. Tanley. Cremwell, now, actually. "Haley, what happened?"

I don't know why I feel weird about showing up with a guy, but for some reason I do. "We were working on a Civics project at O'Connor's, and he had a reaction to something."

Tate's mom leans down to look Fletcher over. "Hey, Fletch." She raises her head and says to the doctor. "Tree nuts and peanuts, eggs, dairy, wheat, and shellfish."

Our whole crew is walking through the automatic doors now, heading toward an exam room with a curtain for doors. My heart quickens, my brain working hard to process all this information. "Wait…you're allergic to all of those things? How is that possible?"

Fletch tosses a glare my way, like I've asked the worst question ever. Maybe my timing sucks. Yeah, my timing definitely sucks.

"Which did you have contact with?" the doctor asks him.

From his seat in the wheelchair, Fletch stands and makes his way onto the exam table. He lifts a finger and points it at me. "Ask her. Whatever is all over her hands."

I'm frozen in place again. My eyes probably wide with my panic. My legs tremble, and something rises in my throat, my lunch threatening to make a reappearance. "But…I didn't…I don't…"

And then I replay the last moments at O'Connor's, replay my hand on Fletcher's mouth, his tongue tickling my skin.

Tate's mom steps in front of me, and a curtain snaps closed behind her. I hold my hands out, staring at them like they're covered in blood. "I killed him, didn't I? We aren't even friends, not really…but we were just talking about murdering people and—oh my God."

Tate's mom steers me by the shoulders toward a giant sink. "You didn't kill anyone, Haley, I promise." She turns on the water, urging me to place my hands under them. I'm too in shock to do anything, so she places the foamy soap on my palms and scrubs them together. "It was an accident."

I look up at her when she hands me a sheet of paper towels. "I feel sick." I wipe sweat from my forehead and force back the urge to vomit. Mrs. Tanley shoves me into a chair and places a cool rag on the back of my neck. "This is my fault. He kept trying to get away from me, and I wouldn't give in… How can someone be allergic to that many things? What does he even eat? Is he fed with a tube or something?"

She bends down in front of me, a slight look of impatience on her face. "What did you have for lunch?"

Information scrambles around in my brain, but finally I land on an answer. "Fried shrimp basket. At O'Connor's."

She nods and then turns away, but I grab her sleeve. "And one of Leslie's cheese sticks."

"Anything else?"

I give myself a second to come up with something I'd forgotten, but eventually, I shake my head. Tate's mom disappears behind the curtain where Fletch is hopefully not dying. I yank the cool rag from the back of my neck and use it to scrub my arms. I scrub and scrub until my skin turns nearly as red as Fletch's. I'm diseased. Crawling with disease.

I hear bits and pieces of the doctors and nurses helping Fletch. They started an IV, took blood, gave him antihistamines and breathing treatments. After fifteen minutes or so, no one is rushing around with the urgency from earlier, and I'm shoved out into the waiting room and told I need to put my car in a real parking space. I'd left it running and blocking the ambulance bay.

When I return to my spot in the waiting room, I'm slightly calmer and able to replay the entire incident again. I know I put my hand on his mouth but it was only seconds later that he— Can his allergic reactions really happen that fast? It seems unreal.

I wait another fifteen minutes, and my phone is blowing up thanks to living in such a small town.

*CLAIRE: u left ur cheer book here. Isn't it sacred or something? What happened?*

*ME: omg! Pls keep the book in a safe place! And do you know Fletcher Scott?*

*CLAIRE: Manny's nephew? Yeah, I know him a little. Why?*

*ME: he had some kind of allergic reaction. He's ok now. I think. Seems like he wants to keep it on the DL, ok?*

*CLAIRE: got it. No problem.*


*MOM: what are you doing at the ER??!*
*DAD: What happened?*

*ME: classmate needed to go to hospital. I drove him. He's maybe ok. Not sure yet. Allergy*

*MOM: Fletcher Scott?*

*ME: Yes. How did u know?*

*MOM: grade school. It was pretty bad for him. Didn't*

***know he still had all of those problems. I heard he outgrew them***

"Haley?"

I set my phone down and turn my attention to Tate's mom. "How's Fletcher?"

"You look pale, are you okay?" She holds out a can of ginger ale. I nod, but I take the drink anyway. I don't feel great, that's for sure. I may have contributed to another person's almost-death. How can I feel okay after that? "We're gonna keep him here for a few hours, so you should probably head home."

"What about his parents? Are they coming? He shouldn't be here alone." The urge to take some kind of helpful action won't fade no matter how much I hear that he's going to be fine.

"I left a message with his family. I'm sure they'll come as soon as they get it."

I sink down into my chair, releasing a breath. "So, what happened? I barely touched him and…" Already this sounds sleazy. "I was just reaching for a pen next to his hand, and then next thing I know, he's covered in welts and struggling to breathe."

"I can't discuss his medical specifics with you," she says, glancing over her shoulder at a woman with an infant who just walked through the doors. "But promise me something, Haley?"

"What?"

She gives me the warning-mom look. "Next time, don't drive him or anyone to the hospital yourself. Call 911."

"I tried to," I mumble, but she's already taking off to help the woman and the baby. I know I'm not allowed to go back there and see Fletcher, but I still can't bring myself to leave. I pace around the waiting room, write cheers in my head, mentally draft a dozen to-do lists, and eventually, an hour later, Fletcher's grandfather and a younger guy come racing through the automatic ER doors.

I recognize the younger guy right away. But he doesn't notice me. He's focused on the person shoving off the orderly and nurses, pushing his way past the desk.

Fletcher.

He's still a little red and splotchy, but it's nothing compared to two hours ago, plus he seems to be able to breathe now. His grandpa swears under his breath, but Fletch holds up a pink sheet of paper. "Eighteen now, remember? I can do that AMA thing everyone loves so much on TV."

The doctor behind him gives Fletch a stern look and then turns to his grandpa. "He needs another few hours of observation."

Fletch's grandpa stands up straight and salutes the doctor. He and the doctor stand closer and carry on a conversation full of medical jargon.

I look over at Fletch's brother, noticing him, noticing me. "Coach Braden," I say, flashing him a grin.

His mouth falls open, and he looks me up and down. "No way. You can't be Rhinestone? Last I checked, that girl was four feet tall with a dirty face and a head full of tangled hair."

I laugh, but I'm watching Fletch take this in. His body sways just a bit, probably from the Benadryl.

His grandpa breaks away from his conversation with the doctor and says to Braden, "You two know each other?"

Braden is huge compared to Fletch. He takes two steps and then lifts me off the ground. My face heats up, but I'm quickly put back on my feet and the moment is over. "This girl was on my peewee football team," Braden tells his grandpa.

"The team you had to coach for community service?" Their grandpa looks me over again, like I'm different now than yesterday when he let me into Fletch's room. "You don't look like a football player."

Braden shakes his head. "This kid was the best offensive player on my team. She kicked some ass."

"Well she sure got Fletcher here quickly," the doctor says. "Seems like this young lady has many talents."

"Yeah, she does," Fletch says, his voice groggy. Everyone stops and looks over at him. "She's pretty good at killing people with her bare hands, too."

I flinch and then hold my breath, waiting for all the feelings to taper off. I didn't even know he had that kind of power over me, to make me feel like shit.

Not bothering to look at me, Fletch pushes past his older brother and grandpa. "I assume one of you came to drive me home, right?"

Braden throws me an apologetic look, but both men follow Fletcher out the doors. I watch them go and try to hold off the tears. He's an asshole. No doubt about that. But I pushed him. He tried to get me to back off, and I kept pushing and pushing. To get my way. It's always about me and my way.

Maybe I haven't changed at all. Maybe this *A* in Civics is Juniper Falls Princess all over again.

# Chapter Fifteen

## -FLETCHER-

I wake up from my Benadryl-induced coma, sprawled out on the couch, the TV a faint glow. My head is hammering, and I feel like I've been thrown in the middle of a hurricane. Cole is seated in the recliner, an EpiPen clutched in his hand. I toss the blanket aside and sit up slowly.

"Everyone out in the fields?" I ask.

"Uh-huh." Cole glances at me for a second then back at the TV. "They went out with headlamps and lanterns a while ago. Doubt they'll be back anytime soon."

"Hence the need for the fifteen-year-old babysitter." I stretch my arms and look around for my glasses—they're on the coffee table.

Cole shrugs. "I don't mind."

With my glasses on, the TV picture appears clear right in front of me. Cole is watching audition rounds for *So You Think You Can Dance*. I'd tease him about this if it weren't for the fact that (1) he's probably been stuck here for hours making sure that I don't die in my sleep, and (2) I'd be a big fat hypocrite. Not that I watch the show.

"Did my mom blow up my phone?" I ask.

Cole is focused on the show. A guy way too old to audition is attempting to tap while dressed as Nigel. "I talked to her. She's making you an appointment with the allergist or something. Call her tomorrow."

I nod and rub my eyes. "Thanks, man."

The show finally goes to commercial, and Cole spins to face me. "Did Haley Stevenson really drive you to the ER? Braden said—"

"What? No." My response is more knee-jerk than fact-based. But seconds later, the events of the day are rolling over me in one giant tidal wave. "Wait…maybe."

"So, you guys were like…" Cole twirls the EpiPen some more, not looking right at me. "…hanging out?"

"I don't know." My forehead wrinkles. I scrub my hands over my face. "I was at O'Connor's waiting for my car…" I jump to my feet. "Shit. My car is still at the shop."

"It's here," Cole says. "Your dad and Braden took care of it."

I sit back down, relaxing. "Tanley was talking to me at O'Connor's. Haley was there with her friends—"

"Leslie and Kayla," Cole fills in a little too quickly.

"Dude, no." I roll my eyes. "Please tell me you haven't moved up to stalking?"

He doesn't say anything about the fact that Tate Tanley and I had a conversation outside of school or hockey—and I don't even think we've had a conversation *inside* school or *during* hockey before—but maybe he's too focused on Haley information to make note of this big event.

Cole looks down at his lap and then sighs.

"What?" I say, my pulse quickening. He's keeping

something from me. I bet Tanley and Claire saw me blowing up like a balloon and told everyone. Cole shakes his head, so I press him harder. "What, Cole? Seriously?"

"Nothing." He sighs again and then rests his head against the back of the chair, finally making eye contact with me. "She likes you."

"Who?"

"Haley," he says finally.

This answer is so unexpected, I burst out laughing. "Are you kidding me? No way."

He shrugs and goes back to watching the TV.

It takes a couple of minutes for me to process that thought of Cole's and come down from my laughing high. "What makes you think she likes me?"

"I don't know," he mumbles. "Just stuff."

"Stuff that's probably all in your head." I pull myself up to my feet again and tap his shoulder with the remote control. "Watch your show and yell for me if there's a really hot girl auditioning. I'm gonna get some food. You want anything?"

"Nope, I'm good."

After stuffing myself full of smoked ribs and rice, I head for the shower to scrub the hospital and medicine smell off of me. Cole's theory about Haley liking me is still stuck in my head the second I step under the hot water. Something about it is bugging me, like there's a reason I know it can't be true, but it's lost in a hazy memory of the day's drama.

I'm turning the knobs, shutting the water off, when I'm hit with a recap of my exit from the hospital. Braden had hugged her, I think. And he called her some weird nickname...Rhinestone. What the hell? Maybe that was a Benadryl-induced dream. God, I hope I'm not having dreams about Haley. Or Haley and my twenty-six-year-old brother.

Haley's sunny expression comes back to me—a look she had while we sat in that booth together at O'Connor's. Then I get a flash of that smile fading, of her looking completely crushed. By my words. What had I said to her?

*"She's pretty good at killing people with her bare hands."*
Shit.

Her intensely focused face—the one she wore while speeding through town toward the hospital—comes back to me, too.

Man, that girl can drive a stick shift like a pro.

Guilt twists in my stomach along with the big meal I just consumed. Jamie Isaacs is probably going to kill me after he finds out what I said to Haley. And he'll probably end our extra practice sessions.

But it isn't Jamie's warnings or even fear of his fists that has me hurrying to get dressed and grabbing my keys. It's Haley. I hurt her. And as much as I'd like to forget it and move on, I can't.

I shoot Jamie a quick text.
**ME: what's Haley's address?**

**JAMIE: OK, well that's one way to handle things...**

**ME: she left something at my house. I'm going to drop it off.**

**JAMIE: why don't u ask her?**

**ME: fine. Don't tell me.**

**JAMIE: it's on Prairie LN, don't know the number. White house, blue shutters, 3rd from corner**

**ME: thanks**

I slide my shoes on and then toss Cole's into his lap.

"Come on, I'll take you home."

He stands, but then glances wistfully at the TV. "Save this for me, okay?"

"Yeah, okay." I work hard not to laugh. In fact, I take a second to study the ballroom dancers currently auditioning. Mary Murphy is yelping like she's about to put them on the hot-tamale train—yes, I know the show basics. I point a finger at the dude wearing number 276. "Look at his shoulders—bad technique. And he's got no chemistry with his partner. He's looking at the judges way more than her."

"Yeah," Cole agrees. "I think he'll get cut in Vegas. The girl will probably make top twenty."

The girl is blond, leggy, and perfectly toned. She reminds me a little of—

I shake the thought from my head, not allowing its completion. Jesus Christ, no.

The air outside is both warm and cool, with a nice breeze from the lake. I'm beginning to feel normal again. The hives and swelling are mostly gone. But my stomach twists with nerves. What am I going to do exactly? Apologize? She might get pissed and slam a door in my face, tell all her friends I'm horrible, and join Kayla in calling out "nerd alert" next time we're in the same place.

I spot the dogs over by the barn and whistle for Vixen. She's brushing my thigh with her nose seconds later. "Hey, girl. Want to go for a ride?"

Cole stares at me, faking shock. "You're letting a dog in your precious car? Are you sure you're fit to drive?"

I open the back door for Vixen and toss a blanket over the leather seat. "I'm training her to save me if I'm dying of an allergic reaction."

"Seriously?" Cole says.

I shrug. No, not seriously, but she's my dog, she's gonna

flip her shit if I'm passed out, not breathing, so maybe she'd pull a Lassie and run for help. I could tell Cole the truth, that Vixen is backup for me, a way to keep Haley from slamming doors, but for some reason I don't want him to know I'm going to her place. Besides, she might not even be home. She's probably at a party or practicing cheers.

After dropping Cole off, I get even more nervous heading toward Haley's house. I park across the street, under a tree, and sit there for several minutes giving myself a pep talk. Her front door opens and closes a few times, one of her parents emerging each time to put items on the driveway— suitcases and bags. Maybe they're going on vacation? But Haley wouldn't be able to miss summer school and still get full credit, so she must not be leaving.

Her dad squints into the dark, looking in my direction. Now I have no choice but to get out of the car. That or look like a stalker. Vixen and I head up the driveway, and both Stevenson parents greet us.

My face heats up before anyone even utters a word. "Is Haley home?"

Through the front windows, I can clearly see the TV playing the same show that Cole was just watching at my house. Haley's blond ponytail is moving up and down from the couch.

Her mom looks me over and then glances into the windows. "Um…yeah, she's here."

"I'll get her," Mr. Stevenson says, eyeing the dog.

He's allergic. Damn, I forgot. I back up a few steps until we're on the sidewalk again, and then I glance at Vixen. "Sit, girl."

She plops down in her spot, keeping her distance. I take another look at the items on the driveway. "Are you guys headed somewhere?"

Haley's mom is still studying me. Maybe she remembers me from grade school. She was my music teacher. "Mr. Stevenson and I are going on a bird-watching expedition." She waits for me to respond, and when I don't, she adds, "It's our twentieth anniversary in July."

I don't really know what to say to her. The girls I talk to—and do other things with—don't have parents hanging around. Ever. "Haley and I are in Civics together."

"She mentioned that."

"We're partners for the Constitution project." God, this is unbearable. Maybe I should call it a night?

Finally, Haley steps through the front door. Her hair is wet, and she's wearing pajama shorts and a tank top. Several feelings—too many to even process—sweep over me, and it takes every bit of focus I have to keep my face cool and calm. What the hell is going on here?

Whatever it is, it needs to go away. Like now.

# Chapter Sixteen

## −HALEY−

The sight of Fletcher, normal-looking with his usual messy hair and sexy glasses, has my stomach doing flip-flops, but I plaster on my poker face the second my parents leave us alone on the sidewalk.

I fold my arms over my chest, smashing the urge to sit on the ground with Vixen. Fletch needs to know that pushy and selfish me bugging him constantly isn't a good enough reason to treat me like shit. Or anyone for that matter. I refuse to enable these defense mechanisms of his. So, all I say is, "You seem better."

"Yeah." He looks down at the dog. She's wagging her tail now but staying seated on my sidewalk. He takes a deep breath, and when he looks up at me again, I'm fighting the urge to step closer, to breathe the same air. "Haley…thanks for what you did today."

"You're welcome." I stare back at him, forcing my expression to stay neutral. "Did you need anything else? If not, I should go back to studying—"

"I'm sorry," he says, so fast the words smash together. "I didn't mean what I said about—"

"About me killing you?" I finish for him. He cringes. "Fine. Apology accepted."

I turn to leave, but Fletch reaches out a hand, stopping before actually touching me. "Wait…" His gaze darts toward my house and then back to my face. "Can we—I mean—do you want to go for a walk?"

I'm about to say no, but Vixen gives me those sweet doggy eyes and her little wet nose turns up toward me. I sigh. "Fine, let's walk."

I'm barefoot but don't feel like going inside for shoes. I give Vixen a good twenty seconds of petting before I lead us down the sidewalk, past the O'Connor's house, and toward the park in my neighborhood.

"I really am sorry," Fletcher repeats. "It was an accident and…well, I should have never said any of that to you."

I count to five before responding, not wanting to give an impulse-driven answer. "Okay, thanks for telling me."

Both of us are silent, walking the remainder of the block. Our feet touch the edge of the playground, and Fletch says, "So, we're cool?"

I kick at a chunk of mud in the grass with my toe. "No, we're not cool."

Fletch tenses beside me. "We're not?"

"No." I head over to the swings, picking the one on the end to sit down on. I'm exhausted. It really has been a long day for me. Fletch hesitates, but eventually he follows and sits on the swing beside me.

"I apologized, and you accepted it," he says. "So why can't we go back to the way things were?"

Here is another reason dating in high school scares me.

Not with Tate, it wasn't like this with him, but if I found someone new, I could get sucked down the rabbit hole of forgiveness, even when it's undeserved.

I twist my swing to face Fletch, my toes digging into the sand below. "You know Kayla, right?"

"The girl devoted to saving the world by giving off nerd alerts," Fletch says, rolling his eyes.

My face flushes. I hate that I was part of that conversation. Still, that has nothing to do with him being an asshole to me at the hospital. "Kayla's been my best friend since preschool. But I don't hang out with her much anymore—Jamie's temporarily taking her place—because her boyfriend has done some stuff that I don't think he should be forgiven for, and until she agrees with me and does something, I can't be around her like we used to be."

But I was clear with her about my feelings; even today, I reiterated them when we talked about her and Stewart taking things further. It's a gray area. He's a gray area. But I think he pushes her too hard and doesn't respect her nearly enough. Love is blinding. That's what I've learned from all this. And how can that not scare the shit out of someone?

"You mean Stewart?" Fletch's face wrinkles in confusion. "What does that have to do with me?"

"I just mean that if you want to continue to be friends with me or whatever…" I stop there, hoping not to give him wrong ideas. "You can't treat me like crap. I might forgive you, but I'm going to keep my distance."

Fletcher leans away from me. He's stunned. I've stunned him. I'm half expecting him to get up and leave, but instead, he faces forward again and sits in silence, gliding the swing back and forth.

After a couple of minutes, he speaks again. "This bird expedition…what's that about?"

I contemplate calling him out on the subject change, but I decide to go with it. There's no harm in answering this question. "My parents are into spotting rare birds in the wild. The trip is a group tour. They've wanted to do it for years and probably waited for me to be old enough to stay home alone."

"Where are your parents going on this tour?"

The sand feels amazing on my worn-out feet. I continue pulling them through it. "They fly to Portland in the morning, and the group of twenty-or-so couples meets tomorrow night. I think they head south from Portland, through California... they mentioned something about the Redwood Forest. They'll eventually end in upstate New York."

"This must be a long expedition."

I nod, even though he's not looking at me. "They'll be gone a month. They're skipping the week in New York, though, 'cause my dad plays in Roger Cremwell's band and they booked the Summer Fest."

"Right," Fletch says. "Didn't they perform at the ball?"

"You didn't go?"

He shakes his head and silence falls over us again until Fletch takes another deep breath. "Hypothetically speaking...if I wanted to, you know, fix this thing with us, what would I need to do?"

I smile down at my feet. He's kind of adorable. He's not Kyle Stewart. I smooth out the grin and lift my head. "Well, I think you'd need to behave in a manner that shows you're thinking about my feelings and being considerate."

He looks at me like I've told him to mutate into a different species. "Like how?"

"Relationships—" I start, and then shake my head. "Friendships are built on trust."

His nose wrinkles. "Trust?"

I nod. "Like trusting me enough to tell me you're allergic to my cookies."

Fletch snorts out a laugh and then tosses me an apologetic look. "Sorry. I can't help it."

"Like telling me you're allergic to the baked goods I've offered you," I correct, but I'm smiling, too.

"I'm allergic to your cookies, Haley," Fletch says. He manages to hold a straight face for exactly five seconds before cracking up.

"God, you're such a guy." I roll my eyes. "But think about it…if you had been honest with me, maybe all the drama today wouldn't have happened."

His grin fades, and he nods. "You're right. It's just that I've had some bad experiences with telling people these things, and well, it's easier to…"

"Protect yourself?"

He shrugs but doesn't agree outright. Maybe it makes him seem too vulnerable.

"You aren't worried that I'm gonna like, poison you on purpose, are you?"

He pokes his toe into the sand and stares down at it. "It's happened before."

At first, I assume he means earlier today when I accidentally poisoned him, but the way his face darkens, I quickly realize this is something that goes way back.

"Really?" I say, and he nods. Okay, well this explains a little more about Fletcher Scott. I replay that day in Civics when I waved the granola bar at him, how he'd raced out of the room. I give him a few seconds to explain the details, and when he doesn't, I have no choice but to let it go. Obviously, he doesn't want to rehash that memory tonight. I wonder if my mom knows anything about this…

*No, Haley. That would be untrustworthy.*

Unable to sit any longer, I hop up, and Vixen bolts up, too, then stands in front of us, panting like she's asking for permission to run around. Fletcher gives her a little nod, and she does exactly that—circles the playground happily.

I turn to face Fletcher, who is still sitting in his swing. "Okay, so would you like a shot at redemption right now?"

His eyebrows lift, his face weary. "Right now?"

"Yep, right now." I twist my fingers together, my stomach fluttering for no apparent reason. "Tell me again what you're allergic to."

His face grows even wearier. "Tree nuts, peanuts, and shellfish are the kill-me-quick ones."

I nod, urging him to continue. I did some googling this evening. I have a slightly better grasp on food allergies now.

"Dairy can be really bad, too. It just depends. Usually it's more hives than obstructed airways." He draws in a breath and then blows it out quickly. "Eggs and wheat are different than the others. I can eat them and not die, but I'll end up puking…"

Even in the dark, the flush of his cheeks is clearly visible. He's embarrassed to talk about this. But why?

"Why did Jamie say that you have asthma?" I ask, remembering Jamie's poor imitation of an asthma attack.

"I do have asthma. It's part of the reaction, or it might be exercise induced. I think it's a little of both. Things I'm allergic to float around, and my airway constricts as a defense. When I'm working out, I'm breathing more, so…"

"You bring in more bad stuff," I finish for him. "That makes sense. But your doctors let you play hockey?"

"They don't love the idea," Fletch admits. "But lots of people with asthma participate in high-level athletics, even Olympians."

"Yeah, I guess that's true. But isn't there some kind of

cure or better treatment than EpiPens and ER trips?"

"We've tried everything out there to make some of the allergies go away." He stands up and busies himself twisting his swing into a knot. "Years ago, my mom and I even spent a few months in Minneapolis at this experimental clinic."

"Experimental clinic?" I dig a hole in the sand with my feet, making myself even shorter. "Like a drug trial or something?"

"Not a drug trial," he says, still twirling his swing. "They gave me tiny amounts of peanut protein every day to get my body to build up a resistance. It worked for some people. Maybe a little for me, too, but I wasn't cured. Obviously."

I run through his offensive food list in my head again. "So, what *do* you eat?"

Fletch laughs. "You want an inventory of everything I've ever eaten?"

I roll my eyes. "Don't be a smart-ass. What did you have for dinner tonight?"

"Ribs," he says. "And some rice…broccoli…two apples."

"Okay." I pull myself out of the sand hole. "Are you ready now?"

He turns to face me. "To go?"

"No, to redeem yourself."

"I thought that's what I was just doing." He looks more worried now than ever. "You mean there's more?"

"Oh yeah, but you're on a roll. Don't stop now." I step closer, and he immediately steps away. We've definitely moved backward in the figurative sense, as well, because Saturday he let me hug him and Sunday, he grabbed me out of thin air and prevented my death from falling off his barn roof. Wait…that means we've both saved each other's life. Weird. Although both were my fault. I shake my head and refocus. "I'm now informed on all the items that could lead to your death. Do you trust me to not kill you?"

Fletch lifts an eyebrow and takes another tiny step back. "Maybe…"

"Or maybe not." I fold my arms over my chest and move farther away from him. "That's all right. You're not ready to be my friend. Maybe not anyone's. I get it."

"I have friends," he snaps. Then he scrubs a hand over his face. "Haley, this isn't anything against you; my own grandpa nearly killed me once. It takes knowledge and practice and lots of scary moments to wrap your head around everything I can and can't be exposed to."

He's probably right, but based on all the panties in his pockets yesterday and the fact that he held me down against the roof and he grabbed that pen from me during the first day of physics, I know he's touched girls before. I know he can put himself safely back in that zone. I want him to know I'm not gonna be the one to poison him if that ever happens again. I hold out my fingers and wiggle them. "I swear on the Bible that I won't kill you."

And maybe I need to do this for me, too. After I got home from the hospital, the first thing I did was jump in the shower and attempt to remove all the offensive things from my skin.

Fletch catches sight of a red patch of skin on my forearm and points to it. "What happened?"

I look down at it. "I got kind of freaked out earlier. Went crazy scrubbing myself."

His eyes soften, and he takes one tiny step closer.

My heart picks up speed. I'm nervous, but I'm not sure exactly why. I guess I'm still afraid of killing him. But surely I've gotten all the shrimp off me between the three showers I've taken.

It's not until I place a hand on his chest, feeling his heart, that I notice his T-shirt of the day, which says YOU READ MY T-SHIRT, THAT'S ENOUGH SOCIALIZING FOR ONE DAY.

I smile at the shirt and take note of the fact that the heartbeat beneath my hand has sped up considerably.

"Relax," I say, but I'm not managing this so well myself. My free hand touches his wrist, like I'd done today at O'Connor's. His chest freezes. He's holding his breath.

I slide my fingers up his arm, counting slowly inside my head. I reach his collarbone at twenty seconds. "So far, so good," I whisper.

My index finger glides up to his cheek, brushing over the scruff. My stomach is turning a dozen somersaults, my pulse picking up even more. Fletch's heart does the same, thudding with such force against my palm. Beneath his glasses, those blue eyes meet mine, and I'm stuck in this place where I can't move or breathe.

*No, no, no, this isn't happening. Not now.*

Vixen barks at something in a nearby tree, jolting me back to earth. I slowly creep my fingers to the right and then, before he can stop me, I snatch up Fletch's glasses, just like I did during our first Civics class.

I spin around and take off running, but he catches up to me, grabbing me around the waist and lifting me off the ground. "What's the verdict?" I ask. "Are you dying or not?"

"I'm having trouble seeing…" With what seems like very little effort, he hoists me up onto his shoulder and walks quickly across the playground, heading straight for a tree. "It's too bad I can't see where I'm going. Hopefully I won't run into anything…"

I squeal and try to worm my way off his shoulder, but his grip on me is firm. Instead of running into the tree, he spins in a circle, gaining momentum and going faster with each revolution.

"Oh my God, Fletch, stop!" I'm laughing too hard to punch him or pinch him or something. The world moves quickly all around me, shades of green and brown and bright primary colors bursting out through the dark. "How are you not dizzy?"

Outside of the spinning and laughing, I take note of the fact that Fletch's feet don't shuffle beneath us, there's no rise and fall to his turning, it's smooth and easy. I look down, and his heels are raised. He's on the balls of his feet. This should freak me out even more, the lack of stability, but I'm not scared. I'm stable. Perfectly stable.

"Okay, okay, you can have your glasses back," I concede, the spinning getting to me now.

Fletch makes a sharp stop, and I brace myself for a fall, but I remain perfectly balanced on his shoulder. He wraps his free arm around my waist, turning me and pushing me forward at the same time. I slide down the front of his body, and my laughter is immediately cut off. My heart takes off in a sprint. He's all warmth and hard muscles beneath his shirt. I wait for my feet to touch the ground again, but Fletch keeps his arm tight around my waist when we're eye level.

His heart thuds against mine. "You were right. You didn't kill me."

"That's a good thing, right?" I wonder if he can see well enough to read my thoughts. I hold his glasses up in surrender. "You can put me down now."

My feet make contact with the ground, but Fletch doesn't take his arm from my waist.

The world is still turning a bit, trying to straighten itself out. I unfold the glasses and place them back on his face. "You're lucky these didn't go flying into the sidewalk or the swing set."

He grins. "I trust you, Haley."

My mouth falls open in shock. Fletcher Scott just made a joke. Before I can call him out on it, I become preoccupied with the proximity of our mouths. "What if—hypothetically—someone ate a fried shrimp basket and then decided…" I lean in closer, even though my face and neck heat up. "To kiss you?"

His grin vanishes, and he swallows. "Could be a great way to go."

"Oh, come on." I almost push away from him but can't bring myself to do it. "You flipped out over my finger coming near you. You'd probably have a heart attack if I leaned any closer."

"Try me," he challenges.

Butterflies take off in my stomach. What the hell is happening here? I reach behind me for Fletch's fingers, and the second I begin to pluck them from my back, he releases me and steps away.

"You are so confusing," I snap. I look around for Vixen. I need a distraction. She's standing guard under the tree, probably waiting for a squirrel to come down.

"*I'm* confusing?" Fletch leans against the post of the swing set, completely at ease. Me, on the other hand, I'm a ball of nerves. "I think what you meant is that you're confused. You wanted to kiss me. You were thinking about it."

"No, I wasn't." I fold my arms in defensive mode again, but one lift of Fletch's eyebrow and I'm dropping them at my sides "So? I'm not going to do anything."

"I know that, too." He studies my movement until I decide that frozen-in-place is safest. "Do you ever think that maybe you make too big a deal out of little things?"

The thought *has* occurred to me before. "Like kissing? That's kind of a big deal."

He shrugs. "Only if you make it one."

"Why are you pressuring me about this?" I shake my head. "Jesus."

Fletch holds both hands up in front of him. "I'm not pressuring you to do anything. I'm just picking up on your signals. You were looking at my mouth, and you wanted to kiss me."

"My signals. Right." I roll my eyes, but he's not buying it. I think maybe this is that Other Fletcher. The one who wins multiple pairs of panties in one night.

"All I'm saying is…" He pushes away from the post and walks closer. "If you want to do it, then do it. It doesn't have to be a big deal. We won't have to go on a date or ever talk about it again."

I plop down on the ground and pick at the grass. "Yeah, I tried that once. It didn't go well." Jake Hammond. I tried to make him a random one-night stand, just to stop thinking about Tate. It was weird and fast and really depressing. "Can we talk about something else?"

Fletch shrugs and sits beside me. "Sure. If you want."

I lay back, cover my face, and groan. "What are you doing? Are you messing with my head on purpose?"

"I hate to say it, Haley, but you're messing with your own head." Fletch lays back and leans on one elbow. My face is mostly covered, but I feel him watching me. "When you want to kiss someone, you do it and then move on."

"Is that what you do, Mr. Panty Collector? You just go around kissing whoever you want?"

"If the feeling is mutual," he says.

I remove my hand from my face. Finally, I have an edge in this conversation. "Is the feeling mutual, Fletch?"

He maintains his confident smirk, but I can tell I've surprised him. "You're asking if I want to kiss you?"

I nod, waiting for him to derail. This is way too direct for people our age, especially the socially invisible like Fletch.

"I probably wouldn't hate it," he says, and I smack him in the arm. "But you don't have the balls. And I'm not gonna do it."

"Because *you* don't have the balls," I accuse, pointing a finger at him.

He grasps my finger and pulls my hand down to my lap. "I promise you, I do, but not with things all complicated like you're making them."

I bolt up to a sitting position. "You're the one making this a big deal. I wouldn't have brought it up." Like ever.

"But you would have been thinking about it and then made it into some big thing in your head," Fletch says. "And either you'll get all weird around me or you'll turn into Cole and hang on every word I say."

I'm about to spew some choice words at him, but the warm smile on Fletch's face makes it clear that he's joking. I relax a little. "Okay, I see your point. Maybe I *could* stand to lighten up a little."

He holds a hand out and nods. "That's all I'm saying. It might help you next time we're taking a test in Civics. Take it one question at a time. A kiss is just one kiss. A question is just one question."

Confidence overpowers the nerves. "Fine. I'll do it. I'll kiss you."

Fletch's eyes widen. "Sure you haven't been eating any more shrimp?"

"Not gonna answer that. It's a violation of my trust." I only brushed my teeth about five times after my three showers. Plus, I flossed and gargled mouthwash twice. I cover my face with my hands. I can't believe this is happening. "How did we get here from the shrimp question? This is insane."

Fletch tugs my hands from my face, his eyes full of genuine concern. "It's okay, Haley. Let's just study instead. I'll help you get ready for tomorrow's quiz. We can pull an all-nighter." He closes his eyes briefly. "A studying all-nighter. Not any other kind."

"Uh-uh." I shake my head. "I can't back out now. I'm kissing you, and you're gonna let me. And then we can study."

He sits up again, turning to face me.

My mouth goes dry, my hands shaking. God, it's like I've never kissed anyone before. What's wrong with me? Maybe I do need to do this more often. Desensitize myself or something.

I rest my palms on Fletcher's thighs and lean in. But I stop before our lips can touch. "Aren't you going to take off your glasses?"

He reaches up and removes his glasses, resting them in the grass beside us. "Better?"

"Much." My heart is up to my throat when I lean closer again. I can feel his toothpaste breath against my lips. It should be so easy. But this slightly less than an inch of space between us might as well be a thick brick wall. I squeeze my eyes shut. "Do it for me, please?"

I can't see him, but I feel him shake his head.

My body is shifted so far forward, nearly off-balance, a big gust of wind could probably knock me over, and I'd be on top of Fletch, our mouths forced to touch. I lick my lips and try to brave closing that space again. My stomach flips over, and I release a defeated sigh, using my hands on his legs to push away. "Come on, let's go study."

Fletch climbs to his feet again and walks beside me. I can't look at him. I'm too afraid of the smirk he's probably wearing. Finally, I glance over my shoulder for a split second and do a double take. There's no smirk anywhere in sight. He's calmer than I've ever seen him. Looking exactly how I imagined he'd look when all those defensive walls dropped. Other Fletcher.

And yeah, I still want to kiss him.

# Chapter Seventeen

## -FLETCHER-

"Dig it out of the corner!" Leo shouts at me from across the rink. "Come on, man, get your head out of your ass!"

To my credit, my head is nowhere near my ass, but the large mass that makes up Jamie Isaacs happens to be fighting for the same puck. And neither of us has pads on. Leo's brilliant idea.

My stick tangles with Jamie's as he closes the gap between us. My breaths come quicker, heart thudding loud in my ears. *Get out of this, get out now!* The panic is too much, and I can't resist the instinct to push my way out despite the fact that Leo specifically ordered me not to—

"No! What the hell are you doing, Scott?" Leo wedges himself between Jamie and me. He sets his hands on my chest and shoves hard enough to send me sliding back a couple of feet. "Did you not hear me say like five minutes ago absolutely no hitting?"

Silence falls over the rink at this early hour. My mind is still racing, my heart pounding.

Behind Leo, Jamie cracks up laughing. When Leo turns to glare at him he says, "Sorry, I think I just had a preschool flashback. No hitting, Jamie! I said no hitting!"

The tension falls from the air. Leo works hard not to grin, and when he turns back to me, he's much calmer. "You might be playing defense, but knocking Jamie over isn't your move. That's Red's. You do that, and you give Bakowski no choice but to compare you side by side. Who do you think wins that contest?"

I don't answer that. Instead I stare at the corner of the rink Jamie and I had just been locked in, attempting to envision a new way.

"Plus, you're not gonna plow me over," Jamie adds. "Hate to say it, but it's true."

"Again?" Leo prompts.

I stare at the empty corner a beat longer and then nod. The puck is slid in front of me, and I take off with it. Seconds later, I'm pressed tight in that corner again. I force my heart to slow and my brain to remain calm. This time, instead of trying to go through Jamie, I turn in a smooth but quick circle, the puck following me in a blur of black against the white ice. Jamie's stick reaches in to steal the puck back, but he's too late. I've already sent it sliding along the outside, to no one today, but in a real game, to a teammate awaiting the chance to breakaway for the goal.

Leo skates toward the puck, stopping it with his own stick. "Not bad, Scott. Not bad at all."

I pull my helmet off, set it on the wall, and then lift my jersey up to wipe sweat from my face. "Thanks. That felt pretty good," I admit, and then worry creeps its way back into my stomach. "Of course, it's much easier to think without Bakowski screaming from the bench and stands full of people staring at you…"

"Just takes experience," Leo says. "Lots of varsity practices and games, this shit will be second nature."

Yeah, but unfortunately, I'm a senior, and that kind of experience is expected. I gotta find a way to skip over all the mental shit and get things figured out. But I don't say that out loud, because Leo and Jamie are already doing enough for me. The rest is my deal.

We do a few more drills, and I even attempt to teach Jamie the move I just did on him, but his turns are too slow and Leo takes the puck from him every time. I'm exhausted but feeling pretty good about my game by the time a group of kids shows up for a figure-skating class and kicks us off the big rink.

On my way to the locker room, I hear voices coming from the small rink. One very familiar voice.

Haley.

My stomach turns and knots in a very different way than it had moments ago when I was all doom and gloom over my hockey future.

Okay, what the hell is this?

Before I even spot her, I'm replaying the other night, Haley's long hair falling forward as she leaned in to kiss me. And God, I wanted her to. I hate how much I wanted that kiss, but then she got all nervous and down on herself…it wasn't right to push her. I'm not a pusher when it comes to that stuff. Reading body language is kind of a gift of mine, and I prefer to wait until a girl is so worked up, silently screaming with want, before I make any move of my own.

But that's where things get confusing with Haley, because she did want it, I could feel it vibrating off her skin. Or maybe I was projecting? Maybe my wanting that kiss felt like her wanting it?

I don't freakin' know anymore.

Which is why it's good that I closed the door on kissing the other night and suffered through hours of studying Civics, smelling her hair close by, enduring the clear view I had of her legs in those tiny short pajama shorts and pretending like it wasn't doing things to me.

I stop in the doorway of the small rink, and soon Haley and her blond ponytail are in my line of sight. My gaze travels the length of her, from the bright-white figure skates to her form-fitting sweatpants, all the way up to the wide smile on her face. I almost return the smile but then realize it's not directed at me. There's a kid beside her. A little girl maybe nine or ten with messy brown hair, an oversize Otter hockey jersey, and a hole in the knee of her green sweatpants.

"Last time, Maddie," another familiar voice says.

I turn to my left and spot Jake Hammond leaning against the rink wall, waving a set of car keys.

"No way," the kid shouts at Jake. "I'm not wearing that stupid dress!"

"Jesus Christ, Maddie, you promised—"

Haley shoots Jake a look that shuts him up and then turns to the kid. "Why don't you want to wear the dress?"

"Have you seen it?" She lifts her hands in the air, exasperated. "I never wear dresses. Everyone's going to laugh at me—"

"Or say how pretty you look," Jake tries.

"I hate both of those options," the kid says, folding her arms across her chest.

When she stands with attitude on the ice, the family resemblance becomes clear. This must be Jake's sister.

"The thing about weddings," Haley offers, "is that the

bride gets to do whatever she wants, and everyone has to go along with it. Even the ugly dresses. But the good news is that when it's your turn, you can do whatever you want and everyone has to listen to you."

The folded arms loosen a bit on the kid. "Even bathing suits and a Slip 'N Slide?"

"Oh yeah, even that." Haley nods. "I just saw a YouTube video where a couple got married while going down a waterslide."

"Cool," the kid says. And then slowly, as if it's taking every ounce of effort she has to offer, she skates off the ice, snatches a ruffled pink dress wrapped in plastic that I hadn't even noticed Hammond was holding, and storms out toward the lobby.

When she's out of sight, Haley skates over to the wall, and Jake immediately reaches for her, his arms around her shoulders. "God, I love you."

Those words hit me like a punch to the gut. Spots form in front of my eyes. But it makes sense. The Prince and Princess of Juniper Falls. They even look like a couple.

I turn my back to them, hoping to get away without being spotted.

"I owe you big time," I hear Hammond say.

And then Haley's voice rings loud and clear again. "Hey, Fletch, what are you doing here?"

I have no other option except to address them, but before I can say anything, Hammond says, "Another workout with Jamie and Leo?"

Does everyone know about that?

Lucky for me, Jake's phone rings, and with a groan he answers, "Hi Mom…we're on our way, I swear."

I watch Haley watching him leave. There's amusement in her expression, but not much more than that. And I hate the relief I feel discovering this. I don't do jealousy. Ever.

"You really are going for Red's spot, aren't you?" Haley says, probably assessing my sweaty state.

"Maybe." I look her over, evening the score. "What are you doing here?"

"Racing Jake's sister, Maddie," she says simply. "Jake needed something to bribe with to get her in that flower-girl dress for her aunt's wedding."

"Is there anyone in this town whose life you're not involved in?" I ask.

"Yeah," she says, a grin shining in her eyes. "Yours."

My stomach knots all over again.

"Until now, anyway." She gives me a long look that sends my heart sprinting again. "Because of the Civics project."

"The Civics project. Right." I shake off the weird, unfamiliar feelings. "So, who won the race?"

"Tie." Haley pushes away from the wall and skates backwards around the ice. "But I held back a little."

"Really? You holding back? Hard to imagine," I say before I can stop myself.

Her cheeks redden, but she holds my gaze with a determined look on her face and nods toward center ice. "Come on, let's go."

"Okay, sure," I say with a grin. "Three times around?"

Instead of answering, she takes off, flying past me with surprising speed. With my late start it takes half a lap for me to pass her, and even then, I hear her behind me, close on my heels. Before we even get to the second lap, I feel fingers tugging at my shirt.

"Hey! No cheating." I start to turn to face her, grabbing her hand in the process, but my skates come out from under me. My butt hits the ice, and then my back, and then Haley lands right on top of me.

It hurts less than I expected, but still a shock of pain radiates through me. I wait for it to fade before speaking. "Well played, Haley."

Her eyes are wide with concern. "Are you okay? I'm so sorry, seriously. I was just trying to—"

"Cheat?"

"Slow you down," she corrects. "Your legs are much longer. Unfair advantage."

She's even closer now than she was the other night, and it was hard to keep a clear head then. For a moment, I'm sure she's going to do it this time. Her mouth moves closer to mine until I can practically taste her lips. And God, I want to.

But the moment pops like a soap bubble. A sliver of doubt crosses her face, and then she pushes herself off me and sits on her knees on the ice. I pull myself up to a sitting position beside her and stare at her for several seconds. "What are you so afraid of, Haley?"

"Nothing," she says with a shrug. "Just not feeling it, you know?"

I lift an eyebrow but don't call her out on that lie. She was feeling it. I could feel her feeling it.

Maybe I should just kiss her. Maybe then we'll both get out of this weird funk and go back to our regular lives.

"Are you worried you're a bad kisser?" I ask. "Or that I'm a bad kisser?"

"You really want to know what I'm worried about?" she challenges, and then she's up on her skates again. "I'm worried that you *only* want to kiss me. I'm worried about the fact that you barely trust me with anything personal—like where you work and why panties are involved—even though all I do is spill personal shit to you…" She closes her eyes and sighs. "Like right now, for example. And I'm worried that if I kiss you, it won't be fun anymore. It'll be something else, something more. Can you promise me that if I kiss you, it'll just be for fun? That I won't keep feeling things after?"

I can't even promise that *I* won't keep feeling things after.

I open my mouth to argue, but I'm too caught off guard by this version of Haley to offer anything rational. That seems to be enough of an answer for her. She nods, looking satisfied. "See? I do have a reason to hold back."

"Haley…" I stand and skate toward her, but she lifts a hand to stop me.

"This is my deal, not yours. I'm the one with perspective issues." She offers a smile. "And when you're not being a complete asshole, you're fun to hang out with. I like fun."

I clear my throat. "Yeah, I like fun, too."

But as Haley's frustration turns to a more pleasant look directed at me, an uneasy feeling sweeps over me. As much as I hate to admit it, Haley isn't the shallow, superficial girl I thought she was. She's funny and smart and gorgeous…but the idea of trusting someone like her, of kissing and getting personal—I'm definitely not in the market for anything like that.

She's confused, that's all. Attraction and emotional connections tangle easily when you first get to know someone. I watch her retreating form, heading off the ice and away from me, and the feeling in my stomach is there all over again. Hell, I'm probably confused, too. Another reason I should just kiss her.

Next time.

# Chapter Eighteen

## -HALEY-

've just spent two hours doing awesome tumbling and many failed attempts at partner stunting with Jonas. After shelling out fifty dollars of hard-earned babysitting money for the lesson, I'm flying down the two-lane highway from Longmeadow to Juniper Falls. The windows are down, radio blasting, and the place that appears out of nowhere barely catches my attention.

But it does.

I make a sharp turn into a dust-filled, nearly empty parking lot. The building appears to be an innocent storage facility. It has a dull gray exterior, no flashing lights or anything of that nature—things you'd expect at a strip club.

I put the car in park and hop out, walking around to the back of the building. When I spot the flyers on the door—specifically one flyer—I have to work hard not to shout triumphantly and punch the air, *Breakfast Club* style.

I knew it. I freakin' knew it.

Taking up most of the sheet of paper is Fletcher Scott. He's turned around, but I recognize his dark hair and the black dress pants he was wearing last weekend. And his ass. Think whatever you want, but I know his ass, and I'm looking at it right now.

Across the top of the flyer, it says "Scott, Danny, Paco, and Rowdy…The Samba Boys of Summer. Saturday nights. 9 p.m.-1 a.m."

I snap a quick picture and text it to Jamie.

**ME: Told you he's a stripper**

**JAMIE: wtf?? Where is this?**

**ME: some sketchy warehouse looking place near Longmeadow**

**JAMIE: r u still there? If yes, leave. Like now.**

My heart picks up. I glance around and then make a run for my car. I'm back on the road, speeding away, when Jamie calls me. I told him about my weird night with Fletcher and the almost-kiss and then the second almost-kiss that followed days later. Surprisingly, he was a decent listener and hasn't gone too crazy teasing me about not having the balls to kiss Fletch.

"We have to check it out," I say right after I answer. "He keeps denying it, and I think he needs to see that we're in on his little secret, and the world is not going to end."

"So, you're cool with Scott being a stripper?" Jamie says. "I thought you were into him?"

"I'm not—" I stop, trying to find the most truthful answer. "I'm not sure what I am. And he had his pants on when I found him passed out with the panties and the money. Maybe he only strips a little?"

"If he only strips a little, then he must not be very good at his job," Jamie says. "And you don't really expect me to go watch dudes striptease, right?"

"I'm not coming to any conclusions until I see whatever it is that happens on Saturday night with my own eyes." I blow out a breath. I have a fake ID. A great fake ID, actually. I can get in, no problem. But I really don't want to go alone. And Jamie's the perfect accomplice—he knows how to keep a secret. Unlike my best friends, Kayla and Leslie. "You don't have to look. You can cover your eyes."

Jamie is quiet for a long minute, and then finally he sighs. "You gotta let me bring Leo."

I hesitate, not wanting to blow any trust Fletch has in me, but I know Jamie and Leo will keep it to themselves. Whatever *it* is. "Yeah, okay. Bring Leo."

Before he hangs up, I add another warning. "And delete that picture from your phone. I know how you get when you're wasted, leaving your phone lying around for anyone to look through."

"Yeah, okay."

It isn't until I get home to my empty house that it really hits me: Fletcher Scott—the quiet guy who sits behind me in Civics, who stayed up until two in the morning reviewing all the quiz material with me—does some kind of…performing arts…while women (or men?) stuff money in his pants. And his coworkers call themselves the Samba Boys of Summer. Okay, how can I *not* assume he's a stripper? Is there any other way to connect those dots?

I flop onto the couch and stare at my phone, working hard at coming up with a text that doesn't sound too leading or too forward.

**ME: Got a B- minus on yesterday's quiz. Thnx again**

*for helping me study*

**FLETCH: no prob**

**ME: I owe u one. We could do something…like Saturday night. I can make dinner?**

Oh shit. That sounds like I'm asking him out. Uh-oh. That is likely to send Fletch running or telling me to butt out again. And yet it's weird how easy it was to type those words. It's like I didn't realize until right this very moment that I have the power to ask someone on a date. I keep thinking I'll have a moment of connection with someone, and this will lead to being asked on a date—in college, of course, because JFH is not bringing me any new boys anytime soon—but really, *I* can *ask* someone. Go out with him, and either it works or it doesn't.

Is that what Fletch was trying to tell me with the kissing issue? I do make too big of a thing out of this stuff. I had Tate and me married and our photo hanging in town hall when we were only fifteen. At least inside my head, I had accomplished those things. So of course, my life is over when something I want doesn't happen. And then I quickly become obsessed with making it happen anyway.

My phone buzzes, causing me to jump.

**FLETCH: I can't. I work Saturday. Plus that sounded a lot like a date. I don't do that.**

**ME: wait…u don't date? Like ever? 'Cause love is obsolete, right?**

**FLETCH: have u ever seen me on a date? Or heard about me dating anyone?**

**ME: no, but u do take college classes. I've heard the**

*college girls are highly skilled*

*FLETCH: and 40something with minivans and mom jeans. Have u been to Juniper Falls Community before?*

*ME: ok, I get it. U don't date. Whatever*

*FLETCH: why do u seem pissed?*

*ME: I'm not pissed. Just...frustrated.*

*FLETCH: sexually?*

*ME: lol. Stop.*

*FLETCH: u started it. And that's a real thing. It happens.*

*ME: is that how u end up with all those panties in ur pockets.*

*FLETCH: butt out, Haley*

And we're back to where we started again. I toss the phone onto the love seat so I'm not tempted to keep pushing him. What am I even trying to accomplish? Is it that hard for me to accept that one person in this town won't open up to me? Doesn't like me enough to trust me? Yeah, it is that hard to accept. If Fletch won't tell me his secrets, then I have to find out so I can prove myself trustworthy.

Saturday. It'll all be out in the open.

# Chapter Nineteen

## -FLETCHER-

After rehearsals for tonight, I sat on the couch in the back room and fell asleep. Too much hockey practice, extra running, extra training with Jamie and Leo, plus helping both Haley and Jamie study for Civics has wiped me out. I'm working hard to peel my eyes open when a warm body lands in my lap.

"Rosie or Henrietta?" I say. When there's no answer, I know I'm supposed to play the guessing game. Henrietta has been on a long no-panty streak, so I could walk a hand up her skirt and find out that way—God knows the other guys would do it—but instead, I go for the hair.

I was wrong on both accounts.

"Brittney."

She laughs, and I open my eyes and have to endure the sting of hairspray wafting into my breathing space. Brittney ruffles my hair and then slides off my lap. "You look like a little boy when you're asleep."

"Thanks?" I stand up to my full height and take in the commotion around me. I must have really been zonked. Angel is seated in a chair nearby—pale and bent over, her head between her knees. Her fiancé, who is one of the club's bouncers, is cradling their screaming toddler.

Paco walks into the back room and immediately covers his ears. "Hey, Scott! Braden wants you."

I brush past Angel and give her a pat on the back. She hasn't said so, but I'm sure she must be pregnant again. She's been my longest partner, except when she was über-pregnant, so I know the signs. Ricky—the club's owner—didn't want any issues, since I was under eighteen when I started, and Angel is very professional and practically married, so that's why we've always been paired up together.

I stumble through the doors and walk across the center-platform stage to where the bar sits. Braden has several shots lined up for the staff. It's so strange how different it is for me here than at school or any public place in town. All it took was Ricky saying once, "Don't bring any of these foods in the building, or you'll kill Baby Scott" (that's been my nickname for a while, unfortunately. Partly because of my age when I started working here, but mostly because my brother bartends. He's Big Scott, I'm the baby), and everyone followed Ricky's orders without question.

"Enjoy your nap?"

I rub my face and debate slapping myself awake. "I need something."

"Booze or uppers?" Braden asks.

"Uppers," I say. "Definitely uppers."

He produces a pot of coffee from under the bar and fills a wineglass. "Sorry, the mug is missing."

Apparently, mug is singular here. Whatever. I don't care. Coffee is coffee. I hate it, but I love the side effects. I choke down a long sip and then fall onto the barstool. "I think I might have a problem."

"You mean Angel?" Braden says, lowering his voice. "She looks…"

"Glowing?" I supply, though it's quite the opposite from what I saw moments ago. More like about-to-puke.

Braden nods. "Ricky will pair you with Rosie, probably. She says Henrietta will corrupt your innocence."

I smirk down at my wineglass of coffee.

Braden tosses a dirty wet rag at me, and Ricky emerges from her office and glares at him. "You ruin the talent's shirt, and you're fired."

I look up at Ricky. "I get to wear a shirt tonight?"

She attempts a stern look, but grins anyway. "If you're good."

Braden waits for her to go back into her office and then leans in. "Seriously? Henrietta?"

I shrug. It was one time. Several months ago. "Angel isn't my problem. It's Haley."

"Haley Stevenson?" Braden is all ears now. "What about her? She's not into Cole?"

"No, definitely not into Cole." I shake my head. "I think I might be into *her*, though…" I sigh again and wish I were still sleeping on the couch. I don't know what's going on with Haley, and that's the part I can't handle. I have a handful of people I'm close with who I share shit with, and I have a larger handful of people who I share, um, physical closeness with, but never both. Aside from Angel and her fiancé, I haven't really even seen both before. I don't know what it looks like or how it works. And then toss in the Princess-of-Juniper-Falls factor and the gossip circle that comes with that…yeah, I'm a little out of my comfort zone even thinking about it.

"You stay away from that sweet girl," Braden snaps. "The thought of you and her…I'm getting physically ill here."

"Shut the fuck up." I roll my eyes. "She's not ten or whatever anymore. She's my age. We grow up. We hook up. It happens."

Hook up with Haley? Now that's one option.

"I need to dig up that team photo," Braden says with a grin. "If you could have seen her then. She was constantly dirty, with the messiest hair I've ever seen in my entire life. Her mom chased her around with a hairbrush and kept bedazzling her football socks with pink rhinestones."

Well, that's definitely not the Haley Stevenson I know. But then again, she did roll around in my driveway, letting all three dogs cover her in mud.

"You know what?" I force down another big swallow of lukewarm coffee. "I'm gonna forget about that tonight and focus on collecting some more cash."

"And panties." My brother flashes a grin that looks way too much like Grandpa Scott's.

I return the grin. He's right. All I need is a room full of other women to stop thinking about Haley.

# Chapter Twenty

Jamie holds the large warehouse door open for Leo and me. "If they start playin' 'It's Raining Men,' I am so out of here. You two can get your own ride home."

I grin up at Jamie. "What about 'We Are Family' or 'YMCA'?"

"Stevenson," Jamie warns.

We've walked into an almost-dark, club-like atmosphere. The place is packed with jittery people dressed for dancing. Women and men—though the female count appears to be much higher than the male count.

The three of us squeeze into a spot in the back. My stomach is bubbling with nerves and excitement. I want my answer. My proof. I'm just not sure if I want Fletch to see us here, or if I'd rather tell him later what I've learned. Either way, I'm glad I came prepared to fit in—black dress and platform heels—that way I'm much harder to spot.

There's a long stage down the center of the giant room,

like a wide runway, and then two shorter stages on either side of the long one. Definitely a strip club.

What if they do the whole frontal-nudity thing? Or what if they have man-thongs? I might see Fletcher's—

Jesus Christ. I'm such a baby.

I smack Jamie in the chest. "You've been to a strip club before, right?"

"Yeah," he says drily. "With women and poles."

"Did they—" My face heats up. I'm never gonna make it through this. "You know, take everything off?"

Jamie laughs. "Only in the private rooms."

Okay, well that sort of makes sense. You have to leave a little to the imagination. I heard somewhere that male strippers put socks in their, um, underwear, anyway. Oh shit, what if a sock falls out during the *performance*?

The remaining lights dim, and everyone in the building lets out a gasp. Jamie and Leo both move in closer to me, and I feel a surge of courage. These guys are practically bouncer size. If that's not adequate protection, then I don't know what is. And if I get really freaked out, I can just hide behind one of them. I glance around for exits and spot the door we came in and another one across the room with a bright-red exit sign.

Everyone is completely still, and then music blasts through the speakers. Luckily, not one of the tunes forbidden by Jamie. It's something Spanish or Latin. I can barely see over all the people, but then a bright spotlight shines on the two shorter stages. And standing in each light are both a guy and girl. The couples are in a tight embrace, the girls in sequined dresses and high heels, the guys in dress pants, heeled black shoes, and button-down shirts.

I push onto my tippy toes, trying to get a better view. Neither of those guys is Fletcher. Maybe they're the other

Samba Boys of Summer? Paco or Rowdy or whoever.

The music is slow and dramatic. The couples quickly shift to a new pose. Then female voices rise above the others in the crowd, and a unified chant of "Scott, Scott, Scott!" begins.

The music gets faster, and then a bright spotlight shines on the long center stage. And right there, in the midst of maybe a hundred screaming women, is Fletcher Scott.

My stomach does a super-complicated cheer stunt, and my hands are trembling. Oh my God. He's here. Front and center. About to do…God knows what. But he's not alone. A thin, dark-skinned, completely gorgeous woman is wrapped around him. She's wearing what looks like half a dress and heels at least an inch taller than mine.

The music shifts again, dynamic, dramatic, and then much faster. Fletcher lifts the girl's leg all the way to his shoulder and dips her backward. When he pulls her up again, their eyes lock, and the way they look at each other… it's intense and heated. Goose bumps pop up all over my bare arms. Then all three couples begin dancing in unison, their moves crisp and confident. The way Fletch takes control of the girl he's dancing with, the way he holds her with such preciseness and…well, I don't know what else, but I know it's been there all along. I've noticed the way Fletch held himself, never awkward or unsure, but I had no idea why or what exactly that translated to.

The women scream louder, and a small group in front of me has a shouted conversation.

"He picked me last week," one girl yells to another over the music.

"Which is why he's mine this week," her dark-haired friend snaps. "I paid Ricky for private time."

My stomach drops. *Private time…?*

"You're not allowed private time with Scott!" one girl exclaims.

"Am now." The other one smirks at her friend, flipping hair over one shoulder. "Someone had a birthday."

"No way! He's legal?"

All four girls in the group look over at Fletch again, and the lust meter is high enough to require daily confession for an entire month. I glance up at Jamie. I'd forgotten he and Leo were beside me.

Jamie's forehead is wrinkled, and he's combing a hand through his hair. "I have no idea what I'm looking at."

"They still have their clothes on," Leo says. "That's good, right?"

"The show just started," I point out. "Maybe it takes a while to get to the stripping part."

Jamie pats his rock-hard stomach. "Maybe Scott doesn't have the abs for topless dancing."

I look from him to Leo and then ask both of them, "Does he have the abs? Shouldn't you know? I thought you guys wandered around naked in the locker room."

Or at least that's what I've always imagined when I've gone in there to decorate lockers.

"No one walks around naked," Leo says. "Where are you getting your information?"

"Except Stewart," Jamie mumbles. "He's got balls the size of—"

I plug my ears and squeeze my eyes shut, forcing out that image. "There go my locker-room fantasies."

Leo, always the practical one, waits for me to uncover my ears and then says, "He was JV until state. Different practice times."

We turn our attention back to the stage, and it's as if someone heard our question and decided we needed an answer. Fletch backs away from his partner and does this slow tease of unbuttoning his shirt. The screams grow louder, so much that I fight the urge to cover my ears. But at the same time, I debate joining them.

The girl Fletch is currently teasing dances her way closer and finishes off the last button, tossing the shirt in the wings. When he spins around, his partner behind him, my jaw nearly falls to the floor.

"Okay, then," I say.

From the corner of my eye, I see Leo nod. "I'd say he's got the abs for topless."

Jamie wrinkles his nose at both of us. My brain hasn't even fully processed the fact that Fletch, who I almost kissed—twice—has this secret life and secret talent, but regardless, my feet are making their way forward, moving closer to the stage.

# Chapter Twenty-One

## —FLETCHER—

Angel survives the opening number, but I can tell she's struggling. I keep a tight hold on her and wait for Ricky to give us the nod. I spin Angel and then pull her close. With her mouth right next to my ear, she whispers, "I need to go. Now."

I dance us toward the wings—it's either that or get barfed on—and let the curtain fall around her. I grab one of the vests that sit backstage, just to look like I had a purpose to my excursion into the wings. Of course, with Angel racing off to the bathroom, I'm forced to solo. I head downstage and then drop down, sliding the rest of the way on my knees. It gets me a few super-loud screams.

Ricky is standing by the bar, near Braden. She shakes her head and then gestures toward the crowd. She's letting us mingle early just to cover Angel's exit. Paco and Henrietta hop off the stage, and each chooses a new partner. I glance around the room, gaining a few more screams. Ignoring the aggressive girls, I jump down and choose a nonthreatening middle-aged woman to dance with. We fall into a polite salsa, plenty of space between us. It takes me back to days when dancing was just something I did with my grandmother. Before she passed away. Before I realized it could make me some decent money.

Dancing breaks out all around me, those who brought a partner pulling out their best salsa moves. Ricky's about to give me the signal to move on to a new partner—"spread the love so they come back for more" is her motto—and several small soft hands are already groping me from behind, crinkled bills making their way into the waistband of my dress pants. I give the middle-aged woman my most charming grin and a slight bow before I scope the room for my next partner. I sift through the crowd, bumping hips with a couple grinding and swaying together like pros. I continue my search for someone to dance with and spot a blonde with a messy bun piled on her head. I'm less than ten feet away when she snaps around to face me.

Haley.

Holy shit. Haley Stevenson is here.

I nearly have a heart attack right there on the dance floor, but I recover and keep my hips moving to the music. What the hell is she doing here?

My first reaction is to turn around and head for the other side of the room. I almost do it, too. But a large hand lands on Haley's shoulder, another on her hip. My gaze moves upward, and I meet the hard stare of some thirty-something dude with a leather jacket despite the summer heat and a jagged scar across his cheek.

Without thinking it through, I reach for Haley, tugging her away from Mr. Wrong. Later, I'll process all this. Later I'll come up with some plan that may or may not include moving to a new town. But for now, sweet, innocent Haley Stevenson is about to get down and dirty with me.

# Chapter Twenty-Two

## −HALEY−

"What are you doing?" I hiss at Fletcher, when his front presses against my back. "I don't know sambas or salsas or whatever."

"Not yet."

"But—" I protest, despite my entire body heating up from his touch.

He reaches around and touches a finger to my lips. "No talking."

A thrill shoots through my body. I have no idea what's about to happen, and I really like this feeling. All around us, people are watching the dancers less and becoming dancers more, getting into their moves and the music. Fletch keeps me turned around, my back to him. He lifts my arms around his neck, and then both his hands are locked firmly on my hips.

His feet move in a pattern that I don't know. I watch them closely, trying to keep up, but Fletch slides a hand up my body and lifts my chin so I'm now looking at a couple dancing in front of us.

"Eyes up," he whispers into my ear. A shiver runs down my back. "Feel it, don't watch."

My stomach is a ball of knots, but I draw in a deep breath and close my eyes. With Fletch's hands guiding my hips, it's not difficult to fall into a rhythm with him.

"Good. You got it." Fletcher's hands leave my hips, and then he's sliding closer, pressing us together. I swallow back a gasp at the close contact—I mean the couple in front us is basically going all the way with clothes on. Fletch's fingers glide down my arms, his warm breath against my neck. He unclasps my hands from his neck and spins me around. It isn't until we're face-to-face that I notice his lack of glasses. My own cheeks warm. I don't know what's happening, but it's a lot. Maybe too much.

I drop my gaze to the space between our feet. "I'm not putting money in your pants."

Fletch lifts my chin again until I have to look at him. He's got a hand around my waist, and then he clasps my other hand in his. "Come on, Haley. Relax. Let go."

The fear rises up in me again. It's exactly the same as when I couldn't kiss him. It's like 90 percent of me is dying to do it and the remaining 10 percent just eats the rest in one big bite.

But you know what? Not tonight. This whole situation is practically otherworldly. I don't have to be my normal self here.

"I step in, you step back," Fletch says, not breaking eye contact.

I misstep a couple of times, but I quickly fall into the pattern with him. He recites counts into my ear, keeping me in time. Moving in unison like this, it feels like flying. Fletch lifts my arm over my head and spins me in a half circle. He's behind me again, our hips grinding together. I close my eyes and allow the faces and noise to dissolve around me. Fletch's warm fingers grip my hips and then journey upward. This is not how he danced with the middle-aged lady only moments ago.

When he turns me around again, our eyes lock, and he's staring so intensely, like he'd done earlier with the girl who vanished back stage. I melt into him, close enough for my lips to brush his neck.

"I could do it now," I whisper right into his ear. "I could kiss you."

"Don't." He presses his hand more firmly against my back, bringing us even closer. "It's against the rules. The bouncers will toss you out."

The faces appear all around me, and I'm suddenly self-conscious all over again. All these women are watching me, wondering why I have no idea what I'm doing. Fletch must have sensed my nerves, because he brings me close again and says, "Want to show off a little? You trust me, right?"

My trust has never been the problem.

My mouth barely falls open, preparing to answer, when Fletch hoists me up on his shoulder like he did in the park the other night. He spins around, and two of the other dancer guys appear beside Fletch—either Paco or Rowdy or Danny.

From up high, I spot Jamie and Leo watching us with their mouths hanging open. They're both standing up straight and alert like they're poised to intervene if needed.

Fletch slides me down the front of his body, like he did the other night, but this time, he wraps one of my legs around his waist and pulls the other up to his shoulder. Before I catch my breath, he's dipping me backwards, some of my hair dangling loose from its bun. I laugh. I can't help it. Everything about this moment is so bizarre, so unplanned and unlike the rest of my life, so far out of my comfort zone, and yet it's the most fun I've ever had.

He brings me back up again just as the final beats of the song play out. He's holding me in place, our foreheads touching, hearts pounding together, both of us breathing hard. And this time, it takes everything I have to not close that gap between our mouths.

God, those eyes…is that how a guy is supposed to look at a girl? If so, I don't think I need to see anything else in my entire life ever again. His hand drifts to my cheek, he leans closer, but stops. Disappointment washes over me. Fletch releases my leg, letting it fall back to the ground, preventing me from flashing the crowd. I finally peel my gaze from him just in time to catch two women behind him, stuffing bills in his waistband and a pair of red panties into his pocket.

An older woman with a long, brightly colored skirt pries Fletch and me apart and then shoves him toward a tall, dark-haired girl, probably college aged. Fletch immediately grabs hold of the girl, grinning at her and grasping her hips like he'd done with me. I stumble backwards, a lump rising in my throat.

It's a show. It's all a show.

My cheeks are flaming, from the workout and from the dozens of pairs of eyes looking me over. I spin quickly and head for the door. I'm pushing it open when I feel the presence of Jamie and Leo behind me. The cool summer night air hits me in the face, and I walk as quickly as possible across the crowded parking lot to a picnic table in the field behind the warehouse.

I'm a calm person by nature, but I'm not immune to a

temperamental outburst. And that's exactly what happens—me outbursting.

"God, I fucking hate my head sometimes," I snap at anyone who's listening. A few tears tumble from my eyes, infuriating me as I plop down on top of the picnic table and look at Jamie and Leo. "Why am I crying? What's wrong with me?"

Leo shakes his head, and Jamie lifts his hands in surrender. Both guys look extremely uncomfortable.

"He did dance a lot closer to you than with the forty-year-old soccer mom," Jamie says.

I laugh and wipe the remaining loose tears away. "Thanks."

"It's not a strip club, apparently," Leo says, sitting beside me. "Private rooms are for lessons with dancers."

"So they say," Jamie adds. "Some chick just asked me to dance, and then said she'd give me some private lessons."

Everything inside my head is so confusing, I'm not ready to chat about it. "Why don't you guys go back inside and scope it out some more. I just need a minute of fresh air, okay?"

Leo glances longingly at the building, but Jamie hesitates. "You shouldn't sit here alone."

I hold a hand out. "Give me my keys and my phone."

Jamie removes the items I'd stowed in his pockets earlier and hands them over. I hold up the tiny spray bottle and my phone. "Pepper spray. Cell phone. I'll be fine. I won't go anywhere, I swear."

They head back toward the building, and I lay across the picnic table, staring up at the stars. The temperature is probably sixty or sixty-five, clear skies. God, I love summers in Minnesota. I keep the pepper spray clutched in one hand and try my best to relax and enjoy the distant music.

A while later—I have no idea how long—I hear a familiar voice. "You stole my spot."

I sit up quickly, adjusting my dress, and Fletcher hops up onto the table beside me. I look him over and slide back, putting more distance between us.

"You found your shirt," I say. "And cleaned out your pockets…"

"Two really big hockey players made fun of my vest." His words are casual, but his face reveals some concern.

"Jamie and Leo won't tell anyone," I reassure him. "I know they won't."

He's got a nearly empty water bottle in one hand and an unopened one in the other. He hands it to me and waits for me to take a drink.

"So…" I have a million questions for him and no idea how to start. "Where did you learn to dance like that? Is it ballroom or what?"

"My grandmother," Fletch says, and as if sensing that tonight especially I need more from him, he goes on. "When I switched to homeschooling in third grade, she decided I would take dance lessons from her every day. Said it would make me more confident." He shakes his head and laughs. "I never thought dancing would do any good with schoolyard bullies, but I didn't mind learning. As long as I didn't have to practice with Braden around."

I pick at the buckle on my shoe. "It's like you have this whole different life here. Is that why you don't tell anyone?"

"Maybe. But it's also just Juniper Falls, you know?"

"No, I don't know."

He hesitates, then with a sigh explains. "Our town lives for gossip, and that's all fun and games if you're not the center of that gossip. My family prefers to stay out of the town's daily news, only…"

"Only what?"

"Only that didn't happen," he says, a hint of anger in his voice. "My grandmother nearly got deported years ago after a bunch of people in Juniper Falls started gossiping about her legal status and questions surrounding it."

"Her legal status?" And yeah, I'm on the edge of my seat now.

"She came here from South America with her dance troupe for a tour when she was a teenager. Against her family's wishes. And then she decided to stay," Fletch says. "Even after she married my grandpa, people talked about whether it was real or just a hoax to win her legal status. And then my mom…"

His voice trails off. He can't do it. Even after everything I've done to prove myself trustworthy, he can't open up. We stare at each other for a long moment. Something in my expression must have offered him enough confidence in me, because to my surprise, he finishes what he started to say. "My mom got pregnant with me in high school. I mean, she was eighteen. But still in high school."

I work hard not to laugh. "Seriously? Our town is no stranger to pregnant teens, never has been from what I've heard."

"Yeah, I know that." Fletch nods like he'd expected me to say this. "But my dad is twenty years older."

The hint of a smile falls from my face. No wonder he made a point of mentioning that she was legal age. "I guess that's different."

Fletcher studies me. "You didn't know?"

I shake my head. "It's old news now."

Other than the texting between my mom and me from the hospital after I drove Fletch, my parents haven't been around for us to have a conversation where Fletch's name gets dropped in. But I know exactly how it would go. I can even hear my mother's voice inside my head, "Fletcher Scott? Haven't heard that name in a while. You know there was quite the scandal surrounding that boy's birth back in the day. Grandma must have lit a hundred candles at mass for her family."

Then my dad's voice follows Mom's. "Everyone had it out for Scott, said it was criminal, going after a high-school girl. And you know his mother was an illegal…"

"And just when things had calmed down for their families, someone goes and tries to kill that poor little boy," imaginary Mom adds. "But with all those allergies, it's a wonder he even made it that long in school."

I close my eyes, guilt punching me in the gut. Guilt for a conversation that doesn't even exist. But it could easily exist. I know this for sure, because similar conversations happen nightly in my house. And I'm always right there, taking it all in. Now I get that saying about gossip. That even letting yourself hear it is toxic. Look what it's done to Fletcher's life…he doesn't trust anyone in Juniper Falls. This explains so much. The weight of accepting responsibility for the wrongs done to Fletch's family on behalf of my entire town is a bit too much, and I have to change the subject before I end up hating myself and where I come from.

"What's with the panties in the pockets?"

He gives me a weary look, his cheeks heating up. "It's a long story."

"I'm all ears." I lean back on my elbows, forgetting that he probably has to go back in there. It's not anywhere near midnight yet.

"I'll give you the short version." He runs a hand through his hair. "It wasn't legal for anyone to get too *intimate* with me. So, it became this thing…handing over their panties so

I could see how turned on—"

I slap a hand over his mouth and close my eyes briefly. "Okay, I get it."

Fletch takes my hand from his mouth and holds on to it. His eyes search mine. "Want to come back inside? Dance with me again?"

"Yes," I say immediately and then shake my head. "No. I mean no."

"No?" He pauses like he's waiting for me to explain. I totally would if I could figure it out. "What's wrong, Haley?"

"You." I pull my hand away from him. "You and your stupid hands and stupid mouth. And your stupid abs."

He leans closer, the corner of his mouth popping up into a sexy half smile. "You liked dancing with me. Admit it."

"Yes! I liked it. It was fun. So fun." I jump down from the table and move farther away from Fletch. "And then it turned into this big deal inside my head. And you…you can slide up behind anyone in the room and look like I feel right now."

His jaw tightens, and I exhale before retracting some of my words. "I'm not judging you, Fletch. I wish I could be more like you. That's all I'm saying."

His eyes lock with mine again. "You should kiss me."

"What?" I fold my arms over my chest. "No way. Besides, we already know how that will go."

"I think you can do it now," he says. "You danced with panty pushers—that's what we call them backstage, by the way—and you were totally hot. Totally in the moment. I think you're ready for this. No strings attached. Just a kiss."

A grin spreads across my face. "I was totally hot? Really?"

He nods. "Way, way hot."

I walk a couple of steps in his direction, my pulse pounding. "Hotter than your flexible partner?"

"Without a doubt."

I press my sweaty palms against my dress, drying them discreetly. "You were hot, too."

"Really?" he asks, less confident than I've seen him all night.

I nod. "I totally get the panty thing."

Fletch arches a dark eyebrow. "Yeah?"

"Yeah, but I'm keeping mine." I take a deep breath and stand right between his legs, my hands resting on his thighs again.

"You only have a little farther to go." He whispers the words right against my lips, and they're magnetic, pulling me in.

I close my eyes and try to be here and now. Not five years in the future. Not naming our future children or plotting career plans for us. But then I freeze up again. "Should I use tongue, or maybe it should be really quick?"

"Do whatever you feel like doing," he says.

Okay, but what if he does whatever he feels like doing, and I'm left trying to keep up or match skills?

"Don't move okay?" I order. "Keep your hands on the table."

His fingers curl around the edge of the picnic table, showing his willingness to do this my way. I count to three inside my head, sixth-grade spin-the-bottle flashbacks playing on repeat. Then I lean in and touch my lips to his. A millisecond later, I'm pulling back again. There. I did it.

Fletch's eyes are still open, and when I stare into them again, a fire builds inside me and the invisible brick wall falls down around us. I reach out and grip his face, pulling our lips together again and muffling the really sexy noise that escapes from the back of his throat. With even less inhibition, I slide my hands down his neck, enjoying the feel of his skin beneath my fingertips. His fingers brush my elbows, forgetting my earlier command, but then he quickly returns to gripping the table. I pull away again to tell him he doesn't have to keep holding the table, but then I look from his face to his now-white knuckles, and a surge of power zaps through me. I kind of like calling the shots. My fingers find their way to the back of his hair. and I bring our lips together again. A groan escapes Fletch's mouth, and his lips part, allowing our tongues to mingle.

Fletch slides farther back on the table, and I follow him. His hands attempt to lift several times, and then he re-grips the table. Finally, with both of us breathing heavily, our pulses racing, I tell him he can touch me.

In no time at all, his arms are around my waist, lifting me up onto his lap. My dress gets hiked up, and my legs wrap around Fletch. He leans my head back and plants kisses up and down the front of my neck until I'm ready to go completely crazy.

"*Jesus,*" he mumbles. "You are so beautiful."

My insides warm at those words, and then we're kissing harder, more intensely, the stars twinkling above us. Then something twists inside me, a weight pressing against my chest. I slow down my movements and eventually we pull apart.

I squeeze my eyes shut, willing away the feelings. All the feelings that aren't supposed to be here.

*Be gone. You're wrong. Go away.*

Fletch rests his hands on my cheeks. "Haley?"

I shake my head, refusing to open my eyes.

"You're not supposed to cry." Concern leaks into his voice.

I didn't even know I was crying, but the evidence is clear when I feel his thumbs brush under my eyes, wetness beneath them. "I'm sorry. I told you, I suck at this."

"It's just a kiss, Haley."

I nod and then open my eyes. Any remaining anger fades when I see all the worry on Fletcher's face. He's just as confused as I am. He doesn't want to hurt me. He wants to be honest. I get it. It's other things that I don't get.

"You don't feel this…?" I hesitate, grappling for the best words. "This weight on your chest." I rest a hand over my heart. "Like you've just screwed up something or lost something you cared about."

"No." He slides a hand into my hair, working his fingers all the way through it. "I feel light, actually."

My forehead wrinkles as I study his face. How could we kiss like that—equal passion—and have completely different feelings? "Maybe it's the blood draining from your head to…lower regions."

He laughs. "That's possible." In one swift movement, Fletch stands with me still on his lap and turns around to give me my seat on the table again. He sits down on the bench and brings me to the edge so he can keep his arms around my back. "I have to go back inside soon. I only get a thirty-minute break."

"Yeah, okay." The weight presses harder on my chest, imagining all the girls he could dance with or kiss like he kissed me. *What is wrong with me?* I give his shoulders a shove and force a smile. "Go, before you get in trouble."

"Come with me," he says. "Please."

"I'll probably cry again." I meant that sarcastically, but it's totally possible.

"You won't cry." Fletch stands and leans in, his mouth hovering near mine. "But you will look hot and sexy and probably feel hot and sexy, which is never a bad thing."

I'm smiling now. I mean, how can I not be? I reach up

and touch Fletch's cheek. "I like you like this."

"Like what? Hot and sexy?" he guesses.

"Not an asshole." I get brave and pull his mouth to mine again.

Fletch responds by parting my lips and lifting me up off the picnic table. He continues kissing me, my feet dangling a couple of inches off the ground, his mouth working mine like he's got all the time in the world, like he's not on the tail end of a thirty-minute break. I pull away before my panties become completely ruined. He's way too good at kissing for me to come out of this alive.

"For someone who was afraid to touch me," I say, "you really seem to like picking me up."

Fletch grins and places my feet on the ground. "You're easy to lift. And my partner is pregnant, so I don't get to throw her around as much."

My mouth falls open in shock. "You got your partner pregnant?" Oh my God, this is so *Dirty Dancing*.

Fletch rolls his eyes. "Her fiancé did. And she hasn't actually told me yet, but the signs are all there. I know they want two kids. She's already got one."

"So, you and her aren't like…?" I turn away and look at the building.

"Uh-uh," Fletch says.

I glance sideways at him. "But you looked so…convincing."

"It's an act." He takes my hand and pulls me in close like he did on the dance floor. "We make up stories, and we get really into the characters."

"Just like *So You Think You Can Dance*," I say, already feeling my stomach flip over again from being in Fletch's arms. The realization behind his answer hits me hard, and I sink back into that weighty feeling. "So, it's probably like that with me, too."

"Haley," he warns. "Stop doing that. I'm good at convincing other people it's real when it isn't. And you're good at convincing yourself it's real."

"But we're not working together," I point out. "We've been flirting since I nearly tumbled off your barn roof. It's not all acting. So, what is it?"

"Attraction." Fletch slides a hand up my back and into my hair. "Curiosity." He dips me back again and kisses my neck. "Hormones."

"But isn't that how most relationships start?"

"Maybe, if you let it," Fletch agrees. He stands up straighter and presses a hand between my shoulder blades, forcing my spine to straighten. "You've got a decent frame."

"And you don't?"

"Have a decent frame?" Fletch says, though I can tell by his face that he knows what I meant. "My frame is excellent. My grandmother made me practice with a back brace and weights on my shoulders."

I shake my head. "I meant you don't let relationships begin."

"No, I don't," Fletch says firmly.

I don't press him for more details—he's already spilled a lot tonight—but I know, beneath that answer is a story. Maybe Fletch and I have more in common than I realized.

# Chapter Twenty-Three

## —FLETCHER—

Okay, so I'm not being 100-percent truthful with Haley. I *have* let relationships begin before. I know what she means about a weight pressing on your chest. But I haven't felt that since I was sixteen and fell hard for a twenty-year-old dancer—a mistake both Grandpa Scott and Dad warned me against. To say that I get what Cole feels like with Haley is an understatement. But after talking with her tonight, I think all the feelings I've been having make sense. Yes, that kiss was fucking amazing. But it's just attraction and hormones and all those pre-relationship things. Stuff that I can shut down anytime I want.

I think Haley could, too, if she worked at it. I know what she's going through, and I want to help her.

Before she can press me with any more questions, I bring her back inside. The music pumps hard through my veins, and soon I'm surging with energy. Hard to believe I was asleep on the couch earlier.

Just to prove to Haley that dancers can act, I grab Paco and pass Haley over to him. She's startled at first, but I nod my encouragement, and she must trust me or have decided not to trust herself tonight, because she lets my friend sweep her up and move her around the dance floor like putty. I turn my back to them and laugh to myself after Paco pulls her in close and shares one of his famous long looks. He's got me beat in that area, too. And considering Leo is more his type than Haley, she's bound to believe me about dancers being actors after this.

Angel's claiming to be recovered, so Ricky puts us back on center stage, and we do a couple more routines. She doesn't ask me to, but I leave out all the big lifts, and by the time we're closing out with the last dance, I'm sure she's guessed what I've guessed. But still, nobody says a word.

I head backstage to shower and change, and when I return to the main room, Jamie is in the corner flirting with some woman who might be thirty. Leo is at the bar, drinking what looks like a soda and having an animated conversation with Braden. Haley is seated beside him, but her head is resting on her arm, and from across the room, it looks like she might be sleeping.

I walk over to them and assess Haley: she's definitely asleep. "Man, you guys must be really entertaining."

Leo looks over at her, does a double take. "Oh shit." He glances at Braden. "You didn't serve her anything, did you?"

Braden practically glares at Leo. "Seriously? This girl is still ten to me."

Leo snorts out a laugh. "Guess you didn't see her and Fletch dancing?"

I hold up my hands. "She came here on her own."

Jamie appears behind me—he must have decided against a hookup with the woman he'd been chatting up. "Think we should bring her to your place? How big is this tent?"

I assume he's talking to Leo, but quickly realize he's looking at my brother. "Who's sleeping in a tent at our house?"

Jamie claps a hand on my shoulder. "Us, man." Jamie scratches his head. "You've got two tents, right? Because Leo's invitin' his boy over, and you know, third wheel and all that…"

"We have four," Braden answers. "And a barn."

I step behind Jamie and attempt to silently converse with my brother, but it's no good. He's already invited them. What the hell is he thinking? I don't do this sort of thing—mix work people and town people. Like, ever. And I could really use some downtime to process the fact that three people from my school now know where I work and what I do on Saturday nights.

"All right." Leo claps his hands together. "Let's get the princess and take off."

"Let me do the honor." Jamie moves beside Haley. "She's so cute when you wake her up."

He shakes her shoulder and leans down to whisper something to Haley. With her eyes still closed, she lifts a hand and shoves his face back. "Fuck off."

I crack a smile, but then my protective side kicks in. I step around Jamie and scoop up Haley, turning both of us toward the door. She's surprisingly heavier in this ragdoll, sound-asleep state.

Paco and Henrietta are at the door; both move to hold it open for me. "We goin' out, Scott?" Paco asks.

I roll my eyes in Braden's direction. "Apparently there's a campout in my backyard."

"A campout?" Paco wrinkles his nose. "Like Boy Scouts?"

Jamie elbows me in the side. "Dude, she's invited, right?"

He's eyefucking Henrietta. I look right at her and grin, but lean in to whisper to Jamie. "Just be careful. She bites."

"What about beer?" Leo says, tossing another log onto Grandpa Scott's expertly built bonfire. "Doesn't that have wheat?"

"Only if it's wheat beer," Braden answers before I can.

Thanks to Grandpa confiscating all the offensive snacks the guys brought over as a hospitable gesture, my allergies have become the hot topic of discussion.

But maybe it's not as bad as I think. Leo is taking off for Michigan U in a couple weeks, and Jamie's leaving for college soon, too. Assuming he passes Civics. And when we're not talking about my personal shit, I kind of like hanging with Jamie and Leo.

"Well that's fucking good." Jamie knocks back the tail-end of his can of beer. "'Cause if you couldn't drink beer…"

"I don't drink beer," I say with a long sigh. Not wanting to explain how beer has gluten, and gluten won't kill me, but it does bother me.

"He's a hard-liquor guy," Braden says.

"Didn't know you still had all that shit going on," Jamie says. "Thought it was just the breathing thing…asthma. Keep forgetting that word."

I glance at the house, wondering if Haley is enjoying her spot in my bed. I'd like to be in there right now. Not with her. Okay, maybe with her?

God, I don't know anymore.

I stand up and brush the grass off my shorts. "After someone from school tried to kill me, I decided being the allergy kid wasn't in my best interest."

This is what happens when you tell people in Juniper Falls your secrets. Not only do they tell everyone, but they use it against you, too.

It was my half birthday in third grade—summer birthday kids always got to bring treats on their half birthdays. My mom baked Fletcher Allergy-Approved cupcakes for the occasion, and we passed them out in such a rush at the end of the school day that I didn't get a chance to eat mine. Mrs. Lewis, my teacher, gave me special permission to eat on the bus—usually food wasn't allowed.

I sat in my seat and opened the container, pulling out a sprinkled cupcake. The tiny crushed nuts someone—we still don't know who did this—had added blended in well enough with the nondairy sprinkles my mom had special ordered for the occasion to fool me. But a couple seconds after my first bite, I was in full-blown panic mode. Much of the minutes that followed are either a blur or completely blank. I remember hearing laughter from the back of the bus briefly, but then screaming and crying followed. I think the bus driver nearly crashed getting the vehicle to a stop, and that probably freaked everyone out. Then she broke the only EpiPen we had before being able to use it. My throat was so closed up, the paramedics had to cut a hole in my neck to get air in. I still have a scar from the incision.

"Someone tried to kill you in elementary school?" Leo says, pulling himself upright again.

"Oh yeah, I remember that." Jamie holds up his empty beer can. "I was on the bus that day."

I spin slowly to face him. "You rode my bus?"

Jamie nods and lifts his empty can higher. I don't move to get him another, though I was planning on doing just that seconds ago. "Do you know who did it?"

Jamie studies me like he can't decide if it's a serious question. "What if I do?"

"Who was it?" I demand.

"Okay, raise your hand if you're confused," Paco says, his arm shooting up. He's laughing, probably to lighten the tone—which has abruptly shifted to ice-cold.

Henrietta lifts a hand in the air. I glance at her for a split second then stare at Jamie again. "Was it you?"

Jamie tosses his can into the fire and sits up straighter, all amusement gone from his face. "What are you gonna do, Scott? Go kick someone's ass for stupid shit they did when they were nine or ten or whatever?"

I squeeze my fists at my sides. "Maybe."

"Then I'm not fucking telling you anything." Jamie stands up and walks away from me, toward the cooler of beer Paco brought with him. "You cool your shit down, and we can talk about it like fucking adults." He looks over his shoulder and grins. "Well, not fucking adults—like the verb."

Leo shakes his head. "Dude, that joke is getting old."

I'm about to take off, go for a ten-mile run to cool down, but I'm distracted by Grandpa butting into the conversation. He's got an ax, and he's been busy several feet away from the fire pit chopping wood.

"I bet it was a hockey player," Grandpa says. "I've always thought that. The way we treat you boys around here…we're grooming devils."

"So, what you're saying is," Leo presses, "your grandson is the devil?"

"Oh no," Grandpa says. "My boy is an angel compared to you lot. But he barely made varsity, so he's not been ruined yet."

"Thanks, Gramps." I shake my head and turn to Leo, who looks confused as hell. "He played football for JFH. So did my dad and—"

"Me," Braden adds. "But I'm not a complete hockey cynic. I'd have played if I could skate like Fletch."

Grandpa points an ax at Leo. "You boys are always into trouble. I don't hear nothin' about the football players stirring up trouble."

"Wait, there's a football team at JFH?" Jamie jokes, returning to his seat around the fire.

I'm still watching Jamie carefully, trying to decide if he really knows who nearly killed me on that bus years ago. In my head, I've always imagined that person grew up to be a giant prick who could probably use some ass kicking. I mean, what else would someone who could do something like that grow up to become?

"What was that big ordeal last winter, over at O'Connor's?" Grandpa asks. "As I recall, one of the hockey boys—that Tanley kid—beat the shit out of someone out back and got off without even taking a trip down to the station. Is that what you consider an evening out on the town? Fightin' and gettin' the sheriff involved?"

That drama happened last February during the sections tournament leading to state finals. I hadn't been moved up to varsity at the time of that incident, so I'm not exactly sure what happened. Now I'm rooted to my spot, waiting for Leo's or Jamie's comeback. They don't really have to defend the Otters anymore, so I'm expecting them to laugh it off or joke about it.

"It wasn't a fucking hockey-team brawl at the bar, if that's what you're thinking," Leo snaps at Grandpa.

"If it walks like a chicken and bawks like one…" Grandpa says.

"You're not even close to the truth." Leo glares at Grandpa and then stands up. He walks toward the lake, his phone emerging from his pocket.

Grandpa opens his mouth to call Leo back—Gramps can be a pain in the ass to argue with, but he means well—but Leo is busy on the phone.

"It's a sore subject for him." Jamie sighs. "For me, too."

"So, what happened?" Paco and Henrietta both ask. They've been so quiet watching us like a reality-TV show, I almost forgot they were here.

"Claire O'Connor went out back to the dumpsters," Jamie says, his eyes on the fire. "I guess she was gone for too long, so Tanley and Leo went looking for her. Some crazy fisherman had her up against the dumpster, his hand over her mouth. Leo and Tate came after him, Claire took off, and then Tanley beat the shit out of him."

I move toward the fire and take my seat on the log. "And Claire...was she hurt? Did anything..."

Jamie shakes his head. "She was fine. But Tate...I mean, you should have seen him after. I didn't think he'd ever snap out of it. Scared the shit out of me. Leo, too." Jamie throws some blades of grass into the fire, causing it to rise up and glow brighter.

"You know who was the real savior that night?" Jamie says when Leo returns from his phone call. "Fucking Haley."

"Yep," Leo agrees. "It takes a lot of pride-swallowing to be the one to comfort your ex's new girlfriend."

Both of them stare at me, so of course Henrietta and Paco do the same. I lift my hands up. "What?"

Jamie narrows his eyes at me. "Are you fucking with Haley's head?"

"We are definitely not down with that," Leo adds.

This whole situation has taken a turn for the worse. I didn't ask to be in this spot. "Haley's pretty good at fucking with her own head."

The words fall out of my mouth without much thought, but after, I brace myself for a potential Jamie/Leo beating. They both stare me down, but finally Jamie says, "Yeah. True."

I silently release a breath and glance at Paco. His eyes are wide, and he gives a little shake of his head like he's telling me I'm nuts. I probably am.

"She's also not so bad to be around," I admit, earning a bit of a glare from Henrietta, though I'm not sure why; she and I are not a thing. Both Jamie and Leo have quirked an eyebrow, waiting for something, so I add, "And you guys aren't too bad to hang around, either."

"'Course we're not," Jamie says. "And Haley's not too hard to look at, right?"

There's no point in lying. I look him straight in the eyes. "Definitely not."

"All right, I'm here. Now where the hell is here?" a voice says from behind me.

I turn around to see who else I'm gonna have to deal with tonight. I'm greeted with the snide and arrogant face of Kennedy Locust, future senior class president.

Kennedy points a finger at Braden. "You? This is your house?"

Braden rolls his eyes. "I'm really beginning to regret the crime I committed years ago that forced me into coaching peewee football."

"Another peewee player?" I guess. Might be nice to focus on Braden a little and less on me and Haley.

Kennedy folds his arms over his chest. "Player is a bit of a stretch, considering I was benched 90 percent of the time."

Jamie falls off his log from laughing so hard. "Oh man, talk about harsh. Benching the gay, nerdy, unathletic kid in peewee football. Did the moms all riot against you?"

Even I'm surprised by this revelation, but if I know my brother—

"That's right." Braden stands and throws his own can into the fire, signaling that he's done. I'm shocked he stayed up this late. "I'm the ass that ruined your football career. Sorry about that."

Grandpa waves a finger at Kennedy. "I know you. That little punk who made those other kids quit. What'd you say to them, anyway?"

Kennedy shrugs. "It's not my problem that they were all emotionally weak and couldn't handle a little teasing. Considering Fletcher's years of hiding out, I guess your whole family was a little sensitive to the issue, though. I should have realized—"

I'm not even a bit bothered by Kennedy Locust pressing buttons—it's what he does best—but apparently Jamie is. One second he's rolling on the ground laughing, the next, he's got his hands around Kennedy's shirt and is lifting him off the ground.

"God, this is so fascinating," Paco says. "Homeschooling can never compare."

Paco is one of the few coworkers who I know from when I was a kid. My mom joined a homeschool group that combined our entire county, which includes Longmeadow. Like me, Paco suffered teasing a bit in school—apparently, he was extremely flamboyant in his youth—but he's completely different now. Also a product of Grandma Scott's dance lessons.

"Enough." Leo cuts in between Jamie and Kennedy, prying them apart.

Jamie is fuming. "Dude, I'm at my limit."

"Okay, okay," Leo says.

"I'm just sayin'…" Jamie looks over at Braden and

Grandpa. "Where'd you say those tents are hiding?"

Grandpa tells him where to look, and before Jamie takes off, he adds, "Hey, thanks for clearing up that story about the hockey team and the bar fight."

Jamie gives him a beer salute. "It's what I'm here for." He looks over at Paco and spreads his arms out wide. "Paco, my man! Sleeping buddies, what do ya say?"

I turn around quickly to avoid Jamie seeing me laugh. While everyone is setting up tents on our property—Leo and Kennedy kept at a safe distance from Jamie—Grandpa hands me his ax.

"Got any of that rage left in you, take it out on the wood. My stock is depleted."

I stare at the ax, and I'm already picturing myself taking a swing—this is how we deal with misplaced anger in my family. And town gossip, if I'm being honest, because that almost always seems to be the source of anger in my family. Grandpa taught me wood chopping. Dad and Braden taught me boxing. And Grandma taught me Latin dances. So far, Grandma's skill is the only one with capital gains.

He gives my shoulder a squeeze. "You dig all the money out of your pants already?"

"Yeah." I laugh. "Making Grandma proud, huh?"

"Hey, you damn sure are," he snaps. "You're doing exactly what she told you—making women feel special and powerful. That's something. Look at all those girls your brother coached at football back in the day—like Haley. And all the little girls on the hockey teams, how many of them are playin' in high school? None," he says. "We're doing that. We're doing something around here that makes them think they can't keep up with the boys. You're giving them the power back."

I scratch my head. I don't really feel like I've done any

of that, unless letting Haley kiss me while I kept my hands on the table counts as relinquishing power. God, that was fucking awesome.

"Look at you, Grandpa." Henrietta comes sidling up behind me. "Leading a feminist rally."

"Well someone ought to," he says, and then before Henrietta can get her arms around me, he tugs her away. "He's just a boy. He can't handle you."

I laugh, because even though I've been there, done that, Grandpa is sort of right. He takes Henrietta into the garage and gives her all the best sleeping gear—inflatable air pad, sleeping bag, and camp pillows.

I head inside, sneaking through my room quietly. I still have my contacts in, and my eyes are starting to burn. After I've got my glasses on again, I take a minute to stare at Haley asleep in my bed. I have the tiniest urge to crawl in there with her. I mean, what would it feel like to fall asleep with all of her wrapped around all of me? Maybe I wouldn't even be able to sleep. Maybe she kicks and I'd get nailed in the nuts. The only person I've ever shared a bed with before is Braden, when we've been out of town somewhere and stayed in a hotel. I search my memories and can't even come up with one time I saw my own parents in bed together sleeping.

I glance at the clock beside the bed—it's nearly five in the morning. An idea forms in my head, and seconds later, I'm shaking Haley, waking her up.

# Chapter Twenty-Four

## —HALEY—

"Haley? Wake up," I hear Fletch say. I'm half convinced it's a dream, but then I notice the unfamiliar scent around me, that the covers aren't mine, either.

I bolt upright, my eyes bouncing around the mostly dark and spotless bedroom. "Oh God, my parents—" I pause, allowing my brain to catch up, "…are bird watching."

Fletch tosses back the covers, exposing my legs. "Come on, I want you to see something."

He's back to regular Fletch, with his glasses and gym shorts. I hop out of his bed and start opening dresser drawers. "What are you doing?" he asks.

"I need something else to wear besides this dress." I spot his grammar-correcting T-shirt folded neatly in a drawer and snatch it up. I find a pair of sweatpants in a drawer below the T-shirts—luckily with cinched bottoms—and Fletch watches with amazement as I manage to put both the shirt and pants on *before* wiggling out of my dress. I'm talented like that.

Thanks to long bus rides with the hockey or basketball team, combined with a strong desire to get out of my cheer uniform. I toss my dress on the floor and dig through my purse until my fingers land on the travel toothbrush. Fletch goes behind me, remaking his bed, snatching my dress off the floor and folding it, picking up bits of paper and tissue that fell out of my messy purse. No wonder his room is so clean.

I wiggle the toothbrush in front of his face and grin. "Just in case I decide to kiss you again. You never know."

He rolls his eyes and points to the bathroom door. After I've finished—and Fletch has wiped the sink down—we walk out into the backyard, me with a thick blanket I stole from the couch wrapped around my shoulders. Several tents are scattered across the yard, the glow of flashlights and laughter emerging from each one. There's a fire going in the fire pit. Seems like I missed a lot tonight.

"How many people are here?" I ask, following Fletch over to the barn.

"I don't know. Too many." He takes the blanket from me and wraps it around his neck before nudging me toward the grooves I used last week to climb onto the roof. "Go on, I'll be right behind you."

I make the climb quickly despite my half-asleep state, and when Fletch sits beside me, he wraps the blanket around my shoulders again. "You want to share?"

He shakes his head. "I'm fine."

"What's the big thing?" I ask. "I've been up here already."

Fletch glances at his cell phone and then puts it back in his pocket. "Sunrise. Soon."

"Wow, and you haven't even gone to sleep yet." The air is a bit chilly. I pull the ends of the blanket together, not letting in any air. Fletch's gaze is fixed on the lake, so I take several seconds to stare at his profile. He's got amazing bone structure. Perfect skin tone. Perfect lips.

My stomach does a backflip, and I force myself to inhale a long, slow, deep breath. Maybe I'm supposed to tell him he's beautiful. He said those words to me, and it was with no strings attached or whatever. Maybe if I say exactly what I'm thinking, stuff won't build into big imaginary relationships inside my head. A guy can be hot and sexy without being a marital prospect or a soul mate. Right?

"Hey, Fletch?"

"Hmm?" He turns to me for a second but quickly refocuses on the lake.

"You're…" I try to say the *B* word, but it doesn't want to exit my mouth for some reason. "Nice to look at."

"Um, okay?" He faces me again, his forehead wrinkled. "Thanks, I guess."

My cheeks warm, but I smile anyway. "You're welcome."

"So…" Fletch leans on one elbow, stretching out over the slanted roof. "How was your dancing session with Paco?"

"Great." I lean on my elbow and face him, my eyebrows wiggling. "Actually, it was sexy, erotic, completely mind-blowing."

Fletch fights a smile. "Oh really?"

"Yep, I'm gonna be fantasizing for weeks about Paco and the way he loves to stare at *your* ass."

Fletch bursts out laughing and then glances over his shoulder at his own backside. "Didn't know that did it for him."

"It is a really nice ass," I say. "I recognized it right away on the flyer."

"So that's how you found me."

"I take tumbling lessons in Longmeadow," I explain. "Your, um, *place of employment* is on the way."

"That's right, tumbling was on your 'Hump Day To-do List,'" Fletch teases.

I grab his side, preparing to pinch it. But I'm distracted by the close proximity. I pull away. "How does this thing work, Yoda?"

He turns to check on the horizon, but it's still dark. "What thing?"

"The thing where I want to kiss you and you tell me that I should do it." I pick at my fingernail. "And then I do it—"

"It was a great kiss," Fletch says.

"It was." I brave looking up at him. "But now I'm wondering if I'm allowed to do it again."

He cocks an eyebrow. "You're asking my permission?"

"I don't know." I shrug. "You're the expert here. I'm the one trying not to make a big deal out of nothing. I assume you've kissed more girls than me?"

"A few," he says, not elaborating further.

"And do you often have repeat kissing with the same girl?"

He holds my gaze for a beat and then turns forward again. "You know what's cool about sunrises and sunsets?"

"What?"

"You have to actually make a conscious decision to watch them," he says. "Or else they just happen, and you barely notice."

I allow his words to hang in the air between us for a minute, and then I force him back to my question. "Fletch?"

He scrubs a hand over his face. "I don't know, Haley."

"I think you know something."

He sighs and lays back against the roof. "I don't usually… I mean, it's never just kissing."

I almost ask him what he means, but then my brain catches up. Talk about a punch in the gut. "Oh."

He sits up again, his face full of worry. "Not that it couldn't be, it's just that…I'm sorry. I shouldn't have said it like that."

"Don't apologize." I shake my head and study my hands again. "You were being honest. And I asked the question."

"I'm sorry," he repeats, despite my clear instructions to not apologize.

Silence falls between us, and we both lie back on the roof—me with a big weight on my chest again and Fletch with God-knows-what? Guilt I forced on him?—and watch the orange and pink emerge on the horizon.

After the sky has brightened considerably, I can't help mumbling, "It really is beautiful."

Fletcher nods his agreement.

We both sit perfectly still, our silence growing more and more comfortable by the minute. I relax into my space and allow the reality of kissing a boy who isn't and probably won't ever be in love with me to sink in fully. The sun is rising. The world hasn't ended over this revelation. And it really was an incredible kiss.

I turn to Fletch. "Let's make a pact."

Relief washes over his face, maybe seeing that I'm calm and not crying again. "What kind of pact?"

"The kind where we're allowed to do whatever we want…" I say. And when he lifts an eyebrow, I add, "Mutually, of course. And we promise to be completely open and say whatever we're thinking or feeling. And that's it. No drama, no miscommunications. Simple. Not complicated or imaginary."

"This is all having to do with the Constitution project, right?" He flashes me a devious grin. "Because I thought that was the only reason we were forced to hang out."

I lay back down and stare at the rising sun. "God, doesn't that feel like a century ago?"

"It's summer," Fletch says. "It's like because the days are longer, every event seems further apart from the last."

"But it still always goes by so fast." My hand extends out to him, my pinkie waving in front of his face. "Are you in? The pact?"

"Okay." He wraps his little finger around mine and gives it a squeeze. "I'm in."

"Can I ask you something?" I say, and Fletch nods. "What goes on in the private-lesson rooms?"

He laughs, his eyes crinkling in that adorable way. "No idea. Ricky, the club's co-owner, won't tell me, and she won't let any of the guys tell me, either. She has a way of threatening people that makes requests impossible to ignore." He flashes me a grin. "But I do know that there are locks on all three doors…and yet, we do get a larger number of skilled dancers each Saturday night, so maybe actual lessons are happening."

"Some girl in front of me paid for private time with you," I say, since we're doing that honesty thing.

"Really?" Fletch pops up, his eyes wide. "That must be for this week. I haven't gotten the schedule yet."

I laugh and smack him in the shoulder. "Don't look so excited."

"I *am* excited. It's a hundred dollars an hour."

My mouth falls open. "Seriously? You have to tell me what happens. Will you tell me, or would that be weird?"

He traces a finger over the roof shingles. "I'll tell you… if you tell me about these UCF tryouts. What's UCF? Is that Florida?"

"Hey!" I say accusingly. "How do you know about UCF?"

"'Hump Day To-do List,' remember?" Fletch lays back, his hands resting behind his head. His shirt creeps up, revealing a strip of those abs. "Your teeth look great, by the way. How's your underwear drawer?"

"It's very clean. Thanks for asking." I curl up on my side again, with the blanket tight around me.

"And UCF?" he prompts.

I spill way too many details regarding cheer tryouts and out-of-state tuition waivers and partner stunts. When I finally finish talking, we're practically in sunglass-needing territory. "Am I boring you?"

Fletch shakes his head, but his eyes are half closed. "I think UCF is about as illogical as me wanting to play varsity hockey this year. I could be in college now if I wanted to. I might end up sitting on the bench more than not, and yet…"

"You still want it," I finish for him. "I'm not even sure I can see myself going to college in Florida. But I really want to visit campus this summer. Maybe meet the coach and the squad."

"If your cousin lives there, can't you stay with her? Then it's just a plane ticket to Orlando, right? That's nothing."

"For you, maybe." I poke him in the stomach. "But not everyone gets cash stuffed in their pants every Saturday."

"And panties," he reminds me.

"Some of those thongs looked expensive. Maybe you can stow them up for a few weeks and have a rummage sale."

He turns to flash me another grin. "It'll be the Haley Stevenson charity sale. All contributions go to your college trip to Florida."

I pinch him again, but I'm laughing. He's pretty funny like this. Other Fletch. And suddenly, my mouth is hovering an inch from his. Without thinking it through at all, without all the worry and fear from before, I press my lips against his. It's incredible how quickly my body can shift from this low, dull buzz of relaxed energy to full-on electric current.

Fletch kisses me back with warmth and gentleness, but then he pulls away, his forehead still against mine. My entire body is left screaming for more.

He rests a hand on my cheek, holding my gaze with his. "You're sure this is okay?"

"Positive." I pull him to me again, and he responds with even more enthusiasm.

His body presses into mine until my back is flat to the roof and I'm feeling all of him against all of me. I slip my hands beneath his sweatshirt and let my fingertips glide over his skin. Other Fletcher doesn't mind if I touch him—he's an open book. I don't let myself think about what this might mean, what might become of it. Right now, it's just me and this beautiful, sexy boy and the sun beating down on us, the thrill of kissing on a slanted roof.

After a while, Fletch's rough fingers find their way to my lower back, and then he whispers in my ear. "Haley? I think the shingles might be giving you a rash."

"Huh?" My foggy brain is slow to catch up. "You think I have shingles?"

Fletch laughs, and his whole arm wraps around me, covering my back. "The shingles on the roof. They're rubbing against your skin. You have bumps."

"Huh."

He plants a kiss on my cheek and then my lips. "Let's go in my room."

In his room. Where the more-than-kissing likely happens. Not sure I'm ready for that today, especially since it took Tate and me nearly a year to finally decide to have sex. I sit up quickly, nearly knocking Fletch off-balance. Then I grab his phone to check the time.

"Uh-oh." I swing a leg over him and head for the ladder. "I'm late."

"Late for what?" Fletch calls after me.

I flash him a grin on my way down the ladder. "Church."

"Church?" Fletcher laughs.

"I know, right?"

When we get to solid ground, I'm about to go in search of Jamie's keys. He won't mind. I'll have his car back before he even wakes up. But then I catch a glimpse of Fletcher standing there with his hands in his pockets but still looking oh-so-open, and I'm scared of him turning back to his other self and never seeing this version of him again.

I move closer and loop my arms around his neck. "Last night was…"

"Enlightening?" he offers when I seem to be digging for the right word.

I laugh. "I was going to say fun, but definitely enlightening, too."

For a moment, I don't know why I'm here so close to him again, and then I remember my fear of this Fletcher vanishing. I push up on my toes and kiss him until we're both breathing heavy again.

"Sure you don't want to go inside?" Fletch asks.

I push away from him. I need air. Space. "To your room? To do what, exactly?"

He looks me dead in the eyes, no hint of a joke or amusement on his face, and says, "Anything you want, Haley."

The air whooshes from my lungs; words are lodged in my throat. Such a simple answer, and yet I can tell that Fletch means it in a way I probably can't even wrap my head around. Yet. And I'm so tempted to figure it out…

I give him a look that hopefully says *hold that thought*. "Not today."

He just nods, not uttering another word of protest or offering any excuses. A few minutes later, I'm driving Jamie's truck toward my house to change, and already it feels like the moment might have passed, like last night was its own universe and there's no way to teleport back.

And maybe I just need to figure out how to be okay with that.

# Chapter Twenty-Five

## —FLETCHER—

*HALEY: random Q...don't u ever worry about someone eating shrimp or peanuts and then touching u at the club*

*ME: yeah. But there's no food in the building. Alcohol washes away a lot. Ricky is a germaphobe so she's got hand sanitizer everywhere too*

*HALEY: I did notice the hand washing stations. Have u ever had a reaction at work?*

*ME: mild ones. No ER trips thus far*

*HALEY: good*

*ME: is that all?*

*HALEY: yep. I'm just bored.*

*ME: at 5:45am?? I'd be sleeping if I didn't have*

*practice in a few minutes*

*HALEY: I'm waitin for my girls to show up for our morning run*

"Keep the pads in your lockers, boys," Bakowski says when I'm finishing tucking my phone away, preparing to suit up. "No skates, either. Apparently, the ice is melting. They're getting it fixed, but in the meantime—"

"No practice!" Stewart says, punching a hand in the air.

Bakowski glares at him. "Just for that, you get an extra mile. Shoes on, we're running with the cheerleaders. Any of them beat any of you, we come back tonight and do it all over again."

Beside me, Tate glances down at his Nike slides. Red has the same pair on, and he says, "What if I don't have running shoes?"

"Go barefoot," Bakowski snaps.

I leave my dri-FIT shirt on and grab my tennis shoes from the top of my locker. This sucks. I'd been looking forward to showing off my back crossovers. With Jamie and Leo's help, I'm flying around the cones now.

Several of the guys file out of the locker room, and Bakowski corners me before I can follow. "You can sit this out if it's…you know, too hard for you."

My stomach sinks. I glance around to see if anyone is within hearing distance. Several guys are. Bakowski never lets anyone out of anything. No exceptions. This can't be good for my position this season. It means he's not concerned with my preparedness level.

With my jaw tense, my whole body stiffened, I slide my feet into my shoes. "I'll be fine."

"Sure about that?" he asks, cocking an eyebrow. "Bring your breathing thing just in case."

I snatch the inhaler from my locker and stuff it in my pocket. This sucks. This completely sucks. Maybe Bakowski won't ever see me as anything but weak no matter what I do.

When I get to the track outside, there are at least ten or twelve cheerleaders out there — all of them wearing nothing but sports bras and tiny shorts. Several of the guys whistle, and Haley rolls her eyes. "The one activity I let the girls show their stomachs for, and we're invaded by hockey players."

Bakowski pushes past me and blows his whistle. He smacks Red in the back of the head when he reaches out a hand for Leslie's bra strap. Seriously? Is he in middle school? "You can't act like a decent human being, we'll put a blindfold on you and send you out to run in the road."

All the guys shut up and look at Coach. No one ever assumes Bakowski is kidding. Coach gestures to Haley, who spends a minute explaining the route. I'm being very well-behaved and not checking out her legs, but I do space out for several seconds, replaying Saturday night at the club and Sunday morning on the roof. Definitely could go for a repeat make-out session with her. My gaze bounces from Cole (who is silently in love with Haley) to Tate (who she used to love) to Hammond (who is the most likely candidate for Haley's next love), and my stomach twists in a ball. Any repeat sessions with Haley will definitely need to be in a covert location. I should have talked to Cole about this already. I should talk to him now. And yet I don't want to ruin this idealistic world Cole still gets to live in.

"…we've been running this route for several weeks now, so don't pace yourself with us. You'll want to save some energy for the last mile because the hills are killer." Haley signals to the other cheerleaders, and they file behind her.

Beside me, Tate steps out of his sandals with a sigh and a shake of his head. "Guess he's not worried about me being able to put on skates tomorrow."

At least five of the twenty guys are going barefoot. The cheerleaders all have on identical white tennis shoes with little silver and green triangles on the sides. I keep my jog slow and even at first. I do quite a bit of cardio on my own—at least I have been since the state game—but it's on my own, so I have no idea what pace I'm running. I do know that cold weather triggers more asthmatic flare-ups, and with the mild temperatures outside, I'm likely better off than on the ice. Maybe I should have played football like the rest of my family.

Another glance back at Coach, and I'm suddenly fired up to prove him wrong. Instead of holding off until the last second to discreetly use my inhaler, I take a few puffs now, at the beginning, to keep my airways open and ready.

Tanley is on one side of me, Hammond on the other, Stewart and Red a few paces in front of us. I look through the crowd in front of me and spot Cole, working his way toward the front, where Haley is. I suppress a groan and shake my head. I can't tell him about my make-out session with Haley and not crush him in the process.

I'm so deep in thought that I don't even notice when we hit the two-mile mark, or that Haley's blond ponytail is now bobbing right in front of me. I look over my shoulder and see that Cole and several of the guys in front have fallen back. Several of the cheerleaders, too.

I tug Haley's ponytail and then move beside her. "You've

got some slackers way back there."

She seems to pull herself out of her own haze, and then she spins around, jogging backwards. "Let's go, girls! Pick it up!"

I don't turn around to see their reaction, but I do hear several groans. She faces forward again and elbows me in the side. "What are you doing all the way up here, Asthma Boy? I figured you'd be huffing and puffing in the back with the smokers."

I shake my head. "Don't know. I just phased out for a while, and then here I was."

"Same thing goes for me. I zone out, and it turns out I'm in the zone, you know?" She flashes me a grin. "This last mile is a bear. Sure you don't want to slow down?"

My chest is a little bit tight, but my fingernails are still pink and not blue. I take another hit of my inhaler. "I'm going all out. Even if I pass out."

Without further words, Haley and I both lengthen our strides, her shorter legs taking nearly twice as many steps as mine. The rolling hills a mile from the school, ice rink, and the main strip appear before us, and my legs flex in response, my muscles already burning.

"Bakowski told me I could sit this out," I explain to Haley, my breathing much more labored now.

"And…? You didn't want to?"

"He never lets anyone sit out. He doesn't put me in the same category as the other players."

"And you need to be," Haley finishes, understanding.

"Yeah, I need to be." All people are not created equal. I understand this philosophical concept just fine. But I can't help the fact that all I've ever wanted was to be considered equal among my peers.

The amusement drops from Haley's face, and she's all business now. "Relax your arms. And keep your head up. It increases oxygen circulation."

I almost crack a joke, but the intensity of the workout is too high for that. I do as I'm told, and both of us pick up our pace once again. The push uphill is grueling, so much that neither of us can speak a word. Haley's cheeks are flushed, sweat pouring down her body. I'm sure I'm just as red.

We're pumping our legs downhill, the busy strip of main street with the Sparkplug, the ice rink, and O'Connor's Tavern now in our line of sight.

"A quarter mile left," Haley says.

"Got it." I wave a hand, my chest too tight to say any more words. One quarter mile. That's all. We pass the shops and turn in to the high school, making our way behind. My elbow is literally rubbing Haley's. I kick it up a notch, and she does the same. *Damn it, Haley. Slow down.*

I suck in as much air as my lungs will allow and push harder, my longer legs taking the unfair advantage and running—literally—with it. Leaning against a bench on the side of the track are Coach Bakowski, Coach Ty, and Mrs. Levitt, the cheerleading sponsor.

"Uh oh…" I hear Bakowski say. "Looks like we're gonna be back tonight."

My feet move quicker, eyes focused on the finish line, and a few seconds later, I can't see Haley from the corner of my eye anymore. I cross through the end marker. My chest feels like a truck is sitting on top of it. Haley's white tennis shoes show up beside me, her own breathing heavy and ragged.

"Put your hands on your head," she says, huffing out the words. "It helps with—"

I nod, cutting her off. I already know this. I take another puff from my inhaler and then walk in a circle with my hands over my head.

"Jesus." Haley bends over, hands on her knees. "I should have eaten something before that run. I don't usually push that hard."

I spin around, expecting to see my teammates and the rest of the cheerleaders behind us, but the track is still empty; only the coaches are there, off to the side.

"What happened?" I say to Haley. "Did we make a wrong turn or something?"

She stands back up and moves beside me. "I made the route, remember?"

I clasp my hands behind my head. "But where is everyone?"

"Back there." Haley smiles and points down the main road. "Way, *way* back there."

I stare at her. "Wow…"

Bakowski is watching us. He doesn't say anything from where he's standing, but he looks at me for a very long time, his eyes narrowed like he's thinking hard. Then he shakes his head and jots something down on a clipboard.

"Did you see that?" I ask Haley.

"I saw it." Haley is looking at me like a proud parent now, but then her grin fades. "Tate would have beaten both of us if he'd had shoes on."

"Jake, too," I agree. But they didn't have shoes, and they didn't beat us. I'm just gonna let myself enjoy that. Olympic gold medals are won under similar circumstances—the leader falls, and the underdog takes advantage.

I step behind Haley and wrap my arms around her shoulders, half leaning on her for support. "I owe you breakfast, okay?"

The lack of oxygen must be getting to me, because next thing I know, right before anyone else rounds the corner heading toward the track, I plant a quick kiss on Haley's temple. Then I release her and step back before anyone sees us together.

Haley's gaze drops to the ground, but I can see her smiling. "Water?"

"Yeah, water." I nod.

And we both head for the drinking fountain near the bleachers, keeping a healthy distance between us.

# Chapter Twenty-Six

## –HALEY–

"Haley!" Fletch says in a way than indicates he's done this several times already.

I flop onto my back on my bedroom floor. "What?"

"The conclusion?" Fletch sighs. "What do you think of it?"

I make eye contact, giving the appearance of listening, but the paragraph he reads to me from his laptop turns into nothing but mushy sounds. My fake-listening doesn't fool my Civics partner.

He sighs again and then snaps his laptop shut. "Let's finish this later."

"Wait!" I cross the room and grab his computer. "I'll look at it. That'll be easier."

"Will you promise to stop tapping your pen?"

I let the pen in my hand fall to the ground. "Sorry. I didn't know I was tapping."

"Clearly I'm the most boring person on the planet." Fletch fights a grin. "I've been saying things for thirty minutes, and none of it has stuck."

*Welcome to my world.* And he's not boring. He's kind of stuck in my head, just not this Fletcher who's reading me boring Civics Constitution project conclusions. The other Fletcher who promised to do anything I wanted in his room. Alone. Does he say that to all the girls? So yeah, I'm pretty distracted this afternoon. Probably from the knowledge that Fletch has his very first private-instruction victim (I mean customer) tonight. I get why this is bothering me, but I don't get why logically thinking it through isn't helping me not hate that he's doing this lesson. He isn't my boyfriend. He doesn't owe me explanations for everything. And dancing is his job.

I open the laptop, and the bright Word document flashes in front of me. I read it through twice, but still nothing sticks. I glance at Fletch and grin. "It's great."

"So, you liked my reference to Barbie's disproportionate figure?"

"What?" My eyes snap back to the screen, and I quickly reread the paragraph. "Where is Barbie—"

"Kidding," he says. "I was just testing you."

I close the laptop and shove it back at him—a little harder than I should. Fletch grunts from the force and looks around for space on my messy desk to place it. He finally decides to tuck the computer away in his backpack.

"Maybe you could concentrate better if your bedroom wasn't attempting a shot at *Hoarders* fame," he says.

I roll my eyes. "My bedroom looks like the bedroom of a teenager. Your room, on the other hand, is freakishly clean."

Fletch eyes the five-foot-high pile of magazines in the corner. "That is not normal."

I rest my hands on my hips. "Well, what do all those other girls you hook up with have in their bedrooms? Steel countertops and see-through drawers?"

He shrugs, his eyes on his cell phone. "I haven't really gone in any girls' rooms before."

See? He can't insult me without anything to compare to. But wait… "Never? Do you hook up at your house, then?"

Fletch looks like he'd rather discuss the economy or tax forms. "I don't bring girls to my bedroom, either."

"Your dad wouldn't like it?"

"Hard to say," he admits. "He wouldn't forbid me or anything, but I'd be subjected to interrogation after, and I'd rather not be."

But he invited me to his room. What does that mean? *Stop analyzing every little thing!*

I shove the throw rug over with my big toe, exposing the wood floors so I can practice turns. I've done this so much that I've actually caused the wood to discolor, hence the need for a throw rug. "So not at your place or her place…but you've had sex, right? Or are you one of those 'everything but' people?"

"Why does it feel like I'm walking into a trap?" Fletch is straddling my desk chair, sitting backward in it. He lays his arms over the back and rests his chin there, watching me.

"You're a great big mystery to me." I successfully pull off a double turn and put myself in position to try again. "And I'm curious now about how everyone else goes about their sex life. I'm not a virgin, in case you were wondering."

"I wasn't," he says. "Keep your shoulders down on those turns."

I stick my tongue out at him but drop my shoulders anyway. "Tate and I had sex, and then Jake and I—"

"Haley," Fletch says, raising a hand to stop me. "You

really don't need to tell me this stuff. And I kind of assumed you and Tate had…you guys were together for what? A year?"

"A year and a half." I spin to a stop and face him. "But that doesn't mean we had sex. Kayla and Kyle Stewart have been together for two years, and they haven't done it."

Fletch stands up, and just as I'm mid-turn, he grasps my shoulders and holds me in place. Relief washes over his face. "Can you just stand still for a second, please? I'm getting nauseated watching you bounce around."

I break out of his grip and plop down on my bed. "I'm sorry. I suck at being anyone's partner when it comes to school stuff. I'm kind of an idiot, in case you haven't noticed."

Fletch returns to sitting in the chair and looks me over. "Have you ever considered—don't take this the wrong way or anything—but you seem like one of those ADD people."

"One of those ADD people?" I repeat like he's just told me I'm ugly or have three boobs. "What does that even mean?"

"Maybe more like ADHD." Fletch runs a hand through his hair. "I had an ADHD kid in my homeschool group. He couldn't get any of the assignments completed, but he made these amazing castles out of toothpicks…"

"Toothpick castles? That sounds like it's got savant written all over it. Now I'm an unfocused genius?" And yeah, my defenses are all flying up at once. I don't like hearing anything that I can't change. If I do poorly, I can work harder, study more. If my brain is wired to be this way for all eternity, well, I may not be able to do anything about it.

"He wasn't a savant or whatever," Fletcher argues. "Eventually his mom put him on medication, and he was like, the best one in the group. I think he's going to med school now or something."

I close my eyes and groan. "So, you think I need Ritalin?"

"There are plenty of other medications besides Ritalin," he says.

I bury my face in a pillow. It's Friday of week three of summer school. Only two weeks to go. Jamie has a *C-*, maybe a *D+*, either way, he's passing. I'm passing. I have a *B-*, actually. Not an *A*. But whatever. Kill me now. I can't take any more of this. "Can we please be done studying?"

"Haley?"

"Yes, Fletch. The answer you should give me is yes. 'Cause I'm seriously studied out, and I'm driving you crazy. I promised to never drive any more guys crazy, so it's best if we end this session right now."

"I'm going to answer your question from earlier," he says, surprising me enough to get me to lift my head. "The one where you asked me if, when, and where I've had sex…"

I scrunch up my nose. "God, did I really ask that? I'm sorry."

"I don't mind answering." He shoves his glasses back to the bridge of his nose, indicating that he might actually mind. "It just felt like a leading question, or like there was something else you wanted to ask me, but you're avoiding it for whatever reason."

Jesus. Add mind reading to the list of Fletcher Scott skills. I put my face back in the pillow. I'm braver like this. "I really want to know if you're gonna have sex in the practice room during your private lesson today."

He's so silent, I get all nervous and squirmy. "Not that there's anything wrong with that… Well, there might be, actually. Since she's paying you, that could be a form of prostitution—" I shoot upright, my eyes wide. "Okay, I did not just say that."

Fletcher's mouth twitches, the right corner slowly rising.

"You're right. Civics study session is over. How about I give you an example of what might occur during a private dance lesson?"

My eyebrows lift up. "Two girls in one day. Sure you have the stamina for that?"

"First…" Fletch stands and then pulls me to my feet. "I would establish a no-talking rule."

"What about moaning and other nonword sounds of pleasure?"

"In a real lesson, definitely not. But for you? Negotiable." Fletch smirks.

"So, I've earned special treatment?"

"Maybe a little." He gets back to business. "Next, we need to find a more suitable space because this room is… not acceptable."

I glance around. It would be hard to fit two sets of feet in my turning spot. "Basement?"

He shrugs, and I lead him out—Fletch flips the light switch off and closes my door. Tomorrow we're going to have a chat about *his* neurotic behaviors. Maybe I'll even google some medication suggestions for him.

My basement has low ceilings, but it's pretty clean and empty for the most part. We've got a giant flat-screen and a sectional sofa, but that's it. Lots of empty carpet space. Unlike my bedroom.

"Okay, Yoda, what are you gonna teach me today?" Personally, I wouldn't mind stretching out across the couch while Fletch strips off his shirt and dances in front of me, but would that really be a lesson?

"What are you in the mood to learn?" He steps back from me, assessing me head-to-toe like I'm going to need a costume change depending on what I pick. "Something fast and complicated, or maybe slow and sexy…?"

"How about somewhere in the middle of those?"

He nods. "Okay, cha-cha, then."

Fletch jumps right into a basic explanation of this style of dance, but unlike with the Civics project, he keeps the words to a minimum and uses mostly demonstration and hands-on assistance. And honestly, I figured he was doing this little "dance lesson" as a method of flirting or pressing my buttons, and I'm almost disappointed that he's actually teaching. But then I get into the challenge, and watching him move with such ease—it's something completely other for me—and eventually the goal of moving together wins my attention.

He has music on his phone that we play at a low volume due to lack of speakers, but it helps to hear the beat along with moving to it. After I've got several eight counts mastered and even a turn, Fletch says, "Want to add a trick?"

Based on the way his face lights up, I can tell he likes the tricks. So do I. He grabs his phone and shows me a video of him and Angel, pausing it in the middle. I watch the move carefully—it involves Angel turning upside down and Fletch keeping her head from crashing into the ground. He replays it a few times and then waits for me to say something.

"So, it's like a cartwheel, but I use your legs as the floor?"

"Exactly," he says, surprised.

I shrug. "Cool. Let's try it."

He places me in a spot where I can't kick the TV or the sofa, then he slides a couple of feet to the side. "The most important thing is to go all-out. Really kick into it, and I'll do the rest, okay?"

"Okay, Yoda." I replay the video in my head, and then I kick into the cartwheel, reaching for Fletcher's legs and pressing my hands against his thighs. I'm standing upright on the other side of him seconds later.

"Not bad, Stevenson," he says, flashing me his biggest grin. "It took Angel two rehearsals to learn that one."

"Really?" That's hard to believe considering how amazing of a dancer she is and the fact that I thought it was pretty simple. Unlike the cha-cha steps.

Fletch shrugs. "She's a tad bit too tall for me. It works out fine, but that does a number on her confidence. Ricky doesn't care, though. She says our chemistry makes up for it and then some."

He's back on his phone again, searching for more tricks. But I'm still sitting on this chemistry thing. "What does her fiancé think about all that chemistry you guys have? Or are they like, open or something?"

Fletch glances up at me, likes he's checking to see if I'm serious. "I already told you that it's not like that with Angel and me. Chemistry, like actors have. It's not actual chemistry."

"I think I get it." I begin going through the steps Fletcher taught me on my own. "To you—all the long looks, the caressing, the hip grinding—it's all just work. And for people like me, who make a social experience out of it, it's one long, hot foreplay session."

"Maybe," he says, tossing his phone onto the sofa. "Maybe a woman I dance with gets all riled up, and then she goes home and screws the hell out of her husband. Nothing wrong with that, right?"

"I don't know." To me, it's a gray area. "If I were the husband whose wife needed to be turned on by someone else in order to feel like having sex with me…" But Fletch isn't the husband or the married woman, so he doesn't really need to hear my opinions on this gray area.

"I see what the problem is now." He steps into my dance space, getting his arms around me, moving through the steps with me. "You're looking at it the wrong way. Me leading someone around the dance floor isn't about me and how I'm affecting them."

I completely disagree. I was 100 percent affected by him leading me around the other night. In fact, I'm feeling a little bit of that right now.

"Is there an employee handbook at your job that provides these perfect answers?"

"Relax your shoulders." Fletch pulls me in close, his hand pressing between my shoulder blades, forcing my back straighter. "And no, my answer didn't come from a work handbook, it came from my grandmother, and also Grandpa Scott."

I look at him, one eyebrow lifting. I'm waiting for him to explain further.

"Allowing me to lead, it's a gift," he says, his voice low and sexy. "Respecting that gift means respecting my partner. She is the reason the dance is happening; she is the reason I have someone in my arms. I never forget who's really leading."

His breath tickles my ear. We've fallen into a new pattern—a waltz or maybe a rumba—that involves being completely pressed together, and I stop the jolt my stomach takes, the flipping and flopping, the goose bumps…it's exhilarating.

Fletch steps forward, and I step back in time with him. "For most women," he continues, "handing over control in a dance is empowering. Whatever pleasure they gain from it is one they sought out and took for themselves. It has nothing to do with the partner. The partner is interchangeable."

As much as I'd love to fall into a trance right now, this speech is too much bullshit for me to be able to do that. "So, all those women yelling out "Scott, Scott, Scott" every

Saturday night…have you let them know this yet? That the partner is interchangeable or whatever?"

"When you dance with someone, you get a thrill out of it, you get turned on, and then you give him all the credit, well where does that leave you?"

I shake my head.

"Powerless," Fletch answers. "Your pleasure, your success, your sexiness, are not only uncredited to you, but also reliant on a specific person that you can't control. It's perfect grounds for codependency, self-esteem issues…"

I stop dancing and scrub my hands over my face. It's like I've stepped into an alternate reality. I can't decide if I should call bullshit or reprimand myself because maybe I've been the closed-minded judgmental one, assuming what all the screaming women were after last Saturday night.

God, I'm confused.

I drop my hands and stare at this strange creature in front of me. "So, you never get turned-on when you're getting down and dirty with someone? You don't have certain partners that do it for you more than others?"

"The laws of attraction…some people draw you in more than others. Why that is and what we're all attracted to is getting into some complicated psychology and brain chemistry theories."

"I want inside your head, for like five minutes," I say. "Just to take a peek around and make sure these are all your thoughts."

"Come here." He tugs my hand, pulling me in front of him. "I'm gonna show you something."

He's behind me, his front against my back. "Close your eyes."

I lean against Fletch, and he drapes an arm around my waist. I'm expecting a dance move to come, but instead, his free hand glides slowly up my thigh and over my stomach. I sigh and then clamp my lips shut, not wanting to give away any more signals. Light as a whisper, his breath tickles my neck, lips brushing my skin so perfectly. A shiver races down my spine.

"What are you doing, Fletch?" I mumble. "Is this a Juniper Falls samba or something?"

Those amazing fingers glide down my arm and then lace through mine. He lifts my hand and slides it over my midsection, creating more goose bumps. My head falls back against his shoulder, my eyelids relaxing on their own. God, this feels amazing. Best study session ever.

"Okay," I concede, when Fletch moves our linked hands over my boobs. "You can have my panties. You've earned them."

"But I'm not doing anything."

"Bullshit." I think if he just moved our hands a little lower… "I have a new goal for myself."

"What's that?" Fletch says.

"To figure out how to dance with you and have *you* get this turned on."

He rests our linked hands on the waistband of my shorts. The muscles in my stomach quiver with anticipation. "Why does it matter? So long as you're turned on."

"Because it'll make me feel powerful," I say. "Getting you all hot and bothered."

He laughs against my skin. "Fair enough."

I feel like I'm on the verge of insanity. I can't think clearly. I want to do a whole bunch of things I've never done before.

"Haley?" he whispers. "This feels good, right?"

"Hmmm."

"Open your eyes."

When I do, the normally dim basement lighting is offending. I squint at the brightness. From the corner of my eye, I notice first that it's not Fletch's hand on my cheek, it's my own. And it's also my own fingers that are teasing the waistband of my shorts. Okay, so that's a little surprising. I don't even remember him releasing my hand. How did it decide to move on its own?

"See?" he says. "You can take full credit for all of that."

If only that were true…

I laugh because he's pretty cute, trying to give me lessons in touching myself. Thanks, Fletch. "I was imagining you doing it."

"Yeah, but that's all within your control. You can pick anyone."

"Even Channing Tatum? I've got a thing for male strippers." I spin around to face Fletch just in time to see him grin and then laugh. I've made him laugh. Not an easy feat. "So, who do you pick?"

"Easy," he says. "Blake Lively."

I roll my eyes. "She's way too tall for you."

When he flashes me another grin, I'm literally putting all my energy into not grabbing the front of his shirt, tossing him onto the couch, and…well, doing whatever may come next. Instead, I press my palms against his shirt and shove him back a foot or two. "Can we practice more cartwheel things or something that doesn't involve you whispering in my ear, telling me I have sexy girl powers?"

He studies me for a long moment, making my face heat up for the first time since we came down to the basement.

"What about the pact? I thought we were pledging against denying ourselves things we want."

I laugh really hard. "Okay, yeah, I'm gonna have to add an amendment or addendum or whatever it's called.

Kissing is one thing, but where my head was going, that's not something you just do on a whim." Fletch opens his mouth like he might protest, but I cut him off. "Maybe it's something *you* do on a whim, but not me." Except that one time, I did it on a whim. "There are consequences with sex that aren't there with kissing,"

He lifts a hand. "Okay, that makes sense. I was just checking to make sure you weren't subconsciously hoping for a nudge from me."

"Of course I'm hoping for you to push me further," I snap. "Cartwheel things. Now."

# Chapter Twenty-Seven

## -FLETCHER-

I work hard at forcing all the built-up tension between Haley and me into flipping her around her basement—and not in the way I've imagined inside my head.

I feel like a phony. Well, sort of. I mean, in theory, I believe all the jargon I've spit at her about dancing and being powerful. But I don't really think I'm part of that movement yet. The thing is, I need Haley to believe all this. She's the one letting go, opening all these doors for herself. The last thing I'd ever want to do is take credit for that.

"Hey, Fletch?"

I shake out of my haze. "Yeah?"

"Let me show you what I'm working on." She plops down on the couch, typing in a search on YouTube on her phone. She's calm and at ease now. So unlike the riled-up state I put her in moments ago. I close my eyes briefly, hating the screwup. Correction: *the state she put herself in*. Although she did say they were my imaginary hands touching her...

"Fletch? Sit," Haley orders.

God, I think she has more self-control than I do. I honestly didn't think that was possible.

I take a deep breath and fall onto the couch beside her. She plays a video for cheerleaders wanting to prepare for UCF's tryouts. I watch the stunts closely, studying each one. "Wow…that doesn't look easy."

She sighs. "I know. It's, like, impossible to prepare when we don't do any of this stuff here. I mean, we don't have guys on the squad."

Her face is turned toward me now. I don't think I've ever wanted to kiss anyone so badly in my entire life. But unlike some of our other recent encounters, I don't get that kiss-me vibe from Haley right now. She's put a wall up on that activity. I settle for gliding my fingers over her cheeks inside my head. I take my time feeling every inch of skin on her face and neck, and then I lean in, taking the smallest taste of her lips, savoring it—

"Oh shit!" Haley jumps up after reading something on her phone. "I forgot about Andi!"

As if on cue, the doorbell chimes. "Andi?"

"Mike Steller's little girl. I'm babysitting her tonight." Haley is already heading for the stairs.

I follow behind her. "I should probably go, anyway. I have a lesson soon."

She groans and then glares at me. "You had to remind me, didn't you?"

"I didn't realize you were trying to forget." My stomach twists with more confusion. "Sorry."

"Don't apologize," she snaps. "I hate when you do that. It's not you."

"Why not? I apologize for all kinds of things."

"Okay, clarification needed." She rests a hand on the front

door, preparing to open it. "It's not like you to apologize for how you choose to spend your free time. You're only doing that for my benefit, because I have some weaknesses in this area."

Okay then. Guess someone is working on her self-awareness. "I think what you mean to say is that we know each other well enough that I don't have to be polite for your benefit."

She flings the door open, plasters a grin on her face, and greets Mike Steller. The Otters' former starting goalie who became a bit of a town outcast when he walked right out of the ice rink during the first home game of last season. To be a father, apparently, though it wasn't public information at that time. Mike saunters in, a baby car seat dangling from one hand, a diaper bag from the other.

Then Haley turns to me. "Yes, what you just said. Exactly. But I'm still pissed that you brought it up again, and I'm totally ready for you to go so we can *not* talk about it anymore." She flashes me her cheerleader grin. "How's that for honesty?"

My cheeks warm; even my ears heat up. "Civics project," I tell Mike. "Hard to agree on ideas sometimes."

"Mike," Haley says, "do you know—"

"Fletcher Scott," Mike says, giving me a nod. He looks like he wants to shake my hand, but his hands are full. "How's it going? How's summer practice?"

He sounds so genuine, I'm too shocked to say much. "Um…good. It's pretty good."

I can't exactly leave Haley all pissed, so I stand by the door while Mike gives her some instructions on sleeping and feeding before taking off. She lifts the baby out of the seat and holds her at arm's length. "Look at you, getting so big. How much do you weigh now? Fourteen, maybe fifteen pounds?" She ignores me and keeps up the baby voice. "We're going to have so much fun tonight, Andi. We'll go for a walk to the park, you'll watch me eat left over pot roast, maybe I'll paint your toenails again."

Haley shifts the baby to one arm and opens the front door. "Don't you have somewhere to be? Unless you want to stick around and change a diaper?"

I glance at the formula can in the bag. It's the regular kind. Made from cow's milk. The second I go near that baby, she'll probably barf that up all over me. I shake my head. "Can't. Babies and me…we're not compatible."

Haley nods like I've said something wise. "Well, then Andi here is reason number one not to have sex on a whim, right?"

I pinch the bridge of my nose. Is she saying that as a warning for my lesson today, or is she giving me reasons for her earlier reluctance? Whichever it is, something has gone wrong. Really fast. "Haley…?" I say slowly, grappling for words. "Are we okay?"

She closes her eyes and pats the baby on the back. "Look, Fletch, your speech about taking what I want and running with it was lovely. But I'm not like you. And right now, I feel extremely powerless, and I don't know what the hell to do about it."

I'm momentarily stunned to silence. Clearly, I don't know what the hell I'm doing anymore, either. "Maybe we should—"

"Just go, please." She looks at me in a way that says she means it. "Mike has way too much pride to ask for free help unless he's completely desperate, so I don't get much time to hang out with Andi, and I'd like to enjoy it."

And there it is. That weight Haley mentioned the other night. It's sitting on my chest, heavy as a truck. I take a second to assess my breathing, make sure I'm not having an asthma attack. Then I finally manage to whisper the word "okay" before walking out the door and jogging to my car.

I'm definitely in need of an outside opinion.

"Clearly, he shouldn't do this lesson," Angel says to Ricky after I've spilled my most recent drama to both of them.

Ricky waves a hand, shutting up Angel. "I have no reason to believe anything but dancing happens in those lessons." She covers her ears for a second, showing how much she'd like to be left in the dark. Angel rolls her eyes. Ricky turns her attention back to me. "You know how much I love your dad and Gramps, right?"

I nod and reach for my shoes below the backroom couch. I've got fifteen minutes before my private shows up.

"And I adore everything they've tried to teach you. And look at you. Your grams made you strong and confident and observant. You listen to people," Ricky says. "Women at the club all adore you."

"But…?" I prompt, knowing her compliment sandwich habit.

"But." She nods. "This girl has spilled how she feels about you, and then you've gone and told her that she's wrong. That what she's feeling isn't real."

"Women do want to feel powerful," Angel says, "but we also want to be heard and have our feelings taken seriously."

I sink back into the couch, the weight on my chest growing heavier. "So, you do think Haley's into me? Like for real?"

"Why is that so hard to believe?" Ricky asks me. "You have women after you every weekend."

I shift uncomfortably on the couch. "Yeah, but they just want the guy dancing with them, not the other versions of me. The confidence, the leadership, being in the moment... that's what they're into."

"But not Haley," Angel says. "She's different."

"Pretty sure she's into that version of me, too," I retort, though I know it's not completely true. She might be attracted to that me, but she doesn't seem to trust him as much as the guy who confided in her outside the club and on the roof of the barn last Saturday night. "God, this is so confusing. What am I supposed to do? Give her space so she doesn't get the wrong idea? Apologize even though she said not to?"

They both exchange looks, and then Ricky says, "I think you should suggest that she hook up with someone else, have a little fling of her own, dissolve some of that tension."

My stomach drops. My heart picks up speed, my hands clenching the couch cushion below me.

Angel and Ricky are both silent, watching me. Then a grin spreads across Angel's face. She points a finger at me. "I knew it! You hate that idea, don't you?"

Yes. Very much. "I d-don't..." I stutter. "I don't know."

Ricky's eyebrows shoot up. "Well, I bet you do know a little about how she felt, thinking about you in my practice room..." There's a narrow-eyed warning to go with that statement. Clearly Ricky wants me to focus on teaching dance during the private lesson. I had planned on doing that anyway.

"The point is," Angel says, bringing us all back on topic. "You're trying to simplify something that isn't simple."

"Here's a completely insane idea." Ricky flips her long,

slightly graying hair over one shoulder and rests her chin in her hand. "You could ask her out."

I look between the two of them. "Um, no. There's no way I'm gonna be the guy who went on a date with Haley Stevenson."

"Better than the guy who screwed around with Haley Stevenson and didn't even ask her out," Angel says.

I shake my head. "It's not like that…I mean, we're not going to—"

"Tell anyone?" Angel suggests. "Yeah right. In that tiny town of yours, this is gonna spread like wildfire."

Exactly what I've been afraid of all along.

Ricky stands up and smooths some of my disheveled hair. "Time to join the grown-ups, Baby."

I make a big show of messing up my hair again, but I don't have any words of protest. Even I admitted to myself the other night that I didn't feel like a grown-up. Maybe I'm not acting like one, either.

"I know what we should do," Angel says, perking up. "I'll do the lesson with you. Will that help?"

I toss her a grateful look. I'm not gonna ask Haley-fucking-Stevenson, Princess of Juniper Falls, on a date, but that doesn't mean my brain isn't working on overdrive right now. I'm not in a good state to handle an overenthusiastic student. If that's even what I'm going to get.

The girl who shows up for instruction in Argentine Tango is one I recognize from Saturday Latin Nights. She's pretty, not at all shy, and clearly disappointed by Angel's presence. But once we really get into the lesson, she's working hard, sweating, and even listening to pointers from my partner. I force Angel to take half the cash for the lesson, and then I make a joke about her needing to buy two sizes of diapers soon.

She holds a finger to her lips and says, "Don't jinx it. I've got a few more weeks before I can celebrate."

Okay, well that explains the lack of information.

I sit in my car staring at my phone for nearly an hour until I finally figure out the right words to say to Haley.

*ME: it's possible that I might be a little bit confused too*

*HALEY: Okay...?*

*ME: Just didn't want you to think I have it all figured out.*

*HALEY: Ok*

*ME: Is that a good ok or a bad ok?*

*HALEY: The fact that you asked automatically makes it a good ok*

*HALEY: Here ☺ does that help?*

*ME: Yes, very much. Still pissed at me?*

*HALEY: Kind of. But I will get over it. Eventually*

My fingers are itching to keep going, to make this conversation last, and that in itself scares me enough to stuff my phone out of reach and start the car.

At home, I use Grandpa's advice and take my frustrations out on the wood. He and Dad are both suckers for angst, so of course, I end up killing my back chopping while explaining this whole drama to both of them.

"Maybe Ricky is right," Dad says from his seat on the tractor. "She feels how she feels. You can't really change that. Just like Cole feels how he feels."

Oh shit. Cole. I drop the ax and plop down in the grass. "Maybe I should go back to homeschooling?"

"Call your mother," Dad says sarcastically. "She's great with encouraging you to hide out and not have a real life."

"You know what people are like around here," I remind Dad and Gramps. Both have been on the victim side of town gossip. Gramps for his alleged hoax of a marriage to an illegal and Dad for getting a high-school girl pregnant. I've talked a lot with Gramps about what happened to Grandma, but Dad and I have never talked in detail about what he went through. It would be easy to place judgment on him, but the truth is that I wasn't there. I don't know what that relationship was really like. But I do know my dad, and he would never ever talk a woman into something that she didn't want. At one point, my parents were very much in love. I know that for sure. My mom has told me as much.

"I think you should buy her a present," Gramps says, ignoring my mention of town gossip. I'm already shaking my head. That's way too superficial for Haley. But he raises a hand to shut me up. "You can get her something to show that you don't disregard all of her interests."

"That's not a bad idea," Dad says. "Maybe this is so confusing for both of you because you consider her a friend now."

Could that be the real issue? Haley is my friend? Weird, but maybe not so weird.

I point a finger at Gramps. "Genius award for you tonight. I'm gonna get her a present. That's perfect."

Of course, this revelation leads to me sitting in my bedroom, staring at the ceiling, trying to think of the perfect gift for Haley. Being the meticulous student that I am, this task includes me creating a list of everything I know about Haley. I jot it down in reverse order, from the most recent acquisitions to the more distant bits of information, so it takes a while before I'm writing down the items that had been on her "Hump Day To-do List."

The second I recall the task of looking up info on UCF tryouts, I know exactly what to buy Haley.

# Chapter Twenty-Eight

## −HALEY−

The doorbell rings at seven in the morning. On a Saturday. I'm not wearing enough clothes to answer it, so I wait fifteen minutes and then walk outside to see if it's the hair ribbon I ordered from Amazon a few days ago. There's a tiny box at my feet, but it's not from Amazon or even the UPS man. I glance around, looking for the owner, but no one is nearby. I take the box into the kitchen and pour a glass of orange juice.

There's a folded-up note taped to the outside. I open it first and recognize Fletcher Scott's perfect print right away.

Haley,
Okay so maybe I can't wrap my head around your idealistic views on love and relationships, but this UCF thing? I would hate myself if you applied my cynical views on love to something like this. I did some research on the school and the cheer squad, and I really think

you should give it a shot. In fact, you should probably visit the campus soon. Hope you like the gift.

Your friend,

Fletch

My forehead scrunches up. I'm more confused than ever by this note. Did he give me his research in a box? I pull away the strip of tape and remove the printed pages inside. After a quick glimpse, my heart does a little flip.

Plane tickets. Fletcher got me nonrefundable, use-in-the-next-six-months, fly-anywhere-in-the-continental-U.S.-on–United Airlines, plane tickets. Two of them.

I blow out a long sigh and reach for my phone. I want to call, but at the same time, I don't want to have any hesitancy in my voice.

*ME: u r amazing. But I can't take these. My parents would never let me accept a gift this big from anyone*

*FLETCH: ok, well good thing it wasn't a big gift then*

*ME: um…right. I just price searched. It's $250 round trip to fly to Orlando right now so $500 for the pair*

*FLETCH: I didn't pay $500*

*ME: how much did u pay? I know it's rude to ask but I have to know*

*FLETCH: $30 each. My mom recently developed a phobia of flying. She gave me all her airline miles a while back. She had enough to cover most of it*

*ME: wow. I don't know what to say*

*FLETCH: go, have fun. Take one of your parents or*

*Jamie or Leslie or whoever*

*ME: ok, you've talked me into it! I'm gonna do it! After Civics is over in 2 wks of course.*

*FLETCH: can't wait to hear how it goes*

I'm too stunned by this development to even think straight, but after a few seconds of processing, trying to decide if I should talk to my parents or my cousin first, I type one last text to Fletch just to be sure where we stand.

*ME: you could come with me?*

*FLETCH: Haley…*

*ME: It's fine. I get it. Too much too soon. Just being spontaneous. You did tell me we could do anything I wanted*

*FLETCH: Yeah, in my bedroom*

I stare at my phone, a bit shocked by the words, and then it rings, Fletcher's name flashing on the screen. I pull myself together and fake calm when I answer. "Hey, Fletch."

"Haley," he says with an edge to his voice. "I'm sorry. I didn't mean it like that. And that day I really meant anything—watching TV, reading, sleeping."

"Just not leaving the state," I say for clarification purposes and to make sure he doesn't think I'm crushed, even though I am just a little bit.

"Right," he says. "And just so you know, I really like hanging out with you—"

"But I'm Haley Stevenson, Princess of Juniper Falls, and you're Fletcher Scott, a guy who doesn't want anyone to talk about him. Like ever."

There's only silence on the end for a long time, and then

he clears his throat. "How did you—I mean where did you…"

If I weren't feeling like I just got punched in the stomach, I would probably smile at the surprise in his voice. "You're not that hard to figure out, Fletch. But don't worry, I'm keeping your secrets."

"I don't want it to be like this," Fletch says. "I mean I still want—"

"To be friends?" It's rude to cut him off, but my pride can only take so much. "Done."

"Haley—"

There's something in his voice that almost stops me from ending this, something that says he might be falling as much as I am. But again, pride. It's a necessary evil. "Hey, it's fine. It's all fine. I should probably go and call my mom and my cousin."

We hang up shortly after, because I don't let him get another word in besides "okay" and "bye." And I give myself a couple of minutes to feel crushed all over again, and then I shut it down. This is why I said no guys until college. This is exactly why. Imagine if things had gone further, if we were in deeper. I definitely don't need that kind of heartbreak in my life right now.

I actually have the day free, so I take my time, calling my mom and asking if I can use the tickets to visit my cousin. I'll have to ease them into the UCF thing, though visiting a college is something they always want me to do anytime we go anywhere. I mean they are teachers, so yeah. That's all this is. A campus visit. And maybe I can meet the cheer coach.

Before I can even get all upset or weird about Fletcher's gift and slight dismissal, I'm whipping up a mega to-do list.

*Saturday To-do List*

*1. Call Serenity about visiting.*

*2. Civics! Civics! Civics! Test on Monday. Study note cards.*

*3. Jamie! Civics!*

*4. Email UCF cheer coach.*

*5. Ask Jonas to double up on private lessons.*

*6. Ask Mom/Dad, Grandma, Aunt Cathy, and whoever else for b-day and Xmas advances to pay for extra privates.*

*7. Figure out something I can give Fletch as a thank-you.*

*8. Google cooking for ppl with food allergies.*

*9. Make thank-you notes for Junior League board (pre-sucking up for college letters of rec).*

*10. Google ADHD.*

I start at the bottom of my list and quickly find an ADHD checklist online. Before I read it, I make myself promise to look at it objectively, like an outside party.

*Runs or climbs excessively.*

I mean, I did climb on Fletcher's barn roof. And I have been forcing my cheerleaders to run three mornings a week.

*Unable to play quietly.*

Play what quietly? Poker? I did that just fine the other day at the nursing home when I volunteered.

*Has difficulty waiting his or her turn.*

Like when I'm in line at the Sparkplug waiting to get

fresh muffins? I guess that's true.

*Easily distracted by extraneous stimuli.*

Is it me or does this list sound really dirty? Maybe the fact that I'm thinking this means I'm distracted by extraneous stimuli.

*Fidgets with or taps hands or feet.*

The image of Fletch grabbing my pen during that first day of summer school pops into my head. Check for that one.

In the sidebar of the web page, I notice a link to "ADHD checklist for Adults." Okay, that explains a lot. I click the new link and begin reading this list.

*History of academic underachievement.*

Check. I swallow a gulp of orange juice and scroll further down through the list.

*Poor ability to complete household chores, organize things…*

I glance around my cluttered room, and my stomach drops. Even my underwear drawer has returned to its previous I-can't-find-the-pair-I-want state.

*Reluctant to engage in tasks that require sustained mental effort.*

The bookshelf and pile of novels on my messy desk call out to me. I can handle a million tasks in one day—babysitting while baking cookies and talking Leslie down from a crash-diet ledge, but I can't seem to get myself to read any of these books. Books I've bought or asked people to buy me. I've started many of them. Some I've even made it past the midpoint. But I can't remember the last time I finished an entire book.

*Relationship problems due to forgetting important things or getting upset over minor things.*

This item hits a little too close to home, and part of me wants to slam the laptop shut, while the other half of me is leaning closer, wondering if I'm about to find my mothership full of people like me.

*Chronic stress and worry due to failure to accomplish goals and meet responsibilities.*

Check.

*Chronic and intense feelings of frustration, guilt, or blame.*

Check.

I close my laptop and pull my knees to my chest, the weight of being disordered or whatever hitting me all at once. But really, what does having this knowledge change? I still need to accomplish all the goals I've created for myself, so what has the research done besides tell me that it's possible I may be destined for a lifetime of relationship problems and many different varieties of inabilities and poor abilities? I guess I could use this as an excuse if/when I fail at anything. But again, what good does that do? Excuse or not, I'm still not getting what I want in the end.

And it isn't like I haven't come to realize that I drove Tate crazy when we were together—though I never forgot important things; quite the opposite, I made a huge deal out of every little thing. And I'm aware that I've occasionally been a pain in the ass to Fletch, as well. I know my grades would be better if I studied longer, took better notes, paid attention more in class. But my grades aren't terrible, either. I get by. My ACT score is a different story…23 is not exactly winning me any merit scholarships or acceptance to selective schools. Maybe not any out-of-state tuition waivers, either. Mr. Smuttley, the guidance counselor, said that he's sure I can do better. I'd planned to do a small number of practice lessons from the ACT study guide every day this summer, but we're three weeks in and the ACT prep book my dad bought me has yet to be cracked.

Okay, this is unbearable. I can't sit here and let myself

melt into a big puddle of failure and doubts and more doubts.

*Chronic stress and worry due to failure to accomplish goals.*

I jump up from my bed and dig in my laundry for a sports bra and shorts. I change quickly, scarf down a banana, and then grab my cell and headphones before hitting the pavement.

*Runs or climbs excessively.*

"Haley!" A hand reaches out and crosses in my path. I stop quickly, breathing hard, sweat running all over me. After assessing my surroundings, I panic for a second. I'm standing on the sidewalk that crosses Tate's driveway. Oh shit. Did my subconscious send me to the house of my ex in order to repair our failed relationship? God, this is so Dr. Phil.

I yank the headphones from my ears and force a grin at Tate. "Hey, what's up?"

Tate returns the smile. I feel a little better after seeing that he's also sweaty and covered in smudges of grease. His hands are practically covered in black stuff.

"Not much. Where'd you run from?" He lifts his T-shirt to wipe sweat from his forehead. *Don't look, don't look.* I turn my attention to the open garage. Tate's stepdad, Roger, appears to be beneath an old beat-up car. I know it's him because I recognize his battered work boots.

"From home," I say in response to Tate's question, but when I glance at my phone and see that it's ten in the morning, I know I've done more than the two-or-so miles between our houses. I can't even remember where I've been.

"But also around…I think I got a little too into the run."

I bend over after feeling a rush of dizziness.

"Need some water?" Tate asks, concern on his face.

"Yeah, that would be great." I stand upright again and walk toward the garage in an attempt to get out of the sun. "Maybe some sunscreen, too? I totally forgot."

"Got it," Tate calls over his shoulder.

"Maybe a granola bar or something if you have it," I add.

Tate turns around before going inside. He's laughing. "Anything else?"

I scrunch my nose up, slightly embarrassed. "Nope. I think that's all."

He finally goes inside, and I give Roger's boot a tap. "How's Midlife Crisis? Surviving without your drummer?"

Roger started a band last winter and invited my dad to join. Despite my original hatred of the idea, they are surprisingly good.

"It's not bad." He slides out from under the car and sits up on his wheely-thing. "Your parents having a good time bird-watching?"

I'm still sweating like crazy, but I'm breathing normally now. I show him a few of the pictures Mom and Dad have texted me recently. They're heading across middle America.

"I'm supposed to be checking up on you," Roger says. "I've failed at my duties. Have you been staying out of trouble? No big parties every night?"

"Trouble and parties. That's basically all I've done since they left." I find a folded-up lawn chair against the wall and pop it open before sitting in it. I know this isn't my boyfriend's house anymore, but I can't help it if I'm beat and I happen to know where things are. "Last night, I partied until 8:20 and then passed out on my couch with a baby beside me. It was wild."

"Andi?" Roger guesses, and I nod. "She's getting so big, isn't she?"

Tate returns and dumps a pile of stuff in my lap—three water bottles, a box of cereal bars, two apples, a couple of string cheeses, and a giant bottle of SPF 70.

"Are you trying to win the pit-stop-of-the-year award?"

"No." Tate grabs one of the water bottles and a cereal bar. "But I decided that I'm hungry, too."

"What's Claire up to today?" I drink the water first, downing half a bottle in no time.

Tate finds another chair and sits down in it across from me. "She's practicing something for an audition. I don't know what it is because she won't tell. But it requires several hours of solitude and nonjudgment."

He attempts to add some sarcasm into this, but I'm not fooled. He's all about supporting Claire and her big dreams.

I dump sunscreen into my hand and spread some over my nose. "Actors are very superstitious. She probably doesn't want to jinx anything."

Tate opens his mouth to reply, but we're interrupted by Olivia, Tate's six-year-old stepsister, bursting into the garage dressed in a two-piece polka-dot swimsuit.

"Who's taking me to the pool?" she sings. "I ate my beanie things, and someone is taking me to the pool!"

"You did not eat those beans, did you?" Tate asks. "After they sat out all night?"

"Beans?" I ask.

"I bribed her with a trip to the pool last night," Tate explains. "If she ate all her black-eyed peas."

"Add babysitter of the year award to your accomplishments," I say.

Bribery is Tate's style. He used to offer me all kinds of things while we were studying. I shake those thoughts from my head. It's weird to think about us together like that. And for a long time, I had the opposite feeling—it was strange to think of us not together.

"I'll go to the pool." Roger pushes up to a stand. "You stay here and hang out."

"You sure?" Tate asks. "I don't mind as long as Livi doesn't ask me to take her to the bathroom. I had to blindfold her last time."

I roll my eyes. Amateur child-watcher in the room. "Just ask another mom around to take her in the women's restroom. I'm sure you can find someone you recognize at the only public pool in town."

"I'll go, it's fine." Roger says to Tate, and then he looks over at me and scratches his head. "Why didn't I think of that?"

I reach for Olivia and pull her in front of me. "Stand still. I'll do your sunscreen."

"Get under my straps." Her blond curls flop around while she manages to keep her feet planted but still bounces up and down. "Last time, Tate forgot and I got burned and now I'm all peely and itchy."

Tate lifts his hands. "I can't do that. It's creepy, right?"

I try really hard not to laugh while giving Olivia a thick coat of sunscreen. Minutes later, she and Roger are climbing into the van, towels tucked under their arms. I finish off my water bottle and wait for Tate to say he needs to leave or something. But he's relaxed in his chair, looking completely at ease.

"So, the whole stepfamily adventure is going okay?" I ask. This is something I should have talked to Tate more about when we were together. We broke up literally days after he and I were witnesses to his mom and Roger's courthouse wedding. We signed the marriage certificate and everything.

I made a huge deal out of that, too. Well, a huge deal out of the fact that Tate didn't think it was monumental and life changing like I had.

*Relationship problems due to getting upset over minor things.*

"I can't believe she ate the black-eyed peas." Tate shakes his head. "Those things are nasty."

"I see." My eyebrows rise up. "So, you weren't encouraging your little stepsister to eat healthy, you were daring her to swallow something nasty?"

"When you put it like that…" He grins and reaches over to snatch an apple from my lap. "But yeah, things are okay with them."

I'm honestly happy to hear this. I know Roger really cares about Tate. I've seen that with my own eyes. He's not in this family just to be with Tate's mom. I set an empty water bottle on the ground and go for one of the cereal bars. I've recently developed a label-reading habit—not because of the calorie counter app I downloaded and rarely remember to use—but because of Fletch. Every time I eat something that has a label, I'm curious to see if it's on his do-not-eat list. From what I've gathered, more is off-limits than on for him.

*Contains: wheat, milk, and soy ingredients.*

Soy is one allergy that was mostly cured when he did that trial thing. But I asked him about it the other day, and he said he still mostly avoids it, just in case. Soy is apparently in a lot of processed foods, and after much prodding, Fletch reluctantly admitted that he avoids processed food because he gets random unidentified reactions from them and can't pinpoint the cause. I can't imagine being scared every time you ate something.

I squeezed all that out of him in less than ninety

seconds before we began studying yesterday. But then he got uncomfortable and changed the subject.

"So…what's going on?" Tate says after I unwrap the cereal bar and begin eating it.

I shrug. "Not much. Just running and, you know…doing stuff."

He looks me over and relaxes further into his chair, like he's planning to be here a while. "I meant what's wrong? You've got your pretending-to-be-okay look on."

Not a very good make-believe face, apparently.

I pick at a loose string on my shorts, my eyes on my lap.

"Haley?" Tate presses.

I exhale and look at him again. "You look comfortable."

"I am comfortable." He refuses to break this eye contact he's got going on. "Why wouldn't I be comfortable?"

I shift in my seat. "I don't know. It's kind of a chore dealing with me now. Maybe it's even a little weird."

"It was weird." His gaze travels to the ceiling. Finally. "At first. But now that we've had time and…I don't know, it's just not weird, okay?"

I laugh. "Okay. It's not weird."

He flashes me a grin, and then next thing I know, he's swiping my phone from my lap. "You're about to reveal your deep, dark angst to me. If I know you well—and I do—then you took off running because you were stressed about something, and then you decided to make a playlist of whatever songs pop up that represent your current angst."

I glare at him and fold my arms across my chest. I don't think he's referencing the most humiliating playlist I've ever made intentionally, but that's the first thing that comes to mind. And yes, I did this today, but I don't remember what all I picked. However, it feels so random and displaced inside my head, Tate's not going to hit anywhere near the mark. My secrets are safe.

"Aha!" His eyebrows shoot up. "Playlist made Saturday, June twenty-first."

"'Nirvana' by Sam Smith," he reads, then he pauses and eventually moves on. "'I'm a Mess' by Ed Sheeran, 'Halfway' by Parachute, 'Crazy for You' by Scars on 45, 'Stolen Dance,' 'Sleeping With a Friend'…"

I watch as his forehead wrinkles, his thumb scrolling farther down. Eventually, he sighs and tosses the phone back into my lap. "I got nothing from that list."

A satisfied grin spreads across my face. I'll take it as a sign that Shallow Haley is still stuffed in a far corner inside my head.

"Unless…" Tate says, assessing me again. "Sleeping with a friend…maybe you and Jamie—"

I throw the box of cereal bars at him.

"I'm kidding." He retrieves the loose packages that spilled from the box and sets it all on the ground. "Jamie would tell me.'"

"He would not." Okay, maybe he would. Tate and Leo are kind of his people to go to when he needs to talk about who he's sleeping with.

"You could just tell me what's going on," Tate suggests. "Then I don't have to make up false accusations."

We've come a long way since our breakup last fall, but I can't lay all of this tangled web of things on Tate. I bring my knees to my chest and hug them. "Can I ask you something? And by that, I mean will you answer honestly?"

The amusement drops from his face. "I'll try."

"You and Claire…" I keep my eyes trained on the old lady across the street watering her garden. She's in the Juniper Falls Women's League. She's probably going to tell all the ladies at bridge club tonight that I was hanging out with Tate in my bra today. "Do you ever think about, you know, like the future? Where you guys will be in several years?"

He grips the arms of his lawn chair, looking less comfortable now. "You mean, like, separately or together?"

"Both, I guess."

"I think about all of that," he admits. "More like, I worry about it."

"Because you're here and she's at Northwestern?" I ask. This is a side of Tate I've never seen before—attached, insecure...

"That musical Claire was in this spring?" he says, and I nod. "A producer for a Broadway show that's currently in Chicago saw her and wants her to audition for something new that's being workshopped to maybe open up in New York City next year—"

My feet drop to the ground, and I sit up straighter. "Oh my God. That's incredible."

"Please don't repeat that," Tate warns. "Claire's all worried about jinxing it. Anyway, I'm applying to Northwestern, but Claire might not even be there when I would start. And then there's the Rangers—"

My jaw drops. "The New York Rangers want to draft you? They want you to play for them?"

"No." He shakes his head. "For their junior team. I'd rather play college than juniors, I think. But some players go to juniors after high school, and then college, and then pros."

"Can you imagine if you and Claire were both in New York City?" I sit back again and let this sink in. "Two kids from Juniper Falls making it big in New York. That's just... wow."

"Or she could get really into her career and not have time for a relationship, especially with an athlete who lacks artistic integrity," he says.

"So, you worry about that, too?" The weight of all the impossible falls back onto my shoulders. "But you love her, right?"

"Yeah." He looks down at his hands. That can't be an easy thing for him to tell me. "But I love her being out there, doing what she does best, too. So, I don't know what will happen."

"Well, I'm not gonna lie," I say. "I want to go to New York and see Claire on Broadway and tell everyone in the seats nearby that she's my friend, so you'd better not do anything to stand in the way of my dream."

We sit in comfortable silence for several minutes, and then my mind drifts to one of the rehearsals we had for the ball. "I still get goose bumps thinking about Claire singing at the ball. I don't think I've ever done anything like that."

"Like what?" Tate asks. "Sing? I've heard you sing; you're not terrible."

I roll my eyes. "I'm not Claire, either. But not singing, just something—anything—where I put myself out there completely. Something uncalculated and from the guts, you know?"

"You mean from the heart?"

I shake my head. "The heart is pretty. Guts are raw and ugly. It's different."

His eyes lift to meet mine, and he stares for a long moment, like I'm someone else right now. "Yeah, it is different."

"I should probably get going." I untangle my headphones and start to stand up.

"Haley?" Tate says, letting out a breath. "I just want to...I mean—"

I adjust my shoelaces and then look down at him. "What?"

"We never had that chat I promised you, and…" He rubs his hands together, and I'm already shifting, uncomfortable with where this is headed. "From your perspective, it probably seems like I never confided in you and then I went and told Claire everything…but honestly, it wasn't like that."

I nod. "What was it like, then?"

"What I'm trying to say is that I was happy most of the time with you. You made me happy. It was fun. We were fun." He gives me that famous Tate Tanley smile. "I never got nervous around you. You're competitive like me, not afraid of a challenge, you were always fine playing video games or touch football in my yard. It wasn't all bad."

"It wasn't?" A lump forms in my throat. How did he know that I really needed to hear this? Am I wearing a sign that says please tell me if I've ever done anything nice for you?

"I think it was mostly good, if I'm being honest." Tate has finally dropped those walls he'd put up during the last couple of months of our relationship. "You were kind of my best friend for a while."

I look down at my fingernails. "Maybe that's what we should have done. Stayed friends."

"Maybe." He shrugs. "But then everyone would have said we were dating anyway if we hung out all the time."

I shake my head. This is so true, but I've never thought about it that way. "Toss in some hormones and sexual curiosity, and basically we were doomed."

"Exactly." Tate laughs, his cheeks flushed a little. "I don't think we'd have any trouble with that now."

"Maybe not." I take another drink of water. I'm going to need it for the run home. "Can I ask an extremely intrusive question?"

He rubs the stubble on his cheek. "Sure?"

"You and Claire..." My face heats up just thinking this question. "Are things better with her? Like, *things*."

"Oh." His eyebrows lift. "Things."

"I mean have you guys—"

"Yeah, we have." He looks down at his lap. "I wouldn't use the word *better*."

"You mean you're afraid to use the word *better*," I laugh.

He lifts his eyes again, forehead wrinkled. "I'd say evolved. It's evolved. Which has a lot more to do with experience than the actual person."

So most likely, a person who is awarded multiple pairs of panties on a weekly basis from various women and who can practically unravel me just by standing close and barely touching me would be considered sexually evolved.

Though, now that I think about it, Fletch never actually answered my virgin question yesterday.

"But I'd say it's definitely a different experience than, say..." Tate pauses, searching for a word "...sleeping with a friend. In case you're contemplating anything in that realm."

I snort back a laugh and toss my water bottle at him. Why is that even on my playlist? I'm about to throw a few choice words his way when Claire pulls up in front of the mailbox. My whole body tenses, my face flushing brighter. Why didn't I wear a T-shirt? What is she going to think about me sitting here in a sports bra, laughing with her boyfriend?

Claire is practically skipping up the drive. When she spots the two of us, she stops and then makes a big show of tiptoeing backwards. "I can come back later."

I jump to my feet. "It's fine. I was just..." In the neighborhood? Which is the truth, but it's way too cliché to say out loud.

Tate looks over at me. "I told her that I wanted to talk to you. She's probably thinking we're in the midst of a serious chat."

Guess we sort of were, but I think he's said what he needed to already. "It's fine, Claire. Seriously, I'm heading home."

"She's been going to my therapy sessions," Tate explains, though I'm still hovering over the realization that Tate is in therapy. I didn't know. But I guess it makes sense with all the stuff with his dad. "I just didn't want you to think I sit around talking about you to other people," he adds in a hurry.

"Oh, well, I'm quite fond of being on everyone's minds."

He rolls his eyes. "I've still got a lot of pieces to sort through. We've made good, bad, and gray-area piles. You're in the good pile, by the way. Even my mom didn't make the cut for that one."

My mouth falls open, but I have no idea what to say. Jesus Christ. Things were even worse for Tate than I realized.

Claire is in the garage now. She's heard Tate's comment about his piles and his mom. She lays a hand on the back of his neck, rubbing it gently. The lump in my throat grows bigger. I don't want them to end up apart somewhere. I don't want Tate to feel the terrible weight of heartbreak after everything he's been through. Or Claire. She'd have never gone through with that audition if it weren't for Tate. And she was in a pretty bad place last fall, too. After her dad's surgery and all the stupid town rumors about her and Luke Pratt.

I'm about to turn around and take off, but a few tears leak from my eyes before I get a chance to. Which is just great. Now it's gonna seem like I'm crying over them. I mean, I am, but not like people will think.

I swipe the tears away with my hand, but Tate is already out of his seat, walking my way. "Haley? What?"

"Nothing." I shake my head. "Nothing bad. I mean, I

*was* having a bad day, but this is good." I take a deep breath, pulling myself together again. "Thank you. For what you said. I needed that."

"Yeah?" He looks skeptical still.

"Yeah," I say as earnestly as I can. Tate moves closer like he's going to hug me, but I step back. "Don't. I'm all sweaty."

Tate gets his arms around me anyway, and my cheek is suddenly pressed against his grease-smudged T-shirt. When I finally escape Tate's hold, Claire looks like she might hug me, too. I say good-bye and leave before that happens. I don't want to take a chance of breaking down. And with all those new developments, I really need to run again.

Maybe I didn't screw up my and Tate's relationship? Maybe lots of people have a Tate. The question is, how many get to have a Claire? I'm not desperate to fall into an intense relationship or anything—quite the opposite—but I want to know if, by chance, it does happen, am I destined to ruin it? According to Tate, I didn't ruin us. We just grew up. We became the people we're going to be forever.

Which brings me to another problem: Tate is destined for hockey greatness, Claire is headed for Broadway. Fletcher is…well, I don't know what he's going to become, but I'm sure it will be amazing. He's really smart, and he works really hard. Jamie and Leo are headed off to play college hockey. Jake Hammond will be our next NHL star, probably an Olympian, too.

And me? Well, it's quite possible that I'm destined to be the girl who peaked junior year of high school when she won Juniper Falls Princess.

# Chapter Twenty-Nine

## −FLETCHER−

"What's going on? Where's Haley?" Jamie rubs his eyes, the red from a weekend of partying still hanging on.

I have an hour between practice and Civics class this morning, and I tricked him into getting here early. I told him Haley had an emergency.

"She's probably running with the cheerleaders." I open the door to the school building and wait for Jamie to walk through. "We're working on a surprise for her, okay?"

He grumbles but follows me toward the library anyway. "Love how you use my extra hour of sleep to make up for you being an asshole to Haley."

The lights in the library are off, so I switch them on before choosing a table in the center. Jamie sits beside me and leans on one arm like he might doze off again. I pull two cans of Red Bull from my bag and slide them his way. Then I spread all the test materials out in front of us.

"Here's what we're gonna do…" I show Jamie my game plan and dive into teaching him the Civics-themed plays I've created. Haley said the other day that Jamie needs a *C* on this test to get his passing grade and head off for college glory. I tried texting and calling her over the weekend, but she's kept her distance, which I get after that phone call we had, but I still wanted to help her study.

The only thing left for me to do was help Jamie. I know that'll lighten Haley's worry load considerably.

Jamie chugs Red Bull and shakes his head. "I'm swimming in words. I can't do this."

"Yes, you can." Three weeks ago, I wouldn't have said that. But he's a whiz with hockey plays, I've learned. He can memorize. He just needs it to feel like a necessity. "If you do what I'm telling you, you'll have a high enough grade that you can take all zeroes for next week and head to Minnesota State."

His eyes widen. "No way. Seriously?"

I nod. I emailed Mrs. Markson a bunch this weekend. She's a stickler, but she did make Jamie a very fair offer. "It's teacher approved. She'll even put your final grade in early so you'll have credit."

"And my diploma?" He looks like I've just offered him a million dollars.

"Yes." I smack the paper in front of him. "But shut up and pay attention. We're down to fifty-five minutes."

"In case I run out of here celebrating later without saying this," Jamie says, "thanks, man."

"Not yet," I warn. "We've got work to do."

Jamie nods and downs more Red Bull. This is the most serious I've ever seen him.

. . .

I'm trying to work through my own test—which is thirty percent of our grade in the class—while keeping an eye on Jamie a few rows over and Haley right in front of me. I answer a couple more questions before looking over at him again. Mrs. Markson is blocking my view now. She's been pacing up the aisles, but has now stopped beside Jamie, looking over his work. She leans in and whispers something. I hold my breath. Is she telling him he's missing too many points or…hell, I don't know. I've never been in Jamie's position before. I've never even gotten a *B* on anything.

Jamie nods along to what she's saying. I take that as a good sign and turn back to my test. I flip to the final page. I've got eight more multiple-choice questions to go, and then I'm done.

In front of me, Haley is tapping her pen in an even more neurotic rhythm than usual. She shifts in her seat, her foot joining the tapping pen. My stomach twists in knots. I want to tell her to relax. Rub her shoulders, make her close her eyes and take a few deep breaths.

I lean over a few inches, just to see which question she's on. Only one page of the five-page double-sided test is flipped over. She's on number twelve. Fuck. She's not gonna finish. There's no way. She tugs at her shirt collar and wipes sweat from her forehead. Her cheeks are a scary shade of pale.

Before I can even whisper the words "are you okay," Haley is out of her seat, rushing toward the classroom door.

Shit.

I glance around and see Jamie start to rise from his seat. I hop up and walk quickly down his aisle. I press the back of his head, forcing him to look at his test again.

"Don't move," I whisper.

Mrs. Markson is still staring at Haley's retreating form. She snaps around to face me when I reach the front of the room. "Where are you going?"

"I'm just gonna…" I point to the door, hating that everyone is looking at me. "I mean…"

"I'm not an idiot," she says, pressing a hand to my chest. "You can't leave until you're done with your test."

Jesus Christ. My jaw clenches but I nod. "I'm done. You can take it."

She releases me immediately, and I race out the door, looking around the hallway for signs of Haley. Two girls' bathrooms are of equal distance from our classroom. I pick one, and I only have to crack the door before I hear sounds of someone puking. A younger girl, probably a soon-to-be freshman, is at the sink, applying lip gloss. She wrinkles her nose at the sounds of retching. I walk right into the first stall where Haley is leaned over the toilet. Long blond strands are falling out everywhere. I quickly sweep them off her neck and out of the line of fire. With the hair in a pile in my hand, it's clear I didn't get here soon enough. While Haley is clearing out the remains of her stomach, I grab some toilet paper and attempt to clean off her hair.

I wait for the heaving to stop and then reach up and flush the toilet. I'm still holding her hair in one hand as she leans against the stall door and lifts her T-shirt to her face to wipe it clean. Very ladylike.

"Fletch, what are you doing in the girls' bathroom? You're gonna get in trouble." Her eyes are closed. She looks completely miserable. My stomach twists again.

I place my free hand under her arm and pull her to her feet again. "Come on. Let's get you cleaned up."

Haley shuffles out the stall door but freezes when she spots the girl at the sink. The freshman goes all wide-eyed at the sight of Haley then practically runs out the door.

Haley swears under her breath. "Great. I hope you're prepared to be pregnant with my baby by tomorrow." She leans over the sink and turns the water on.

I release her hair and move to the other sink. "I don't think I'd look good in maternity clothes."

Haley splashes water on her face and in her mouth, then she lifts her head. "I meant I'm pregnant with your baby."

A girl from our class appears in the doorway of the bathroom just as Haley says this. She goes completely deer-in-headlights. "Uh…Mrs. Markson told me to bring you these."

She drops Haley's purse and backpack by her feet and takes off.

"Fucking hell," Haley groans. She tosses more water on her face and then sighs. "At least I have my toothbrush now."

I wait for her to find the travel-size toothbrush and toothpaste she'd had at my house before I turn the faucet on to wash my own hands. The second I look down at my hands, currently under the stream of water, my heart jumps up to my throat. Hives. On my hands, maybe my neck.

God, I'm an idiot. A fucking idiot.

I dump a pile of soap on my hands, frantically, but not so much that Haley notices. The last thing she needs right now is another Fletcher-is-dying-and-it's-all-your-fault episode. It's not her fault.

"I was bombing that test, Fletch," Haley says, her mouth full of toothpaste. "I kept reading the same question over and over again, and I couldn't—" She shakes her head. "I studied. I really studied."

My chest is tightening, but it's not full-blown anaphylaxis

yet. Wheat. It's probably wheat. Or maybe dairy. I just need to help her get out of here and then take some Benadryl.

Haley rinses her mouth and then catches sight of the tips of her hair. "Oh God, that's nasty." She looks down at her shirt and groans even louder. She's got the shirt off in a second, a purple bra back flashing in my line of sight, and then she digs in her backpack, pulling out her Otter cheer tank.

I tug at my shirt collar, scratching my neck hard. I can ask Jamie for a ride home after I triple dose on antihistamines. I reach behind me until my fingers land on the pouch that holds my two EpiPens.

Haley sticks the ends of her hair under the faucet and attempts to reach the soap dispenser, but it's too far. "Great."

On instinct, I jump in to help, putting a pile of soap in my palm. I lay my other hand on her back. I don't know what I can say that's worthwhile, but I want to do something. To be something. "Haley, I'll talk to Mrs. Markson for you. I bet I can get her to let you take the test over."

"Yeah, that's exactly what I want. To repeat that experience." She takes a glob of soap from my hand and lathers up her hair, but she keeps the hair a distance from me. "Be careful, you probably shouldn't—"

She bolts upright, her eyes wide. "You already touched me, didn't you?"

"I'm fine," I say quickly.

I'm not fine. I'm not dying, either. But my throat is closing. I need my inhaler. And the Benadryl.

"Jesus." She carefully ties her hair up, scrubs her hands again, and then turns to me. "What do you need?"

I stick my hands behind my back, but Haley reaches for them. She pushes me until I'm walking backward and eventually plopping down on the bench underneath the window. I'm working so hard at staying calm, keeping all the breathing difficulties not emotionally or panic driven so I can assess how bad this is.

Haley shoves the window open and then squats down in front of me. "You can breathe?"

I nod.

"Swear to God?"

I nod again, making a big show of inhaling. A breeze from outside swoops in, and fresh air fills my lungs. I close my eyes for a second and feel Haley's small fingers behind my back. She unzips the pouch and grabs my EpiPens. "You hold one, I'll hold the other, and I'll go get your bag, okay?"

I grab her shirt to stop her. "You aren't going to…I mean what are you gonna tell—"

She rolls her eyes. "Give me a little credit."

The second she's out of the bathroom, I pull the cap off the EpiPen and hold it above my thigh. I recite my action plan going through each system in my head. I didn't eat anything. It's skin contact only. Though I could have inhaled particles.

Haley returns so quickly I have to look up to make sure it's her and that she has my bag. She does. But she throws it to the ground right away and goes back to the sink, scrubbing her hands hard again. She frantically scrubs between her fingers and under her nails, then she squeezes her eyes shut and scrubs her entire face with soap.

Shit. I've made her OCD now.

"Haley, it's fine. You don't have to—"

She's drying off with paper towels now. "Yes, I do." She plunges a hand into my backpack and emerges with a bottle of Benadryl. She squints at the bottle's label, trying to read the dosage.

"Just give me four," I say. "Maybe five."

She dumps the pills into her palm and holds them out for me to take. It occurs to me that her hands are probably cleaner than mine. I tug her closer and put the pills right into my mouth from her hand. I head over to the sink again, take a drink from the stream to wash the medicine down, and give my hands and arms another scrub.

"New shirt?" Haley says, holding up a folded T-shirt from my bag. Obviously, sports participation has provided an advantage for both of us today.

I'm shaking my hands dry while Haley brings my T-shirt over my head. She tosses the dirty one as far across the bathroom as she can, then steps back to look me over. "Maybe just go without one."

I sit back down and laugh. Haley hands over my inhaler, and I take a few puffs. My lungs open up immediately. Okay, this is a good sign.

"Better?" she asks.

I nod, counting to five in my head before exhaling.

"Your lips aren't blue," she says, leaning in to look me over. "Or like big and swollen."

I turn my hands over. "The hives aren't too bad. Was it eggs?"

"Muffins." She wrinkles her nose, her face heating up like she's humiliated by this whole event.

"Hey…" I rest a hand on her shoulder. "I'm the one having an asthma attack in the girls' bathroom."

"Well, they can't really blame you, can they?" She bats her long eyelashes. "I mean, you just found out you're going to be a father."

I drop my face into my hands and start laughing. This is seriously the nightmare I've protected myself against for years, and now I'm laughing about it. Oxygen deprivation is a bitch.

Seconds later, Haley is sitting on the floor laughing harder than me, tears forming in her eyes. "On my God," she says, her shoulders shaking. "We are so screwed."

"It's summer school," I point out. "Gossip has to move slower in summer school, right? Only five percent of the student body is here."

"You sound better already," she says. "If you had just left me alone and stayed in your seat…"

"I'm fine, I swear."

From outside the door, the sounds of students walking the hall get louder, indicating classes are out. A high-pitched voice says the word "baby" loud and clear. I look at Haley, and we both start laughing again.

A few minutes later, the bathroom door opens and Jamie bounces in, his fist in the air. "Guess who is fucking done with this place!"

Haley looks up at him and grins. It's only then that I notice she's still pale and sick looking.

Jamie skids to a stop and takes in both of us. "What the hell is going on?"

"Fletcher's pregnant," Haley says, straight-faced.

I nod. "I am."

"I thought I heard something about that." Jamie walks back to the door, sticks his head out, and shouts, "It's my fucking baby!" Haley slaps a hand over her face, and I start cracking up again. "Oh, hey, Mrs. Markson."

"Shit," Haley mutters.

I kick her foot. "Look sick."

Our teacher comes in, heels clicking against the tile floor. She holds both hands up. "Please tell me no one is pregnant."

"Fletcher is," Jamie says, closing the door and coming back inside.

"No one is pregnant," Haley answers.

"Thank God," Mrs. Markson says. "Because I skipped the special workshop we had on dealing with those situations."

"Haley needs a retest," I say immediately. Our teacher's eyes grow to double the size, and I quickly realize my mistake. "A retake of the Civics test. Maybe a less time-pressured retest."

"Go finish now," she tells Haley. "I'm here until five. Is that long enough?"

Haley's face goes from pale to bright red, but she scrambles to her feet. "Thank you so much. I swear, I studied, I just—"

Mrs. Markson waves a hand. "Go. Before I change my mind."

"Haley," I say, catching her hand. "You know that stuff. I drilled you on Friday, and you were ready. One question at a time, okay?"

She nods and then passes by Jamie, who smacks her on the ass. "Go, Stevenson! You got this!"

"Hands in your pockets. Now." Mrs. Markson points a finger at him and then turns to me. "Are you all right, Fletcher? You've got hives. You didn't have hives when you left my classroom. And where is your shirt?"

"She really is ready for that test," I say on Haley's behalf. I have good clout with the teachers, and I feel like I should take advantage of it. I reach for the T-shirt on the floor and pull it over my head. "And I'm fine. I took Benadryl."

"Okay. Do you need a ride home? Should I call your father?"

"I got it covered," Jamie says. "That's my man over there."

Okay, this is weird. Whatever. As long as I can get out of this girls' bathroom sometime soon, I'll be fine.

"I just have one last thing to do," Mrs. Markson says, then she turns to face Jamie and holds out her hand.

"Congratulations, Mr. Isaacs, you are now a high school graduate."

Jamie's usual goofy expression falls, and he stands up a bit straighter before shaking our teacher's hand.

"Good luck in college," she says before sweeping out of the room.

Jamie takes a breath of the fresh air Haley allowed in. "I always wanted to graduate in a girls' bathroom."

I snort back a laugh. "Check the hallway, will you? See if anyone's out there."

Jamie pokes his head through the door. "It's just Clooney."

"Shit, Cole needs a ride, too."

"Yeah, I figured. Little wingman's probably got a lot of questions for you." Jamie lifts an eyebrow, and my stomach sinks again.

But the Benadryl has caused a calm feeling to wash over me. My limbs are like Jell-O. I manage to make it out to Jamie's truck without too many balance checks. The Russian judges would have probably deducted points, but whatever. Cole sits between us, and I lay my cheek against the cool window.

Jamie's down the road, tapping his fingers against the steering wheel, matching the beat on the radio, when he says, "You may have heard some rumors…"

Cole's mouth falls open, but he snaps it shut again, sinking back against the seat. Okay, he's not happy.

"But just so you know, Fletcher is *not* pregnant. It was a straight-up blue line. All three tests."

Cole's gaze bounces between the two of us, his face tense. "It's not funny," he mumbles.

"It's a little bit funny," Jamie says. "At least the first time, and that was the first time for you."

I squeeze my eyes shut, pushing away the sleeping cloud floating in front of me. "No one is pregnant."

"So, you and Haley are…" Cole stops, his voice cracking.

I open my eyes. "We're not anything."

Jamie clears his throat, obviously disagreeing. Then he coughs the word "bullshit."

"It's fine. Whatever," Cole says, staring straight ahead.

"Cole, seriously, I'm not…"

"Better finish that sentence before you pass out," Jamie says. "You're not what? Screwing her?"

"Nope," I say.

"Dating her?"

"Nope."

"Becoming her new BFF?"

I think about trying to sit beside Haley and watch the video on her phone. I didn't last five seconds before I began the imaginary make-out session inside my head. Definitely not best-friend behavior. But friends, maybe? "Nope, not BFFs."

"What else is left?" Jamie says. "Are you thinking about her naked? Wait…I do that sometimes, so it can't count for anything."

Cole shakes his head. "I don't care."

Even tactless Jamie has the sense to put an end to this conversation, and Cole and I are forced to listen to him tap the same beat against the steering wheel all the way to my house. I stumble out of the car, and Cole pushes past me and heads for the back, where Grandpa Scott is using the ax again. I'm sure he'll give Cole an education in anger management.

"Have fun with that, man," Jamie says, sympathy on his face. "Little dude over there is a romantic. What can you fucking do?"

Yeah, what can I fucking do? I was a romantic at Cole's age, too. It was a very short-lived state of mind for me, one I can hardly recall.

Even though I'd love nothing more than to fall into my bed and give myself over to the sleep cloud hovering over me, I walk carefully down the driveway and into the back. Grandpa's got his know-it-all look on. He stares at me for a long moment—maybe an attempt to transfer his advice silently—and then he hands the ax to Cole and stalks over to the barn.

I sway and reach for something to grab on to, but unfortunately, I'm outside in the open. I plop down in the grass. Good. The ground is flat and stable. Not tilting like the rest of the world in front of me.

"Look, Cole," I start but pause when he takes a whack with the ax. For such a good shooter, he has surprisingly bad aim with an ax. "I didn't mean for anything to happen with Haley."

"I told you she liked you." *Whack, whack, whack.* Grass blades fly up everywhere.

"It helps if you aim for that big hunk of wood," I suggest.

Cole glares at me, his long, skinny arms dangling from the weight of his chosen weapon. "She's different than you thought, isn't she? Not so shallow and superficial after all?"

Huh. Now this is surprising. I always imagined Cole to be infatuated with Haley Stevenson, Princess of Juniper Falls. It's possible I may have underestimated him. "You're right. She's different than I thought."

He takes another swing and makes contact with the tip of the tree branch.

"Good one," I say.

Cole gives the wood a satisfied smirk. When he looks over at me, he's much calmer now. "I'm glad you figured it out."

"You are?" This is definitely surprising, considering the fact that it took some close personal interaction with his current crush for me to figure this out. Maybe Cole doesn't know about those things. Surely, he suspects something happened between us.

"I am." He nods. "But what if…"

"What?" I press.

Cole shakes his head, his gaze focused on the wood. "Never mind. You'll think it's pathetic."

"Your axman skills are pathetic." I roll my eyes. "But whatever you're thinking isn't."

"I like Haley," he says with a sigh. "She's beautiful and just…so much. And obviously I'm too much of a kid for her…but Jesus Christ, don't you think there's someone else who wants her like I do, and what if…" He looks away from me, probably preparing for my judgmental or teasing side. "What if she's too hung up on you to meet that person or whatever?"

"Cole, did you just say, 'Jesus Christ'? I think that's a new swear phrase for you."

He drops the ax, shaking his head. "Forget it. I knew you would think it's stupid."

"It's not stupid." I groan and flop back into the grass. In fact, I think my fifteen-year-old cousin just displayed more maturity than me. Truth is, I don't want this responsibility. I don't want the power to affect or effectively ruin someone else's life—someone outside of my family, anyway. I've managed to avoid putting myself in a position like this for a very long time. I allow these responsible thoughts in for a few seconds, and then I shut them down quickly, reverting back to my defensive mode. If I can make Cole believe me, maybe I can make myself believe me. "I wasn't lying about what I said in Jamie's truck."

"You mean about not screwing her?" he says, and I flinch hearing my little cousin speak those words so bluntly. "And you're not dating her? But you know she likes you, and you keep hanging around her, messing with her head…"

"I'm not messing—" I stop myself. It's true that I wasn't messing with her head in the beginning, but now, I fucking rushed off to the bathroom and then held her hair while she barfed.

"If you're falling for her, then you should just tell her," Cole says.

Falling for Haley? How is that possible? We haven't done anything except make out. Twice. Of course, there're all the times I wished we were kissing, wished we were doing more than kissing. And right now, we've been apart for twenty minutes and I already want to see her again.

Jesus Christ, I'm screwed.

"Fletch?" Cole says, leaning over me now. "You're starting to turn a little bit blue, what does that mean, again? I can't remember? Do I get the EpiPen?"

I tug my inhaler from my pocket and take a puff.

"I'm not mad at you," Cole offers.

I nod like this is great news, though honestly, it's kind of the least of my worries. Not that I don't care about his feelings, but he's supposed to be the *only* one with feelings.

"It's not like you were trying to go after Haley because I like her, right?" Cole presses.

"No, definitely not," I manage to say.

Some of the worry fades from his expression, which means I must be less blue. He sits down in the grass. "I'm not an idiot. I know Haley isn't going to go out with me— assuming I'd ever have the balls to ask her out—I mean, I didn't know that at first but after a while, I got it. So, you don't have to, you know, pretend to help me or anything."

He diverts his eyes from mine, embarrassed to admit all this, I'm sure. "Look, Cole, I only knew how this would play out because I've been there. I was into this older girl, Tia, when I first started working at Ricky's. We even danced together sometimes, so of course I confused her performance feelings with real feelings and…" I stop, not wanting to relive that, especially now with all this other shit out in the open. "Anyway, I'm sure you can guess how it turned out."

He's quiet for a minute, absorbing this news, or maybe he doesn't know what to say. "That actually sounds worse than me and Haley. Sounds like you put yourself out there. I did the opposite of that. Crushing on Haley from a distance was pretty damn safe, no risk at all."

"When did you get so smart?" I stare at my younger cousin, scrutinizing him. It seems like only weeks ago that he was this twelve- or thirteen-year-old kid who I had to protect, had to hide details about my job from, and edit swear words out of everything I said. Now I can't hide anything from him.

Cole beams with the compliment. "It's weird, isn't it? How you had everything figured out about me and Haley right away, and I had you and Haley pegged right away…"

Vixen comes barreling over, panting right in front of me. I think she *is* learning to sense distress on my end. I stroke her back trying to calm her, and then Cole's declaration hits me. "Wait…what do you mean you had us pegged?"

He shrugs, stands, and grabs the ax again. "In the hallway after that first day of summer school…you didn't see how she was looking at you? And I could tell she'd pissed you off, which meant there was a chance."

"A chance for what?" Where the hell is this coming from? No way did Cole see all of that after two minutes in the hallway.

"A chance that she could shake you up a little." He turns red at that and focuses on swinging the ax instead of looking at me. "You have patterns when it comes to girls. You just needed someone to force you to change those patterns."

"What books have you been reading? Or are you watching *General Hospital* again?"

Cole ignores this jab. "I mean, I didn't want it to be Haley. At first, anyway. But I wanted it to be someone."

"Right." I roll my eyes. "You've told me your feelings about hookups without relationship. I get it."

"Not just that." He finally holds the ax still and looks at me. "It's really cool having you at practices. I just thought maybe if you went out with someone from town, then we could hang out more together, like with the team or just people from school. After you played at state, I was sure things would change, but you're on the team now and things sort of haven't changed, and that sucks…for me at least."

I don't know what to say. Or how Cole kept all of that stuff inside his head. Until now. Never in a million years would I have guessed that he'd want something like that from me. Maybe because I can't imagine myself as someone hanging out in Juniper Falls on Friday or Saturday nights.

"What did you think would happen?" I ask Cole. "That we would suddenly start spending weekends loitering at Benny's wearing our varsity jerseys, flirting with cheerleaders? First off, Benny's uses peanut oil in their fryer. I can't step foot near that place."

"I know that," Cole says. "But didn't you have a party here? With Jamie and Leo and Haley? If you just explained stuff to people, they'd understand."

"Some of them," I agree, thinking of Haley. She really was a rock star today, coming to my rescue. "But not all of them. How am I supposed to know who to trust? Plus, do you know what people say about my dad? About Braden? My mom? And then there's Grandma Scott…"

"No one ever talks about any of that," Cole argues.

"Yeah, not now. But my mom moved out of town, and the rest of us stay out here in the middle of nowhere most of the time. But if things changed—"

"Things *have* changed. You're just not ready to accept any of it." Cole drops the ax, clearly disappointed. "I guess you figured out what to do about Haley?"

My forehead scrunches. "I have?"

"Yeah." He nods. "Nothing. Absolutely nothing."

With that, he scoops up the ax and heads for the barn, probably to put it away. And all I can do is just sit here, frozen in place. Because he's right. I'm not willing to change all of the things he mentioned. Being in a relationship with someone like Haley—a town socialite—is impossible without being under the microscope. Look how fast the pregnancy rumors spread through the summer-school crowd today. And would any girlfriend be okay with her boyfriend spending Saturday nights smashed against other women? For money?

Cole's right. The only thing I can do about these newly discovered feelings for Haley is, well, nothing.

The answer I'd been digging for makes my chest ache. I never thought doing nothing could hurt so much.

# Chapter Thirty

## -HALEY-

tap my foot impatiently while Mrs. Markson flips through my test. It's after three in the afternoon. I've been in this classroom since nine this morning. I'm so ready to be out of here, but I couldn't *not* take advantage of her giving me as long as I needed on the test. Somehow that gave me this sharp tunnel vision I rarely have when it comes to school stuff.

I glance at my cell phone and nearly scream out loud when I read the first of the slew of text messages I've gotten during the day.

*LESLIE: u had sex in the girls bathroom??? During summer school? Hope you took the bathroom pass! U drop a whole letter grade for ditching 1 day*

*KAYLA: I'm confused...did u hook up with Jamie or the mystery guy in the bathroom? Or was it Mira Sylveski? Someone said they saw her taking ur stuff in the bathroom.*

*AMANDA: U would tell me if ur gay right? I'm cool with that, btw*

*BAILEY: Mira is kinda hot. Just sayin* ☺

Jesus Christ, what is wrong with these people? And mystery guy? That has to be Fletcher. I guess the girl who saw him didn't know his name. Well, at least one good thing came out of that mess. I check on Mrs. Markson—still grading—and then with a heavy sigh I type a heated text to Leslie. Hopefully this won't come back to bite me in the ass.

*ME: Truth—I got test anxiety, ran to the bathroom to barf, Mrs. Markson asked Mira to bring my stuff, and then Jamie came in to check on me. That's it. I'm a little busy trying to save my grade so can you just be my best friend and fix this asap?? You know I would do it for you.*

So yeah, I left Fletcher out, but it's still the truth. Mostly. I wait the longest thirty seconds of my life for her reply and then sigh with relief when I see it.

*LESLIE: Of course. I'm on it \*hugs\**

I stuff my phone way down in the bottom of my bag so I won't be tempted to check for more updates. Finally, Mrs. Markson flips back to page one of my test and scribbles a score on the front—a score I can't see from my seat. I'm in the desk right across from hers, so there's really no excuse to stand and peek yet.

"The PowerPoint you and Fletcher turned in over the weekend," she says, her impassive teacher face plastered on. "How much of that was your effort? Be honest, I've already logged the grade, so it doesn't make a difference either way. I'm aware that Jamie Isaacs did none of his assignment."

That's not completely true. His partner, Trinity, asked

him to make up a really old person's name, and he said, "Harold."

"I have no clue what the conclusion says," I admit. "But I do know that Barbie isn't in it."

She shakes her head, confused probably. "But the rest?"

"I helped with all the rest. I mean, Fletcher is the one who knows how to outline, and I got caught up on the individual sections, and he made sure we had all the pieces at the end…"

"Give me an overview of your project, then," she says.

Even though I'm dying to know my test grade, I attempt to explain the project in as much detail as possible. We won't present it until tomorrow, but we had to turn in the hardcover for a grade by Sunday night.

Basically, our PowerPoint was a timeline of voting progression from the signing of the Constitution to present day. Who voted then—the demographics like ages, marital status, gender, race—and now. And then we included each amendment to the Constitution and how that affected voting demographics.

"Okay." She nods like I've managed to satisfy her with my response. "I gave you two a hundred and four percent on the written part. Now I can sleep at night knowing you didn't bribe my best student into doing it for you."

"I wouldn't do that," I protest. Is that so hard to believe? I may have sought out a brainy partner so that I could actually learn something, in addition to getting a good grade. And I did. Learn something. Organization of thoughts never comes easy to me. Fletcher gave me a basic template to use for any project in this realm.

"I'm sure you'll do well presenting the material. You've got a knack for public speaking." She finally hands me my test. A big red 90 percent is written across the top.

I look up at her, my mouth hanging open. "For real?"

"I checked it twice." She opens a desk drawer and removes a folder with my name on it. "I've noticed that you've been leaving questions blank on all your tests and quizzes."

I take a deep breath and nod. Oh man, is she gonna dock me points for having all this extra time compared to everyone else? It would make sense. It should be the same circumstances for all students. "I almost never finish tests in time. Same thing happened to me on the ACT. I left a bunch blank on each section."

"So, this is a continuing problem for you?"

I nod, hoping I haven't opened an ugly can of worms. I don't have the best grades in the world, but I'd rather they didn't get any worse because Mrs. Markson looked into my files a bit too carefully.

"Well, unlike the teen-pregnancy workshop I skipped out on, I did attend the test-anxiety workshop," she says, flipping the folder open. "If you can get a diagnosis from an approved professional, the school and possibly even the ACT board will allow you to have extra time."

I sink back into my seat. "What kind of diagnosis?"

"Have you had any trouble reading? Or been diagnosed with dyslexia?"

Does having an unread pile of novels in my room count as reading troubles? I shake my head.

"Are you sure? You'd be surprised how many dyslexic kids go undiagnosed," she says.

"Guess I don't know for sure. But I know I could read really well in preschool, and no one else could," I explain. "I got picked all the time by the teachers to show off my skills. I think it gave me a complex."

Mrs. Markson cracks a smile. "Probably not a reading

issue slowing you down."

"I do have to reread the questions a lot," I admit. "What else is grounds for extra time?"

"Mood and anxiety disorders, like OCD, autism spectrum, ADHD," she recites. "Any learning disability may qualify with proper documentation."

"ADHD?" I wasn't expecting that. "People get extra time for being hyper?"

"I believe so," she says. "Mr. Smuttley can give you more specifics and tell you what's required as far as documentation. Definitely talk to him."

"Okay." I nod even though I'd been poised to deny any ADHD labels.

"But right now…" She drops a quiz from two weeks ago onto my desk. "Answer those last three questions for me."

I stare at her, not sure if she's serious. But when she doesn't stop me, I flip to the last page and read the first blank question. My adrenaline is still pumping from all this grade drama, so I get through it quickly. Mrs. Markson takes the paper, gives two questions a red check mark and one a red X. Then, on the front of the test, she changes my 76 percent to an 83 percent.

I open my mouth to respond, but she drops our first exam onto my desk. "You left seven blank on this one. Want to take a stab?"

"I'm not sure—" I start to say, my cheeks warming. Maybe Fletcher waved his magic perfect-student wand and bribed her. As much as I want to take the advantage, I'm not sure it's right. "I mean, isn't this cheating?"

"No," she says, and when I still look doubtful, she explains, "Haley, what do you think the purpose of a high school class is? Try to push through the hazy mixed signals we like to send around here."

"To get a good grade," I say.

She shakes her head. "Try again."

"To pass?" I suggest, less sure.

"Uh-uh." She flips test one to the page with all the blank answers. "The purpose is to be proficient in the material presented. Mastery. All the grade and test mumbo jumbo is because we teachers have to provide proof of that proficiency or, in some cases, not. And the proof often isn't an accurate portrayal of proficiency. Are you following me?"

My forehead wrinkles. "Sort of."

"I take my course material very seriously," Mrs. Markson says. "God forbid any of you students walk away from my class claiming God as the founder of our country."

I laugh. "Or the first lady as successor to the vice president."

"Or that." She nods. "We haven't even finished our class, and already those are two mistakes you will no longer make, correct?"

"Correct." Though I would have never missed Jamie's George Washington question.

She taps the page in front of me. "Then it's settled. You've learned. Now prove your mastery, and we can both move on."

I stare down at the test. I'm exhausted, but it doesn't feel like the academic world is out to get me right now. This helps a lot. The empty classroom without other students flipping pages and shifting around helps a lot, too. And my grade is decent at the moment. I can walk out of here whenever I've reached my limit. I'll just think of these questions as bonus points.

"I'll give you half credit for any wrong answers you correct," she says. "I do this for everyone on the last day, but maybe it will help you to have a jump start?"

• • •

I t's after five by the time I walk out of the school. I'm in dire need of food and beverage and probably a nap, but I'm flying high. My grade in Civics is now a 91 percent, and it will go up higher after Fletcher and I present the Constitution project. I even had a chance to talk to Mr. Smuttley after I finished with the tests.

He didn't act like my concerns were strange or disordered. He did say extended time with an ADHD diagnosis is tricky if the documentation and testing are less than three years old. I guess kids try to cheat the system. Obviously, I need my parents' help on this one, but I'd been planning to retake the ACT in October, and Mr. Smuttley said that would give us plenty of time. In the meantime, he suggested I gather any evidence of attention problems in my childhood— old report cards showing underachievement or disciplinary notices. Anything before age twelve.

So, after I hit up Benny's for a double bacon cheeseburger, fries, and a chocolate shake, I take my food home and drag out the container from the basement labeled "Haley's School Stuff."

My mom, who has no organizational disorders, has these sorted by school years, beginning with day care when I was eighteen months. I'm munching on my fries—the burger already devoured—and sifting through piles of daily reports with Little Lamb Nursery across the top. Reports that let my parents know how many times my diaper was changed and any unusual colors that presented in said diapers. I'm sure I'll find this information extremely useful at some point in my life.

I set aside the Little Lamb box and move on to kindergarten. The report card marks reveal very little. All they expected of me was alphabet reciting, shoe tying, holding scissors properly…real genius production going on in our elementary schools. But in the comments section of the report card, Miss. Jenny—who I don't think lives in town any more—wrote "Haley is a very sweet girl. She continues to struggle with remaining on her cot during naptime and often spends too much time talking to peers when she should be getting work done. But she has shown exemplary reading skills and is such a wonderful class buddy for Rowen."

I smile to myself. I remember Rowen. He was autistic, didn't speak at all, but I figured out ways to play with him. Six-year-olds are creative in that way.

I move on to first grade, and the comments shift to me getting out of my seat too much. Me not finishing daily work. Still nothing too big. Just tiny hints here and there. But when I compile all of them, it does add up to a lot of the same thing over and over. Several teachers mentioned what a great athlete I was—only in Juniper Falls does that make it onto an academic report card—and even drew the conclusion that my constant movement correlated with my athletic abilities. I played every sport when I was a kid—hockey, football, basketball, soccer, swimming…

My middle-school report cards brought much fewer comments and more inconsistent grades. Mostly *A*s and *B*s, but some *C*s, too, and usually in major subjects. In home ec, art, drama, and PE I had all *A+* grades with positive comments from teachers. Maybe I'm destined to be a Stepford Wife with soccer-mom potential? But that would require home organizing skills, and it seems I may be stuck with "poor ability" when it comes to those.

I close the lid to the middle-school box, but when I move to do the same to my Little Lamb Nursery box, a sheet of pink paper stands out amongst the sea of soft yellow daily reports. I tug it from the pile and read the heading: "Incident Report."

Scandalous. An incident at the Little Lamb Day Care center.

Explanation of incident: During morning snack, Haley chose to place Cheerios into another student's nose. When asked to stop, she continued the behavior.

Resolution of Incident: After the standard two warnings, Haley was given a three-minute time-out (one min. per year of age) in the red classroom time-out chair. The boy left for the day, and Haley was unable to apologize for her behavior. We discussed apologies and practiced apologies on Waffle, the classroom mascot.

Who Was Notified of Incident: The boy's family through phone call, and Haley's parents through this incident report and a conference during pickup time today.

I shouldn't laugh. I really shouldn't. But I can't help it. He was right. And who would have ever thought we'd have actual proof? Given the fact that my parents have documentation of every single diaper change I had from eighteen months to potty training, I should have known there would be something around here.

It says the boy's family was notified by phone and mine wasn't. And that he left for the day before I could apologize. Left following morning snack.

I jump up from my spot on the living-room floor and head for the kitchen pantry. I dig around, shoving things aside until my fingers land on a nearly empty box of Cheerios. I scan the label, and right there at the bottom it says "Contains wheat."

From what I've read, the more severe food allergies

almost always present themselves in the toddler years. Most likely, Fletch was already allergic to wheat. Among many other things.

So basically, I've been poisoning him for years.

The doorbell rings, offering me an excuse to set my guilt aside. I don't even have to get up to answer it. Jamie walks right in after only a few seconds.

"What if I was walking around naked?" I demand.

"Saw you through the window. Fully dressed." He flings himself across the couch, shaking the cushions and the foundation of the house in the process. "Don't you have something to say to me?"

I pull myself upright from my spot on the floor. In all my drama, I completely forgot that today was a big day for Jamie. "Oh my God, what happened? How did you do?" Why hadn't I just asked Mrs. Markson? I was with her all afternoon.

He leaves me in anticipation for three whole seconds and then a grin spreads across his face. "Passed! Graduated. All that shit. Done."

I've watched Jamie accomplish some amazing things—winning or almost winning state the last four years, getting a hockey scholarship—but never have I seen him look as proud as he does right now. I think I get what Mrs. Markson was trying to explain when she talked about what grades really mean—it's about leaving the class knowing more than when you came in. Jamie succeeded at that, and it was good enough for the strictest teacher at JFH.

A lump forms in my throat, and my eyes start to well up. Jamie sees me and immediately shakes his head. "No crying! Jesus. You and my mom both."

"Okay, okay." I pull myself together and offer him my best smile. "I knew you could do it."

"No, you didn't," he says, but he's still smiling. "No one saw that coming. Couldn't have done it without you. And Fletch."

Hearing Fletch's name sends my heart racing all over again. I don't know what's happening with us. "Did you—I mean, you gave Fletch a ride home, right? Was he okay?"

"He was doped up, but fine." Jamie reaches for the remainder of my french fries and pops one into his mouth. "You know it's not gonna work with you two, right?"

"What's not gonna work?" I say, playing dumb.

Jamie rolls his eyes. "It's all fucked up. You have to know that. I've talked to his friends from the club. He's into some wild shit."

"Oh, I see." I stretch out on the carpet and toss Jamie a look. "I'm too innocent for all that wild shit. Thanks for the inaccurate label."

"Well, you are sort of innocent," Jamie agrees. "But I just mean that Fletcher's not a one-woman man. Never has been from what I hear. And you are definitely not the kinda girl to share your man."

"What man?" I say, releasing a frustrated breath. "I don't have a man, and I don't want one. Not now and not in the near future!"

Jamie allows my heated reply to fall into the space between us until it's calm and silent again. "But you want him."

I swallow back another angry reply and rest my head against the floor. "Maybe."

"Great, that's just great." Jamie releases his own frustrated groan. "I'm gonna have to stop being his friend now."

"Why?" I sit up. "Not for me, I hope. I'm fine with you and Fletch being…whatever you are. Besides, he hasn't exactly rejected me…"

Jamie gives me a look that says you've-got-to-be-kidding-me. "Dude's not gonna change for you. Not that much. You're a catch and all, but he's stubborn as hell and kinda paranoid, if I'm being honest. You guys are at one of those, what's it called when it's a tie in chess?"

"A draw," I say.

Jamie nods. "A draw. That's exactly it. You made a move. He made a move. You and then him. But neither of you got anywhere, and it's impossible for anyone to win."

"But technically we could keep playing..." I say slowly.

"You could." Jamie pops another fry into his mouth and studies my face. "But what's the point? No one wins. Plus, we aren't talking about chess. Fooling around without it going anywhere...that's not for everyone."

It's not for me. That's what he's trying to say.

But Jamie's not completely right about all of this. Fletcher does care about me. I saw that today with my own eyes. But does he care enough to make big changes in his life for me? Jamie's probably right about that being too much too soon. Especially for Fletch, who seems to have an extra aversion to change. I glance at my phone. I'd been about to text him before Jamie showed up.

But maybe I shouldn't?

# Chapter Thirty-One

## -FLETCHER-

"You are getting way too fit for me," Angel says, panting after our closing number.

I'm about to roll my eyes, but then it occurs to me that it's been weeks since I used my inhaler backstage. It used to be an every-time thing. I may not be as winded as Angel, but I'm hot, sweaty, and in need of hydration. I grab a water bottle and take a long drink.

"I bet you're a blast in bed, with all that endurance," she says.

I choke on my water, spraying it everywhere. "What?"

Angel looks at Brittney, and the two of them crack up. Brittney shakes her head. "It's just too easy."

Henrietta joins them. She's already taking her hair down. "He's all rattled from the mere mention of hooking up."

"Since when?" Rosie says, butting in.

"Who's rattled?" Paco shoves the curtain back in place after stepping through, then he lays a hand on my shoulder.

"How'd you do tonight, man?"

Neither of us have shirts on, so the bills are pretty easy to spot. I've got plenty. So does Paco.

"What he means to say is," Brittney adds, "how were the middle-aged women tonight? I didn't see you within hip bumping distance of anyone under thirty the whole night."

I flash them a grin. "What can I say? The money's good in that age bracket. It's like they know they're funding my college education."

Henrietta moves behind me and sticks her hands into my pockets. I feel her cheek against my back. I try to sidestep her and move away, but she holds me in place. Boundaries, like respecting personal space, don't really exist in my job, unfortunately. "You're all messed up over that girl, aren't you? The passed-out blonde?"

I guess all she saw of Haley was her sleeping, but still she wasn't like *passed out*. I open my mouth to protest, but Rosie interrupts me. "Haley, right?"

I shoot a glare at Angel. "Thanks."

She shrugs. "Come on, we all saw you guys dancing together a few weeks ago."

Rowdy pries Henrietta from me. "Leave him alone. If he wants your input, he'll ask for it."

I give Rowdy a nod, and before anyone can jump on my back again—literally and figuratively—Ricky comes floating backstage, a little tipsy from bartender's cocktails.

"Quick staff chat," Ricky announces. She hates the word "meeting." Says it takes the fun out of our jobs. "Sixty-nine—"

Danny lifts his hands into the air and shouts, "Sixty-nine!"

Ricky rolls her eyes. "Sixty-nine private-lesson requests for next week. Forty-two of those are specified, and you'll get a notice on your calendar. The rest of the open lessons are on the board in my office," Ricky says. "Any ideas for Friday-night themes in the fall? We're gonna need to change it up. There's a reason why disco only lasted a short time."

"Sock hop!" Brittney shouts.

Ricky shakes her head. "Too town-hall family night."

"What about Ginger and Roger?" Angel suggests. "We can play Gershwin and waltz."

"Can you waltz?" Ricky says, looking at the guys more than girls.

I glance at Paco and Rowdy, and we all silently decide to shrug. Of course we can waltz. It's not rocket science. But it's also a bit…snooze worthy.

"Maybe," Ricky says, her face scrunching. "I like it, but does it really scream Friday night?"

"More like Sunday after church," Paco says. "Before the early-bird specials."

Ricky looks like she wants to scold him for judgment against the older crowd, but she also seems to agree.

I keep my mouth shut. I'm never the idea person.

"What about *Dirty Dancing* night?" Henrietta suggests. "We can play all the hip-grinding, heartbreaking fifties and sixties hits without going PG sock hop."

Ricky's whole face lights up. She snaps her fingers and points at Henrietta. "Yes! We'll call it 'Time of Your Life.'"

Almost everyone squeals and begins tossing around more spin-offs of this theme. I scratch the back of my head. I really need to see that movie.

I'm about to head for the shower in the staff bathroom when the new bartender Ricky just hired comes backstage. "Fletcher? Who the hell is Fletcher?"

Paco smacks me on the back. He's laughing almost too hard to talk. "I forgot that's your real name."

I shoot him a glare. "Scott is my real name, too. It's

called a last name."

"But it's also a first name," Rosie points out.

The new bartender—Joey? Maybe Jackson?—tells me a couple of guys are looking for me in the parking lot.

"That never ends well," Paco mutters.

The new guy gives a brief description, and I know exactly who it is. I change quickly and grab my stuff before heading outside.

I glance around and spot Jamie and Leo leaning against my car. "Hey, what are you guys doing here?"

"Dancing," Jamie says, like duh.

"Really." I unlock the car, and Leo opens the door to the backseat. "You guys were in there earlier?"

"Yep," Jamie says. "It's our new hangout. We did disco last night."

I spin around to face him. "Seriously?"

Leo rolls his eyes. "We stood at the bar for three hours watching the disco dancing."

"Leo's got a lead on a new man."

"A lead on a new man?" Leo punches Jamie hard in the shoulder. "It's not the FBI."

Jamie rubs his arm. "Feels like it around here."

"Come on." Leo nods toward his truck. "You're going out with us. We gotta celebrate our last night as big fish in the small pond. Also, Jamie's bathroom graduation."

I shake my head. "I'm beat. I was just about to head home."

"No, you weren't." Jamie shakes his head and tugs my sleeve.

My feet skid a bit in the dirt parking lot.

"Jesus," Jamie says, then he looks at Leo. "I told you he'd be like this."

"I'm sure you guys have plenty of people who wanna

hang out tonight, right?" I suggest. "Someone has to be throwing a party in your honor."

"'Course they are." Jamie pulls me a few more feet, and I finally give in and walk. "But we'll get to them later."

"Why don't I just follow you, then?"

"We can pick your car up on the way home," Leo says.

Clearly, we're not going to Juniper Falls. That makes this seem 90 percent less painful.

I end up seated between Jamie and Leo with no access to a door. Right away, Leo jumps on the two-lane highway, heading toward Longmeadow. Now I really have no idea what we're about to do.

Jamie tosses me a brown paper sack, and I open it and peek inside, glancing briefly at the sandwiches in ziplock bags before closing it up tight.

"Your Gramps made those," Jamie says. "We stopped by to pick up your gear, and he said to give you this."

"My hockey gear?" What other gear would it be? "Why are we going to Longmeadow?"

Leo shrugs. "Rink time is rink time."

My stomach growls. I'm starving. I open the sack again and remove a sandwich, but I keep it sealed in the clear bag. I lean close and try to examine it in the dark. It looks like Gramp's oat-flour bread and my turkey. And I'd pulled the same kind of tomatoes out of the garden this morning.

"Dude, seriously?" Jamie is staring at me, his mouth hanging open. "We're not trying to kill you."

"We didn't even open the bag," Leo adds.

I pretend to scratch my back, but instead I'm feeling for my EpiPens, just in case. "It's cool," I say, but there's a clear hesitation on my part before I muster up the nerve to take a bite. This is why I never eat in restaurants—you have to trust strangers, take their word when they tell you they followed instructions. Some people don't get that I'm not on some weird fad diet or making a social protest, or that it's not something I can have a little bit of without noticing.

I chew the sandwich slowly, counting in my head. So far, so good. Longmeadow is only a couple of miles from Ricky's club, so we're at the rink in no time.

"You sure we can get away with this?" I ask. "I still have to play these guys this season."

"You'll be fine," Leo promises.

It's after midnight so I'm pretty tired, but I can't pass up the chance for some more defensive help. Especially knowing that Leo and Jamie are taking off tomorrow. My bag is sitting in the back of Leo's truck. I grab it, but Jamie tells me that I won't need to suit up all the way.

"The goal is for you to outskate your larger counterparts. You don't need to take any hits tonight."

The rink is only half lit when we walk through a back entrance. But there are a few people on the ice. People I recognize right away. Tate Tanley, who is suited up in goalie gear, Claire O'Connor, Mike Steller—also in full goalie pads—and Haley. Gramp's sandwiches churn in my stomach. I shouldn't have eaten two.

Since the bathroom drama (that my name miraculously stayed out of), I haven't sent Haley even so much as a single text, and she hasn't sent me one, either. In class, we've just been polite acquaintances. She must know where I'm at with things. She's perceptive; she may have guessed.

Mike Steller's girlfriend, Jessie, is in the penalty box, baby car seat on her lap.

Jamie shoves me from behind. I hadn't even realized I'd stopped walking.

"Dude, I get it. You like to keep your circle of friends tiny, so I had to improvise so we could play a real game." He glances over at Claire, who is flipping her helmet around, trying to figure out how to put it on. "Well, sort of a real game."

Haley's got a tiny pair of beat-up hockey skates on and a helmet with a mask. Her stick is like half the length of Leo's. She waves when she sees me. My whole body tenses, even more so when Haley skates over to the wall.

"Hey," she says, her cheeks pink from the cold. "I'm here strictly on business, I promise."

"Haley—" I start to say. I owe her some kind of explanation.

She holds her hands up. "It's all good. We're all good. Now get your skates on. Jamie promised me a chocolate shake from Benny's if I played on his team."

"Wait," Claire jumps in. "You're getting a milkshake?"

Jamie rolls his eyes and snatches the helmet from Claire before placing it correctly on her head. "Fine. You get one, too."

I sit down and lace up my skates while Jamie and Leo give out assignments. I'm having a hard time believing this is a legit game. But I can't exactly say that without possibly offending Haley and/or Claire.

Jamie takes both girls to his end of the goal with Tate, and it looks like he's about to attempt passing drills. I shake my head. This is insanely weird.

Leo has me playing defense while he shoots at Mike's goal. Despite our practice sessions, I've never actually gone one-on-one with Leo, not like this, and I'm surprised by how good he is.

"Take it out wider," Mike suggests. "Whenever you're behind the net, sweep it out wider. Puts you in a better position to pass to the outsides." He draws a diagram in the ice using his skate blade.

The next time, I'm able to get around Leo after stealing the puck, and I sweep it behind the net.

"Yeah," Mike says. "Like that, man! Nice one."

On the other side of the ice, a puck bounces off the glass and flies toward the penalty box near us. Mike takes off, jumping up in the air like an outfielder instead of a goalie. He snatches the puck in his glove and lands hard on his side. Jessie stands slowly, having ducked at the sight of the flying object.

"Jesus Christ, Isaacs!" Mike shouts. "Are you trying to kill my kid?"

Haley puts her arms on top of her head. "Oh my God, oh my God…I can't believe I did that. I'm done. I'm a baby killer." She skates across the ice, twists to a stop in front of the penalty box, and leans over to look. "Andi, I'm so sorry. Are you okay, baby?"

"Haley, damn it," Mike says. "You've got a wild slap shot."

"I have an idea," Jessie says, before an argument breaks out. She lifts up the baby car seat. "How about I move to those seats behind the glass wall."

Mike nods and then hands her a spare glove. "Put this on, would you?"

Jessie gives him a bewildered look but agrees.

"I'm sorry," Haley says again to Mike.

He finally smiles at her. "Yeah, I know."

"Can we play now?" Claire says. "I want my milkshake."

"Like my wingmen?" Jamie asks me when we're lined up. "See, you're not gonna check them. This'll keep you from trying to play enforcer when you're not. Even better than just having no pads, right?"

Maybe, but how hard is it gonna be for me to steal the puck from Claire or Haley? As if to prove my point, before Claire passes the puck, Tate shouts, "Other way, Claire. Flip your stick over."

"Oh, right." She turns her stick and then stares down at it like it's a foreign object. "Are you sure? I like it better the other way."

Tate laughs. "I'm pretty sure."

"Put it however you want," Haley tells her. "You're not being graded."

Sure enough, Claire passes to Haley with the stick backward. I intercept it easily and take a shot from the point. Tate stops it with such ease I'm almost embarrassed.

"Too predictable, man." Jamie sends the puck back up toward Haley.

She's flying down the ice—even faster than the day she and I raced—but I catch her and my instincts kick in, and I have to stop myself from attempting to plow her over. Instead, I get in front of her, working on those back crossovers Jamie and Leo have made me do millions of times. Haley fakes left and then sneaks around me, breaking away for the goal. She shoots, but Mike catches it in his glove.

I stand there stunned for several seconds. I look over at Jamie. "Did that just happen?"

"Yeah, we uh, hustled you." Jamie grins. "She is a little rusty, though. All that cheerleading."

"Shut up," Haley snaps.

I refocus, and this time I don't underestimate my opponent. Well, Claire mostly stays out of the way. Leo gets a goal past Tate, and I come close. Twice.

No one scores on Steller.

"Get low, Fletch!" Mike shouts from his end. "Take it and turn."

I do what he says, and next thing I know, I'm spinning in a half circle, the puck in my possession, while Jamie is still moving forward, not yet aware of his loss.

"Yes!" Leo shouts. "That was awesome. Exactly what we've been talking about."

Okay, so maybe Leo and Jamie are right. I'm not moving around in as many directions as I should be.

A few minutes later, I try the same move on Haley. It works, but she's ready for me and quickly turns herself so she can steal the puck again.

"Take it wide," Mike repeats. "Get it turned around and then move it toward the outsides."

I steal the puck from Claire a little bit later, and she shouts after me, "At least I can do a sit spin in my skates."

I try not to laugh and focus on moving past Jamie. When I do, Tate is distracted by Claire—she's most likely sit spinning in her rental skates—and I take a shot. The hesitation on Tate's part is enough to let the goal in.

Leo jumps up and cheers like this was done under normal conditions.

"Tanley, what the hell?" Jamie says. "This is why we don't let our girlfriends play hockey."

I'm high from my goal, regardless of the circumstances. Claire finishes her decent-looking sit spin and does a little curtsy after. "Fletch paid me to throw the game."

"That was Steller," I accuse. I glance at Claire and say, "Watch this."

I skate backward in her direction and throw a double jump. I don't know my axels from sal cows or whatever, but I spend a lot of time on Grandpa's lake in the winter trying shit like this. Always in hockey skates. I land on one skate, but I have to put the other one down right away to get my balance.

"Dude, what the hell was that?" Jamie says.

I shrug. "Don't know. A jump-spin thing."

"I think it was a double axel," Claire suggests. "Maybe

not because you didn't face forward first…I don't know. Do it again."

I shake my head. "Just when I score a goal."

"Which means we might never see it a second time," Claire retorts, then she quickly realizes what she just said. "No, I didn't mean it like that—"

"You don't take back your trash talk, Claire," Tate says.

"We don't trash talk in theater," she explains to me. "It's all about saying something super nice and then jinxing them. Like 'You're going to be so great, I'm sure you'll hit all the big notes.'"

"Nasty," Jamie says, shaking his head.

"All right, next goal wins," Mike says. "My baby is awake at two in the morning. She's gonna revert back to up all night, and we just got that shit figured out. Mostly."

"I rode with Mike," Haley says. "I leave when they leave."

"Okay," Jamie agrees. "Last goal."

It takes ten minutes for Leo to score on Tate. I think Claire distracted him again. Either that, or later activities with Claire motivated him to get the game over with quick.

Before Mike takes off, he says to me, "Bakowski is a dumb-ass if he doesn't use you more this season. And we all know he's not an idiot. So, I'd say your chances are looking good."

I'm pretty much stunned by this, so all I can do is mumble thanks. Haley is quick to grab Jessie and race out the door, maybe to avoid an awkward good-bye with me. That weight presses down on me again, watching her leave. We only have a week of class left. Will I run into her much after that?

The baby worms around and fusses from her car seat. Mike quickly unbuckles her and holds her in one arm, the baby seat in the other. Andi snuggles against Mike's shoulder, her fist in her mouth, drool running down her chin. Her blue eyes are wide open, staring at me and Jamie. A red rash around her mouth, chin, and cheeks catches my attention.

"She's got hives or a rash or something?" I tell Mike.

"Yeah, I know." He sighs. "She's had it on and off since she was a few weeks old. The winter was terrible. Her doctor said it's eczema."

It takes me a second to shut off the panic that comes at the sight of hives. For me, it's almost always sudden and emergency related. This is different, but still not something I'm unfamiliar with. I've practically become a dissertation of food-allergy knowledge. My mom is capable of writing an actual doctrine on the subject, and she has zero medical degrees or certificates. The diaper bag and can of formula flash in my head.

"Dairy can cause eczema," I say, despite a large part of my brain protesting this out-of-character information sharing.

Mike looks at me, his forehead wrinkling. "Well, she's barely started on baby food, so she hasn't had dairy…"

"It can be passed through breast milk." Did I just bring up breast milk to Mike Steller? "And regular formula is dairy based."

"No shit?" Mike says, surprised. "Jessie asked the doctor like a dozen times if it was anything she was eating. I thought Jessie was nuts but…huh. Okay then."

"General practitioners aren't usually great with food reactions. They treat symptoms mostly and rarely dig for the cause." I know this all too well.

"It got so bad they put her on steroids for a while," Mike says. "Have you ever seen a baby juiced up on steroids? It's like we put a double espresso in her bottle."

Jamie is watching this exchange a little too closely. I shift around, uncomfortable with the topic, and Mike takes the hint.

"Thanks, man. I'm gonna look into that dairy shit." He gives me a nod. "Good luck this season."

He's whispering something to Andi on his way out the door, words I can't understand, but whatever he says, she seems to relax against him more, her eyes fluttering shut.

I'm still staring after them when Jamie says in a low, hesitant voice, "That's your bully, Fletch."

I snap around to face him. "What?"

"That's who nearly killed you on the bus in grade school."

"No way." I'm shaking my head, but I don't know why.

"You wanted to know, so I'm telling you." Jamie gives me a shove from behind. "Go on, go kick his ass. I bet he's not even to the car yet. Then it'll take a minute to get the baby all strapped in…go on! Now's your chance to get revenge."

My mouth falls open. No words exit. I look at Jamie and then back at the propped-open door. But I don't go anywhere. My feet stay rooted to their spot.

# Chapter Thirty-Two

## −HALEY−

I thought this late-night activity was a terrible idea, and then it turned out okay and actually fun. But now I'm mourning its loss, reminding me why it was such a bad idea.

I'm smashed in the front seat of Mike's SUV between him and Jessie. Tate, Claire, and Andi are in the back. Probably, my vacant stare and glazed-over eyes are cause for concern, but I'm not the only one silent and staring out a window at nothing on the drive back into town.

Mike is beside me—Jessie's driving—and he's leaning against the window, looking pensive. I've never had a good enough reason to use the word "pensive" until right now. Obviously, I'm going to assume his state of mind is due to Jamie and Leo leaving town, going off the play college hockey and become something Mike himself was set up to become. I feel a pang of regret for him, and then allow myself to sink back into my own confusion and pensiveness. But then Mike says something totally out of left field.

"I don't care if Andi plays hockey or not," he says.

"She has long fingers," Claire points out. "I think you could have a musician on your hands."

Mike shakes his head. "I don't care if she's good at anything. I just want her to be the nice kid, you know? The one who likes everyone, no matter what. I don't ever want to worry about her hurting someone else."

"So basically," Tate says, trying to make light of the grim mood in the car, "you want us to tell you if your kid is giving people shit."

Mike points a finger at him. "Yes."

"Consider it done."

"Think about it," Mike says. "All these competitive sports, competitive-whatever shit we worship in our town...don't you think it's making us into monsters? How many of us in this car were pushed into something as a kid—sports, or music, or dance...?"

Everyone but Jessie lifts a hand.

"See?" Mike sits up, his face more animated and less blank. "And who in this car considered themselves the nice kid in school?"

"Define nice," Claire says.

I'm racking my brain, trying to answer honestly. I did have all those nice-girl comments on my reports over the years, but I was a competitive trash-talker on the athletic fields, and don't even get me started on the manipulation and backstabbing involved with Juniper Falls Princess nominations...

"Not jealous or vindictive, not wishing someone would keel over dead so you could have their spot." Mike swallows and shakes his head. "Not wanting to give someone shit just to prove you have power over some aspect of your life."

"I would raise my hand, but I had too many 'let's bash the

stupid people' sessions with Jody," Claire admits. "We were pretty tactless and judgmental, though rarely to anyone's face."

"I'd raise my hand, but too many fights over the last year would disprove that," Tate says.

I shake my head. "I'm out, too."

"Me, too," Mike says, quietly. "And that leaves…"

"Jessie," we all say in unison.

"You were totally the nice girl," Claire says.

Jessie smiles but keeps her eyes on the road. Mike reaches across me and gives her thigh a squeeze. I immediately feel in the way.

"She got my angry ass to mellow out," Mike admits. "And she didn't get to play hockey or anything like the rest of us. No one breathing down her neck to play better, no one beating the shit out of her when she didn't meet expectations."

"Well, the limits of trailer-park life do have their positives," Jessie jokes. But I can tell by her wistful tone that she may have enjoyed a bit of that parent-breathing-down-her-neck stuff.

"Hey," Mike says to her. "I'm not saying your shit life didn't suck, but it did make you awesome, and that's all I'm sayin'."

"I know." She flashes him another smile.

"We can't go back and undo shit," Mike adds. "All we can do is make sure that our kids are never like that."

Silence falls over the car, and I grow more and more down. About me, about Fletch, about the pieces of my life that feel incomplete and undefined.

When we drive past city limits, Claire tugs on a strand of my hair. "Your parents are still gone, right?" I nod. "Want to stay over at my apartment?"

I turn around to look between Claire and Tate. Tate's mouth opens, possibly in protest. I shake my head. "I don't want to interfere—"

"It's fine," Claire says, throwing Tate a look.

"It's fine," he repeats.

I laugh. "You guys are such bad liars."

"I need a girls' night," Claire says. "He's got me hanging out with jocks all the time, playing hockey, I mean what's next? Scratching my balls?"

Tate bursts out laughing. "You did not just say that."

"Come on, Haley, please," Claire says.

I hold up my hands in surrender. "Fine. I'll stay over." I glance at Tate. "Just note that I did turn down the offer initially."

"Noted," he says, giving Claire that I-would-have-made-it-all-worthwhile look.

She must really be desperate for me to dish the Fletcher Scott gossip. And I know whatever's happened between me and Fletch isn't meant for the town gossip mill, but I think, unlike with Leslie or Kayla, talking to Claire is safe. I need this. I really need this.

"So, you really did put Cheerios up his nose?"

I nod.

"I had no idea that he's allergic to so much," Claire says. "I've seen him at the bar, in the back booth studying and ordering nothing but bottled water...I just figured Manny told him he could hang there without buying anything. If my dad knew this stuff, he'd definitely figure out how to serve him something without killing him."

"I don't think it would matter to Fletch," I say with a sigh. "He doesn't trust restaurants. Like ever. I spent eight hours scrubbing my kitchen top to bottom and removing any food particles from anywhere—I was going to make him some allergy-safe cookies or a pot of soup as a thank-you for the tickets, but I couldn't go through with it. Even I'm scared of killing him."

Claire curls up on her side, facing me. Both of us are pretty zonked, especially after we've polished off a bottle of pink wine Claire swiped from the restaurant kitchen downstairs. "Okay, so Fletch is afraid to trust people, but he gives amazing speeches about empowering women and encouraging them not to get infatuated with him, but to instead get infatuated with being in control over their lives and their feelings. Am I giving an accurate summary?"

I exhale. "Yeah, pretty much."

"And do you feel infatuated with your control or…"

"Not," I admit. I flop back onto Claire's bed and stare at the ceiling for a long minute. By the time I'm looking her way again, her eyelids are fluttering.

"Let's sleep on it, okay?" she mutters.

I yawn, which counts as agreeing. If I don't fall asleep soon, I'll end up witnessing another sunrise. But when I roll onto my side and close my eyes, I'm still wide awake. I pull out my phone and stare at it, the half bottle of wine swimming in my blood and removing inhibitions. If I hadn't seen him tonight, it would be easier to resist.

I type a quick text to Fletch. It's likely he'll be awake. Tomorrow I'll have willpower to ignore any response he may send. Although he hasn't called or texted me since I decided to text him. It's almost like he knew my plan.

**ME: hey, I'm sure u r asleep. Just wanted u to know**

*that Mrs. Markson ended up giving me an A- in Civics*

    *ME: I still feel a little weird about the extra time she gave me and letting me go back and finish the other tests*

    *ME: But she wouldn't do it if she didn't think it was fair…it's not like she's an easy teacher, right?*

    *ME: OK I'm done. 3 texts with no reply means: Haley=pathetic. Oops make that 4 texts*

I start to send a fifth text to apologize — yeah, the wine is getting to me — but my phone vibrates in my hand. I roll over to make sure Claire is still sleeping before glancing at it.

    *FLETCH: Haley=unpathetic and no worries, I'm up*

    *ME: Why? Did Jamie and Leo keep u out all night?*

    *FLETCH: I'm home. Just couldn't sleep*

    *ME: b/c ur lovelorn?*

    *FLETCH: why r u up? R u lovelorn?*

    *ME: no, I'm pathetic, remember? Ur turn*

    *FLETCH: I'm…idk. Hard to explain*

    *ME: doesn't have to be. Complete this sentence: "I'm feeling _____"*

    *FLETCH: conflicted, retrospective, unsatisfied*

    *ME: this has lovelorn written all over it*

I slide carefully out of Claire's bed and head for the back balcony. I dial Fletch's number and wait for him to answer.

"Hey," he says. Already I hear the hesitancy, the walls up.

But he did answer the phone.

"So, what happened? You were thinking about how lovesick you are over me and couldn't sleep?"

He laughs, cutting the tension. "No, it's not that. Jamie told me something tonight—something I thought I wanted to know, and now…"

"You're not so sure," I finish for him.

"Right. I should feel angry or some kind of satisfaction, but I don't." Fletch goes on to explain the reason he left school for a couple years, the incident on the bus and how he didn't know who did it all this time. I keep very quiet, listening to the details, but already my heart is racing, feeling the panic younger Fletch must have felt, the fear of going to school or doing anything normal. And all that is after his parents and grandpa suffered through some nasty side effects of Juniper Falls gossip. "I figured Jamie was just messing with me a few weeks ago. I didn't think he knew who it was."

"Wouldn't they have asked all the kids? It's not hard to scare nine- and ten-year-olds into ratting out a friend," I say, trying to keep from shouting, *oh my God it was Mike Steller!* And now I'm seeing that conversation in the car from a whole new angle. "Conflicted" isn't a strong enough word to describe these feelings. Obviously, this incident stayed with Fletch all this time, but it stayed with Mike, too.

"Jamie says he didn't know until right after," Fletch explains. "I guess a couple of middle-school guys dared Mike to do something to me. They told Mike the whole allergy thing was bullshit and I was just trying to get extra attention at school."

"Okay, but after, wouldn't Mike have told on those guys or something? Stuff always comes out eventually with little kids," I protest.

Fletch sighs. "Jamie said Mike couldn't say anything because his dad would have beat the shit out of him. Of course, I was like, well, my dad probably would have done the same to me if I'd done that. He wouldn't have settled on a lecture and a time-out, that's for sure. And then Jamie said, 'no, he would have *beat* the shit out of him.'"

Yeah, this is probably true. I've heard as much from talking to Jessie. Both she and Mike are determined not to be like either of their parents. That's a tough task in this town.

"I thought I'd find out who did it and everything would make sense. Someone who grew up to be a punk-ass loser," Fletch continues. "But Mike Steller...."

I debate telling him about the conversation in the car. Will it help? Or will it make him more conflicted? "Here's the thing. Not to discredit what you felt on the bus that day, but look at it from Mike's perspective. He had to watch you nearly die and know that he caused that. What do you think that does to a person?"

"He was really cool tonight," Fletch says. "Didn't even think twice about helping me. You'd think he'd be bitter, considering Jamie and Leo are off to college and he was the big talent last season. Or he should have been, at least."

"Why would he be bitter? It was Mike's choice to quit the team and drop out of school." I respect his choices, but I never thought he needed to sacrifice everything just to prove he could be a better parent than his parents.

"I don't know. Guess I don't know much about Mike." Fletch yawns loud enough for me to hear through the phone.

"Look, Fletch, I can't solve this puzzle any better than you can, but I will say that Mike would take it back in a second if he could." I decide to explain Mike's gloomy state on the drive home and his declarations about Andi.

Fletch is silent for several moments after, but he finally says, "If he's thinking about it right in front of me, why doesn't he have the balls to say anything?"

"I'm sure he has the balls to tell you it was him. Jesus, this is the guy who walked out of our arena mid–home game. That's grounds for lynching. He probably saw that you were okay and maybe that his encouragement meant a lot. If he told you, it would devalue that." I lean on the railing, feeling the cool breeze hit my bare legs and arms.

"Haley?" Fletch says. "This thing with us…"

Confidence — and probably alcohol — surges through me, and before he can finish what he'd started to say, I blurt out, "Go out with me."

Oh God, did I just do that? I did. I totally did. "What I mean is that I need a date. For the end-of-summer dance. I'm on the planning committee, and it looks really bad if I show up alone."

"And I'm the right person for this job?" Fletch says, not even trying to hide the disbelief in his voice.

My hands are literally shaking. My insides are twisting into a tight ball, but still I reach for the most honest response I can offer. "You're the only person I wanted to ask."

Silence of the absolute worst kind falls between us. And then finally he says, "Haley, I can't do that. I just…"

Okay, so this hurts a little more than I expected. Maybe because I've never really asked anyone out before. Maybe because this is the first time I've put myself in a position to be rejected by Fletch.

"Is there anything you would do with me? Like on a date?" Clearly, I'm a glutton for punishment. "A movie?"

"I haven't been to a movie theater since I had my first anaphylactic reaction," he says. "Look, Haley, you're beautiful and smart and funny, and I love hanging out with you, but — "

"You can't be seen with me," I finish for him. "Or in the town you actually live in. You can't ever be the one to kiss me. You never kissed me, did you know that? I always made that first move. You can't put yourself out there."

"It's not that simple, and you know it."

There's a finality in his voice that I know means we're done. With this conversation. With hanging out. With everything. But I already knew that. Our talk earlier was just more moves that went nowhere, that led back to this inevitable draw.

"Okay," I concede. "You win. Or it's a draw or whatever. I'm officially done trying. I didn't even want to try in the first place, but here I am, four weeks of summer school and half a bottle of wine later..."

"Haley, wait—"

"See you around, Fletch." I hang up before he can say something sweet or cute or sexy. Or infuriating. It's done. Like summer. Like a bag of cotton candy at the circus. Eventually you hit the bottom of the bag.

Even I'm smart enough to walk away while my head is still up, my heart mostly intact. Mostly.

# Chapter Thirty-Three

-FLETCHER-

"Scott," Coach shouts from his office when I pass by his open door. "Get in here!"

Tanley, who just appeared at my side from the locker room, lifts an eyebrow. I'm frozen outside the door, my heart racing. What does he want with me? Did I screw up in practice this morning? I replay the entire two hours. I did some kick-ass maneuvering around Stewart, but Bakowski didn't say anything to me about it. He just barked insults at Stewart.

Tate gives me a nudge. "It's fine, man."

I shuffle into the small office and stand awkwardly in front of Coach's desk. Ty is seated in a chair in the corner of the room. He's the head JV coach, so I'm more skilled at reading his face than Bakowski's. Ty makes eye contact and nods to the empty chair across from the desk.

I don't sit until Bakowski barks, "Sit, son."

My backpack falls to the floor, and my ass falls into the

chair. I try not to fidget with my hands. Bakowski stares me down, his fingers drumming on the desk.

"I'll be frank with you, I wasn't planning on keeping you on my team after the summer," he says. My stomach sinks, my face heating up. Seniors can't play JV, so this means I'm out. "But…"

Ty's pen freezes in his hand. He exhales at the same moment as I do.

"You're a scrapper," Bakowski says. "And you aren't taking no for an answer. That goes a long way with me."

I don't even attempt to mumble thank you, because I still have no idea where this is going.

"The Longmeadow scrimmage game next month is how I pick my lineup. Always," Coach says. "As of now, I'm tossing Johnson back to JV. He's young, I figured that would happen but wanted to test the waters. Now it seems we've got a space open when the real season starts. If the scrimmage goes well, then maybe…"

I stare at him for a good five seconds before saying, "Wait…so I'm in? For the game?"

"You're in," he confirms. "Now let's see how you do."

"Yes, sir." I nod.

Bakowski leans forward, his hands clasped on the desk in front of him. "But you need to keep your personal stuff personal, understood? Longmeadow or any other team in the division gets ahold of that information, and I wouldn't be surprised if they use it against us. I can't have that kind of trouble on my team."

Yeah, I get it. I worry about this every single day of my life.

"Don't talk about it with the other guys, don't talk to myself or Ty except in private situations like this one. Think you can handle that?"

"Yes, sir," I say with another nod.

"Go on." He waves a hand, dismissing me. "Give Beverly at the rental counter your info. She'll get you a varsity uniform."

Still dazed, I head out of the office, and my first thought is to go right to Civics and tell Haley the good news. Except Mrs. Markson canceled our last class. She said we'd covered everything and didn't need it. Haley's at cheer practice right next door, I'm sure. But she made it clear that I'm either in her life fully or...not. And I don't even know how to begin being someone who hangs around town with Haley Stevenson. I can't give her what she wants.

I walk outside alone—Cole still has Health class today—and head for my car in the near-empty lot. Practically the entire summer thus far, I haven't been able to avoid having Haley or Jamie pop up in my personal space out of nowhere, making me anxious and on guard. I just didn't realize how much I'd grown to expect and even enjoy them being around. Makes it a little harder to go back to my old ways.

And then before I can stop myself, I shoot a quick text to Jamie and Leo.

**ME: *Bakowski gave me a varsity spot for the Longmeadow game***

Both guys respond at some point during the ten-minute drive home from practice.

**JAMIE: *about time***

**LEO: *you earned a spot. Nobody gave you anything.***

• • •

don't know exactly why Haley's at the club tonight. She couldn't have known I'd be here, because up until twenty minutes ago, I didn't know I'd be here. I've never felt the urge to step through these doors on Manhattan Club nights.

I slide behind a tall guy and prepare to work my way to the door. Haley wouldn't be too excited to find out that I'm here, considering our last conversation. Plus, she's brought girlfriends—Claire, Leslie, and Kayla. The last thing I need is Leslie and Kayla telling everyone in town about my job. I glance down at my clothes and remember that I'm not dressed for work—no dress shirt and pants, no heeled ballroom shoes. If any of them spot me, it wouldn't be social suicide. Tonight is definitely designed for cool people. Yet another reason why I'm never here on Thursdays.

Haley heads over to the bar alone. I keep an eye on her while she orders. My mouth falls open in shock when, after flashing an ID, she receives a tray of shot glasses. I'm about to go over and question this new bartender, but someone taps me on the shoulder.

I spin around, and I'm face-to-face with literally the last person I ever expected to see here—Tate Tanley.

"Dude, what are you doing here?" he says.

"Uh…my brother. He's a bartender." My gaze flits to the bar and back to Tanley. "Just finished up his shift. I'm on my way out, too, actually."

"You're leaving?" He looks disappointed. "I'm dying here. Claire dragged me. She and Haley have been coming the last few weeks, but she says she's sick of dancing with girls."

So, this isn't Haley's first Thursday-night club night. "Was that your way of asking me to stick around?"

Tate nods. "Pretty much."

On the other side of the bar, all four girls down shots,

and then they head for the middle of the dance floor, making it even more difficult for them to spot me. It's weird being here without the stage, without everyone noticing me, just another guy in the club. It's more like the School Me.

"I'm gonna need a drink for this," I tell Tate, and we head toward the bar. I order a vodka tonic and hand the bartender one of Braden's old IDs. Luckily, he doesn't look too closely, because I don't resemble my brother at all. I ask Tate what he wants. He shakes his head and holds up a set of keys.

He's just moved up to martyr status in my book, taking on the job of getting four drunk girls into the car and home later on.

We shift away from the bar and hang back off to the side. Tate just stands there, looking painfully uncomfortable, his hands stuffed in his pockets. He should probably be the one drinking.

"If Jamie and Leo knew I was here, I'd never hear the end of it."

I stare down at my drink, trying not to laugh. "They might surprise you."

He gives me a long look like he knows I'm keeping some big secrets. Then he nods toward the dance floor. "You into this?"

I shrug. "Sometimes."

I can't exactly say no. Kinda creepy showing up here alone just to watch. Especially considering that I don't have a girlfriend who coerced me into being a designated driver.

"Well, I'm not," he states.

"Which part are you not into?" I take a long drink. "The loud music? Crowded floor? Handsy dudes with exposed chest hair? Or the dancing?"

"Mostly the dancing," he admits.

But even while he says all this, he's focused on Claire,

probably watching for handsy guys making a move on his girlfriend. We stand there for several minutes not talking. It's pretty hard to carry on a conversation at this volume. Tate is busy watching the girls, and I'm busy polishing off my drink, trying to decide if I wanna risk helping him a little. Normally I wouldn't consider it. But I think being at the club—I mean it's kind of what we do here—makes things a little different.

"This music," I tell Tate, half shouting now. "It's either about jumping up and down a lot or being loose. Don't overthink it."

He scratches the back of his head. "Yeah, that doesn't help at all."

From the corner of my eye, I can see Angel in Ricky's office, the black dry-erase marker we use to update the calendar poised in her hand. She stops when she spots me. I nod for her to come out here.

Soon she's in front of me, all curious and nosy. I point a finger at Tate, who's trying to figure out what I'm doing.

"This is one of my teammates," I tell Angel. "Tate, this is Angel…she's a friend of my brother's."

Her eyebrows lift. "Right. A friend of Braden's. That I am."

"Tate's a dance virgin," I tell her.

"I'm not—" He protests but then stops, probably wanting to see where I'm going with this.

I turn Angel around so her back is to me. I'm about to show Tate where to put his hands, but she stops me. "Wait…I need to channel my eighteen-year-old self for this music." I give her a second, and finally she says she's ready.

"Hands here…" I direct, laying them on Angel's hips. I give him a few more tips, and Tate listens about as intently as I do when Jamie and Leo are helping me with hockey stuff. This kind of dancing, this music, not exactly my scene, but still, it's not rocket science.

Angel turns to Tate after our short little demo. "See? It's easy. Now which girl do you have your eye on? I can feel out the situation for you."

"That would be the tall redhead in the center," I answer for Tate. "His girlfriend."

"Your girlfriend?" Angel says, and then she gives Tate her most warm smile, the motherly one. "You've got nothing to worry about. She already likes you. Effort goes a long way."

Claire looks over this way, goading Tate with her eyes. I give him a shove in that direction, and he surprises me by walking straight over there, no hesitation. Angel and I lean against the wall, watching him and Claire dance together. Claire is smiling a lot, and Tate surprisingly shows no signs of being rhythmically challenged.

I hold a hand out to Angel, and she slaps me a low five. "Nice work, partner."

"What would the world do without us?"

Angel goes back into Ricky's office, and I stay in my spot, my gaze glued to Haley in her short pink dress with lip gloss to match. Her hair is down and flowing everywhere in a sexy, I just had a hot make-out session way. My pulse quickens just thinking the word make-out with Haley in sight. Soon, I'm pushing off the wall, heading in her direction. Even though I shouldn't. Even though it was me who turned her down a couple of weeks ago. But Tate would have outed me anyway, right?

She sees me when I'm still a few feet away, and the smile drops from her face. I almost disappear back into the crowd, because that isn't the reaction I'd been hoping for. But who am I kidding? She doesn't owe me any reaction at all.

But then she's right in front of me, arms crossed,

eyebrows lifted. "How did you know I was here?"

I shake my head. "I didn't. Tate caught me leaving and asked me to hang out."

For a long moment, we look at each other, both of us trying to decide how this will go. Finally, Haley wraps her fingers around my shirt and tugs me toward her little crew. She gives me this stare from over her shoulder, rolls her eyes, and says, "Same old Fletch, huh?"

Same old Fletch. Unwilling. Being dragged into Haley's life. That thought sits heavily in the pit of my stomach, and suddenly I don't give a fuck about her friends watching. Or Tanley being here.

I reach for her, drag her body against mine, feel her breath catch, her mouth fall open in surprise. But she doesn't stop me. The music gets faster, louder, like it's inside me and all around. I stop thinking about eight counts and posture and downbeats. Haley molds herself to me, and we easily move together. I press my face into her hair, inhale. Her hands are everywhere—sliding over my chest, my back, under my shirt.

Soon I'm consumed by thoughts of the last conversation we had, Haley saying I didn't even have the balls to kiss her. She's the one who did it first. She's right. And now all I can think about is proving her wrong. I step out of her hold, grasp her hand, and head her off the dance floor.

Normally, I'd never pull a girl away from her friends or take her somewhere alone without asking first. But with Haley, I don't have to ask. I simply think the question, and I can feel her answer.

My heart is pounding, my thoughts in a haze, as I lead her through the dark backstage and fumble around for the dressing-room doorknob. And then I fling it open, tug her inside, and press her against the door. The music is faint in the background. Even in the dark, I see her chest rise and fall with rapid speed.

*You've never even kissed me, Fletch. You won't do it. You won't put yourself out there.*

We both take a quick breath together, our hearts pounding in the dark. And then I lift her off the ground, her dress hiking up, her legs wrapping around me. Maybe I haven't made the first move before, but I sure as hell have imagined it.

# Chapter Thirty-Four

My back collides with the wall the same moment Fletch's mouth collides with mine.

I can't breathe. I can't think.

All I can do is feel. All of it. Everything. Like Fletch's arm locked around my waist. His other hand in my hair. The softness of his lips. The thudding of his heart. I barely remember walking in here. Not that I even know where here is. It's dark. I don't care. I just want…need…

"I need…" I breathe out the words without meaning to. My legs tighten around his waist, my dress sliding higher up my thighs.

"You need?" he prompts. Fletch moves his mouth to my neck. "Need to stop?"

"God, no."

He shifts me, pressing more of my weight into the door, freeing one of his hands. Warm fingers brush over my satin panties. I inhale sharply, the scent of fresh flowers filling my nostrils.

"This," he says.

Not a question. Tonight, I'm with Decisive Fletch. Observant Fletch. The Fletcher Scott who takes context clues to a whole new level.

His mouth is on mine again, my fingers slip into his hair, and I'm so far from nervous, far from self-conscious. I couldn't find my way back there even if I wanted to.

His hand moves into the little space between us, beneath my dress, and his fingers find their way to my breasts. I pull my lips from his, a sigh escaping. Fletch pauses, his body tensing. Then he takes a few steps sideways, and suddenly I'm perched on the edge of what feels like a shelf.

Lips are on my shoulder now, my collar bone, the straps of my dress slipping down. I dig my heels into Fletch's back and drag him even closer. Just when I'm about to grab his hand and put it back in the vicinity of my panties, he does it himself, gently moving his fingers over the thin satin material, while his lips are much more rough against mine. The dark world blurs all around me and then sharpens, allowing me to see the angles of his face, the muscles in his arms, gripping me tight.

I'm lost. A million times lost. Hurtling toward something new. And just when I'm a heartbeat away, I realize what's happening. "Wait…"

But it's too late. It hits too fast. My fingers press into Fletch's back, my head falling against his shoulder. The blood pumping in my ears makes it hard to hear him whispering to me. At first it sounds like he's calling me baby, which doesn't really seem like a Fletch thing. And I realize baby rhymes with Haley, and then the idea of Fletcher Scott whispering my name while *that* is happening brings me even further over this cliff.

I'm soaring too high to have any control. I grab Fletch's

face and kiss him. Hard. My fingers knot in his hair, and I don't even know what I'm saying, but I'm saying something against his lips.

He laughs, light, sexy, his warm breath touching my lips. "Was that English?"

Now I'm waking up from the haze. Almost as quickly as I got there. My face heats up. Maybe he didn't notice? *Just kiss him again.* I'm leaning toward him, ready to dive in, when the door opens a crack. Without warning, light fills the space we're in. I squint and look around—it's a dressing room, I think.

Fletch has this puzzled look on his face like he's trying to figure me out. My cheeks burn all over again.

"Anyone in here?" a female voice says. "Counting to five and then I'm entering. With a child."

I press my hands into Fletch's chest, shoving him back, and then I hop down, righting my dress. I look at him again and have to look away. God, he must think I'm...

But I don't know what. Desperate? Loud? Great at moaning?

Jesus Christ. I gotta get out of here.

Fletch says something to whoever is trying to enter, and the door shuts again. But I've got it open in two seconds. "I better go back—" I stop because I don't want to make this worse.

"Haley, wait."

I give him one last look and then turn beet-red again. "Sorry," I mutter before stepping out of the door.

A small light is now on backstage, and I almost knock over Fletch's dance partner, Angel. She's got a dark-haired crying toddler in her arms. She opens her mouth to say something, but I get embarrassed all over again and walk away, practically at a jog.

Kayla and Leslie are still busy dancing with each other,

they might not have noticed me leave. And Tate and Claire haven't moved spots, either. I head straight for the bar, hoping I don't get carded again, because Leslie has my purse. I step in line behind a few people. I can't get my heart to slow down. I close my eyes and draw in a breath, but this just puts me back in that dark room, Fletch lifting my dress, his skillful hands moving over me.

*Fuuuuuck.*

I shake out my arms and give myself a pep talk—be cool. No big deal. God, I don't think I'll be able to smell flowers again without seeing—

"As your designated driver," Tate says, appearing out of nowhere, "it's my duty to advise you to drink lots of water with your booze."

"Water," I repeat. "Got it."

He's standing beside me. Not going anywhere. And then I realize he's studying me. "You look…have you been—"

"Shut up," I snap. "Just don't."

"Yeah. Okay." Tate turns to face forward again. "You might want to fix your dress."

I glance down. My dress is shifted so far over, my right boob is practically hanging out. That was probably what Angel tried to tell me before I took off.

While I'm adjusting my clothing, I sneak a peek at Tate—for Claire's sake—and his eyes are trained on the head in front of him. Good boy.

I exhale. Fletch is probably back there laughing at me. Or comparing me to all the other much older, much more experienced women he's been with.

# Chapter Thirty-Five

## —FLETCHER—

Angel knocks on the door again. I'm sure she's figured out that I'm in here. Maybe wondering why I haven't followed Haley out. But I'm in no condition to leave. I shake my arms out, trying to calm myself. And then I lean over the sink and splash some cold water on my face.

"Baby Scott," Angel says in her the-kid-is-with-me voice. "If you're gonna be a while, can you just toss the diaper bag out in the hall?"

Josie is crying now. Loudly.

My breathing hasn't returned to normal yet, but other parts of me have. Mostly. Crying babies certainly help the cause. I exhale and then open the door and stand half behind it. Angel steps inside and immediately turns to face me. "That good, huh?"

I glare at her.

She dumps the crying kid on the floor and goes digging for a pacifier in the diaper bag. "I'm completely jealous. I haven't had dressing-room sex in forever."

Angel hands Josie the pacifier and then lifts her up again. "I have got to ask Bobby why we never have dressing-room sex anymore."

I'm still not breathing normal. I know I'm gonna get hell for this, but I have no choice but to pull out the inhaler and take a puff. I point a finger at Angel. "Don't."

"Nope. Not saying anything," she mutters. Josie popped that pacifier in, and now her head is on her mom's shoulder, her eyes closed.

My lungs expand, my breathing deeper and more solid. I could go back out there now. Talk to Haley. Check on her. But something stops me. Confusion. I don't know what just happened. I glance at Angel then back at the door. This repeats a few times.

"What?" she says, rolling her eyes. "I know you want to tell me."

I toss the inhaler back in my bag and lean against the wall. "I'm not sure—I mean..."

"This must be a feelings question, because you don't usually have any trouble talking about more physical topics," she concludes. She lays Josie on her belly on the couch and pats her back in this hypnotic pattern.

"It is physical," I say eventually. "Did Haley seem upset when she left?"

Angels thinks for a moment. "She seemed embarrassed."

"That's what I thought, too." I walk a few paces. "I mean it was weird...good. Really good. But weird."

"What was weird? The sex?"

"No sex." I shake my head. "We were just kissing, but I think she...I mean I know she..."

Angel's eyebrows rise again. "Oh. No wonder she was embarrassed."

I stare at her. "Orgasms are embarrassing to girls?"

"Sometimes." Angel laughs at my expression. "Wouldn't you be embarrassed if things went prematurely on your end?"

"Well, yeah," I agree. Been there, done that. Grew out of that, thank God. "But it's different. Most girls would want that to happen, so it can happen again. Later."

"You're comparing Haley to Rosie and Henrietta—"

"Haley is nothing like Henrietta," I say. Jesus. What the hell?

"I just mean all the girls in your life are too busy playing your teacher to be self-conscious. I'm glad I stayed out of that game, but I'm not an idiot. I know what's going on. I know who you hook up with and exactly what went down." She wrinkles her nose. "Or *who*."

I open my mouth to protest but decide there's no point. Not a lot of secrets around here. Plus, outside of my crush on a dancer way too old for me a couple of years ago, I've never been embarrassed about anything I've done in that realm.

"I'm sure we've all given you an unrealistic perspective. Plus, how old is Haley? Sixteen? Seventeen? When I was her age, orgasms were not a part of sex—"

"Wait…what?"

She laughs. "See? We messed you up. First sexual experiences are not pleasurable for most girls, especially if you're young like Haley."

I let that sink in for a second, but then I remember something. "She's not a virgin. And she seems to be into honesty in that area. Guess that could be a new thing?"

Angel's face lights up. "Oh! Maybe Haley is having one of those sexual awakenings, where it's all about being physical and owning her body and her pleasure. Could be her summer project." She waves a finger at me. "If that's true, she picked the right guy. You refused to date her but will make out with her. You're attentive, yet detached."

It's like someone sucker punched me right in the stomach. For a second I can't breathe, and my stomach ties up in knots. I barely register Angel standing in front of me, offering her water bottle. I shake my head.

"That bothers you, doesn't it? Being her boy toy." She gives me that know-it-all look. "This *is* about feelings, Fletch."

I close my eyes and pinch the bridge of my nose.

"Look at me." Angel rests a hand on my arm and waits for me to turn my head. "You're gonna fall in love with this girl. You can't stop it from happening, no matter how hard you try. But I promise you, it'll be okay. We've all been crazy in love. We've all had our hearts broken. You. Will. Be. Okay."

"But what about everyone else and my town and—"

"It won't matter. Just tell her how you feel, that you're ready, and none of that will matter anymore."

I want to protest, to give her a list of carefully thought-out, logical arguments to everything she just claimed to be fact. But I can't. I'm too busy freaking the fuck out. I need to find Haley. I leave Angel standing there in the dressing room, and I'm out the door, back in the club in no time. I search the dance floor, the beating music hitting me right in the heart.

I'm frozen for a moment, the memory of Haley's fingers pressing into my back, her incoherent words against my lips. I don't want to love her. I don't want to fall in love with anyone.

But I'm not sure I have a choice with this girl.

Haley is nowhere in sight, so I look for Tate. He's taller, and I know he wouldn't leave if any of the girls were still here. But he's not here. Still, I keep searching, even asking a girl to check the bathroom for me, but no Haley. Or Claire or

Tate. I send Haley a quick text asking her if she left, but ten minutes later, no answer. I head back to the dressing room where Angel is waiting patiently for me to return.

"Well?" she prompts. "How did it go?"

"She's not here." I turn around, checking the room, as if Haley may have hidden here or something.

"Do you know where she went?"

"No idea." I shake my head, but then I remember. "I do know who she's with. Technically I could call him—"

Angel gives me this look, and I shut my mouth and dial Tate's number.

"Hey, Fletch…did we leave something behind?"

"Um, no, I don't think so. Is Haley with you?"

"Uh-huh. We're heading to Wilson's party. He's got that big house near Lake Cameron." Tate seems to turn down the loud background music and protests follow. "If you want to stop by."

"Okay, thanks, man." I hang up before he can ask me why I really called. I turn to Angel. "Whatever I was gonna tell her will have to wait until tomorrow. She's going to some jock-infested party."

"Well, aren't you a jock? Can't you go to that party and talk to her?" Angel presses.

I eye her warily. "Tomorrow sounds better."

"Yeah, because it feels real good to sit on that kind of embarrassment for fourteen hours."

The arguments turn over and over in my head until I finally release a groan and say, "Will you give me a ride? I just had a vodka tonic."

She smiles. "I'd love to."

# Chapter Thirty-Six

Claire shifts on the blanket beside me. "How do you know he's laughing about this?"

I roll over and press my face into the blanket, feeling the cool grass beneath it. Music drifts from Nick Wilson's house. We came outside to escape it, but the *boom, boom, boom* of the bass carries farther than I'd thought possible. And all it does is take me back to the dance floor with Fletch. Why did I dance with him? Why did I let him take me backstage? Why can't I stop hanging out at his place of employment?

"Haley?" Claire prompts. "How do you know he's laughing at you? How do you know what he's thinking if you just ran off?"

"I don't know that he's laughing at me, okay?" I admit, and then I turn over to look at her. "But that doesn't mean I don't wish it had gone differently. That I'd been more in control of the situation. More experienced. I mean I just let him…"

"What?" Claire asks, a grin sliding across her face. "Pleasure you? Meet your every need—"

I reach up and cover her mouth with my hand. Why did I have to tell her? I shoot a glance at the two guys standing near the lake, only about twenty feet from where we're sitting. "Tate is right over there," I hiss. "It's already weird that I told you."

Which is why I couldn't tell Claire that what happened with Fletch was kind of a first for me. Yeah, Tate and I had sex when we were together, and he definitely tried his best to be considerate and unselfish, but still that never really happened for me. We were too young, too inexperienced for it to be amazing. But in the event that Claire and Tate are having mind-blowing sex together, my own pride is a bit too fragile to explain to her why tonight was more monumental for me than it may seem.

"Still don't get how Leslie and Kayla missed you disappearing with Fletch," Claire says.

"I know, right? What's the point of safety in numbers if your numbers don't notice that you're missing?" Although, if I'm being honest, had it been the other way around, had any of them disappeared, I wouldn't have seen a thing. I was way too absorbed in Fletch.

God, Fletch.

He's still on my skin. In my head. In my panties.

I groan and return to pressing my face into the ground. My head is throbbing. I've had too many drinks tonight. And a lot of excitement. "No more club. Don't let me go back there no matter what I say, deal?"

"We can revisit that request," Claire says. "But first, what if we employ a little basic logic? Fletcher made it clear he can't do the girlfriend/boyfriend thing with you—"

"Oh, so clear," I say. A lump forms in my throat thinking

about that last phone call, my stupid idea to ask him out. Like I'm so great that I can make anyone say yes. Didn't work with Tate; sure as hell didn't work with Fletcher.

"But," Claire offers. "He's obviously into you. He wants you in some way, maybe not in the way you want. But if we're being logical, this means you can have something from him, just not everything. The question is—"

"Is that enough for me," I finish. I sit up, slowly allowing that question to sink in. In the moment, I didn't need anything else. Couldn't think about anything but the feel of him, the taste of him. But now...?

"If you're enjoying yourself," Claire says, "what's the harm in continuing?"

"That's the thing, it is fun," I admit. "Well, it was until I asked him out and he shut down all hope of anything in the future. But if we go back to that, what happens when things in my life aren't so fun? What if I'm in a crisis and I really need someone?" I look her in the eye. "What if Tate was only willing to be the guy for you who shows up after closing time at the bar for hot make-out sessions? What if he wasn't willing to stick around when your dad got sick or when that guy tried to attack you? Would that be enough for you?"

Claire's face grows serious. She shifts her gaze to her hands. "No, it wouldn't."

"That's what I thought." My heart drops to the pit of my stomach. "So yeah, I definitely can't go back to that club."

"But is it like that for you and Fletch?" Claire says, her forehead wrinkling. "Is it just hot make-out sessions after closing time?"

As if someone hit the rewind button, I replay the events of my summer. Fletch trying his best to explain complicated outline structures to a distracted me. Fletch showing up at my house with Vixen to apologize for being an asshole. Fletch admitting to me how much he loves to play hockey. Watching the sunrise on the roof of his barn. Dancing in my basement. Him holding my hair while I barfed and pleading with Mrs. Markson to give me a retest. All the details roll over me in layers upon layers.

Slowly I shake my head. "No, it hasn't been all about the make-out sessions, but he said he didn't want—"

"To go to a stupid town dance with you," Claire points out. She's got that look on her face that people get when they think they've figured out something before you have. "My mom used to tell me not to judge a guy by what he says, but instead to pay attention to what he actually does. I think she wanted to make sure I didn't fall victim to some sweet-talker, but what I'm saying is that Fletcher hasn't promised you something and then broken that promise, right?"

Something about that advice and the way she worded that last thing about promises sends a punch of guilt through me. She's right. Fletch didn't promise me anything. But still he gave and he gave on many occasions. And then I pushed him. Like I always seem to do when I really want something.

And I really want him.

"It wasn't fair, was it? When I asked him out?" I say to Claire, though I'm really talking to myself. "I knew he wasn't ready, and then it's like I gave him an ultimatum—either date me or never speak to me again."

Claire opens her mouth to argue but instead bites down on her lower lip, likely seeing my point.

I spring to my feet, feeling both guilty and energized. I free my phone beneath my dress strap where I'd stowed it. "So, I'll call him. I'll tell him I'm sorry for running off and for pushing him and just…" I look at Claire for more, but she's focused on something inside the house. "And whatever.

We'll just go from there. It's a good start, right?"

"You could call him," Claire mutters, her eyes now wide. "Or you could just tell him in person."

I pivot to face the house and, sure enough, Fletcher Scott is pushing through the crowded living room, heading for the back-patio door.

# Chapter Thirty-Seven

## -FLETCHER-

This living room is packed to the brim, worse than the club on Saturday night. My stomach is churning, my heart racing, my neck beginning to itch. The urge to turn around and flee the scene grows stronger with each pair of curious eyes that lands on me. But it's too late. I've already decided. Angel is right. My only job right now is to tell Haley that I want to be with her. The rest will sort itself out later. But damn, I wish she hadn't taken off like she did. It would be so much easier if we could have this talk at the club. On my home turf. Because a big high-school party at a football player's house is so far from home turf for me, I might need a passport.

I spot Leslie standing near the sofa, but before I can ask her if she knows where Haley is, she points a finger at me, her eyes narrowed. "Hey…I know you!"

Her words mush together in a drunk and disorderly way. The chances of her being helpful are slim to none. "Yeah, you called me an elf once."

"God, Haley's right, I am a bitch," Leslie says, and then because I needed more shit to deal with, she dunks her head and starts shaking with sobs.

Jesus Christ.

"Don't beat yourself up over it." I give her a small pat on the shoulder and quickly turn my back.

When I've got some distance from Leslie, I scan the room for Haley and come up empty. But right near the back door, my gaze lands on someone who I hadn't anticipated being here.

Cole.

He's got a beer in one hand and appears to be telling an animated story to one of our teammates.

This is great. Just great.

I release a frustrated breath and head straight over to Cole. The look on his face when he sees me, though, is almost worth all the discomfort of being here at this party. Almost. I snatch the beer from his hand and pass it to a girl standing a few feet away.

Cole's face reddens, but he separates himself from the little group he'd been chatting up. "What are you doing here?"

"Babysitting you, apparently," I say. "How did you get here—" I stop myself and refocus on tonight's objective. "You know what? I don't care. Just don't move from this living room. No one at this party is giving you a ride home, got it?"

His gaze darts left and right. He scratches the back of his head, clearly embarrassed, but he nods.

Maybe I should just call Braden to come pick us up now and call it a night. But then I remember what Angel said about Haley stewing in her embarrassment or whatever for fourteen hours. Truth is, I don't know exactly what's going on in her head. I just know that she was with me and she left upset, and I can't wait until the morning to fix this.

Even though it goes against all my instincts, I exhale and then say to Cole, "Have you seen Haley?"

"Yeah, she's out—" He stops, his eyes wider than when he spotted me here. "That's why you came? For Haley?"

"Maybe…I mean yes." I scrub a hand over my face. "I just need to talk to her."

Before he tells me where she is, I spot her through the glass back doors. She's standing on a blanket in the grass, her cell phone clutched in one hand. My heart picks up speed. My hand is on the doorknob. But I turn quickly to Cole. "I meant what I said. Stay right here."

By the time I get the door open, she's spotted me.

And suddenly this is all so much more real. She knows I'm here. I came to say something. My chest tightens, my steps grow heavier, but my resolve is still intact. All the eyes at this party could watch me, and I'd still want to tell her what I came to say.

Claire had been sitting on the blanket in the grass, but she scrambles to her feet as if preparing to make an exit. Tate, who probably doesn't have a clue what may have gone down between me and Haley, lifts a hand to wave at me.

"Hey, man. You came!"

Claire rushes over to stop him from coming closer, and soon I'm standing in front of Haley, scared as hell, but here.

Her hair is still tangled from our make-out session, her dress is a bit wrinkled now, but she looks gorgeous and perfect and so many other things I can't seem to articulate. Freakin' hell, Angel is right. I am definitely falling in love with this girl.

She stares up at me for several seconds, and I'm about

to dive in to what I came to tell her, but then she says, "I was just going to call you."

"You were?" That's a little surprising.

"I'm sorry," she blurts out.

"Sorry?" I feel my forehead wrinkle. "Don't apologize for…what happened at the club. If you were feeling uncomfortable—"

Her face flames. "No, not for that. I'm sorry for asking you out. Especially the way I did it."

"I shouldn't have said no." Before she can ask for clarification, I step closer and reach for her hand. Slowly, I tangle our fingers until they're locked together. "What I should have said is that I don't know if I can handle a town dance, but I want to be with you. I want to be able to call you and see you and talk to you and all the other yous that we haven't even thought of."

"What about—" she starts to protest.

I touch my free hand to her lips. "Can we do that? Can we just be together and figure out all that other shit later?"

She uses our linked hands to tug me closer and then lifts my fingers up for me to see them. "Your hand is shaking." Concerned, she rests her other hand on my chest. "Your heart is racing."

"Just nerves," I reassure her. "I'm a little out of my comfort zone. And a little too close to a beautiful girl to keep my pulse in check."

A hint of a smile crosses her face. She still hasn't answered my question. "We should make a contract…"

"A contract?"

"You know," she says, looking up at me. "So we can list all the things you're open to and all of your hard nos—big town events, definitely no. Jock parties—maybe. Bondage, nudity, role play…probably."

Relief washes over me. I bring her closer until her head rests against my chest, then I kiss her hair, her temple, her cheek. "No contract. I promise I'll be much harder to get rid of from now on."

The way her body relaxes against mine, I know that I've finally said the right thing. And even with the nosy onlookers, I lift her chin until she's looking at me and then kiss her in a way that most people might reserve for when they're alone.

Eventually, Haley pulls away, glances around, and then says, "Want to get out of here?"

"That would be a hard yes."

# Chapter Thirty-Eight

## -HALEY-

I come out of the shower to find Fletch in my bedroom, spinning in a slow circle, taking it in.

"You cleaned…" He's still gawking at the spot where the magazines had been. "You really cleaned. This is pretty incredible."

After the kitchen-scrubbing session, I moved on to my bedroom. Something I've needed to do for a while. "My parents are gonna flip when they get back." I stare at Fletcher, looking oh-so-sexy in my bedroom. The shock of him showing up at the party hasn't worn off yet, and I'm not sure how much I can throw at him in one night. But the truth spills out anyway. "I just kept thinking about you being in here, and how it's so messy and I don't have a clue what's in this room, and what if you came over again and there were peanut crumbs hiding somewhere—"

The look he gives me is so intense, so welcoming, words get stuck in my throat. He crosses the room in two seconds flat, and then his hands are on my face. And then his mouth is on mine, and I'm in heaven. This is what I've been waiting for from him all along. This kiss. One with layers and layers of us and what we're willing to do for each other.

The towel I'd wrapped my hair up in falls to the floor, startling both of us into coming up for air. Fletch takes another moment to look around at the tidy room. There's actually nothing on my bed except blankets. That hasn't happened in years, probably.

"Can't believe you cleaned your room for me," he says, practically under his breath.

My face heats up, but I brave the honest path. "There are a lot of things I would do for you. Cleaning my room is just one of them."

As if to prove that my new habits are here to stay, I scoop the towel from the floor and hang it over my desk chair.

Fletcher shifts from one foot to the other, looking uncomfortable for the first time since his brother dropped us off here thirty minutes ago. "I guess it bothers me...some."

"It's too much?" Worry eats at my insides. I shouldn't have told him why I cleaned it. He didn't ask. "I mean, it isn't like I meant to announce it to you or anything. You—or more like your situation—got me thinking about being clean as more than just a personal preference. It's a safety issue. Andi is here sometimes, and she's always getting these rashes—"

"Haley," Fletch says, his voice and his eyes full of warmth. "It's not too much at all. Not in that way. Just that I hate that you even have to think about these things. A month or two ago, it didn't matter. And now it does. Because of me."

Suddenly, a whole lot of things about Fletcher Scott make sense. The biggest item being his anti-relationship history. "That's what bothers you? That it might be too much for someone you get close with? Too much for me?"

He releases a breath and then nods. "Maybe not at first, but eventually it'll get old. Dealing with my shit. Never eating in restaurants, probably never here, either. All the handwashing and gargling with Listerine just so you can touch me." He looks away, runs a finger over the quilt on my bed. "I know my family will do whatever they need to, but anyone else? It's always seemed like too much to ask. So, I make a point not to put someone in a position of needing to change."

His eyes meet mine again, steady and strong, a hint of challenge as if he still expects that I might bail. "Not that I sat down one day and made a big decision to avoid…" He gestures from me to him. "Whatever you want to call this. It was all mostly subconscious. This is probably the first time I've put it into words. Out loud."

My first instinct is to say I'll do anything and everything he needs me to do, but even I think that's too heavy. And it won't turn his doubt. Only time will do that. Time spent taking a big risk. "No one can make promises about how they'll feel in the infinite future, not even me, and I love planning for the future. It isn't too much right now. And I'm not easy to get rid of, either."

Fletcher cracks a smile and returns to standing close to me. "You're right. No one can promise that." He touches my wet hair, sliding a lock from the side of my face. "And it doesn't matter, anyway, because I'm definitely falling in love with you, and there are no brakes on this train. Even if I wanted to stop it, I couldn't."

My eyes burn and blur in front of me. I throw myself into kissing him before I start crying. There was so much honesty in his voice, in the actual words he said, it's making my chest physically ache.

Fletch walks backward, his mouth still glued to mine, tugging me with him until he's seated on my bed. My hands are all over him, untucking his shirt, lifting it over his head. He loosens the tie on my bathrobe and slowly, giving me time to protest, slips a hand inside. His fingers glide gently over my back. Then he breaks our kiss, his chest rising and falling rapidly. "Haley…about earlier tonight…at the club…"

I shift closer until Fletch lifts me off the floor and onto his lap. "If you're going to tell me that you can't take credit for any of that, save it. You get all the credit."

He laughs, his breath tickling my neck. "I've learned my lesson regarding that topic."

"Also…just so you know…" I tangle my fingers in the back of his hair and comb through it. "If that happens again, I don't plan on running away this time."

Fletch laughs. "If?"

I smile at that, at the confidence in his voice. Then I kiss him again. "Whatever happens, I don't plan on running away."

He cups my face in his hands. "Me, either."

"Promise?"

"Promise," he repeats with a nod.

And because Fletch has always offered me his most honest responses, I believe him.

# Chapter Thirty-Nine

## -FLETCHER-

I set a steaming bowl in front of Haley and then grab the second bowl for myself. I slide into the seat beside her on my living room couch and watch her carefully.

After spending a couple of hours at her place, we were both starving. I suggested coming here—where else is it safe for me to eat?—but worried about the abrupt change in location ruining the mood. But Haley looks perfectly content. And perfectly gorgeous wrapped up in one of my sweatshirts, her hair tangled from us…well, being tangled together.

She leans forward, sniffs the bowl, and then looks up at me. "Where's the brown sugar? I can't eat oatmeal without at least five cups of brown sugar."

I grin at that. I believe it, too. "Just try it."

"Fine." She lifts her spoon to her lips, takes a bite, chews slowly, and then nods her approval. "Okay, so let's talk contract terms."

My spoon hovers above the bowl, pausing its movement. "What contract?"

"The contract. Of our relationship terms. Your list of Hard Nos and—"

"Hard Yeses?" I suggest, hating the seriousness of this chat. "Because I've got dozens of those."

"Sure," she offers. "All of that."

"For starters, my Hard Yes list includes anything and everything you and I could possibly do alone together."

She lifts an eyebrow. "Everything?"

"I'm open-minded." I shrug and return to eating.

After taking a few bites, Haley says, "So I can tell people that you and I are—"

"Yes," I say quickly before I can get anxious about what that might mean for me. I want to be with her. Enough said.

"What about your job?" she prompts. "Do you want people to know about that?"

I'm pretty sure Tate and Claire already know. Haley says they aren't gossips and won't say anything unless I say it's okay.

My silence speaks volumes.

"Okay, so that's a hard no," she confirms, no trace of disappointment in her voice. "So, I'll say that you hang out there sometimes because your brother bartends."

She questions me for another ten minutes, going over each and every scenario—can I tell people not to bake you cookies with nuts? Are you opposed to all school dances? What about outdoor movies?

My brain starts to hurt, and my chest aches just realizing all the things she has to think about that weren't on her radar before me. I take the empty bowl from her hands, set it on the coffee table, and then stretch out on the couch, pulling her down beside me.

Haley settles into the couch with me and lays her ear right over my heart. "You know what? I'm in charge of assigning locker buddies. So you're mine. Nobody else is baking you any cookies."

We're both quiet for a bit. I tug the quilt from the back of the couch and toss it over the two of us. Haley snuggles against me, her eyes closing. And I'm caught off guard for a second by how good this feels and how scary it is at the same time. I'm definitely past the point of no return. And I'm okay with that.

Drowsiness sweeps over me. My own eyes start to close. But right before I drift off, Haley says, all sleepy and sexy, "The Longmeadow scrimmage is tomorrow, right?"

A jolt of nerves rushes through me. "Right."

Haley must hear the uncertainty in my voice or else she felt me tense, because she lifts her head. "Nervous?"

"It's just a scrimmage, doesn't even count," I try, but even I know it sounds forced. I exhale and try again with more honesty this time. "It feels like Coach only gave me a varsity uniform to test me…like a sink-or-swim situation. Like he doesn't want to waste his time on me during the real season if I'm not worth the trouble."

Saying it out loud, it sounds like athlete insecurity, but in reality, I know it's true. Maybe not a consciously plotted plan on Bakowski's part—because there's no way he spends that much time thinking about me—but it is his plan, regardless.

"I think the solution is simple." Haley has this dead-serious look on her face. "Don't sink."

For the length of a few heartbeats, I'm not sure if she's for real, but then a grin spreads across her face. She leans down and kisses me. "I'm kidding."

"Funny." I squeeze her tighter. "Thanks for the support."

"I'll be there. Cheering you on." She curls against me

again. Her lips brushing my neck sends a spread of goose bumps across my skin. "I am a cheerleader, you know."

Warmth spreads over me. She'll be there. For me. I can't say that doesn't feel amazing.

# Chapter Forty

## -HALEY-

Never in my life have I been this nervous at a hockey game. It's not even a real game. Not for our town, only half of which showed up. The rest are waiting for November, when the season begins for real. But for Fletch, this game is completely real.

Leslie holds out the nachos we're supposed to be sharing, but I wave them away. My stomach is in knots; I can't think about food. My gaze follows Fletch's number seventy-six jersey around the rink while the team goes through warm-ups. His skating is smooth and easy, like all his movements, but his turns and stops are sharp and precise. He looks good. Really good. Jamie says, for Fletch, it will depend on whether or not he can keep his head clear and make smart choices in the game. His skills are all there.

I watch him move from center ice toward the goal, skating backward while Jake attempts to maneuver the puck around him. Fletch nearly gets the puck from Jake but comes up empty-handed, and Jake pulls off a trick shot to the top corner pocket, surprising Tate, as well.

Tate digs the puck out of the net, removes his helmet, and looks over at Jake, his hands lifted, a relaxed grin on his face. "What the hell, Hammond? Where did that come from?"

"Senior year," Jake says, as if that explains everything. Jake's grin mirrors Tate's, relaxed but excited.

The difference in tone between those two and Fletch is likely apparent only to me. Tate and Jake are here to play, literally and figuratively, like a pickup game or a shooting match on the pond during the winter.

On my left, Claire nudges me in the side. "You okay?"

"Yeah," I say immediately and then turn to her and give a tiny nod in Leslie and Kayla's direction.

Claire lifts an eyebrow but says nothing more.

I hear Kayla whisper to Leslie, "We're really not allowed to ask her about…you know who?"

After our public display of affection the other night at the party, news about me and Fletch is buzzing all over town. But when my friends press me for details, I just tell them I don't know. It's new. Too new.

Coach Bakowski blows a whistle and gathers the guys up. My nerves go from a solid seven to a ten.

And if I'm being honest, these feelings aren't just about me caring for Fletch and wanting what he wants. Selfishly, I'm worried that if this game doesn't go well, Fletch will retreat back to his isolated existence, surrounded only by women he can hook up with but never fall asleep together on the couch or watch the sunrise from the roof of his family's barn with. I'm scared I'll lose him if he loses hockey.

The pregame pep talk dissolves, and both JFH and Longmeadow's starting lineup head back out on the ice.

My heart sinks to my stomach. Paul Redman—aka Red—skates out onto the ice. And Fletch climbs over the wall and takes a seat on the bench.

# Chapter Forty-One

## -FLETCHER-

We're halfway through the second period when Bakowski finally says my name, so quiet I nearly miss it. "Scott, you're in."

Three guys. That's how many have played what I've wanted all summer to be my position. And I've just sat on my ass and watched.

Hammond, who's red-faced and drenched in sweat, shoves me from behind, and I jump into action, tossing a leg off the wall and then a foot onto the ice. I barely have time to think about being nervous or the fact that my dad, Gramps, and Braden are here watching.

And Haley.

I make eye contact with the Longmeadow player currently handling the puck, preparing to break away for the goal and then skate quickly toward him, my stick in position. The clock above my head ticks down the seconds.

4:33

4:32

4:31

My heart pounds, threatening to tear itself out of my chest. Despite all the training and pep talks from Jamie and Leo, it's hard fighting the instinct to back this guy against the wall, or to race over and check the teammate he's likely planning to pass to.

Don't go there, I remind myself. You're not an enforcer.

I'm right with the guy, my gaze zeroed in on the puck shifting right to left under the direction of his stick. The goal is right behind me, too close. His gaze flits in the direction of a teammate to his left, and somehow, I know it's a trick — he's not passing anything.

Behind me, I can practically feel Tanley tense up, preparing to block this shot. I wait a beat, let the guy fake his pass, and then when he's about to shoot, I snag the puck right from under him.

Turn it around. Take it outside.

It's Mike Steller's voice that rings inside my head, offering a solution I'm fully prepared for. I spin around, the puck moving with me, and soon my opponent is behind me. I break away and then send the puck sailing along the right side of the rink, right to Cole, who takes control of it and heads for Longmeadow's goal.

"Nice one, Scott!" I hear Tate say from behind me.

A weight lifts off me, and I dive head and feet into this game. Jamie and Leo are right. I have the tools, just need to quit being "so goddamn predictable" and take a little risk, try something new.

Three more times, I follow Longmeadow's best shooters and manage to surprise each of them. I'm dragging the puck around the back of our goal when I see an opportunity too big to not take a chance. Instead of passing right away, I head straight for center ice, where Longmeadow's bulkiest defenders have gathered in my honor. Before I reach any of them, I make a sharp left turn, and luckily speed wins over bulk and I'm around them and only two feet from Cole. I loft the puck in the air, setting him up perfectly for one of his best trick shots. Cole is quick to respond and sinks the puck into Longmeadow's net.

The crowd erupts with cheers, the guys around me celebrate, clapping both me and Cole on the back.

"That's what I'm talking about, Clooney!" Bakowski shouts. "Keep 'em coming, just like that!"

Cole lifts his face shield and grins at me. "Yeah, keep 'em coming," he says to me. "It'd be nice if every goal was that easy for me."

I give him a little shove, but it feels good hearing that, even from my much-younger cousin. Maybe that's what he meant when he said he'd been looking forward to us being teammates this season. There are advantages to family members playing together. We know each other so well.

Cole and I both get into position again. Behind me, Tate says, "Keep it up, Scott. I didn't really want to work hard today, anyway."

I refrain from looking over my shoulder at him, not wanting to take my eyes from the game, but I grin again. Before the puck is put back into play, Bakowski shouts, "Collins, Gordon, Scott...change up!"

Red appears out of nowhere, his shoulder bumping into me. "Thanks for the breather. I'll take it from here."

My gaze flits to the scoreboard displaying our 1-0 lead over Longmeadow and the time remaining in the second period.

2:16.

At least it was more than thirty seconds.

With a sigh, I skate off the ice and toward the empty spot on the bench.

# Chapter Forty-Two

## —HALEY—

Four minutes and twenty-two seconds. That's how long Fletch played during the scrimmage. *Hardly shit.* Jamie's words, not mine. I texted him the moment the third period ended (final score 1-0, Otters). But God, he looked great. And I don't mean his abs, which unfortunately remained concealed by all those ridiculous safety pads. I saw Fletch play during our midnight game, and he seemed good then, but damn, I didn't know he had all that in him. The assist to Cole was unbelievably placed. I nearly strangled Bakowski for not saying anything to Fletch and then pulling him out right after.

I'm wringing my hands now, staring out at the empty rink, wondering what Fletch is thinking, where his head is at. If Bakowski is going to tell him "Thanks but no thanks. I'd rather devote my time to developing younger players than a late-blooming senior."

"Hey, I'm gonna head across the parking lot and check

on the bar," Claire says, startling me. "Are you sticking around?"

I glance up at the stands—only a couple dozen people remain—and then over my shoulder at the entrance to the locker room where the team disappeared twenty minutes ago. So far, I haven't seen any guys exit.

I turn to Claire. "Should I go? Is it pathetic to wait around?"

As if on cue, Fletch exits the locker room, dressed in jeans and a T-shirt, his hair wet from the shower. I'm about to chicken out and make a run for it, but before I do, he spots me from the lobby. Our eyes lock, and I draw in a breath, holding it. His face is blank, unreadable, but there's disappointment in his eyes.

My insides clench, cold dread spreads over my limbs. He's done. With this. With me.

But slowly, his body turns, and he takes a step toward me. The defeat in his eyes vanishes, and he plants his feet right in front of me. From the corner of my eye, I see Claire turn quickly and head for the side entrance of the rink.

"Hey…" I say to Fletch, unsure what else to offer besides that. Unsure where we stand.

A smile spreads across his face, his fingers lifting to brush gently across my cheek, and all my worries and doubts scoot right out the door behind Claire.

"Hey," he says. "Thanks for waiting for me."

Without any hesitation or any checking to see who might be around to watch us, he leans down and kisses me. I'm so relieved I almost cry, but after pulling apart, it's obvious that the defeat I saw moments ago is still there, not on his face but in the way he stands, in the weight he seems to be holding on his shoulders. He's glad I'm here, but things definitely didn't go how he wanted them to today.

I wrap my arms around his waist and hug him tight. "You were amazing," I whisper right next to his ear. "Bakowski is an idiot for not playing you more."

Warm, strong arms wrap around me, and I feel his mouth rest against my temple.

"Thanks," Fletch says, holding me tighter. "You're the perfect person for me to spend the rest of the day with. Want to get out of here?"

Warm fuzzy feelings flood my insides, but I try not to let them get too big inside my head. Try not to let them mean more than they should. But it's hard not to. "Yes, whatever you want to do, I'm in."

"Fletcher Scott?" an unfamiliar voice says from behind me.

We break apart, and both Fletch and I turn to face an older man I don't recognize. And I know everyone in town. My face heats up, and I put even more distance between me and Fletch, but soon I feel Fletch's fingertips tickle the inside of my palm, and then his fingers lace through mine.

For some reason, I never pictured Fletch as a hand holder. Maybe to lead me through a crowd. Or to a dark dressing room at the club. But not just because.

"Great game today," the man says. "That little guy Longmeadow has facing off is something else, huh?"

I glance at Fletch, and when he doesn't respond, I give his hand a squeeze. All he does is offer a polite nod.

"But not as fast as you," the guy continues.

Confusion fills Fletch's face. "I'm sorry, do I know you?"

I was thinking the same thing, but I'd never just blurt that out.

"You're fast," he repeats, ignoring Fletch's question. "Bakowski might be a top high school coach in this state, but he isn't always the best judge of talent. A bit one-dimensional, if you ask me."

I'm confused now, too, but Fletch seems to loosen up hearing that last part.

"One-dimensional as in wanting only giants for defenders?" Fletch says.

The guy releases a short laugh. "How tall are you, son?"

"Five ten," Fletch says right away, and then after earning an eyebrow lift from Mystery Guy, he says, "Five nine."

"A third of my team is your size, some of them smaller."

"Yeah?" Fletch says. "What team is that? Girls' Varsity at Longmeadow?"

The man reaches into his jacket and holds out a business card. I read it quickly before it's in Fletch's free hand.

### SCANLAN CARUSO
### NAHL TEAM MANAGER
### DULUTH EAGLES

"NAHL?" I say under my breath.

Fletch stares at the card then looks up at the man. "Junior hockey?"

"Tier two," Coach Caruso says. "And I'd like you to come try out with us. If what I saw today is any indication of your potential, then I want you on my team. 'Course, I'm willing to wait for February if you want to finish out the high school season…"

"In February?" Fletch says. He looks stunned now. "Even though I'd still be in—"

"High school," Coach Caruso finishes. "Yep, we'll make it work. I've got a couple guys who are only sixteen starting with me this season. Some are as old as twenty." He waits a beat for Fletch to say something, and when he doesn't, he adds, "Talk it over with your family and get back to me either way."

"Yeah, um, sure," Fletch says, stumbling on the words a bit. "Thanks."

We both stand there watching Coach Caruso exit the rink, and then I turn to face Fletch, dying to know his real reaction.

"Did that just happen?" he says, still stunned.

I nod slowly, a smile spreading across my face. "It definitely happened."

Fletch leans against the rink wall and tugs our linked hands, pulling me closer to him. "I think you might be good luck."

"Of course I am." My insides warm again. "What do you want to do today? Go home and tell your dad and gramps about this Caruso guy?"

He glances over his shoulder at the empty rink and then rests both hands on my face. "The whole rink to ourselves, that's hard to resist…" He kisses me gently on the mouth. "I think we need a rematch from our last race. Got any skates lying around?"

"Maybe." I loop my arms around his neck. "But only if I'm allowed to knock you over and end up on top of you again."

"I'm counting on it." He kisses me, longer and slower this time, and while my eyes are still closed, the taste of him still lingering, he whispers, "I love you."

My eyes fly open, and Fletch looks even more shocked than he had a minute ago with Coach Caruso's proposition. "I'm sorry, I didn't…"

"Mean it?" I prompt, blood rushing to my cheeks. "You got caught up in…in…"

He cups my face, closes his eyes, and releases a breath. "I didn't mean to say it out loud." He opens his eyes to look at me, the defeat from earlier turned to determination. "But I meant it."

I nod, more than a little stunned myself. "Ok

"Okay?" He releases a short nervous laugh. "
could be worse."

"I mean, okay as in that's…that's good. Real
I rest my head against his shoulder. "I thought a
game that maybe you were going to tell me that
all too much."

"Haley…" Fletch says in a way that makes my hea
"We're not that fragile. I'm sorry if I made it feel t
All these moments we've had…it hasn't broken us do
made things stronger, more secure. Harder to live wi

This time I can't exactly stop a few tears from fallir
kind of perfect. Even when he isn't. "Okay," I say ag
love you, too."

His mouth collides with mine, and now that no
around, this kiss is more hungry. More…everything.

The summer romance that wasn't supposed to ha
might actually be here to stay. And I couldn't be ha
about that.

# Acknowledgments

I'd like to thank my agent, Nicole Resciniti, for her amazing support over the years. Liz Pelletier at Entangled for always finding a place for me and my stories. Thanks to Stacy Abrams who helped shape Fletch and Haley's characters and their love story. The phenomenal team at Entangled does an amazing job of spreading the word about my books, creating beautiful sexy covers, and listening to readers...Heather Riccio and Melissa Montovani to name a couple. Thanks to my family and their continued support during the writing of this book, which also coincided with my return to college and my family's move from Illinois across the country to California (2017 was a busy year for us) where I'm currently continuing my education at Stanford University. Thanks to the wonderful staff and leaders at Appel Farm Arts Camp in Elmer, New Jersey, where I wrote the ending of this book, special thanks specifically to the photo department whose fan I borrowed during my day off so I could finish the last chapter without heat exhaustion after the air conditioning went out in my room. And special, special thanks to the readers who continue to stick around to see what I'm writing next, I love all of you and wouldn't be here without you.

# GRAB THE ENTANGLED TEEN RELEASES READERS ARE TALKING ABOUT!

## NEVER APART
### BY ROMILY BERNARD

What if you had to relive the same five days over and over?

And what if at the end of it, your boyfriend is killed…

And you have to watch. Every time.

You don't know why you're stuck in this nightmare.

But you do know that these are the rules you now live by:

Wake Up.

Run.

Die.

Repeat.

Now, the only way to escape this loop is to attempt something crazy. Something dangerous. Something completely unexpected. This time… you're not going to run.

Combining heart-pounding romance and a thrilling mystery *Never Apart* is a stunning story you won't soon forget.

## WHY I LOATHE STERLING LANE
### BY INGRID PAULSON

537 rules hold Harper's world together, until spoiled, seditious, self-righteous Sterling Lane corrupts her brother. Worst of all, Sterling has perfected the role of a charming, misguided student trying to make amends for his past transgressions, and only Harper sees him for the troublemaker he absolutely is. As Harper breaks Rule after precious Rule in her battle of wits against Sterling and tension between them hits a boiling point, she's horrified to discover that perhaps the two of them aren't as different as she thought, and MAYBE she doesn't entirely hate him after all. Teaming up with Sterling to save her brother might be the only way to keep from breaking the most important rule—protecting Cole.

entangled teen

an imprint of Entangled Publishing LLC